wahala

The book everybody is talking about, soon to be a major BBC TV series

Named a Most Anticipated Book of 2022 by *Vogue, Marie Claire, Glamour, Oprah Daily, Grazia, RED* Magazine, *Good Housekeeping, POPSUGAR*, and more!

'FULL OF FOOD, HUMOUR AND PITCH-PERFECT OBSERVATION'
Stylist

'ALL THE RIDE-OR-DIE REALNESS OF FEMALE FRIENDSHIP IN THIS FUNNY, JUST-ANOTHER-CHAPTER-BEFORE-YOU-TURN-OUT-THE-LIGHT NOVEL'
RED Magazine

'WITTY, CONTEMPORARY, AND SHARPLY OBSERVED. AN ILLICIT PEEK INTO THE VERY SECRET LIVES OF WOMEN'
Nita Prose, author of *THE MAID*

'MAY'S BREEZY PROSE IS WELL SUITED FOR MOMENTS OF CASUAL INTIMACY, UNFOLDING OVER DRINKS, AT THE HAIRDRESSER'S OR AT THE KITCHEN TABLE, WHERE ALL THE BEST GOSSIP TAKES PLACE'
New York Times

'A FUNNY, TRAGIC, PIERCING PORTRAIT OF MODERN WOMEN AND FRIENDSHIP, WRITTEN IN GLITTERING AND DISCERNING PROSE'
Emma Stonex, bestselling author of *THE LAMPLIGHTERS*

'NIKKI MAY WRITES SO WELL ABOUT FRIENDSHIP, FOOD AND FASHION'
Clare Chambers, author of *SMALL PLEASURES*

Born in Bristol, raised in Lagos and now living in Dorset, Nikki May is Anglo-Nigerian. She ran a successful ad agency before turning to writing. Her debut novel *Wahala* was inspired by a long lunch with her friends. It will be published around the world and will be made into a major BBC TV series.

WAHALA

Nikki May

PENGUIN BOOKS

TRANSWORLD PUBLISHERS
Penguin Random House, One Embassy Gardens,
8 Viaduct Gardens, London SW11 7BW
www.penguin.co.uk

Transworld is part of the Penguin Random House group of companies
whose addresses can be found at global.penguinrandomhouse.com

First published in Great Britain in 2022 by Doubleday
an imprint of Transworld Publishers
Penguin paperback edition published 2023

A CIP catalogue record for this book
is available from the British Library.

ISBN
9781804990872

Typeset in Fairfield LT Std by Jouve (UK), Milton Keynes.
Printed and bound in Great Britain by Clays Ltd, Elcograf S.p.A.

The authorized representative in the EEA is Penguin Random House Ireland,
Morrison Chambers, 32 Nassau Street, Dublin D02 YH68.

Penguin Random House is committed to a sustainable
future for our business, our readers and our planet. This book
is made from Forest Stewardship Council® certified paper.

For Peter. This is half yours. This is ours.

'The axe forgets, but the tree remembers.'

African proverb

Aftermath

Am I strong enough?

The woman sits huddled in the corner of her bedroom. Her dress is ruined – the button missing, the belt ripped. One seam has come apart, exposing her bare shoulder.

She's clutching a sculpture in both hands. It's a head, a little under life-size. She stares into its unblinking eyes, willing it to come to life. She wants it to tell her that this is not her fault. That there's nothing she could have done differently. That she's the victim here.

But it's made of leaded brass. It can't speak.

With trembling hands, she places it gently on the carpet. Then, holding the split halves of her wrap dress together, she clambers to her feet.

Am I strong enough?

She knows the answer. Justice must be done.

She picks up the phone.

'Help me. Please . . .'

Four Months Earlier

1

RONKE

POUNDED YAM AND EGUSI? *Eba* with okra? No, it had to be pounded yam. But maybe with *efo riro*. Ronke ran through the menu in her head as she walked up the hill to Buka. She knew it by heart but that didn't make choosing any easier. As usual she wanted it all.

And as usual she was running late. She stopped at the cashpoint anyway and withdrew a hundred pounds. The girls teased her, told her it was an urban myth, but ever since Ronke had heard the story about Simi's cousin's friend getting her card cloned at Buka, she'd paid in cash.

Ronke had been looking forward to their Naija lunch all week. And not just because of the food. For the first time in ages, when Simi asked, 'So what's new?', the answer wouldn't be, 'Nothing.'

She hustled past the Sainsbury's Local, the Turkish grocery and the Thai nail bar. The Nigerian flag outside Buka was looking a little tatty, frayed at the edges. The green was still vibrant but the white was a dirty beige. Ronke studied her reflection in the shiny mirrored door, yanked at her hair to fluff up some of the curls, patted to flatten some down. As good as it gets. At least once a day someone said to her, 'I wish I had curly hair,' but Ronke knew better – curls meant frizz, knots and chaos. She pushed open the door and stepped out of suburban London and into downtown Lagos.

The smell hit her first. Smoky burned palm oil, fried peppers and musty stockfish. Next came the noise: Fela Kuti blared out of the speakers, struggling to compete with the group of three men at a corner table, talking over each other. And because this was effectively Nigeria, their voices were louder, accents stronger, gesticulations wilder.

The waiter looked up with a scowl. As Ronke turned to shut the door, she knew his eyes would linger on her arse. It felt like home.

She spotted Simi deep in conversation with a striking woman and felt a spike of irritation. 'Just us two,' Simi had said. The stranger had long toned limbs and glossy brown skin; she looked almost sculpted. Something about her profile was familiar and for one heartbeat Ronke was sure she knew her from somewhere. She blinked and the feeling disappeared. She didn't know anyone who showed side-boob at lunch. Or had such an over-the-top blonde weave.

Ronke tried to tamp down her annoyance as she wove between the tables towards them. The men stopped talking and turned to watch her and she realized she was holding in her tummy.

Simi stood and beamed at Ronke. It was easy to love Simi. When she looked at you she made you believe you were the only person in the world she wanted to see. Simi had given Ronke the same grin the first time they met, seventeen years ago, at freshers' week in Bristol. Teeth, dimples, sunshine, joy.

'Ronks! This is Isobel – you're going to love her.' Simi spread her arms out in welcome.

I wouldn't bet on it, thought Ronke. She leaned into Simi's hug and fixed a smile on her face before turning to say hello to the interloper. Still, three people meant three starters. This Isobel had better be a sharer.

Simi poured her a glass of fizz as Ronke unwound her scarf. 'Champagne?' Ronke asked. 'We always have rosé at Buka.' It's not forty pounds a bottle, she didn't add.

Simi nudged Ronke with her knee under the table. 'Iso's allergic to cheap wine,' she said, 'and we're celebrating.'

'Here's to my divorce,' said Isobel, holding her glass aloft, 'and to friends – old and new.'

Ronke thought divorce was a strange thing to celebrate but she smiled and clinked glasses.

The waiter plonked three massive menus on the table. Pages and pages of laminated sheets nestled in faux leather folders. Ronke adored the old-fashioned, over-long menu, the notable absence of words like seasonal, local and sustainable, the bad spelling and dodgy typography. She stroked her menu and a rush of nostalgia flooded through her, echoes of long family lunches at Apapa Club.

'*Wetin* you people want?' the waiter asked, glowering down at them.

'Another bottle of this.' Isobel gestured at the empty champagne bottle. The waiter's frown deepened.

'Thank you!' called Ronke to his retreating back. She tended to overcompensate with waiters. Even rude ones.

'Isobel is embarrassingly rich,' said Simi, 'but she loves throwing her money around, so I forgive her.'

Ronke laughed in spite of herself. 'How do you two know each other?'

'We met when we were five,' said Simi. 'The only half-caste kids in our class . . .'

'Simi! You can't use that word,' said Ronke.

'Oh, come on, this is us. Everybody called us half-caste in Lagos.'

'You can't even think it in LA, unless you want to be sent on a race awareness course.' Isobel stroked Simi's arm. 'It's so good to have my *alobam* back.'

'We clocked each other straight away. You know how it is when you spot another *mixed-race* person in Lagos.' Simi made exaggerated air quotes as she said 'mixed-race'. 'Isobel beat up a boy on our first day. After that we were inseparable.'

'He deserved it,' said Isobel. 'The little shit called you a mongrel. It was only a little tap.'

'You knocked two of his teeth out,' said Simi.

'He insulted us. Anyway, it worked.' Isobel smiled. 'No one messed with us after that.'

Ronke tried and failed to place her accent. 'Is your mum American?'

'Russian. My dad was working in Moscow, that's where they met.' Isobel placed her hand on Ronke's arm. Her nails were electric blue, long and pointy. 'What about you? I want to know everything.'

Ronke fiddled with her scarf and glanced around for the waiter. She hated talking about herself. 'My mum's English. I was born in Lagos, but we moved here when I was eleven. Have you looked at the menu?'

'Ronke is the best dentist in London,' Simi said. 'And an amazing cook.'

'I'm not.' Ronke wished Simi would stop jabbering like an overexcited PR. 'But I do love food. We should order – they're so slow here.'

Simi ignored her. 'She's practically perfect. Apart from her dodgy taste in men.'

Ronke clenched her jaw and looked around for the waiter.

Isobel clapped her hands together and beamed. 'Me too! I knew we'd get on. I always go for the bad boy.'

'Kayode isn't a bad boy.' Ronke glared at Simi and yanked at a curl.

'I love your hair,' said Isobel. 'How do you get it to spiral like that? Is it real?'

Ronke gave Simi one more hard look, then turned to Isobel. 'Yes, it's real.'

'This isn't.' Isobel flicked her blonde mane from side to side.

No kidding, thought Ronke. She didn't want to be mollified. 'Let's order, I'm starving.'

'Quick,' Simi said. 'If Ronke gets hangry, we're in for it. She'll bitch-slap us with these tacky menus.'

Ronke patted her menu as she swallowed down another twinge of annoyance. Hanger was a real thing; she'd read an article about it in the *Sunday Times* just last week.

'I'm not doing carbs – well, apart from wine,' said Simi. 'Fish pepper soup.'

'No carbing in a Naija restaurant?' Isobel's laugh was high-pitched and jangly. 'You're such a coconut. I'll have *amala* with *ogbono* and assorted meat.'

'Jollof rice with chicken for me,' said Ronke. She couldn't bring herself to order pounded yam in front of skinny, glamorous Isobel. 'Are we having starters?' she added hopefully.

∽

ISOBEL AND SIMI PICKED AT their food – they were too busy chatting about the good old days. Their Nigerian childhoods had been filled with swimming pools, beach clubs, air-conditioning, drivers and maids. Ronke's memories were of noisy family gatherings, power cuts, spicy street food, the car breaking down and playing clapping games with her cousins in the dusty courtyard.

Ronke listened as she ate. Simi was wearing a single over-sized earring, which made her look lopsided. Isobel on the other hand was perfectly balanced – shoulders back, head held high, blonde fringe perfectly straight.

Isobel pushed her plate away after three tiny bites. Don't stare, Ronke told herself, fighting the temptation to spear a piece of *shaki* off her plate. Her jollof had been so-so – she should have ordered the yam. Thank God she was getting a takeaway.

The waiter dragged himself away from the TV and sauntered over to clear their table. Ronke watched as he slammed her empty plate on top of Isobel's, squishing the black pillow of *amala*. What a waste.

Isobel's phone buzzed. 'Got to go,' she said. 'My driver's here. I'll get this – my treat.' She went to the bar to pay the bill, sashaying past the rowdy men.

One of them, eating *eba* and *egusi* with his hands in the

traditional way, paused, licked his fingers and called out to her, 'Hello, luscious yellow baby, why don't you come and greet us, *ehn*?'

Ronke froze. Simi tutted. But Isobel was unfazed; she winked and put even more swagger into her walk as she came back to the table. She bent to give Simi a hug, air-kissed Ronke, and then she was gone, the door slamming behind her.

'*Na wa, o!*' said Ronke.

'That's Iso,' said Simi.

'She has a driver? In London?'

'Her dad's loaded. I mean, proper rich. He was in the government *and* in business. Legalized corruption – you know the type. My dad used to be his lawyer, but they had a big falling out. She's been through hell so he's being ultra-protective.'

'What sort of hell?'

'A dodgy ex-husband. The controlling sort. He told her what to wear, who to see, how to spend her own money. Fucked her over. I'm guessing he was violent, but I didn't want to pry.'

'That's not like you,' said Ronke.

Simi held her hands up in protest. 'She was close to tears. I couldn't keep pushing her to talk.'

Ronke tried to imagine Isobel crying, but couldn't. 'But she seems so confident, so self-assured, so . . . shiny.'

'Ronks, you know how it is. We all have faces we put on. I think her dad came to the rescue – saved her from him. Hence Boris. The driver-cum-bodyguard.'

'Boris? You are joking?'

'OK, I made that up. But Boris suits him – he's massive and he's Russian.' Simi said the last bit in a terrible Russian accent and they both burst into giggles.

'I need to order a takeaway for Boo,' said Ronke. 'She's having a major strop with Didier. I'm going to hers after. Come – it'll be fun.'

'I'll pass. I had the oh-poor-me, I-do-everything spiel on the phone this morning.'

Ronke managed to get the waiter's attention and reeled off her order. 'Jollof rice with chicken stew, no chilli. Jollof rice with fried beef. Pounded yam with seafood okra, extra hot, please. Beef *suya*. Chicken *suya*. Two portions of *dodo*. One *moin-moin*, please. Oh, and a Buka fish special.'

'And one espresso.' Simi gave him one of her high-watt smiles. He almost smiled back, remembered himself and went back to surly.

'So what's new?' asked Simi. 'How's Kayode?'

'My dodgy boyfriend?' Ronke narrowed her eyes. 'I can't believe you said that to someone I don't know.'

'Relax. Iso's one of us. She gets it.'

'Well, Kayode is fine. Tomorrow we're going to look at a flat in Clapham.' Ronke had been waiting for this. She was careful to keep her voice level, slipped it in as if it was idle chit-chat.

Simi took the bait. 'What? You're flat-hunting? Together?'

Ronke wanted to stay deadpan but it was too exciting. 'I know. And it's *his* idea. We spent hours on PrimeLocation last night and *he* called the agent to book the viewing. I'm seeing batik curtains, lots of raffia baskets, wooden floors just like Boo's – and a cot.'

'A cot?' said Simi.

'Cat, I meant – cat.' Ronke blushed. 'But yes, I want kids. You and Boo aren't the only ones allowed happy ever after.'

'Of course not. But come on, Ronks – we're talking about Kayode! He can't even commit to a weekend in Paris.'

Ronke blinked at the peeling paint on the ceiling. This was the downside of telling your friends everything: it meant they knew everything. Yes, Kayode had left her standing like a saddo at St Pancras, watching the train pull out without them. Yes, she'd been in bits. But if Ronke could get over it, why couldn't Simi?

'It wasn't completely his fault,' she said. 'I know he didn't handle it well, but we're fine now. Can't you just pretend to be pleased for me?'

'I'm sorry. I just want you to be happy. Let's start again. Show me the flat.' Simi shuffled her chair closer. 'Please?'

Ronke tapped her phone with a short unpainted nail. 'It needs a lot of work, but that's fine – good even. Like a blank canvas. I can move into his flat while the builders fix it up. I thought we could make it more open-plan.' She jabbed at the phone, scrolling through the images. 'It has a yard, south-facing; we can have loads of pots. It's at the top of our budget and we won't get it, but . . .'

'I love it,' said Simi. 'You can do a Kirsty, knock all the walls down and fill it with scatter cushions.'

Ronke laughed. She did have a scatter cushion problem. There were twenty-six in her little flat. Kayode had counted once. All in similar shades of cream and silver. With tassels. With sequins. With pompoms. And one extra special one with tassels, sequins *and* pompoms. Kayode called her the mad cushion lady, but in a nice way. He'd bought her the extra special cushion. It was the only one that didn't get thrown on the floor at bedtime.

Simi chatted with her about houses and builders until Ronke's takeaway arrived. 'Give Martin my love,' said Ronke as she wound her scarf round her neck. No lurid comments from the loud men as they left. Simi hopped into her Uber and Ronke, weighed down with her takeaway, headed for the Tube. She hoped Boo would be a bit more positive about her news.

2

BOO

Boo WAS PISSED OFF. She slammed a mug into the dish-washer and kicked it shut. An occasional Saturday lunch with the girls wasn't too much to ask. Not even the whole of Saturday. God no. She wasn't a monster, for fuck's sake. Just a few hours. Enough time to get to Buka, catch up with her best friends – whose lives revolved around more than cook-ing, cleaning and ferrying – eat food she hadn't made herself and enjoy a glass of wine. A little time-out from being mum, wife and fucking doormat.

But no. How could Didier be expected to remember he'd been *booked* to look after *his* daughter for a few hours? How stupid of Boo to assume he might take a cursory glance at the calendar, the one *she* kept up to date. She'd been ridicu-lous to expect that much of him, not when every morning he stood in the exact same spot and asked, 'Have you seen my keys?' In front of you, moron, she didn't say.

How could someone as important as Didier waste valu-able time tuning in to dull domestic conversation? She'd only reminded him every day this week. 'You know I'm with the girls Saturday and you've got Sofia? Yeah?'

So when this busy, influential, corporate dynamo committed to go to some stupid rugby jolly (sorry, high-powered work function!), could he be expected to tell his wife? Or put it on the fucking calendar? No. Of course not. Best not to mention it until they were lying in bed on Friday night. When it was way too late to find a sitter.

'I'm sorry, *ma chérie*,' he'd said. 'But you can see the girls any time.'

'We're not girls. We're women.' Boo dared him to say – but you always call them the girls. He didn't.

'Sorry,' he said. 'It is for charity.'

Which pretty much translated as: Stop being a selfish cow. Don't you give a shit about Syrian refugees? They hadn't spooned.

The next morning, in penance, he had cooked breakfast for Sofia. Pancakes. About the messiest thing he could have chosen. Flour everywhere. And never mind about the splatters all over the stove. It was such good fun to watch Sofia toss a pancake and miss. Over and over. Tosser.

'*Merde!*' squealed Sofia, as another pancake hit the floor.

'*Houp-là!*' Didier ruffled her hair and slopped more batter over the hob.

Encouraging Sofia to speak French was another of his crap ideas. 'She's half French and it's important she speaks her language,' he'd said. 'Her brain is a sponge at this age.'

Yes, Boo thought, a sponge that was brilliant at soaking up swear words.

'Get Ronke to bring us a takeaway,' he suggested as he left. Like he'd come up with a brilliant idea. 'She won't mind. I'll have jollof rice with beef, nice and spicy.'

'Where's Aunty Ronke?' yelled Sofia. 'When will she get here?'

Thanks, Didier, Boo thought sourly. Now I can spend the rest of the day repeating over and over again, 'No, Sofia, Aunty Ronke won't be here till four o'clock.' And, 'No, Sofia, it's not four o-fucking-clock yet.' Without the F word, obviously. Sofia's spongy brain only soaked up French swear words. Boo's Fs were always internal.

Maybe she was being a bit pathetic when she nudged his wallet behind the cabinet. But it was the principle of the thing. Why were her plans more changeable? What had happened to being equal partners? And why was he always so bloody calm and smiley? Even when he was in a rush and couldn't find his wallet. Even when she was goading him into a fight.

Once he'd left, Sofia gave her a Gallic shrug. Another thing she'd learned from Didier. Head tilted to the right, lips pursed, eyebrows raised, hands thrown dramatically into the air. It said, 'Mama, you're a bitch.' But in French. Boo couldn't fault her reasoning.

Why am I so angry all the time? she wondered. In uni, Simi used to call her Goody-Boo-Shoes. Because she never, ever swore. But over the past few months all Boo's thoughts had been punctuated with profanities. How long before they dripped out of her mouth like poison into Sofia's sponge-like brain? A kid who said '*Merde*' might be called precocious. One who said 'Fuck' was a chav.

She looked at her daughter, sitting cross-legged on the floor, crushing candy on Didier's iPad. 'Fishes! Swimming!' Sofia trilled as she bashed away at the screen.

'Half an hour tops, then we're going out.' Boo picked up a dishcloth and started on the hob.

'Can we go to the park, Mama?'

'Yes, darling.'

'Can I go on the swings?'

''Course you can.' Boo scrubbed at a blackened crust.

'And the slide?'

'Yup.'

'Can we get a dog, Mama?'

'OK.'

'A brown sausage dog? Like Kate's?'

'Don't be ridiculous, we're not getting a dog.'

'But you said.'

'Stop talking. Crush candy.'

Boo spent the next half-hour doing things she hated. Loading the dishwasher, unloading the washing machine, wiping, clearing, putting away crap. Wiping some more.

Sofia's room was a bombsite. Didier had got her dressed. Part of his I'm-so-sorry and look-what-a-great-dad-I-am shtick. They must have tried on everything before settling on her little rock chick outfit. Boo refolded tiny clothes, repaired shoes, made the bed and put a dozen stuffed toys away.

Her child was fucking spoilt. And that was Didier's fault too.

∽

THEY SET OFF FOR THE Common, Boo marching to keep pace with Sofia's scooter. It was a glorious morning, the polar opposite of Boo's mood. Warm, with a clear blue sky and bright low sun. Even the grass looked vibrant – lush and extra green.

Sofia wore a black biker jacket with a red Stone Roses T-shirt, white jeans and silver Aviators – all gifts from Simi, who worked in fashion, got huge discounts and lots of free samples. She was a generous godmother – as long as it involved credit cards, not hands-on time.

Boo was in joggers, her old athletic team hoodie and a puffer gilet leaking fluff. *My child is more stylish than me*, she thought. *I look like her fucking nanny.*

'Sit here, Mama.' Sofia abandoned her scooter and pointed at the bench. 'You can read your book. I won't be long.'

'Ta.' Boo raised her flat white in a sarcastic toast. 'Give me your jacket or you'll roast.'

'No!' Sofia strutted off to accost three boys on the climbing frame. Minutes later, they were under her spell, Sofia shouting, 'Red light, green light,' in some complicated game no one else knew the rules to, winning every round and punching the air in celebration.

Boo studied her little girl, oozing determination with her skinny limbs and copper corkscrew hair. How on earth had she and Didier managed to create a person with such confidence? Sofia was nothing like laid-back Didier. Boo called it apathetic. He called it Zen-like calm. And nothing like her, cautious at the best of times, nervous at the worst.

Boo had bad memories of being five. She'd been an outsider, wished her hair was straighter, her skin paler, her nose narrower. The only mixed-race girl in a small Yorkshire village – white mum, white stepdad, white stepbrothers. Desperate to fit in. Being inconspicuous had seemed the best way to achieve it.

She wasn't much older than Sofia when she decided to change her surname. The register at school was daily torture.

'Boo Babangari?' the teacher would call.

'Bang. Bang. Boo!' the boys at the back would chortle.

So she asked her mum if she could use her stepdad's name. There were lots of reasons for not wanting to be a Babangari. She'd never met her biological dad – he had abandoned her mother before she was born. And it was a daft name, indecipherable and unpronounceable. But it wasn't the best idea she'd ever had.

'Boo Whyte?' said the teacher.

'Oh no, she's not! Boo's brown!' the boys at the back would snort.

She'd never been outright bullied but she was made to feel like a misfit. One day she'd stand out – be picked on and poked at. The next she'd be wallpaper – overlooked and ignored. Boo coped by keeping herself to herself, staying quiet and never making a fuss. Running had helped – she was good at it, won prizes for the school. Best of all, it wasn't a team sport.

Her mum and stepdad loved her, but they didn't understand her. 'A levels?' they'd asked when she was sixteen. 'Why? You can get a job now, start earning money.' They hadn't gone to university so why would she want to? She didn't admit she had to get away. She didn't want to hurt them.

It wasn't until Bristol (chosen mainly for its distance from home), where she met Ronke and Simi, that she started to feel comfortable in her skin. They were the first mixed-race people she'd ever spoken to and to them, being brown was an asset, not a liability. It meant you could always fit in – with black people, white people and all shades in between. They pitied the poor souls with one solitary culture, who used fake tan (or worse – bleaching cream). They were proud of being half Nigerian *and* half English. They loved jollof rice *and* fish finger sandwiches. They had *two* football teams to support.

Determined to fit in, Boo softened her Yorkshire accent and squashed down her shyness. The three of them were soon a unit – The Naija Posse. They were Boo's first real friends. She felt connected. She liked it.

Simi taught Boo how to transform frizzy curls into smooth waves. (Rule number one: There is no such thing as too much hair conditioner.)

Ronke introduced Boo to Nigerian food. She tried to introduce her to Nigerian guys too. That was never going to happen. Boo had learned all she needed to know about Nigerian men from the father she'd never met. They were dodgy, not to be trusted.

Sofia stood in a classic Wonder Woman pose. Hands on hips, feet wide apart, shoulders back, sunglasses perched on her forehead. She read the riot act to a little boy who had dared to question her rules. He looked petrified, nodding, eyes wide, tongue sticking out. Poor kid. He didn't stand a chance.

Part of Boo wanted to freeze-frame this moment. Time goes by too fast. She wanted to keep Sofia little for ever. But a bigger part couldn't wait for her to grow up. Time also goes by too slowly. Boo wanted to be Boo again. Go back to work full-time. Work on challenging research projects, not the stuff no one else wanted to do. Wear suits instead of sweats. Talk about deductive theory instead of the tooth fairy. Go to meetings instead of smelly soft play centres. Get a cleaner.

Boo had left her job at *Tech Times* to go freelance before Sofia was born. She'd got plenty of work but most of it was editing. She had a first in biochemistry and a PhD in bioinformatics – she missed having her own projects, seeing her name in the byline. She resented other people getting credit for her work.

So, when Sofia started school, Boo started job-hunting. She'd been at Modern Science, a think tank, for three months now. She didn't feel like one of the team – she only did two days a week and the full-time team was cliquey. But now she had a new boss and he seemed to have noticed she had a brain.

She pulled out her phone and re-read his latest email. Was it flirty? Did she want it to be flirty? Of course not. But it was nice to be recognized and respected. Valued even. He wanted her to do more days, run her own projects, do innovative stuff – head up a regular syndicated podcast. And he was fit. She read it again. Flirty? Yes. Definitely flirty.

THE DOORBELL RANG AND SOFIA tumbled down the stairs, screeching, 'Got it!'

A minute later Ronke shuffled in, Sofia clinging to her legs, and dumped two massive bags on the island. Boo got a cursory peck on the cheek and a 'Hello, chick', but it was all about Sofia. 'How's my favourite girl?' Ronke slid to her knees and hugged her.

'We're going to play war and I'm going to win.' Sofia tugged off Ronke's coat as she gave a detailed if baffling lecture on what 'war' involved. 'It would be much better if we had handcuffs.' She pointed to where Ronke was to sit and arranged an upended clothes airer around her. 'But don't worry, we can make pretend.'

'Phew.' Ronke held her hands up so Sofia could clamp on imaginary wrist restraints.

'Fancy a brew?' asked Boo. 'I've got that awful herbal stuff you like?'

'No, Mama! You're not allowed to speak to the prisoner,' Sofia barked. 'You sit on the sofa and watch.'

Boo saluted. 'Yes, sir! I'll be a human rights monitor; I think we might need one.' She settled on the sofa with the papers, while Sofia did a frightening Pol Pot impression – patrolling the prison walls and yelling out a litany of ever more violent punishments to be enacted on her POW.

Boo had to pretend to write important notes and take pictures with her phone. She tried to keep Ronke's muffin top out of the shots. Sofia had to approve the photos – she cropped, added filters and sent them to Papa and Aunty Simi. Boo encouraged Sofia to take her time curating the photos; it allowed Ronke to have a break.

At some point during the game, Boo realized she was enjoying herself. Watching Sofia and Ronke together always made her happy. Ronke was a natural. And patient. Boo was a little concerned by her daughter's bloodthirstiness but it could be worse. She could be putting a pink crop top on a blonde doll. Having a little despot was much more progressive.

By the time Didier got home from his important charity thing (jolly), the sitting room floor was covered in toy soldiers, Sofia's goose-steps were getting less exaggerated and even Ronke was starting to flag. When he leaned over and kissed Boo, she didn't turn her face away.

'*Désolé, ma chérie,*' Didier whispered into her ear. '*Je t'adore.*'

Boo rolled her eyes and kissed him back.

'*Merde.*' Sofia pulled a disgusted face.

Ronke collapsed in giggles, knocking over her makeshift prison. Her joy was infectious. Boo started laughing too. 'I know. It's all his fault.' Boo pointed at Didier, who beamed proudly. 'She's got her whole class saying it. I'm dodging mums at pickup.'

'Let Mama play with Ronke now. You help me tidy up.' Didier held the door open for Boo and Ronke. 'I'll bring you some wine in a sec. I've found this new red I want Ronke to try.'

'I'm so jealous,' said Ronke. 'Sexy French husband. Adorable child. Huge kitchen. If I didn't love you so much, I'd hate you.'

Ronke always made Boo realize how lucky she was. Maybe they should swap lives. Ronke would enjoy the cooking and cleaning. And Sofia's endless questions. And Boo would quite like a clean and empty flat.

'I know I shouldn't moan but I get all the boring stuff and Didier gets all the fun.' Boo kicked off her shoes and sank into the sofa. 'Sofia runs into school without a backward glance, leaving me standing at the gate like a saddo. A good-bye kiss would be nice. *Papa* always gets one.' She knew she'd said 'Papa' in a whiny voice.

'Girls love their dads,' said Ronke.

'Not me!'

'My dad was wonderful,' sighed Ronke. 'I miss him every day.'

Boo kicked herself for being so insensitive. Father issues was the other thing the friends had in common. And a subject best avoided. Ronke's – perfect *but* dead. Simi's – alive *but* disappointed. Boo's – non-existent *and* good-for-nothing. 'Didier's obsessed with moving,' she said. It wasn't the smoothest way to change the subject, but it worked.

'You can't move. I love this house.' Ronke slid her socked feet across the parquet. 'I dream of wooden floors.'

'Sofia jumping up and down on them is the sound of night-mares. Anyway, it's Didier's big idea. Sell. Move out of London. Bigger garden, better schools, a dog, a Volvo estate. He wants us to be middle-class, middle-aged, welly-wearing bores, listening to Radio Four and moaning about the commute. He says it's all for Sofia. But we both know it's what *he* wants.'

'Me and Kayode can buy this place. Mates rates?'

'You and Kayode?' Boo snorted. 'The bloke who couldn't commit to two nights in Paris?'

Ronke was silent but her fingers were twisting her hair. Boo felt instantly ashamed. 'Oh, Ronke. I'm sorry. I just wish you'd find someone you could count on, who'd treat you right. Someone white. Or at least not Nigerian. Dull and steady, like Didier.'

'You are so racist, Boo. And Didier isn't dull – how can you say that?' Ronke blinked rapidly. 'Kayode *is* a keeper. And please don't start with your racial profiling nonsense.'

'There is some truth in it,' said Boo.

'Whatever. Me and my boyfriend are buying a place together. We're looking at a flat off Clapham Common tomorrow. So if you don't become a country bumpkin, we'll be neighbours.'

Boo was saved from explaining what a dumb idea it was by the arrival of Didier with the wine. He'd used the posh glasses, as big as goldfish bowls. Didier had a soft spot for Ronke: only the best was good enough. 'Sofia's begging for Ronke to do bath time,' he said. 'I can tell her no?'

'Tell her yes,' laughed Ronke. 'Go warm the food. Being a prisoner is hungry work.' She took a sip. 'Yum, this is good.'

Boo raised her arms and Didier hauled her off the sofa. She fixed her ponytail and traipsed after him. The kitchen was tidy, all signs of battle cleared away. Boo gasped when she opened the takeaway bags.

'*C'est un banquet*,' said Didier. 'Who else is coming?'

'You know Ronke – never knowingly undercatered.' Boo lifted silver carton after silver carton on to the island. She put the trays in the oven to warm while Didier laid the table, using the smart cutlery his parents had given them for their wedding, seven years ago. They could hear muffled giggling coming from upstairs.

'She looks happy,' said Didier.

'You won't believe this . . .' said Boo. 'She's house-hunting with Kayode.'

'About time,' said Didier. 'I like Kayode; they're good together.'

Boo shook her head. The world had gone fucking mad. She was the only sane person left.

∽

'HOW WAS LUNCH?' BOO ASKED fifteen minutes later, spooning *suya* and *dodo* on to Sofia's plate.

'OK. Not the same without you. Simi was wearing this daft earring – just the one. It was as big as an orange. I asked if she got it at Primark and she got stroppy. It was by a designer I was supposed to have heard of. Two hundred pounds! For one earring. Can you believe it? And she brought a friend along.' Ronke whimpered with joy as she swallowed a mouthful of pounded yam.

'Who?' asked Boo.

'Her name's Isobel. Looks like a Bond girl: blonde weave down to her arse and plastic boobs. Posh but slutty.'

'What's a slutty?' asked Sofia.

'Less talking, more eating, you,' said Boo.

'Sorry,' mouthed Ronke. 'She's half Russian, used to live in LA. Now she's freshly divorced and over here. Oh, and her dad's as rich as Bill Gates. Some government big shot with unlimited access to the public purse.'

'Typical Nigerian politician then,' said Boo.

'Yes, but don't start.' Ronke held up a palm and turned to whisper into Didier's ear, 'You should have seen her. Side boob at lunch! The old boys were dribbling.'

'I can't wait to meet her,' said Didier.

'You're in the doghouse, remember.' Boo gave him a poke in the ribs.

'Can I have a dog?' asked Sofia.

'No.' Boo mimed eating movements with her fork. 'How does Simi know her?'

'They were besties in primary.'

'She's never mentioned her,' said Boo.

'They lost touch when Isobel went off to boarding school.'

'Can I go to boarding school?' asked Sofia.

'Now that is a brilliant idea,' said Boo.

3

SIMI

SIMI GOT THE UBER to drop her on the north side of Tower Bridge so she could walk across the river. The champagne at lunch had made her fuzzy. She hoped the fresh air would clear her head, give her the impetus to go for a run, make the sofa less appealing.

But the dazzling sun made it worse and her earlobe was sore – her new earring was gorgeous, but heavy. The cheek of Ronke. Primark! Honestly! At least Isobel knew it was Phoebe Philo for Céline. Ronke just didn't get fashion. Even when it was iconic.

She turned on to Shad Thames and into another world – shaded, silent, still. One more corner and there he was, Jacob the dray horse, the life-size sculpture that guarded their home, black and stark against the bright blue-bricked apartment block.

Right now, Simi lived alone. Her husband, Martin, was in Manhattan, halfway through a nine-month secondment. It meant more money – enough to afford a bigger flat, better views, maybe even a second home. Security. A pension pot. And if Martin had his way, a baby.

She smiled and waved at Ebenezer, the Senegalese door-man, relieved he was taking a delivery. He was a good guy but it was hard to just say hello; he'd tell her all about his family and ask after Ronke, who could do no wrong in his eyes – she remembered the names of his kids (all six of them) and kept him supplied with home-made scotch bonnet pepper sauce. Martin always stopped for a natter; he seemed to actually enjoy it. But for Simi, it was duty; she felt racially obliged to make small talk with a fellow African. But not *every* day.

She opened the door to her flat and took a deep breath. Simi loved coming home after Essie had cleaned. Their flat was never messy these days, she was a neat-freak and Martin wasn't there to wreak havoc, but post-Essie it was pristine. The cushions plumper, the units shinier, the pile of fashion magazines straighter. Even the plants on the balcony glistened. But without Martin, it felt too perfect. Empty and sterile when it was supposed to be minimalist and classy.

She half expected someone to walk in at any moment and demand: *Who are you? What are you doing here?* Her impostor feeling had come back again since Martin left.

The I'm-a-fraud foreboding had happened twice before in her life, but both times there'd been good reasons. She was only eleven the first time, more than a quarter of a century ago. But the memory of being marched out of Ikoyi Club was still visceral, provoking a swell of shame and self-loathing.

The second time was after she dropped out of medical school, halfway through year three. Simi tried not to dwell on that awful chapter. But you can't legislate your thoughts, they have a mind of their own.

The first two years of uni had been everything she'd hoped

for. Freedom, parties, new friends, a city to explore and boys. Skeletons, cadavers, lectures and exams. But year three was different. Clinical medicine, a white coat, live (often barely) patients, disgusting smells, clanging alarms, infected bed-sores, fear, grief and humiliation. It hadn't taken her long to realize she didn't have the compassion to be a good doctor. And one morning she couldn't stomach it. So she didn't go. That day, the next day or the day after.

Ronke was loving dental school and Boo was on track for a first in biochemistry. They wouldn't understand, so she didn't tell them. She didn't tell anyone. If she didn't acknowledge it, she wouldn't have to face it. So why not pretend everything was normal? Turned out Simi was good at pretending.

Medicine isn't quite the same as English Lit – you can't just stop turning up to the ward. Two weeks later, she was hauled into the dean's office, offered counselling (they suspected a breakdown) and told she'd have to repeat the year. She'd already decided to drop out. But still she didn't tell anyone.

Of course, the truth had to come out. And it did, in the form of a letter from the faculty to her father's house in Lagos. Dad had caught the first flight over and read (well, yelled) the riot act. *My daughter will not be a university drop-out. She will not disgrace my family name. Simisola – are you listening to me? You will graduate with honours or I will cut you off. Ehen! Not one kobo.*

Typical Dad – making it all about money. He was a specialist in authoritarian parenting with added blackmail. He assumed he could bully her into repeating year three. He failed.

Simi's mum had cried (she was brilliant at the crying

game) and made it all about her. In between sniffs she tried her hardest to make Simi feel worse. She succeeded.

Deep inside, Simi knew they both meant well. Financial collapse had damaged them and destroyed their thirteen-year marriage – they wanted the best for her.

Dad's arrival (and shouting) meant Simi's secret was out. She had to come clean to Ronke and Boo. They were shocked, upset she hadn't confided in them and guilty they hadn't noticed. They wanted to know what was going on in her head. But how could she tell them when she didn't know? 'I'm fine. I know what I'm doing,' she lied.

With no cash and only six weeks' rent left in their shared student house, Simi took the first job she was offered – as a runner for a photographer in Clifton. She found a cheap (damp and dingy) bedsit in Easton. It was the worst year of her life. True to his word, Dad cut her off – no money, no phone calls, no nothing. Mum called once a week to tell Simi to stop wasting her life. The calls always ended with Mum in tears. 'You're so ungrateful, I can't believe you're doing this *to me*,' was one of her favourite lines.

Simi lived on food parcels from Ronke and 'three for a pound' noodles from the ethnic shop. She put a chair against her door at night – scared of her druggy neighbours.

She hid all this from Ronke and Boo. When she was with them (most weekends) she pretended she was coping, put on her big smile and faked being OK. When she was alone, she struggled, fluctuating between fear and shame.

But then Martin happened. It was a photoshoot in London: corporate portraits of busy professionals hard at work for a finance company's brochure. She was the gofer – tasked to fetch coffees, move props, dab shine control powder on faces and keep track of the schedule.

Martin was the first model. The plan was to photograph him at his desk, staring at a screen of charts and figures, looking like the hardworking forex trader he actually was. But Martin had other ideas, delaying the shoot by pulling silly faces, refusing to stop unless Simi agreed to go for dinner. Egged on by the photographer and Martin's colleagues, she said yes. Why not?

He had a floppy blond fringe and kind grey eyes, was five years older and made her laugh. When she was with him, she felt golden. Martin decamped to Bristol most weekends from this point. She'd stay at Hotel du Vin with him, glad to escape her bedsit. He was the first (and only) person who didn't think she'd made a huge mistake. 'You don't need a degree to succeed,' he'd said. 'You're smart and strong. You can be whatever you want to be. You just have to believe in yourself half as much as I believe in you.'

Three months later she moved into his flat in Maida Vale. And soon she was working as a brand executive for a fashion house run by a mate of Martin's, earning more than a junior doctor. Simi hadn't eaten packet noodles since. She'd done more than survive. She had flourished.

Just when she had life figured out, the anxiety returned. Out of nowhere Simi would be struck by a crippling fear that disaster was impending. It felt physical – like a blow to the chest. It made her edgy and paranoid. She'd be convinced she was going to be caught out as a fake and lose it all – her job, her home, Martin. It went on for months. She never spoke to anyone about it. And then it stopped, as suddenly as it started. Until now.

Simi kept busy so she had less time to think. Monday to

Thursday were bearable. She went to work early, stayed late, met friends for after-work drinks or supper. When she got home, she'd change, head for the basement gym, then fall into bed, mentally and physically exhausted. She was slimmer and fitter than she'd been since she got married thirteen years ago. But weekends without Martin were a drag.

Five p.m. here. Midday in New York. Now was a good time to talk. She went to the bathroom, reapplied her lipstick and ironed her already perfectly straight bob. That was the thing about FaceTime, it made her too self-aware. She took her coffee to the sofa, sat cross-legged and clicked on the app. His face filled the screen, grey eyes twinkling.

'How you dooooin'?' Simi did an awful Joey from *Friends* impression.

'You talkin' to me?' Martin drawled.

'Too *EastEnders*. Not enough De Niro,' Simi laughed.

'You look beautiful. I miss you.'

'I miss you too. Ronke says hello – we had lunch. What are you up to?'

'Off to watch the Yankees with Bill, like a proper New Yorker.'

'Oh God, like Jay-Z. I wish I was there. I could channel my inner Beyoncé for the kiss cam.'

'But it's not football.'

'It beats watching *Strictly* on your own. Get a Yankee cap for Sofia.'

'I will. And one with cup-holders and straws for my Beyoncé.'

Martin talked about work and Simi moaned about her useless brother, Olu, who was broke – again – and wanted another *loan*. When Martin had to go, they argued about who should press end.

There was one upside to a long-distance marriage: travel. They saw each other once a month, in Manhattan or over here. They'd racked up a trillion frequent flyer points, which they spent on upgrades; they both loved turning left.

They explored the short hops from New York – Boston, Martha's Vineyard, the Hamptons. And in a few months' time they'd be in Vermont. She'd booked a beautiful log cabin overlooking the slopes, perfect for a pre-Christmas break.

It was like having a series of mini-honeymoons. They shagged like rabbits, spoilt each other rotten, ate in fancy restaurants and held hands like teenagers. No housework. No DIY. No arguments. They re-enacted *Love Actually* with tearful goodbyes at the airport. They spoke every day and messaged first and last thing. It had made them realize how much they loved each other. Sex had always been good – now it was great.

She finished her coffee and prowled the flat. She was fidgety. Nothing to clean, nothing to put away, no work to finish. She knew that going for a run would help but couldn't be bothered. She flicked on the TV and scrolled through her Sky+ list. A Nordic drama she'd saved for three months (still not in the mood for subtitles); *Question Time* (Martin must have set up a Series Link); *Horizon – Is Binge Drinking Really That Bad?* (God no, way too depressing); and Arsenal v. Everton (Martin again).

Her phone buzzed: a picture message from Boo. Ronke, tangled up on the floor in a wire frame – a drying rack? Hands over her head in surrender as Sofia stabbed her in the belly with a lightsaber. Simi smiled.

She stepped out on to the flat's small balcony and gazed down at the statue of Jacob. Her mind drifted back to lunch. What was it Ronke had said about Isobel? *Na wa, o!* Isobel *was* full on. Sometimes too full on. A trust fund and looks that stopped traffic helped. But the truth was, Isobel hadn't changed since she was five. For six years at Grange Primary, Simi and Isobel had been inseparable in school and out. Isobel had a pool and her parents were never around, so her house was base camp. She and Simi ran feral, bossed the house girls, snooped where they weren't meant to, played dress-up in Iso's mother's clothes and watched movies they were way too young for.

It was their colour that had thrown Simi and Isobel together. Mixed-race kids were unusual in 1980s Lagos. It wasn't that different in 1990s Bristol – that's how she met Boo and Ronke too. It was natural – you had an affinity, a bond – there was nothing prejudiced about it. Simi believed it was impossible to be racist if you were mixed. The more of us the better. If only the world would shag racism into oblivion.

In Nigeria, Simi had been called *oyinbo* or *akata,* but mostly she'd been called *yellow*. It wasn't meant to be offensive, it was a compliment. After all, yellow girls were the hottest, prettiest and richest. Except if you were one of those people who thought they were diluted, wild, immoral or downright wrong.

In Devon, with her maternal grandparents, it was the same but different. As a child, Simi had spent summers in their seaside village. Her grandmother spoilt her, let her choose her favourite sweets in the local shop, where Simi would get her hair fluffed by strangers who asked, 'Where are you really from?' or worse, 'What *are* you?'

'Human,' her mum once snapped. 'What do you think she is? A savage?'

Simi bared her teeth and growled. She and her grandmother thought it was hysterical. Mum didn't agree; she'd
pinched Simi's arm hard as she dragged her out of the store.

When Dad's business nosedived, he blamed Isobel's
father. His hatred was palpable. He changed overnight,
became hostile and angry. Simi once made the mistake of
asking if she could go to Isobel's. He exploded, pounding his
hands on the table and shouting, 'You will never associate
with those people again.' It wasn't difficult to obey – not long
after that, Isobel was sent to boarding school in America.

Overnight Simi's family went from well off – weekends at
the club, driver, cook, gardener, house girls (plural), summers in Devon, Easters further along the coast in Lomé,
Togo – to average. They were forced to leave their detached
five-bedroom colonial house in Ikoyi for a cramped three-
bed flat in Surulere. Mum missed her expat friends, her staff
and her status. She left Dad and returned to England less
than a year later. Their worst fight was over their biggest
asset – their son, Olu. They agreed to share: school in England,
summer holidays in Nigeria. Simi's dreams of Malory Towers
were dashed – they couldn't afford two sets of school fees, so
she went to Queen's College, a selective government-owned
school in Lagos.

In the summer holidays, Simi and Isobel were sometimes in
the same place at the same time – eating *suya* at Glover Court,
hanging out at Mr Bigg's or sitting bored out of their minds at
Murtala Muhammed International Airport. But they never
spoke. It was clear they'd both got the same fatherly diktat.
They pretended not to know each other and went their separate ways, Isobel chauffeur-driven, Simi a lot more pedestrian.

So it was a bolt out of the blue when Isobel called last Thursday. 'I'm in London,' she said. 'I don't know anyone. I need a friend. I need my *alobam*.'

It had been over twenty years since they had last spoken, and Simi didn't recognize the husky mid-Atlantic voice. But she knew who it was. Nobody else called her *alobam*. 'Oh my God – Isobel! Is it really you? How did you find me?'

'On Facebook. I recognized you straight away.'

'But I don't do Facebook.'

'There was a photo of you on Asari's page – at her wedding. I messaged her and she gave me your number. I've missed you. We used to have so much fun.'

It was true. Isobel was fun. And that's what Simi needed right now – a way to shake off this I'm-a-fraud feeling. She went on Facebook and found the picture Isobel had mentioned. It was a lovely photo, with the six of them: Boo giving Didier a dirty look, Ronke gazing adoringly at Kayode, Simi and Martin looking golden. Simi was wearing a Stella McCartney tuxedo jacket that she'd forgotten she owned.

She couldn't spend another Saturday night alone with *Strictly*, a bottle of wine and shitty thoughts. Everyone knew *Strictly* was more fun when you watched it in bed on Sunday morning, fast-forwarding through the boring bits. She punched a quick message. Seconds later her phone chirped.

Frock on bitch! I'll pick you up at 8. Iso x

Simi smiled. Her Stella tuxedo deserved another outing.

THEY PERCHED ON STOOLS AT the VIP end of the long curved bar, sipped cocktails and slurped oysters. Well, Isobel slurped oysters. Simi didn't get the oyster thing. It was like giving a blowjob to a fish. She was quite happy to wait for her squid.

'Will you stay in London?' asked Simi.

'I think so. I'm sick of being a nomad. I've lived in ten cities: Cape Town, New York, Dubai, Abuja, Lagos, Moscow, Hong Kong.' Isobel held up seven fingers and paused. 'I can't remember where else. Oh, LA, obviously. But Chase has put me off that for life.'

'What actually happened?' Simi was dying to get all the dirt on Isobel's divorce, but a waiter arrived with her calamari and a long drawn-out apology for the delay. The moment was lost.

'Your friend Ronke seems lovely,' said Isobel when he finally left. 'Is she always that quiet?'

'No!' said Simi. 'Usually you can't shut her up. Wait till you get to know her. She's a sweetheart – no edges, no sides.'

'How come we didn't know her in Lagos? I don't remember seeing her at the club.'

'They lived in Apapa; they went to the club there.'

'Apapa? I didn't even know they had a club.'

Simi laughed. 'You're such a snob. We can't all live in Ikoyi. Not everyone's as rich as you. Her dad was a dentist, not a politician.'

'Where is he now?'

'Dead. Killed in a carjacking when she was young.' Simi popped a crispy tentacle in her mouth and chewed. 'Now she's looking for him in husband form. It's not going well.'

'How sad. Tinubu . . . That's her surname, isn't it?'

'Yeah. How did *you* know?'

'She was tagged on the Facebook picture. Anyway, enough about her. Tell me what you've been up to. I want to know everything.'

Isobel was a great listener, she always had been, and Simi found herself opening up more than usual. She talked about her family. How disappointed her dad had been when she'd dropped out of medical school. How he hadn't spoken to her for two years – not until she had enough money to sub Olu – her fuckwit brother. How he deferred to Martin but spoke to her like she was still twelve. He didn't have a clue what her job involved – fashion was beneath his notice, marketing wasn't a proper job and anyway, she didn't have a degree – to him, she was an embarrassment.

Isobel talked about her dad – his awful women and umpteen children – twelve and counting. 'A tribe of little bastards. He'll keep trying till he has a boy or his dick falls off – whichever happens first.'

'Do you get on with them?' Simi asked.

'Sometimes. But they're so needy. And greedy. He relies on me to manage the others. So they're either sucking up to me or slagging me off.'

'Ultimate power,' said Simi. 'I've got two stepsisters, Tosan and Temisan. They call me "aunty" and curtsy to me. It drives me mad. I mean, they're lovely, but so timid I want to shake them.' Fresh cocktails appeared in front of them. 'My stepmother is obsessed with church. That's where she met Dad – he found God when he lost his business. She's desperate to convert me. Gives me a prayer book every time she visits.'

'I know all about that,' said Isobel. 'One of my aunts is a

prayer warrior. Kicks off each visit with a two-hour sermon. Tells us to close our eyes and clear our minds. I close my ears and clear my inbox.'

Simi banged on, perhaps a bit too much, about Olu, who as far as Mum and Dad were concerned could do no wrong. A law graduate – not a dropout, even if he did get a third and worked in telesales. Simi knew it was pathetic, but she couldn't help resenting Olu for being the favourite. She just couldn't compete: he was a man who would carry on the family name, much more important than paying his own rent. And he'd made them grandparents – the greatest gift – so who cared if it was Simi (well, Martin) who paid his kids' nursery fees?

Isobel listened, nodded, tutted, laughed and frowned. 'Well, that's one problem I'll never have. I'm the first-born, the chosen one. My mother is the only woman Dad ever loved, his *tsarina*. I remind him of her. He looks out for me – that's why I've got Vadim. To keep me safe.'

Simi had given up on getting her father's approval a long time ago. She didn't need it any more and she relished her independence. But still, it must be nice to know your father would do anything for you. 'Not Boris then,' she said. 'I'd love a Vadim. I hate the Tube.'

4

RONKE

RONKE TILTED HER HEAD and scowled at the picture. Still not straight. She gave it a nudge and stepped back. She'd been fussing round her flat all morning – moving things a few millimetres and then putting them back where they'd been in the first place. She knew she was being ridiculous. Aunty K was one of the messiest people on the planet and would feel more at home with piles of clutter and a thick layer of dust. But Ronke couldn't help herself; she wanted her home to be perfect.

She picked up the framed photo of her parents and wiped it gently. Mum had given it to her when she was thirteen, when Ronke was distraught because she couldn't remember what Dad looked like. This had turned into a full-blown panic attack – sweat pouring off her, heart pounding, shaking like a leaf. Mum had dug out a dusty album and they'd gone through it together, Ronke touching her father's face in every picture. She had chosen this one to keep in her room. They'd bought the frame the next day. It was yellow with red hearts and looked out of place in her grey and silver living room, but she couldn't bring herself to change it.

In the photo, her mother was wearing a mini in a riot of colours and patterns – purple, green, yellow and blue, circles, stars and swooshes. Typical *ankara*, the Dutch wax print everyone wears in West Africa. Thin and leggy as a whippet, shiny blonde hair held off her face by huge white plastic sunglasses, Mum was squinting into the sun, eyes creased, a let's-get-this-over-with smile fixed on her face. Ronke had inherited Mum's shyness. She wished she'd got her figure.

And Dad. This was how she always saw him – wide grin, teeth Hollywood white, skin smooth and dark. He was wearing a crisp white *agbada* with intricate pale grey embroidery around the neck and flowing wide sleeves.

This photo had been taken on Dad's fortieth birthday. Aunty K – his twin sister – had thrown an *owambe* for them both at her house in Apapa. A lavish, over-the-top party – food, music, drinks and people – showing off as only Nigerians can.

There'd been a massive canopy in the garden to shield the guests from the fierce sun. A highlife band with talking drums, steel guitars and accordions. A huge crowd – family, extended family, friends, friends of friends and the usual gatecrashers. And food. So much food. The jollof, cooked over firewood in a pot bigger than a paddling pool, had the wonderful smoky burned smell of party-jollof, a different beast to home-jollof. Ronke had watched in awe as the women pounded yam, sitting cross-legged on little stools, arms bare, wrappers tied around their chests, wooden mortars gripped between strong thighs. Their arms working in unison. *Kpom. Kpom. Kpom.* Dad had told her that their drops of sweat falling into the yam made it sweeter. Ronke believed him. She believed everything he said.

Crates of Guinness and Star beer were stacked up against a wall next to massive oil drums repurposed as ice buckets. Huge blocks of ice had been delivered at dawn. Ronke and her brother, Ayo, had hauled them into the drums, shrieking at the cold. By mid-afternoon the drums were full of water, the ice shrunken into cubes.

Aunty K had a picture of the party on her living room wall: ten-year-old Ronke dancing as her father placed a five-naira note on her forehead. It wasn't a proper *owambe* without spraying. The band played, the young people danced as vigorously as they could and the older guests dealt money like playing cards, sticking notes to damp, sweaty skin. Ronke had done well; she'd always liked dancing. Later she had sat with Ayo under a cashew tree, away from the noise. They drank lukewarm Cokes and counted their cache by torch-light. She'd got loads more and he was pissed.

It was Dad's last birthday.

She gave the picture another wipe. Moved it two milli-metres to the left and then two millimetres to the right.

Mum would have been thirty-five when the picture was taken. Way too young to be a widow with two young chil-dren. *My age*, thought Ronke. *What would I leave if I died today?* A colony of scatter cushions, an obscene number of cookbooks, twenty pairs of jeans (fat jeans, thin jeans and will-never-get-into-again-but-can't-throw-away jeans), a freezer filled with tubs of home-made scotch bonnet pepper sauce and a huge mortgage.

Snap out of it, Ronke told herself firmly. *Today is meant to be a celebration of Dad's life, not a wake*. She and Aunty K always held it in September, the month Dad and Aunty K were born, never in May, the month he'd been killed. Ayo never came. 'It's fucking morbid,' he'd say.

Mum didn't come either. She avoided all reminders of Dad and had as little to do with Aunty K as possible. She'd thrown away all her native clothes, not kept even one *ankara* dress, changed her name back to Payne and hidden all the photographs. She had airbrushed Nigeria out of her life – you wouldn't believe she'd lived there for thirteen years. Ronke's flat on the other hand was full of Nigerian stuff – a Hausa leather pouffe, calabash bowls, a miniature talking drum.

It had confused Ronke when she was young, but now she accepted it was Mum's way of coping. Her husband had been murdered and she survived by blanking him out. And not just him, his family too. This still upset Ronke. Aunty K always sent her love, but Mum never returned it. Was grief a good enough excuse for rudeness?

Ronke was glad she had Aunty K in her life – she was her link to Dad and Nigeria, and they both loved these annual requiems. They played Dad's favourite music (Fela, Sunny Adé, James Brown), ate his favourite food (*moin-moin*, fried rice, banana ice cream) and pawed over old photos. Ronke had attempted to replicate party-jollof and ruined several pots in the search for perfection. It needed a wood fire and she didn't have a garden. Maybe it was just as well she and Kayode lost out on the Clapham flat. The living room might have been big enough for Kayode's huge TV but the yard was way too small for pyrotechnics.

Ronke touched her dad's face and put the photo back on the shelf. It was time to make a start on the *moin-moin*.

∽

As AUNTY K ALWAYS SAID, you can't rush *moin-moin*. It tastes best when you linger over each step. It's a lot of effort, only worth doing for people you love.

First you have to find the right beans. You could use regular black-eyed peas, but Aunty K would kiss her teeth if Ronke did. So this morning Ronke had trekked to the ethnic store in Balham for a bag of Nigerian honey beans and to stock up on other essentials. *Tatashe* peppers, *De Rica* tomato paste, ground crayfish and palm oil.

She soaked the beans for fifteen minutes – long enough for the skins to get loose, but not long enough for them to swell up. She rubbed handfuls of them together, over and over, to remove the skins. Her hands kept moving, into the cold water and out, cupped around as many beans as she could hold. She rubbed her palms together, watching as the beans fell back into the water. Rinsed them to get rid of the brown skins. It was slow repetitive work and Ronke loved it. Simi spent ten pounds a month on a meditation app, when all she had to do was make *moin-moin*. Mindfulness for free. And you got to eat afterwards. Win-win.

Aunty K insisted you had to have good thoughts when you made *moin-moin*. If you were angry or stressed, you'd taste it. So Ronke tried not to think about Kayode. He said he'd be over at five, and he would. Aunty K would love him, and he would love Aunty K. There was nothing to worry about. It was going to be fine.

Ronke let her mind drift back to Lagos. Aunty K giving young Ronke a cookery lesson while Ayo played football with Obi in the red mud, using the cashew trees as goalposts. Ronke still thought of Lagos as home, even though she'd left when she was eleven. She knew Simi felt the same.

'We're special. We get to have two homes,' Simi had said once. Simi could turn anything into a good news story.

Mum had fallen apart when Dad died. She turned catatonic – mute and motionless. Ronke was convinced she was going to die too. Aunty K took over. Someone had to. She abandoned her own children to look after Ronke and Ayo, arranged the funeral and somehow kept them upright through it. She was grieving too – she'd lost her twin brother – but she put it on hold for them.

Mum insisted they leave Lagos straight after the funeral. Ronke begged to be allowed to stay. She'd screamed at her mother, who was still half zombie, 'Why don't you cry? Why don't you care?' She'd pleaded with Aunty K to adopt her. She'd punched her brother when he said they had to leave.

'You don't understand, you're a stupid baby,' he'd told her.

She'd punched him again.

She was ashamed of herself now, understanding that grief hits people in different ways. And it would never have worked. Bringing up two children on your own is tough. Doing it as an expat in a foreign country where you don't speak the language, aren't allowed to own property and attract stares wherever you go, would have been impossible.

So Mum made peace with her parents back in Cookham. They'd cut her off when she'd married *that black man* and ignored thirteen years of photos of their grandkids nestled into Christmas cards. Only God knew what she had to say to get un-disowned but whatever it was, it worked. Two months after the funeral, the fractured family moved in with these strange strangers.

'Don't call us Gran and Grandad. Nancy and Dennis will do fine.'

Those were the first words they'd said to her. And they never said much more.

Ronke had been brought up to respect her elders without question. Three months of living with Nancy and Dennis put her straight. Not all old people were wise. Some were cold, xenophobic and mean.

While Mum was erasing all traces of Dad and Nigeria, Aunty K was busy selling property, cashing shares, lobbying insurance companies and exchanging naira into sterling. Looking back, Ronke realized how hard it must have been for her. Nothing was simple in Nigeria.

Six months later they were settled in Maidenhead. Mum was teaching at the local primary and Ronke and Ayo had discovered *Top of the Pops*. Ronke shivered when she remembered their first winter. She'd only seen snow on TV and had never owned a coat. It was brutal.

But today wasn't about how bad things had been. It was a celebration of Dad's life by the two women who loved him most and were determined to keep his memory alive.

Ronke peered into the bowl; not one fleck of brown skin. She drained the shorn white beans and poured them into the blender with a chopped onion, red bell pepper, half a scotch bonnet and a big glug of chicken stock. The mixture had to be velvet smooth. Aunty K would test it with her fingers – if it was grainy, she'd scowl.

Almost silk – her best yet. She dried her hands and picked up her phone. Two messages, pings missed under the whirring of the blender.

I have been enticed into M&S. I won't be long. God bless. Aunty Kehinde.

Ronke smiled. She'd be ages. Aunty K was obsessed with M&S. She could spend an hour in lingerie, holding up size twenty-two knickers for detailed scrutiny. Tutting at the display of thongs. Whispering 'St Michael' like a psalm.

The other message was from Kayode.

Do NOT freak. Emergency at work. Won't make it. SORRY! Not my fault. Will explain when I see you. Kxxx

Ronke yanked at her hair. There was a lump in her throat; she felt shaky and sick. He should have called. The doorbell buzzed. *Shit, she's here, pull yourself together.* But the tread on the stairs was too light and quick to be Aunty K.

It was a courier. Tall, skinny, top-to-toe leather, visor down. He would have been frightening if he hadn't been holding two bouquets of flowers, stems in his fist, petals dragging on the floor. He shoved them at her along with his device and gestured at her to squiggle.

Despite herself, Ronke melted. A massive bunch of blush-pink peonies, her favourite flower. There had to be at least two dozen, graceful and delicate with a wonderful crisp scent.

The other bunch was smaller. White roses with cerise tulips. The card read, 'For Ronke's Aunty.'

She ripped open her little envelope. The message was handwritten. He must have gone to the florist himself, not ordered online. That meant something. Didn't it?

Boss off sick, had to pick up his meeting. Say sorry to your aunt. I love you! Don't be mad. Kxxx

As Ronke arranged her peonies she realized Kayode must have known he wasn't coming long before he sent the text. Flowers didn't arrive in seconds. He'd known when they talked at eleven – when he promised he wouldn't be late. She bit her lip, told herself not to cry.

The door buzzed again. Slow heavy steps paused at the half-landing, and then Aunty K filled the doorframe. She dropped a bulging M&S bag on the doormat and grabbed Ronke in a bear hug.

'Little Ronke, how I've missed you.'

No one else called Ronke little. She was five foot five and a size fourteen on a good day. Once she'd been released, Ronke helped Aunty K out of her winter coat (it was seventy degrees outside, but freezing according to Aunty K), relieved her of two stuffed plastic bags (double-bagged for safety – the bag for life concept hadn't got to Nigeria yet) and handed her the tulips. 'These are for you. From Kayode.'

Aunty K gave Ronke a piercing look. 'Why can't he present them personally in person?'

'A work emergency.' Ronke felt her cheeks redden. 'He can't make it. It's my fault, I should have planned it for the weekend.'

'Mr Elusive, *ehn*?' Aunty K pursed her lips. 'Not a good

first impression. Does he deserve the hand of my favourite niece?'

'I'm your only niece,' said Ronke. Her accent had become Nigerian. Her voice louder, her syntax altered. It always happened when she was with Aunty K. Boo called it weird. Simi called it being bi-accented, making it sound like an impressive skill. A skill Simi didn't utilize – she only dropped her Received Pronunciation when she was taking the piss out of someone.

Ronke dumped the heavy bags on the counter. '*Na wa, o!* Did you buy the whole of M&S?'

'*Abeg, o! Two* hundred and eighty naira to one pound – can you believe it! Over two thousand for one pair of pants.' Aunty K kissed her teeth impressively. 'Window shopping will be enough for me this trip. I'm saving my sterling for my high blood pressure tablets. I brought this from Nigeria. Only essentials – *Maggi*, *gari* and *Panla* fish.'

Ronke laughed and stepped into the kitchen to put the kettle on. She could get those things in the ethnic shop. And Aunty K could get stopped at customs for bringing fish in. She'd told her often enough.

'How is your mama?' called Aunty K through the open door. 'Please greet her well for me. I always remember her in my prayers. Maybe next time we can visit her together?'

'She's fine. She sends her love,' lied Ronke.

'And what about Simi? And Bukola?' Aunty K pulled Ronke into another hug. She was the only person who called Boo by her proper name.

'They're good. Sofia's growing so fast.'

As always, Aunty K took over the cooking, chatting nonstop about family, petrol shortages and power cuts as Ronke watched. She whisked the *moin-moin* batter, seasoned, tasted, seasoned again.

'It's smooth. You did well.'

Ronke punched the air.

'This is the tricky bit, little Ronke.' Aunty K picked up two banana leaves, rejecting four others in the process. Banana leaves were the one thing you couldn't get in London; Aunty K needed to bring them from Lagos. She always brought about ten times as many as they needed. 'You have to overlay them *well well*, or they will leak.'

Aunty K nested one leaf into the other, flipping them round so the spines faced upwards, then folded them left to right and right to left, creating a V-shaped funnel. She used her free hand to fold up the tail of the funnel backwards. There was a loud snap as the spine of the leaves broke. Ronke loved the sound; it made her tummy rumble.

'Give me a big spoon, Ronke.'

Aunty K dipped three fingers into the funnel, opened it up and spooned in the batter. She sealed the parcel, folded down the tops of the leaves and tucked them in.

'Not too tight, *o*! Or they will burst. And that would be a catastrophe.'

Each wrap took seconds. Soon the pot, lined with banana leaf stems, was full.

'Come and try one, I will guide you. This time I know you will get it.'

Aunty K's *moin-moin* were perfect pyramid-shaped parcels with no leaks. Ronke's attempt took for ever and was, as usual, a disaster. An amorphous blob that oozed pink batter.

Some things didn't change. Which, as far as Ronke was concerned, was a good thing.

～

RONKE WAS ASLEEP ON THE sofa when the buzzer went. She was wearing a cashmere hoodie (a gift from Simi) and bed shorts. Kayode loved her legs. And her bottom. She paused to check her face in the hall mirror; she was going for angry but sexy. He should have called, not texted. But maybe he couldn't face telling her, and the flowers were beautiful. Satisfied, she pressed play on her iPod – Nina Simone, 'My Baby Just Cares for Me' – and buzzed him in.

He came in wearing his 'sorry little boy' look. Shoulders hunched, back bent, trying to make himself look small. A trick he didn't quite pull off as he was eight inches taller than Ronke in her highest heels and she was wearing socks.

'I'm sorry,' he said, handing her a square box. Artisan du Chocolat Salted Caramels. 'Hugo called in sick and I had to take his meeting with a fund manager.'

Ronke raised her eyebrows and glared at him. He winked and pulled a family-sized bar out of his jacket pocket. She couldn't not smile – she loved Aero Mint.

'Come here, you idiot,' she laughed, snatching the chocolates and snuggling into his open arms.

'Was your aunty OK?' he asked. 'Did she like the flowers?'

'She cursed you in Yoruba, called you Mr Elusive and talked about *juju*.'

'It wasn't my fault. Not this time.'

'Yeah, whatever,' she said, handing him a cold beer. She didn't want a row.

'I do want to meet her. What's wrong with this weekend?'

'She goes back to Lagos on Sunday.'

'We could do Saturday?'

'OK, I'll call her tomorrow. Have you had anything to eat?'

'Not since breakfast. Hugo hadn't done any prep. I had to run the liquidity ratios from scratch. I don't suppose there's any *moin-moin* left?'

'I'm not sure you deserve any.'

'I'll work for it,' he said, pulling her down on to the sofa.

5

BOO

Boo was having a shitty day. Another shitty day.

She'd been sure her life would fall into place once Sofia started proper school but the much hoped-for freedom hadn't materialized. Instead, Boo had developed a weird split personality disorder – she was either desperately missing her little shadow or desperate to escape her. When she wasn't bereft, she was smothered.

On Mondays and Tuesdays, she went to work – squashed by guilt.

Guilty. Guilty. Guilty.

For being happy as she rushed out of the house, leaving Didier to get Sofia dressed in her actual uniform, without crazy socks or hat or belt or scarf. For spending ages in front of the mirror, trying on multiple outfits and hating them all. For hoping her boss would be in the office. For staying at work later than she needed to. For praying that Didier would have done Sofia's supper *and* bath before she got in. For wanting a different life.

Guilty. Guilty. Guilty.

Wednesdays to Fridays, Boo was a stay-at-home mum – flattened by resentment and bitterness. Unappreciated and bored. *What do you want?* she asked herself. *A fucking medal for doing the school run? A round of applause for sorting out a wash?*

Getting Sofia and Didier fed and out of the house this morning had been like herding cats.

'No, you can't wear your tiara to school.'

'No, you can't have cake for breakfast.'

'No, we can't FaceTime your grandparents.'

Didier had behaved like a toddler. Playing minigolf in the kitchen, wearing nothing but boxers, his pale doughy tummy wobbling, while Sofia ran around shrieking.

'Mama's favourite word is *non*,' he had said.

'*Oui*, Papa. *Non. Non. Non. Non.*' Sofia giggled like a loon.

Boo had clenched her fists and swallowed a scream.

Things got a whole lot worse when they arrived at the school gate. Boo was about to take command of Sofia's scooter when she heard a voice coming from a two-inch gap in the tinted window of an SUV parked on the zigzag lines, next to the polite sign asking parents not to stop there. She didn't take much notice at first.

But the voice got shriller. 'You! Yes, you. You! Hello? Do you speak English?'

Boo turned. The window lowered a few more inches and a blonde bobbed woman with mirrored shades, bright red lipstick and an enormous phone pressed to her ear pointed a manicured finger at her.

'You talking to me?' Boo pointed at herself.

'I'm trying to. Can you take Figgy in? My nanny's off sick again and I'm late for work. You're not looking for a new position, are you? I could really use someone more dependable.'

Boo had been struck dumb. Which was fine. The woman

didn't want a reply. She hopped out, unclipped a plump child, pressed a business card into Boo's hand, hopped back in, slammed the door, revved her Range Rover and accelerated off, leaving Boo gaping like a guppy fish.

Luckily Sofia had better social skills. 'Don't worry, Figgy, I'll look after you,' she had said, taking the child's hand and marching off to the school gate. 'Close your mouth, Mama. You look silly.'

Boo stomped home with the scooter. Who would call their fat daughter Figgy, for fuck's sake?

She was still fuming when she got home. *Tick-fucking-tock. I hate my fucking life.*

She'd sat down with a brew to make a list of all the things she could (should) be doing when her phone pinged.

Lunch? Today? Bluebird? Isobel says she must meet you and it's been ages since we caught up. Say yes! Simi x

She replied instantly.

YES! YES! YES! What time?

Boo rushed around. Unloaded the dishwasher. Shoved some clothes in the washing machine. Stuffed the pile of paperwork she'd been putting off sorting back in the drawer. Off with the ancient joggers. On with the leather mini – the one she'd worn to work last week.

She felt naughty. *Stop being ridiculous*, she told herself. *You are not a fucking nanny. You* are *allowed to meet a friend for lunch.*

∞

ISOBEL WAS NOTHING LIKE THE glamazon Ronke had described. Yes, she was attractive and slim, but most people were slim next to Ronke. Boo couldn't comment on Isobel's boobs – they were hidden under a cream silk shirt. And her hair wasn't blonde – or down to her arse – it was dark brown, in a neat bun. She was almost austere – no jewellery, no colour. Elegant was the word. Nobody would mistake *her* for a nanny.

Isobel stood to say hello. 'Simi talks about you non-stop. I've been dying to meet you.'

After Ronke's description, Boo had expected Isobel to be taller but they were about the same height. Her voice was soft and her eyes were warm. She touched Boo's arm and sat back in her seat. Boo was relieved. She wasn't a hugger. Ronke and Simi were obsessed with hugging. Boo assumed it was an African thing. Aunty K did it too.

Boo never forced pictures of Sofia down people's throats. She'd had it done to her often enough. Here's Ophelia in the (clawfoot) bath, on the (pristine white) slopes, in her (private) school uniform, on her (rare-breed) pony, on the beach (Rock) in Cornwall. But Isobel insisted – she'd heard all about Sofia and Didier; she wanted to put faces to names.

She was interested in Boo's work, unlike Simi and Ronke who glazed over and called her a boffin. Isobel had actually heard of bioinformatics and the Human Genome Project. She wanted to know all about Boo's paper on the future of personalized medicine.

Simi looked shocked when Boo said how good-looking her boss was, which was rich. Simi was an awful flirt, even when Martin was sitting next to her.

'He looks a bit like Steve Coogan . . . but younger and fitter,' Boo said. Simi and Isobel gazed back at her with blank faces. Neither of them had seen *The Trip*. Why watch it

when you're living it? They didn't spend their evenings veg-
ging out with a lazy husband.

Boo was disappointed when Simi called time, prattling on
about silk blends and hand-rolled seams. You'd have thought
she'd invented penicillin, not a tagline for a clothing brand.
So when Isobel begged her to stay a bit longer, she agreed.

'Another drink?' asked Isobel.

'I shouldn't – I've got to pick Sofia up at half three . . .'

'In Clapham? We'll drop you off.' Isobel ordered another
bottle of wine and moved into Simi's seat. 'Do you still train?'

Simi had bigged Boo up over lunch, told Isobel how she'd
been captain of the athletics team in uni.

'I try to run at least once a week, but I'm out of shape.
Now Sofia's at school, I'm determined to get my act—'

'We can be fitness buddies!' Isobel interrupted.

'I guess . . . I don't know – how far do you run?'

'I'll do whatever you do.'

'Well, we could give it a try, um . . .' Boo felt pressured.
Training and jogging were worlds apart and Boo was dismis-
sive of joggers.

'I'm being too keen, aren't I?' Isobel fiddled with her napkin. 'Sorry. My ex-husband hated me socializing. I've forgotten
how to make friends.'

Boo warmed to her. She knew exactly how that felt. 'We
could meet at the outdoor gym on the Common? It's a great
place to warm up. And it's free.' She realized as she said it
that being free wouldn't be a priority for Isobel.

'Thank you!' said Isobel. 'Now tell me all about your little
girl. How old is she?'

'Five going on fifteen.' Boo launched into her latest

bugbear – Sofia's birthday party. Her sensible suggestions – bouncy castle, balloon animals, pass the parcel – had been deemed dull and boring. Sofia wanted an utterly ridiculous gangster theme. 'Didier has made things worse, as usual,' she said. 'He suggested water pistols and now Sofia has her heart set on guns.'

'How about a rap party?' said Isobel. 'You know, hip-hop.'

Boo was underwhelmed. 'Isn't that a different name for gangster?'

But Isobel was convincing. Her stepsister in New York had organized one last year for her daughter. 'The entertainer was so cool. He taught the kids a dance, backsliding and body-popping; they were so into it.' Isobel moved her hands to demonstrate the moves. 'They did this show. It was awful. But it kept them away from us – and not screaming – for hours.'

'I guess it could work,' said Boo. 'Didier will love it – he's a big kid.'

'You could have a mirror ball, glow bracelets, baseball caps, Kanye West shutter shades . . .' said Isobel. 'How about a graffiti wall with crayons? The kids could have fake gold chains.'

'You're a genius,' Boo said. 'You must come.' She couldn't wait to tell Didier and Sofia. Except there wouldn't be a graffiti wall. As if. Only someone who didn't have kids would even suggest it.

'Only if you let me bring the birthday cake.' Isobel grinned and rubbed her hands together.

Boo decided she liked her. And it would be nice to have a running mate, someone to hang out with during the week when normal people were at work. 'Deal! Ronke usually makes the cake but she won't mind. She'll be doing the rest of the food.'

'Are you sure?' said Isobel. 'I don't want to tread on her toes.'

'She'll be fine. Ronke's cool.'

'She seemed a bit off at Buka, seemed annoyed that I was there,' said Isobel. 'And she got huffy when Simi mentioned her boyfriend. I made an excuse and left early.'

'Oh, Ronke's lovely. You'll see when you get to know her properly. But as for her dodgy blokes . . .' On this topic, Boo had lots to say. 'Akin was a low point. He strung her along for a year and a half, treated her like shit. Then there was Femi the scammer. He borrowed two grand off her and disappeared. Turned out he had a fiancée in Lagos.'

'Men can be such bastards,' said Isobel.

'I wish she'd meet a decent man. She deserves to be happy. But she never learns.'

'Maybe Kayode is the one?' said Isobel. 'What does he do? What's he like? Simi seems to have a downer on him.'

'He's a risk analyst.' Boo was about to launch into all Kayode's faults but she didn't have time. It was three-fifteen. 'I've got to run. Sofia's been teaching her class to swear in French. If I turn up late and drunk at pickup, they might call social services.'

∽

Boo was still buzzing when Vadim double-parked on the zigzag line, next to the polite sign. She hoped the bitch from this morning was watching.

She toddled off to join the pickup queue. The row of nannies, a few mums and a token dad stood to one end of the small playground. Because of course you couldn't just grab your own child and go. Instead the children lined up at the other end, chaperoned by their teacher, and then, one by one, each child was handed to their designated picker-upper. Like some Cold War spy swap.

Up until now, Boo had thought it a sensible system. You did hear about child abductions and peculiar people hanging around school gates. But today it seemed ridiculous. What a palaver. *Give me my bloody child. My feet hurt and I'm dehydrated.*

When Sofia got to the front, she ran to Boo waving her latest masterpiece – a gluey, sparkly picture of something unrecognizable.

'Skirt too short, Mama.' Sofia shook her head in disapproval and thrust the picture at her.

'Beautiful.' Boo yanked her skirt down, squinted at the offering and tried to work out which way was up. 'What is it?'

'A dog, obvs. Where's my scooter?'

'You have to walk today, darling.'

Sofia slumped dramatically. 'Walking's boring.'

Boo yanked her upright. 'So what did you do today?'

'I had pizza for lunch. It was yummy. Better than yours. And I played Duck Duck Goose. And I won.'

'Well, Mama had a busy day too. I met a new friend and we're going running tomorrow.'

'I'm the best runner. Ever. I run the fastest. But sometimes I let Marley catch me. The park is this way, Mama.'

'No park today. Mama's feet hurt. But I've had a great idea for your party.'

'I want gangsters.'

'This is better than gangsters. A hip-hop party! With break-dancing and disco lights and maybe a mirror ball and sunglasses and gold chains. We could even have a ghetto blaster piñata!'

'And guns?'

'No guns,' Boo sighed. 'Hold my hand, Sofia, we're crossing here.'

Sofia obediently took Boo's hand. 'Swords?'

'No guns, no swords. No weapons. How about pizza for supper?'

'I told you we had pizza for lunch. Good pizza. Not like your pizza.'

Nothing like having your food critiqued by a five-year-old to sober you up. Boo rubbed her temples. She needed water. 'Let's stop at the shop.'

'Haribos!' Sofia shrieked.

'OK. One small bag.' Boo smiled at Sofia's shocked face. Sometimes it was easier to say yes.

∽

WHEN THEY GOT HOME Boo did the mandatory thirty minutes of reading practice, as recommended by the school. Boo couldn't recall reading with her mum; she wasn't sure they'd ever spent thirty minutes alone together. She remembered pandemonium, her stepbrothers screeching, her mum running raggedly after them. Boo would escape to the sanctuary of her room till she was called for supper.

Sofia's supper came with the usual soul-destroying vegetable conversation, another thing Boo couldn't remember from her own childhood. Broccoli was now acceptable, while last week's favourite, green beans, were 'eugh, yuck'. But you couldn't give up and squirt ketchup over the fish fingers, not unless you wanted your child to get rickets.

Supper was followed by a strictly controlled half-hour of tablet time, which turned into an hour because in spite of living in jogging pants, it took Boo for ever to find a not-disgusting running outfit. She got lost in Sweaty Betty's online shop, staring at pictures of long-limbed, lithe, toned women with flawless skin and gorgeous messy (on purpose) ponytails. This was so much more than workout gear – these were bum-sculpting, sweat-wicking, life-changing leggings. Add to basket. Click!

She pictured herself doing ashtanga yoga on a manicured lawn, sipping from a silver water bottle as she stretched her hamstrings in a sports-luxe jacket. Add both to basket. Click! Click!

She'd probably need a pair of faux leather leggings for non-gym days – although there wouldn't be many of those in her new toned life – and at nearly a hundred quid, they were taking the piss. Add to wish list. Click!

Sofia pulled her back to reality. 'Mama! Can I go to bed now? I'm tired.'

It had gone eight. Sofia should have been in bed half an hour ago. 'Sorry, darling, I was working.' Where was Didier? Thank God he was late.

Sofia peered at the laptop. 'Looks like shopping.'

'Upstairs. Quick! Wash, teeth, bed. I'll be up in two seconds.'

'I still get a story,' said Sofia.

'A short one.' Boo shooed her up the stairs, then ticked the next-day delivery box. The best thing about PayPal – it didn't feel like spending real money.

∽

'WHY ARE YOU SITTING IN the dark?' asked Didier.

'It's peaceful and I'm shattered,' Boo replied.

'Me too. You won't believe what Robin did. You know that client . . .'

Boo tuned out. She'd spent the evening listening to Sofia talk about Sofia. She couldn't spend the next hour listening to Didier talk about Didier. She closed her eyes and imagined sprinting on a sandy beach. Who was the gorgeous man running beside her, keeping perfect pace?

'Boo! Did you hear a word I said?' asked Didier.

'Sorry, drifted off.'

'Did you pick up my suit?'

'No, I'll get it tomorrow.'

'*O, la vache.* I was going to wear it to the big meeting.'

'Well, tough. You'll have to wear another one.'

'What's for supper?'

'I ran out of time. Let's order a takeaway.' Boo closed her eyes and tried to block him out.

'I could make us an omelette?'

'We're out of eggs.'

'What about croque-monsieur? Or pasta?'

'Didier, stop. I'm tired and my head hurts.'

'OK, OK.' Didier held his hands up in surrender.

'Please stop talking.'

'Sorry. Are you all right, Boo? Time of the month?'

'Didier!'

'Keep your hairs on. I'll go say goodnight to Sofia. She might be pleased to see me.' Didier headed for the stairs.

'It's hair. Not hairs. And don't wake her up.' Boo shut her eyes again. 'Bad wife,' she mumbled. 'Bad wife.' Then she forced herself off the sofa and into the kitchen.

6

SIMI

SIMI LEANED BACK IN her swivel chair and swung her feet on to her desk. She'd done it. She'd won. So why did she feel so flat? She studied her shoes. The iridescent snake-effect leather shimmered from purple to blue when she twirled her foot. Sharp pointed toes, towering four-inch stiletto heels. Ronke had looked horrified when she told her what they cost, but she shouldn't have asked. Simi didn't judge Ronke for eating too much, so why should Ronke judge her for being materialistic? Which she wasn't. She just liked nice things.

Simi wasn't shallow but she kept her depths to herself. Looks mattered. They were a good way of paving over the stuff she was less sure about. She'd once overheard Boo saying she was vain. It was years ago – not long after they'd become friends. Boo had been mortified, she'd stuttered, backtracked and apologized. But Simi wasn't upset. If vanity meant caring about your appearance – tick, she was vain.

Simi knew full well she wasn't beautiful. 'You're almost as pretty as me,' Isobel had said, the day they met. It wasn't true. Even at five, Isobel was stunning. Simi would have been over the moon to be almost as pretty as her, but she wasn't a fantasist. Her nose was too broad, her eyes too small, her lips too thin and her skin still carried scars from pubescent acne (thank God for foundation). Her boobs were non-existent and she had no waist – her brother called her a parallelogram. But she had good hair – wavy, not kinky – and once she discovered the magic of a Brazilian blow-dry, it became pin-straight, white-woman hair. She had OK legs – with the right-length skirt (short) and the right heels (high), she could make her five-foot-four frame look almost leggy. But her best feature was her smile. Her face changed, became decidedly attractive, when it had a smile on it. It was lucky Ronke was a dentist – Simi loved having her teeth whitened. Unfortunately Ronke was obsessed by rules so she never allowed Simi more than two treatments a year.

By the time she was nine, Simi understood how the world worked. In Lagos being light-skinned was far more important than fine eyes, clear skin, a waist or a brain. By the time she was eleven, she'd got used to boys' heads turning when she walked into a room – it was standard, she expected it. She also got used to dirty looks from the girls. She knew what caused it and she knew it was skin-deep.

The first guy she kissed – she was fourteen – told her he 'had a thing for mixed chicks'. She was horrified. But also grateful; he saved her from being a trophy girlfriend to a series of creeps. Her first white boyfriend lasted three months – the time it took to find out that his last two girlfriends had been brown.

Simi developed what Ronke called her *pre-date interview* – questions and prompts about exes. It was shocking how much it narrowed her options. About ninety-five per cent of the Nigerian men who chatted her up would chat up any yellow babe. Over here there was a smaller pool of men who would *ever* date a brown woman, but about ninety-five per cent of them would date *any* brown woman.

Martin made a joke about it in his wedding speech. He had put his hand under her chin, looked into her eyes and said, 'I can pinpoint the exact moment this beautiful woman fell in love with me. It was when she saw a picture of my blonde, blue-eyed ex.' Most people looked confused. Ronke and Boo burst out laughing.

The loud jangle of her colleague's ringtone yanked Simi back to the present. 'On my way,' he said into the phone, then to her, 'Don't forget to go home.'

'Thanks, Gav. You were a star today. And tell your sister I owe her.' Simi twirled her feet again – blue to purple. She'd be last to leave the office. Again.

She'd worked on dozens of pitches and led a few, but this was a biggie. She'd had free rein – complete creative control.

#PooltoParty #BeachtoBar. It was her line. All hers. They'd loved it. The clothes were utterly impractical. Frothy crêpe de Chine dresses that took up masses of suitcase space and were dry-clean only (not great when you were drenched in suntan lotion). But they flowed and billowed, which looked amazing on Instagram. Simi had been determined to do something different – not the bog-standard models strutting the catwalk, frolicking on a beach or swanning around on a yacht. But would she have come up with ballet dancers if Gavin's sister hadn't worked for the English National Ballet? And would she have picked that grime soundtrack if Ronke hadn't banged on about the new song she and Rafa were obsessed with?

She'd won. It was all that mattered. She needed to stop undermining herself.

Her boss, a Queen Bitch, had stumped up for real champagne, not cheap prosecco. Everyone had cheered when Simi had walked into the boardroom. She had felt triumphant. But only for a second, until QB's toast.

'As soon as I saw the brief,' she'd said, 'I knew Simi was right for this. This brand was crying out for her urban vibe.'

Urban was her way of saying black. Simi had downed her champagne through gritted teeth. She wanted to win because she was good – smart, creative, persuasive – not because she was black.

She didn't want to go home to an empty flat. She wanted to hold on to the buzz. More champagne, high fives, well dones. She wanted someone to be proud of her. Boo would be making a meal out of making a simple meal. Ronke wouldn't party on a weekday, and in any case, she'd be in her PJs, waiting for Kayode to not turn up. And Martin was three and a half thousand miles away. Simi knew she'd had too many boozy late nights this week but she couldn't face being alone with her thoughts. She messaged Isobel.

We won the pitch! I want to celebrate. Simi x

The reply came almost instantly.

Of course you did. You're a legend. Come to Gotham. Right now!

Simi swung her feet off the desk and down to earth.

∽

GOTHAM WAS ISOBEL'S FAVOURITE HAUNT. With gleaming black floors, silver tables, chandeliers like giant rhinestone hula skirts and a bat-shaped bar, Simi thought it was trying a little too hard. But arguing with Isobel was hard work, so Gotham had turned into 'their' place.

When Simi arrived, Isobel was at a small silver table, tapping her phone. She was wearing a one-shouldered black jumpsuit, no jewellery and she'd nailed the no-makeup makeup look. Her skin was dewy. Her hair, jet-black today, was pinned in a complicated updo.

Isobel leapt to her feet and pulled Simi into a bear hug, careful not to touch skin and smudge foundation, then stood back and did a slow overhead handclap, followed by three 'we're not worthy' deep bows, her bright yellow lacy bra clearly visible. Anyone else would have looked ridiculous. Isobel looked sassy and sexy. Heads turned. Simi grinned.

Isobel ordered espresso martinis: 'They'll wake us up and fuck us up. Now tell me all about the pitch. I want all the details.'

Simi was happy to oblige. She told her about the dancers from the English National Ballet, the up-and-coming choreographer, the amazing grime track (that Isobel knew – it appeared everyone except Simi did), the ruffles and fluidity of the clothes. 'Even QB was impressed,' she finished.

'Huh?'

'Queen Bitch. My passive-aggressive boss.'

'You shouldn't put up with that kind of crap. They don't deserve you. You're brilliant. My dad uses this excellent headhunter – he owes us a favour. I'll get him to call you. What did Martin say? He must be so proud.'

'He doesn't know yet. It's . . .' Simi glanced at her watch. 'He'll still be at work. I'll call when I get home.'

'What! He hasn't called you?' Isobel's eyes widened in shock. 'Didn't he know you'd hear today?'

'We'll talk later.' Simi would never slag Martin off. To anyone. And there was nothing to slag him off for. He would be proud of her. But she did wish that he'd called. She was cheerleader-in-chief when it came to *his* work.

'You should go to New York. Surprise him. Have a proper celebration.'

Simi laughed. 'Some of us have jobs, you know.'

'Even QB can't begrudge you having one day off – make a weekend of it.'

'It's not that simple. He's in Manhattan, not Manchester.'

'You're making it sound like Mars. It's only seven hours away. People go for weekend shopping trips all the time. Where's the kick-ass, can-do, pitch-winning superstar? Who is this old lady and what have you done with my Simi?'

Simi took another sip of her martini. 'Martin will think I'm mad.'

'He'll be thrilled. You know my motto – celebrate every tiny victory. And this is big. Someone should make a fuss of you. You deserve it.'

'You're right,' said Simi. 'I bloody do.' Isobel's enthusiasm was infectious. 'You know what, I'm going to call him right now.'

Simi downed her drink. She felt invincible. She moved away from the noisy bar into a quiet corridor.

Martin answered immediately. 'What's up? You OK?'

'Better than OK. I'm coming to New York. Tomorrow.'

'Serious?'

'Yes. We've got some celebrating to do.'

'What? What?' Martin sounded excited. 'Tell me.'

'You should be able to guess.' Simi couldn't keep the irritation out of her voice. Typical Martin. Yes, he was busy and under a lot of pressure, but it would be nice if he took her career seriously.

'Oh my God! I'm so happy. And proud. You're amazing. It's fantastic news. I love you.'

'I love you too,' she said automatically. She knew he'd be thrilled for her, but he wasn't usually this gooey.

'How do you feel?'

'Good. A bit squiffy. We celebrated at work. And now I'm with Iso.'

'Should you be drinking?'

'What?'

'Is it safe? For the baby?'

'What?' Simi felt dread wash over her. 'No, Martin. It's not *that*. My pitch. Remember? I won.'

'Oh.' Martin's voice was flat. 'Your pitch.'

They cleared it up. They didn't row. Even managed to (sort of) laugh about it. But it was awkward. It was obvious he was disappointed. She was disappointed too, for very different reasons.

'Look, fly over if you want,' Martin said, 'but I'm working Saturday and I was going to play golf on Sunday. I'll cancel it.'

Simi tried not to sound as flat as she felt. 'No, it was a stupid idea. Forget it. You'll be home soon.'

'We'll have four whole days.'

'Yeah.'

'I was thinking, while we're talking about it . . . maybe we should book to see the GP. You know – find out if there's anything we should be doing. Get a referral maybe. We've been trying for months.'

Simi exhaled dramatically. He was obsessed with making her pregnant. It was like living in Gilead. 'There's nothing wrong with me. Women are fertile for about six days a month. So unless you're planning to give up New York and come home, there's not much a fertility clinic can do.' She got louder. 'It will happen when it happens. And if it doesn't happen when we're back living in the same city, we can talk about it.'

'Sorry.' Martin sounded distracted. 'Look, I've got to go – I'm supposed to be in a meeting. I love you. Talk tomorrow.'

'Fine.' Simi sighed deeply and turned to find Isobel in front of her.

Isobel placed an arm on Simi's shoulder, raised her eyebrows and gave a lopsided smile. 'Everything OK?'

'Yeah, he's good. Made up for me. But he's working all weekend.' Simi started walking towards the bar. 'Hey ho. Let's get another drink.'

'Already ordered,' said Isobel. 'And don't worry, *I'm* going to spoil you. *I* think you're worth it. We're going to Babington House for the weekend. My treat. Cocktails. Spa. R&R. Me and my *alobam*.'

Simi's phone pinged.

Well done on the pitch. I'm a brute. I am proud of you. You're right, it will happen when it's meant to. I'll be home for good soon enough. I love you. Mx

ISOBEL AND SIMI SPENT SATURDAY afternoon in the Cowshed spa. Isobel had booked out the double treatment room for three hours – salt scrub, reflexology, deep tissue massage and a hydro-gel mask facial.

They lay side by side on treatment beds, swaddled in fluffy white towels, and reminisced about their childhood in Nigeria – how they used to hide in Iso's mum's massive walk-in wardrobe, listening to her chatter on the phone in Russian, watching her get ready to go out. Simi had been enchanted by Isobel's mother. She was always beautifully dressed. Always smiling. And always nice to Simi. A complete contrast to Isobel's father, who wore a perpetual scowl. 'Beauty and the Beast' – that's what Simi used to call them. Only in her head though; she wouldn't have dared say it in front of Isobel. Luckily for Iso, she had inherited her mum's cheekbones and not her dad's scowl.

Simi's father had scowled a lot too, when his law firm collapsed. Even at eleven, Simi had more business sense than him. Relying on one client, Isobel's father, had proved to be a risky strategy. And if you took risks, you had to accept responsibility when things went wrong.

'People kept asking, *how come you're still single?*' Isobel was saying. 'I guess I let my guard down. I so wanted to be settled.'

Simi shook her head to clear the bad memories and tuned back in as Isobel launched into the tale of her ex-husband, Chase Adams. He was six years younger than Isobel (Simi had never dated anyone younger, she thought it was weird), a film producer (nothing exciting, just low-budget documentaries). They had met at the gym; he was a total gym rat, superfit, bulging muscles and obsessive – which should have been her first clue.

Chase had pursued Iso relentlessly. He'd been the perfect gentleman: opening doors, pulling back chairs, telling her how wonderful she was, how good she looked. And he paid when they went out – which was novel.

He didn't rush her into bed and didn't let her rush him. And she did try. This was also new. She'd thought it was a good sign. But it was all part of his game. He wanted them to get married, and once they were, it started. He detested her friends, they weren't good for her, they didn't care the way he did – so one by one, she had dropped them. He was worried about her safety – so he drove her everywhere, even if it meant waiting outside the hairdresser for hours. He convinced her she was going mad – making bad decisions, forgetting things, being irrational. He had made her believe she couldn't trust anyone, not even her own family.

'He resented my dad, was jealous of our bond. He gaslighted me. You know?' Isobel said.

Simi nodded, although she didn't have a clue what she meant. She looked it up afterwards. Coercive control – it wasn't even rare.

Isobel's voice had become low and monotone – different from her usual husky, breathless pitch. Simi realized she wanted to get the story out.

Isobel was far from dumb, but she agreed to joint bank accounts. She stopped going out, stopped wearing makeup, stopped smiling. She even stopped taking her father's calls. But that wasn't enough. When Chase's work dried up, he wanted Isobel to finance a vanity project, some documentary about gangs in New Orleans. A hundred thousand dollars. He assumed she'd have it. She didn't. He demanded she get in touch with her dad, ask him for the money. She refused. He got nastier, abusive.

The violence started with rough sex – and she'd gone along with it. Maybe even enjoyed it at first. But it became scary. He'd force himself on her, tie her up, throttle her. She knew he'd end up killing her.

One day she escaped. She ran out of their apartment when he was in the shower. Banged on a neighbour's door. She was barefoot. Thank God they were in.

Her dad ended up rescuing her – got a restraining order, sorted out a divorce, evicted Chase from her apartment and whisked her back to Nigeria to recover.

'I wanted you to know but please don't tell Boo or Ronke.' Isobel sat up, her voice almost back to normal. 'They'll think I'm stupid.'

'Of course I won't.' Simi pulled Isobel into her arms. 'And you're not stupid.'

∽

LYING SLEEPLESS IN BED HOURS later, Simi couldn't work out why she'd opened up to Isobel. She hadn't planned to. She'd considered talking to Ronke, had practised the conversation. But even to her, she sounded selfish and superficial. 'I don't want a baby because I like weekend breaks, size eight jeans, having a flat tummy, my white sofa, lie-ins and being Martin's number one.' Plus, Ronke's biological clock was deafening. And when it came to marriage and babies, she had backward,

African, views – all women wanted to be mothers. Anyone who didn't was a freak.

Talking to Boo would be even worse. Simi frowned at the thought. It would come across as nasty and rude. 'I don't want to end up like you – stressed, pissed off, boring, joyless and frumpy.' And Boo would make it all about Boo – the unfairness of not being able to have another child, how poor Sofia was destined to be an *only*. Simi wished she'd been an only. Olu was a fuckwit.

But the main reason she couldn't tell Ronke or Boo was because it would make her feel like she was failing. Saying *we* don't want kids would be fine. But saying *he does but I don't* was not fine. It meant there was a problem. And Simi and Martin didn't have problems. They were sorted, the perfect couple. Golden.

Maybe it was a mutual sharing thing – tell me your worries, I'll tell you mine. Maybe it was Isobel – she'd always been good at ferreting out secrets, storing them up to use later. Maybe it was being called *alobam*. Or maybe Simi just had to tell someone.

They were sitting in their rustic little cabin, each on her own sofa, facing each other, in front of a roaring fire. It wasn't remotely cold, but the fire had been laid and it seemed a shame to waste it. They both had sections of the Sunday papers on their laps, but they weren't reading, just staring at the flickering lights. Simi was thinking how nice it would be to come here with Martin.

'So what was the row on the phone about?' Isobel asked.

'What?'

'You and Martin.'

'It wasn't a row.'

'OK. But you know you can tell me anything.' Isobel stretched her arms across the back of her sofa and tilted her head. 'I'm your oldest friend.'

'He thinks we're trying for a baby.' Simi blurted the words out before she could change her mind.

Isobel's face was expressionless. No trace of shock or censure. 'And you're not?'

'No. I'm on the pill.'

'Fair enough. It's your body.'

'I hate lying to Martin. It feels like I'm tricking him. He won't stop banging on about bloody babies. He even suggested we see a specialist.'

'Tell him you've been checked out and you're fine. Got the all-clear. That'll shut him up. He'll start panicking he's firing blanks and never mention it again.' Isobel sat forward and clasped her hands together. As if that were the end of it.

Simi felt beads of sweat at her hairline. She'd be deeply hurt if Martin ever talked about her like this to anyone. It was unfair. And disloyal. She knew Martin was worried it might be him. He wasn't blaming her. He was trying to find a solution.

Isobel leapt up and sat next to Simi. 'Stop overthinking this. You've got loads of time.' She laid her hand on Simi's arm. 'Anyway, it's not lying.'

Simi raised her eyebrows. 'Isn't it?'

'Not telling isn't the same as lying. Women get to decide when to get pregnant – at least they do in civilized societies. This is not a big deal. You're worrying about nothing.'

Simi knew Martin would think it was a massive deal. They

were a team. 'Us against the world' was their toast. And he hadn't pushed her into it. It had been *their* plan: Work hard, play hard, build a life. And at some point, have babies. Martin's fortieth was their self-imposed deadline. Ten years ago it had sounded sensible and far off. Simi was sure she'd be ready.

But time had flown and 'at some point' became now. Martin would be forty next year. The last time he'd brought it up Simi had said yes, because it was easier than saying no. She had convinced herself that when she did get pregnant it would be fine, hormones would kick in and make her broody. She didn't expect it to happen for ages. Especially as he was off to New York. It would take a year. At least.

But it did happen, four weeks after coming off the pill. It hadn't occurred to her she could get pregnant so fast. When she saw the two blue lines, all she felt was dread – a horrible sinking feeling in the pit of her stomach. She made an appointment at her GP surgery the same day.

'I did get pregnant.' Simi bit the inside of her cheek.

Isobel didn't miss a beat. 'So you had an abortion. What's the big deal? I've had two. Simi, this isn't the Middle Ages.'

'No. Not that. It was two little pills. But I didn't tell him. He doesn't know.'

'What's the problem? Your body. Your business.'

'Iso, he's my husband. We don't have secrets.'

'Well, you kind of do.' Isobel put her hand back on Simi's arm, gave it a hard squeeze. 'Come on, lighten up. He's not going to fuck his career up. Or get stretch marks and saggy tits.'

'It's not funny. What if I'm never ready?'

'You're only thirty-five. When you get to forty you can panic.'

'So I should keep lying?'

'No. Keep not telling. Bloody men, they can be so primitive, so pathetic.'

'Martin's not like that.' Simi felt uncomfortable. She didn't want to talk about Martin any more, wished she'd never started. She walked to the window and peered into the darkness.

7

RONKE

Poor Rafa. He'd had to juggle two jobs this week – dental nurse and relationship therapist. Ronke had no one else to talk to. She was sick of having her love life trashed by Simi and Boo. They'd be outraged if they found out Kayode had stood up Aunty K. There was no way she could tell them that he'd done it twice. She'd never hear the end of it. They'd make her feel stupid. Even more stupid.

On Monday morning she was angry. Spitting-feathers angry.

'He treats me like shit. No respect at all. He didn't even have the decency to phone. A text! He sent a bloody text. Luca would never hurt you like that. So I'm sitting there like a prize plum with Aunty K calling me "poor Ronke" – I could have died of embarrassment. I'm a prat, aren't I?'

Rafa handed her a face mask. 'No, Ronke. But you're right, he shouldn't treat you like this.'

Rafa spoke perfect English but refused to lose his Spanish accent. His double 'r's usually made Ronke smile. But not this week. She snapped the mask over her ears with a deep sigh.

By Tuesday she'd become sullen. When Rafa asked if she

was OK, she snapped at him, then spent the rest of the day apologising.

Wednesday she was miserable. Grumpy and moany. 'It was *his* idea to visit Aunty K to make up for missing the week before. *His idea*. Not mine. And to accuse me of overreacting!' Ronke took her head out of her hands and looked at Rafa. 'Why can't he just say sorry?'

By Thursday she was panicky. 'Maybe I did overreact. It wasn't his fault his car broke down.' Ronke slumped into her chair. 'What if he never calls?'

'Stop torturing yourself,' said Rafa. 'He's probably afraid you'll scream at him. Why don't you call him?'

'No, not this time. It's up to him – he needs to say sorry.'

Friday was chaotic. The hygienist was off sick. Again. Weird how she only got ill on Fridays and Mondays. So Ronke had to squeeze two clean, scale and polish appointments into an already full schedule. There was no time to grumble until the end of the day, by which point Ronke was past complaining. She just wanted Kayode to call, or better still, turn up.

'Why don't you come out with us tonight?' Rafa said as he flushed the waterlines on the dental chair, his last job of the day. 'Don't stay in on your own. You'll have fun, we're going dancing . . .'

'Ah, thanks – but I won't play gooseberry. Simi's asked me to meet her and Iso for a drink. I might do that.' Ronke had no intention of going. She gave him a peck on the cheek. 'Thanks for listening. I know I've been a cow.'

∽

RONKE HAD USED HER EXPENSIVE cream, the one that was supposed to make your skin shimmer. She was already regretting the sexy underwear. The synthetic thong kept riding up her bum and the bra wires dug into her back. Over the red lace she was wearing a pair of black jeans (her M&S magic shaping ones) and a sheer (might as well show off the uncomfortable bra) jumper. A bit of bronzer. Dab of lip balm. Clean sheets. Scented candle. Low music. She checked her watch. Ten to seven. Any minute now, she hoped.

At half eight she had given up and was rummaging through the kitchen, trying to decide between beans or spaghetti hoops, wishing she'd accepted Simi's invite. A night of slagging off Kayode would have been better than a night waiting for Kayode. She'd just decided on hoops when the buzzer sounded. Three rapid fire taps. She knew it was him; Kayode's buzzes were always impatient.

She tried to look angry when his large frame filled her doorway – scuffed trainers, black jeans, grey sweatshirt, wide open smile, straight white teeth. But when he leaned to kiss her, she felt her body soften. A week of tension evaporated. Just like that.

'I love you,' he said.

'Come in,' she replied.

He had four paper carriers emblazoned with the red Maroush logo. This was a grand gesture. He'd gone all the way to Edgware Road to pick it up. Lebanese was Ronke's favourite food. After Nigerian, Italian and Indian.

He'd covered all the bases. Houmous, tabbouleh, labneh and pitta breads. Falafel, pumpkin kibbeh and cucumber salad. Aubergine stew with rice. A mixed grill (for caveman

Kayode) – skewers of minced lamb and cubed chicken with a spicy sauce and even more pitta bread. A box of rosewater Turkish delight. And a bottle of rosé.

'I should have left the car where it was and caught the Tube. I wasn't thinking.'

'You should have called. Not sent a text.'

'I know. I know.' Kayode slapped his forehead. 'I'm stupid.'

This exasperated Ronke. 'I've had such a shitty week. Why couldn't you just say sorry?'

'You were so angry. I was worried I'd make things worse. You said you needed space. I'm an idiot but you've got to forgive me.' He held her face in his hands and gazed into her eyes. 'Ronke, I love you and I'm sorry.'

'Oh, Kayode.' She kissed him.

They ate picnic-style, on the floor around her coffee table, mopping dribbles off their chins with paper napkins.

On Saturday they holed up, only venturing out to view two flats (both rubbish) and get more food. They curled up on the sofa all evening – Kayode watched the football, Ronke read *The Dentist*. On Sunday morning she watched him play rugby for the London Nigerian Sevens and screamed like a banshee whenever he touched the ball.

But the clincher, and this was a *very* big deal – he arranged dinner with Yetty and Abayomi. A couples' night out. Like normal people in a proper relationship.

Yetty was Kayode's younger sister and they were close. She'd always been polite to Ronke, but a bit distant. Ronke had asked Kayode about it. 'She's protective,' he'd said. 'Give her time – she'll love you when she gets to know you.'

Abayomi, Yetty's (boring) accountant husband, had chosen the restaurant, one of those generic gastropubs, the kind that serves craft beer and average food. Ronke and Kayode were already seated when they arrived.

'Thank God you've forgiven him.' Yetty pulled Ronke up into a warm hug. 'He's been a grump all week.'

Ronke felt weightless. *He'd been miserable. Yes!*

'We're all good now.' Kayode squeezed her thigh as she sat down again. 'She's the love of my life, Sis.'

Ronke did a tiny fist bump under the table. So this was what smug felt like. She couldn't wait to tell Simi. And Boo. *The love of my life.*

'Why did Kayode King go to the dentist?' Abayomi asked.

Ronke had heard his dentist joke before; it wouldn't improve on second telling. 'I don't know?' she replied, trying to look amused.

'To get his teeth crowned,' Abayomi chuckled loudly.

Ronke laughed politely and kicked Kayode – at least she hoped it was Kayode – under the table.

The bland meal was improved by Ronke's take-everywhere home-made pepper sauce. Yetty was a pepper freak too; they both smeared it over their steaks, much to Abayomi's disgust. Ronke promised her a couple of tubs for her freezer. Yetty hugged her goodbye. Ronke hugged her tightly back. She'd always wanted a sister.

They walked back to Kayode's flat hand in hand. Ronke felt small and safe next to him.

ᔫ

RONKE SCANNED THE BAR HOPELESSLY. It was heaving; they'd never get a table. It had been her idea to have a girls' Friday night out – she wanted to tell Boo and Simi all about last weekend's wonderful dinner with Yetty. She'd suggested Lola's, where they usually went, but Simi said Lola's was boring.

Ronke had made a real effort – faux leather leggings instead of jeans, plus mascara and heels. But next to this young cool crowd, she felt like a plump sweaty sausage. She was convinced that her legs looked like a pair of black puddings and was glad her top covered her hips.

She spotted a couple poring over a bill and made a beeline for them, hovering near by with intent, trying not to look like a psycho. They were doing the *who-had-what* thing, which meant they were doomed. Who cared if the seabass cost more than chicken salad? If you couldn't split it equally, you'd never make it work.

The couple glanced at her and Ronke mouthed 'sorry'. She was relieved Simi was late. Simi always got cross when Ronke apologized for no reason.

Ten minutes later the woman struggled into a flowing, fluffy yellow coat – a sad Big Bird. Ronke claimed the table and used her handbag and scarf to stake out two chairs. She ordered three margaritas, which the waiter (obligatory man-bun and waxed moustache), delivered with a bowl of olives. She nibbled hungrily, wishing they were crisps. Lunch had been a rushed supermarket sandwich between appointments. She took a sip from the icy glass and licked the salt off her lips. Delicious.

Simi and Boo arrived within seconds of each other.

'God, I need this. I've had the week from hell.' Simi lifted her glass. 'The Queen Bitch has excelled herself.'

'I trump you. Sofia has been a little madam all week.' Boo popped an olive in her mouth. 'And Didier's French lessons are going swimmingly. *Chienne de vie* is her latest phrase.'

'What does it mean?' asked Ronke.

'Life's a bitch,' said Boo. 'Just what every five-year-old needs in her vocab.'

'*Merde,*' said Ronke. It felt good to be out with her girls.

'Look at this.' Boo shoved her phone in Ronke's face. 'Didier sent it ten minutes ago.'

Ronke peered at Sofia laughing as she splashed in a bubble bath, surrounded by a dozen plastic ducks.

'If he's used my L'Occitane, I'll kill him,' said Boo. 'And if he leaves a mess, I'll kill him again.'

'Aw, poppet.' Ronke passed the phone to Simi. She paused for a moment, wondering whether to bring it up. 'Do you guys remember my creepy patient?'

'I thought he was barred,' said Boo.

'Yeah, he is. Tina's given him details of three other surgeries. But . . .' Ronke paused again. She took a long slow breath. Thinking about him made her anxious. He'd developed an awful obsession with Ronke. It started with unnecessary appointments. When they put a stop to that, he began loitering in reception at lunchtime. He'd follow her to the sandwich shop and back, acting as if they were friends. In the end the practice head warned him off and Ronke had thought that was the end of it. Until this week. She took another deep breath. 'He's started sending me text messages.'

'No! How did he get your number?' asked Boo.

'It's a mystery. I certainly didn't give it to him.'

'Oh my God, is it dick pics?' said Simi. 'Show me. I want to see.'

'No, of course not! You have such a filthy mind. The last one said *No one can keep us apart*. Kayode was livid – he wants me to change my number. Simi, stop laughing! It's not funny. There's something sinister about it. I've been jumpy all week.'

A man in cropped tight trousers and John Lennon glasses asked if he could have the free chair. Ronke smiled her assent.

'No, sorry, we need it.' Boo leaned over and placed her hand on the seat.

'Why?' Ronke had a sinking feeling she knew what was coming.

'Isobel,' Boo replied. 'She'll be here soon.'

'I thought it was just us.' Ronke folded her arms across her chest. 'It's not the same when she's here.'

'Don't pout. I've been running with her three times this week,' said Boo. 'She's been really supportive. Just relax, be yourself.'

'I'm always myself.' Ronke tugged her hair. 'Don't you think it's a bit weird the way she's all over us? I mean, we barely know her. What do you need support for anyway?'

'Give her a chance, Ronks,' said Simi. 'I've known her since I was five. You'll like her once you get to know her.'

'I don't not like her.' Before Ronke could explain that all she wanted was a relaxed night out with her best friends, Isobel made her entrance in a short silver flapper dress, sleeveless with a deep plunge neck. Even in this fancy bar, she stood out. Pretty much everyone watched her glide across the tiled floor in ankle-breaking green heels. Her straight blonde bob swished. Her metallic almond-shaped nails strobed as she waved a hello.

She half-hugged each of them in turn. Ronke was impressed. If she'd bent over in a dress that short, her arse would have been on full display. Even her perfume made a statement – dark, spicy and overpowering.

Isobel slid into her chair and crossed her long legs. 'Thanks for the invite. It's so nice to have you three.'

Ronke ordered a bottle of house white and a jug of tap water. They were not having champagne. Cheap wine allergy or not.

'Ronke's got a stalker,' said Simi. 'And he's sexting her.'

'No, he's not,' said Ronke.

'It's not something to joke about.' Isobel placed one hand on Ronke's arm. 'I had a stalker. I know how it goes. You need to take it seriously. Log every contact, take photos, screen-grab messages . . .'

Wow. Even in the stalker stakes Isobel won. Ronke lifted her arm to dislodge Isobel's hand and said, 'It's just a needy patient. A saddo, not a proper stalker.'

'That's how it starts,' said Simi. 'One day it's *Hello, Ms Tinubu*. The next he's flashing his junk. I hope he does send a dick pic. I've never seen one in real life. I mean, I've seen a dick . . .'

'You're disgusting,' said Ronke. 'And sex-obsessed. Martin needs to come home before you explode.'

Isobel wasn't smiling. 'If he gives you any trouble, Ronke, call me.' She waited until Ronke met her eyes.

Ronke looked away, uncomfortable. 'Don't worry. He won't. Now can we talk about something else. Please?'

'I got stuck on the phone with Mum on the way here.' Simi tipped her head back and downed the rest of her margarita. 'She and my dad have been divorced for a quarter of a century but all she wants to do is complain about him. How her life would have been so much better if she'd never met him. I mean, she's basically saying she wishes I hadn't been born.'

'At least she talks about him.' Ronke leaned over and gave Simi's shoulder a rub. 'My mum never mentions my dad. It's like he didn't exist.'

'I'm sorry,' said Boo. 'But I don't get it. What on earth were our mothers thinking? I'm not being racist . . .'

'Here we go.' Simi rolled her eyes.

'I'm not. Honest. But come on, we're talking the seventies. Why would any sane English woman go for an African bloke?'

Simi sat forward and puffed out her chest. 'I reckon my dad did the *I am a royal prince – my father is the* Akarigbo *of Remoland. Marry me and you will be a queen* routine.' She sat back. 'Mum would have lapped it up.'

Ronke laughed delightedly – she loved it when Simi did her Nigerian accent.

'They must have been mad,' said Boo. 'Knowing how much it would upset your parents, that you'd be stared at on the street, that your kids would be picked on. I wouldn't do it.'

'They fell in love,' said Ronke. 'Colour had nothing to do with it. It's like asking why you married Didier.'

'It's not the same, though. Back then interracial marriage was rare. Not that my father had any intentions of marrying my mum – he already had a wife. It would be like Sofia going off with a Zulu warrior.'

'Zulu warriors are hot.' Isobel placed her long fingers over

Ronke's arm. Again. 'My parents were in love too. She left us and it broke my dad's heart.' Her eyes seemed to darken. 'I'll never forgive her. He's on his fifth wife now – each one younger and more stupid than the last. And they all hate me.'

'I guess I should be glad mine's only on his second,' said Simi. 'Talking about Nigerian men . . . How's Kayode?'

'Good. All good,' said Ronke. She didn't want to bring Kayode into this conversation. 'Are we eating here? Or should we go somewhere else?'

'You're in charge, Ronks.' Simi topped up their glasses. 'Make sure I eat loads. Isobel's a bad influence and I can't have a hangover tomorrow. I've got a casting session. Ballerinas to audition.'

'But tomorrow's Saturday?' said Boo.

'Fashion never sleeps.' Simi winked.

Ronke headed to the bar to pick up menus. Isobel's perfume arrived before her. When Ronke turned, she was at her shoulder. She grabbed Ronke's free hand, her fingers soft and cool.

'We should meet up for a coffee, just me and you. It would be nice to have a proper chat. I think we're going to have so much in common. And not just a weakness for bad boys. I'm particularly foolish when they're tall, dark and handsome. What does Kayode look like?'

'He's tall. And dark. And I think he's handsome.' Ronke picked up the menus.

'He sounds right up my street.' Isobel winked.

Ronke waved the menus in the air, trying to brush off her annoyance. 'Sorry, he's taken,' she said, stomping back to their table.

8

BOO

'A RAT. CAN YOU believe he suggested we get Sofia a rat?' Boo started ranting as soon as Simi walked through her front door.

'Any chance of a coffee?' said Simi, unbuttoning her coat.

'Kettle's on. You'll have to settle for instant; I don't know how to work Didier's machine. A pet rat though? Are you listening?'

'Yes. Yes. Where are Didier and Sofia anyway?' Simi draped her coat over a stool and sat at the island, phone in hand.

'Football and then a kids' party.' Boo handed her a mug. 'Sofia's social diary is more exciting than mine.'

'They say you're never more than six feet from a rat in London. You've probably got one already. Maybe more than one.' Simi did a slow 270-degree scan of Boo's kitchen floor. Boo followed her gaze, half expecting to see a rat run out from under the fridge.

'He's winding you up,' said Simi.

'No, he's dead serious. It's blackmail. He says rats are clean, intelligent and affectionate. And if we don't move . . .'

'What's it got to do with moving?' Simi waved her phone around. 'Is your Wi-Fi down?'

Boo swallowed her annoyance. 'You don't listen. I've told you all this before. Sofia wants a puppy.'

'You said rat.' Simi stared at her phone.

'Yes. But it started with a dog. I'm at work two days a week and I want to add more, so we can't have one. Simi, can you leave your phone alone for one minute?'

'I'm multi-tasking.'

'Well, it's rude.' Boo snatched Simi's phone and shut it in a drawer. 'Didier wants us to sell up and buy a bigger and cheaper house in some godforsaken suburban hellhole.' She drew a house with her fingers, then pointed at herself. 'Little wifey, works part-time from home and turns into his mum – a cake-making, pinny-wearing, green-fingered frump, whose idea of using her brain is crocheting an ugly shawl. While Didier swans off to the City like the big bacon-hunting he-man. And Sofia gets a dog, which muggins here will have to look after.'

'Sounds like hell,' said Simi. 'The country is full of old people. And you can't get decent sushi.'

'It's all because Didier's perfect parents moved to the country when he was little and he had a dog, which made him the wonderful, kind human being he reckons he is. If I won't move, it's a rat. The perfect pet for city dwellers.'

'We had guard dogs. Big vicious things. They didn't come in the house. I was terrified of them.'

'Simi, I don't want a pet dog or a guard dog. And I do not want a rat.'

'What's wrong with the robot dog I gave her for Christmas?' asked Simi. 'That's the ideal pet. Doesn't shed, doesn't shit.'

'Its annoying bark?' said Boo. 'Anyway, that's my point. Scruff the robodog and Sofia were inseparable for three days.

She taught it to sit, stay and bark – in French, obviously. But she got bored and now it lives in a cupboard. Which is what would happen if we got a dog or a rat. Except it wouldn't stay in a cupboard and I'd have to pick up the pieces. Or in this case, the shit.'

'They eat rats in Nigeria,' said Simi. 'Bushmeat. It's a delicacy. They call them grasscutters but that doesn't fool me. I've seen them at the market.'

'Bloody hell, they'll eat anything.' Boo's lips curled. 'I'm surprised Ronke hasn't suggested rat fritters for Sofia's party.'

Simi snapped her fingers. 'Boom! There you go. Sorted. Tell them you can't get a pet rat because Aunty Ronke won't be able to resist cooking it. Same for gerbils, hamsters, even guinea pigs. It's all bushmeat. All yummy as far as Ronke is concerned.'

'She wouldn't.' Boo swallowed, suddenly queasy.

'They don't know that.' Simi did her dirty laugh. 'And she might. Ronke just might!'

'It's not funny, Simi,' Boo sighed. 'You don't get it; they gang up on me. Didier has this idea of happy families. But it's not mine. And Sofia agrees with anything he says. Did I tell you he's already booked our flights to France for Christmas?'

Boo had half listened to Didier and Sofia babbling away in French on FaceTime with Mamie *et* Papy this morning. But she'd understood enough of it to know they'd already planned the Christmas Day menu.

'You always go to France for Christmas,' said Simi.

'Exactly. Why don't I get a say? He takes it for granted that it's my dream holiday too. What if I want to do something different? Or go to *my* mum's?'

'Do you want to spend Christmas in Yorkshire?'

'No, of course not. I can't think of anything worse.' Boo could see it now. All of them squeezed into the tiny front room. Her mother passing round an endless supply of cheese footballs. Her stepdad shouting to be heard over the TV, which was never turned off. 'Don't get me wrong, I love my mum, but we're so different. Didier actually likes his parents. His mum sends him handwritten recipes for stocks and sauces. They're sweet and they adore Sofia, but I don't want to turn into them.' Boo sighed. 'Sometimes it feels like a whole dull future has been mapped out for me.'

'You're being dramatic. Some families are Waltons and some are Lannisters. We got the short straw, Didier got the long. That's life. It's not all bad.'

'If we're not talking about Sofia, Didier and I have nothing to say to each other any more. I want to have some fun.'

'Well, your first gel manicure will be fun. Or you could get acrylics like me.' Simi wriggled her fingers. 'Go on, be brave. If you don't want to be bored, you need to stop being boring.'

Boo blinked. Isobel had said something similar on their run yesterday. Something about changing things up, taking risks, making your own excitement. She made it sound so easy. So enticing.

'We'd better get a move on,' said Simi. 'Isobel doesn't like being kept waiting.'

∽

CLINK. CLINK. BOO TAPPED HER nails on the steel of her laptop. They made a marvellous sound. Amethyst blue (Isobel chose the colour), oval and mega shiny. And, according to Isobel, chip-proof. Boo tried not to think about toxic chemicals.

She took a picture of her left hand and sent it to Isobel.

You were right, it's the perfect colour. Bx

Isobel's reply was instant.

I'm always right! Come out and play – let tubby hubby look after Sofia.

Boo winced. Isobel had coined the phrase 'tubby hubby'. It was a bit mean. But if the cap fits . . .

I wish. I've got a bathroom to clean. I'm not sure who's less toilet-trained – husband or daughter. LOL. Have fun.

Clink. Clink.

Boo was surprised at how excited she'd got about a manicure. She'd always been proud of being low-maintenance. She and Ronke had laughed at Simi with her expensive blow-dries, facials, eyebrow threading, leg waxing, body brushing and teeth whitening. Boo would never turn into Simi – she couldn't afford to. But a bit of pampering and a few new clothes wasn't a crime.

When her first Sweaty Betty order arrived (there'd been another since), Boo had opened it as if it was the gateway to a new life. A silver bag inside a grey box, each item wrapped in pink tissue paper. The accompanying note, on thick cream vellum, felt like destiny:

Boo, you have exquisite taste. Whether you're getting sweaty or going social – nothing can hold you back. You are amazing!

It was an investment, Boo told herself. And it had already

paid off. She had worked out more in the last month than the previous six combined. And it wasn't just about the running. Isobel's confidence was infectious. She made Boo feel better about herself – more attractive, more capable. Not just a wife and mother, but a woman with a brain, a career and a not-so-out-of-shape body.

Clink. Clink.

What to wear to work on Monday? She had a meeting with Neil about the podcast – to scope out potential scientists and researchers she could interview.

Boo lost herself in a daydream. She'd had it twice this week. Didier was dead. She was at his funeral, slimmer and wearing a sharp trouser suit (black, of course), looking haunted but in a beautiful melancholic way. Ronke, Simi and Isobel were beside her, handing her tissues. Sofia was airbrushed out of this fantasy – she simply didn't exist. Boo tried to imagine Sofia standing between her and Neil. She couldn't. She opened her eyes. What the fuck was wrong with her?

The door flew open and Sofia exploded into the room with a (very much alive) Didier.

'Mama! Mama! I've got a tattoo!' Sofia shrieked.

'Don't panic,' said Didier. 'It's not a real one. I'm not the imbecile.'

'It's *an* imbecile,' said Boo. Being irritated by and correcting his 'Franglais' was a new symptom of her resentment, and yet another thing to feel guilty about.

'Yuck! Blue nails.' Sofia threw her coat on the floor. Didier stooped to pick it up.

'Leave it!' Boo felt instantly bad for snapping. She knew

she should stop picking on him. 'Sofia, hang up your coat,' she added in a softer tone.

'But I'm busy. I'm showing you my tattoo.' Sofia pulled up her sleeve to reveal a hideous grey rat with pink ears and a long curly tail.

Boo couldn't help herself. She burst into laughter, crouched down on the rug and pulled her child into a hug.

'He's called Remy. Like in *Ratatouille*.'

'I've watched it.' About thirty fucking times, she didn't add.

'I'm hungry.' Sofia wriggled out of her arms. 'What's for supper, Papa?'

'It's not even five,' Boo said. 'Didn't they have food at the party?'

'Carrot sticks and yucky stuff. Gemma doesn't have an Aunty Ronke to make nice food.'

'Have a banana.' Boo pointed at the fruit bowl.

'I hate bananas.'

'I hate my life,' Boo mumbled.

Didier gave her a disappointed look. She hadn't mumbled quietly enough. 'Eat a banana, Sofia,' he said. 'We'll all go to Pizza Express for supper.'

'Yay!' yelled Sofia, grabbing a banana and ripping off the skin. 'I want dough balls.'

'She's had pizza twice this week,' said Boo.

'It's the weekend. Relax. We'll fill her with junk and send her to bed. I'll make you vongole and you can pretend you still love me.'

Whoosh. Boo undid and remade her ponytail, guilt flooding through her. 'Don't be stupid. Of course I love you.'

Didier did his Gallic shrug. 'Good. You won't have to pretend.'

Boo gave him a peck on the cheek, hoping to make up for her recent peevishness. 'It doesn't matter how good it is. Seafood spaghetti won't make me move to suburbia.'

'I know, *ma chérie*. But a rat might.'

'A rat called Remy,' squealed Sofia, spitting out chunks of banana.

'We'll have to get two rats, Sofia.' Didier squatted and picked up half-chewed banana bits off the floor. 'They're social creatures.'

'Remy and Emile.' Sofia clapped her sticky hands and rubbed them on her jeans.

'You're a pair of barmpots,' said Boo in a broad Yorkshire accent. 'Any more rat talk and I'm abandoning this sinking ship.'

∽

THE FOLLOWING WEEK, BOO COULDN'T wait to see Isobel. She wanted to talk about Neil. She needed a second opinion.

He hadn't been at work on Monday, and wasn't in on Tuesday morning either. He turned up after lunch wearing black jeans, a white T-shirt and a crumpled grey linen jacket. Didier didn't have these sorts of clothes. He had two looks – suit or slob. And Didier wouldn't look like this even if he did. His legs weren't this long. His thighs not this firm.

Neil made a beeline for Boo's cubicle and sat on her desk. Boo's heart started beating faster. Adrenaline and dopamine, she knew, triggered by threat, happiness or lust. But which was it? She was glad she'd put the framed picture of Didier and Sofia in her drawer. No one else had pictures at their workstations. Or a *'J'aime Maman'* mug.

'I loved that piece you did on genomics in medical research. You have a real gift for making complex topics readable.' Neil slipped off his jacket.

'Er, thanks. It's a subject I'm passionate about.' Boo noticed that she was moving her hands more than usual, blue nails flashing. The cubicles were minute and his knee grazed her arm. She felt a tiny static shock and wondered if he felt it too.

'How would you feel about doing an edited version for *The Telegraph*?' he asked. 'You'd have to dumb it down, of course.'

Boo stared at his tanned arms; she wanted to touch them. 'I'd love to.' His knee met her arm again and their eyes locked for a beat too long. Boo's mouth felt dry.

'We need to sort out your review.' Neil tilted his head and smiled. 'Not next week – I'm in Germany. The week after. Let's do Monday, over lunch. I know just the place. We're wasting you, Boo. And I hate waste. I have big plans. We're going to do fun stuff together.'

She'd replayed their conversation a hundred times – reading meaning into words, gestures and pauses.

What to wear for the lunch? She wanted to look professional, but not Hillary Clinton formidable. Attractive, but not Kim Kardashian slutty. Amal Clooney got it right – warm and sophisticated. But while they might be a similar height, Amal weighed half as much as Boo and had a billion times her budget.

Boo couldn't remember what she'd worn to work before Sofia. She'd never cared about clothes before, but now she hated her monotone and uninspiring jumble of black knee-length skirts, grey shirts, joggers, hoodies and over-washed tees.

She couldn't turn to Simi or Ronke for help. Simi had keys to the bank of Martin and wore the most ridiculous things to work. Belts pretending to be skirts, wrap dresses that showed off her non-existent cleavage, slinky scraps of silk that looked like lingerie, skin-tight trouser suits and always those towering heels. Ronke wore shapeless black scrubs. She didn't even have to wash them – they were supplied and laundered by her practice.

In any case, Boo couldn't ask them. They'd want to know why she suddenly cared what she looked like. They knew her too well; they'd be suspicious.

But Isobel she could ask. Not that Boo would ever dress like Isobel. But they were the same height and a similar build – especially now Boo had lost some weight. Most important though, she knew Isobel wouldn't judge.

∾

'A JUMPSUIT. IT'S A NO-BRAINER,' Isobel said as she pushed open the café door.

'Are you sure?' asked Boo. 'Is orange really the new black?'

It turned out that Isobel had a lot to say about jumpsuits. The miracle outfit apparently, apart from the toilet issue. 'He won't be able to keep his hands off you,' she said at the end of her lecture.

'Don't be daft. I want to look credible and current. I want him to take me seriously.' Which was the truth. Pretty much.

'Think of it as a playsuit. Just putting it on makes you more daring. No risk of doing a Simi and flashing your knickers. Best of all, the right jumpsuit will make you five inches taller and half a stone slimmer. It will stretch you – it's remarkable.'

'You had me at taller.' Boo glanced at Isobel; she looked so self-assured. Maybe the right clothes could change the way she saw herself? 'But I don't have a jumpsuit. What about the dress I wore last week – you know, the dark grey one?'

'Boo, we need to go shopping.' Isobel pulled out her tablet. 'Are you an eight?'

'Ten. Maybe twelve . . .' said Boo.

'No wonder all your clothes are shapeless. They're the wrong size. There's no way you're a twelve. You've got a great figure – you need to stop hiding it. And you need to stop buying cheap crap. No offence, but you get what you pay for. Get our coffees and I'll start looking.'

By the time Boo got back, Isobel had added three jump-suits to her basket.

'Best to order a few, then choose the right one. Send me selfies. I love a makeover.' Isobel clicked away. 'God, no, you'd look like one of the Ghostbusters . . . This is gorgeous, but I'm not sure you're ready for tiger print.'

The jumpsuits she did approve of all looked identical to Boo, but Isobel waved off her concerns. 'If you don't like it, send it back,' she said when Boo vetoed a backless thing. 'You can dress it up or down and it won't date. You need to remember you're a woman. A sexy woman. Jump-start his passion with a jumpsuit.' She laughed at her own joke.

'I'm not sure Didier would even notice,' said Boo.

'I wasn't talking about Didier.' Isobel winked. 'Anyway, how did you end up with him? You're so gorgeous. You could have picked anyone.'

Boo pretended she didn't hear that as she got rid of a couple of the more extreme options in the cart – one slutty, the other north of £400.

Shopping done, they chatted about Sofia's party. Isobel asked for pictures of Sofia for the cake – she wouldn't say why: it was a surprise.

'Is Ronke OK?' asked Isobel.

'Yeah. Why?' Boo was startled at the abrupt change of subject.

'I've messaged her a few times, suggested we meet up – I want to get to know her – but she's always too busy. I'm starting to worry she doesn't like me. And she seemed upset the other night.'

'It's not you.' Boo squirmed. 'It was probably my fault with all the dad talk. Hers died when she was young. She never really got over it.'

'Really? What was he like?'

'I've no idea. I know as little about him as I do about mine. But she thinks he was perfect.'

'He wasn't,' Isobel muttered.

'Huh?' Boo cocked her head.

'Nothing.' Isobel waved her hand dismissively. 'Didn't your mum tell you anything about your father?'

'Just once, when she did the birds and bees thing.'

'What did she say?' asked Isobel.

'This is so dull.' Boo stretched her arms behind her and looked towards the exit. She'd only brought up fathers to move the conversation along. She could hardly tell Isobel that Ronke thought she was strange and pushy.

'No, it's not. I want to know everything.'

'OK,' said Boo. 'So Mum moved to London when she was nineteen, got a job as a receptionist in a swanky hotel. Enter this sophisticated Nigerian bloke – he splashed the cash and swept her off her feet. They went to Paris for their first date; he gave her a gold bracelet on the second. She was naive, thought it was true love. He set her up in a flat in Finchley and she got pregnant. He stuck around for a few months, long enough to choose my name, but not long enough to meet me.'

'He named you Boo?'

'Bukola. He said it was his mother's name. Probably another lie.'

'I think it's a lovely name,' said Isobel.

'I don't.' Boo hated the name – it reminded her of her father, the con artist.

'Your poor mum,' said Isobel. 'It must have been so hard for her.'

Boo shrugged. 'She moved back to Pickering and met Terry, my stepdad, when I was four. They got married a year later. She's happy. I'm happy. It's all good.'

'Yes. It is,' said Isobel.

Boo was relieved that Isobel understood. 'Mum was so stupid. She thought something terrible must have happened. She even went to the Nigerian High Commission. They laughed in her face, told her he had a wife at home.'

'And you never tried to find him?' Isobel's forehead was creased with concern.

'Why would I? According to Ronke, one in four Africans is

Nigerian, so it would be like looking for a needle in a hay-stack. And anyway, I don't want anything to do with him.'

'What's your maiden name?'

'Whyte.'

'No, I mean, your father's name,' said Isobel.

'Dele Babangari.' Boo shifted her hips and glanced towards the door again. She knew Isobel was trying to support her but she was sick of the topic and starting to feel pressured. 'Can we talk about something else? He's not my dad. He's nothing to me.'

'You're right.' Isobel laid her hand gently on Boo's arm. 'He's nothing to you. When's your birthday?'

'August,' said Boo. 'Why?'

'I told you, I want to know everything.' Isobel took her hand back and interlaced her fingers. 'That makes you four months older than me.'

Boo laughed. 'Practically your aunt.'

∽

THE NEXT DAY, WHILE BOO was trying to persuade Sofia that courgettes were not poisonous, a massive box arrived. Boo was excited but nervous. Could confidence be sewn into clothes? She made Sofia wash her hands twice before they took it upstairs. Under layers of black tissue were five exqui-site black jumpsuits, each wrapped in more tissue, tied with black grosgrain ribbons.

Sofia stood on the bed, jumping up and down, giving a running commentary while Boo tried them on.

'No, Mama, too tight – you look fat!'

'Too long – you'll fall over!'

And then: 'You look beautiful,' Sofia whispered. 'Like a model. But betterer.'

Boo corrected her absently. She turned in front of the mirror. Isobel was right. Taller and slimmer. And more interesting.

'Take a picture.' Boo handed Sofia her phone and stood on tiptoe. She'd have to think about shoes. Would her smart black ones work? Making an effort was a real effort.

She stepped out of it carefully. £295. It would be the second most expensive item of clothing she'd ever owned. The most expensive being her wedding dress and that was only four quid more.

She ran Sofia's bath and watched her drowning ducks, wincing at the blood-curdling death screams Sofia made as they died one by one, before bobbing back to the surface to be killed again. As per Isobel's instructions, she sent her the photo, then packed the returns, hiding the box at the back of the wardrobe. Sofia would babble about their dress-up session, but Didier didn't need to know it was from a posh designer shop. Not that she needed his permission.

Her phone pinged.

I told you. SEXY! Goodbye Dull Boo. Hello Hot Boo!

9

SIMI

Life was better when Martin was home. And he was here for four whole days.

On the phone Simi crept stealthily through their conversations, cramming omission after omission into her jam-packed box of withholding. Isobel's words came back to her: 'Not telling isn't the same as lying.' Yet again she was right. Martin didn't need to know she'd spent an hour talking to Isobel's headhunter last week. He didn't need to know how often she woke up hungover with a dry mouth and banging head, feeling empty. In the flesh, none of it mattered.

He'd arrived at ten past three the previous afternoon. Simi was at the door waiting; she'd taken the day off work. They stood hugging, swaying on the spot in silence.

It was like being fitted with stabilizer wheels. Then he picked her up and carried her to the bedroom. They emerged at seven and went across the road to Lanterna, their local, for their usual. Seabass with olives for her (he ate the parmesan chips), American hot for him (he ate all of it), two green salads (she ate both) and a bottle of Montepulciano (they shared). They were back in bed at half eight.

'Time to get up!' Simi flung open the curtains. The sky was blue, the sun was shining. Everything was wonderful.

'You cow.' Martin pulled the duvet over his head. 'What time is it?'

'Ten.'

'How did that happen?' He peeked out. 'Come back for a cuddle.'

'We tried that at nine.'

'I think I could try again.'

'You're a pervert. Now get up. Borough Market calls.' She threw his jeans at him.

Simi had invited the gang for supper on Saturday. Martin loved hosting and she was at her best when she was showing off her golden life. He'd suggested pizzas from next door – but there was no way that was going to happen. She'd spent ages flicking through her seldom-used cookbooks. What could she make that would astound her friends? And be edible? She'd considered asking Ronke to help, but Ronke would want to make Nigerian food. She wanted to blow their minds.

'Why are you cooking anyway? You hate cooking.' Martin wriggled into his jeans.

'I've got a cunning plan,' said Simi. 'It's foolproof. As long as you don't overcook the steaks.'

'We'll need to get gas for the barbecue.'

'All done. Your domestic goddess wife has seen to it. And Essie cleaned it yesterday. We just need to get to the shops.'

'Get a move on then.' He rattled his car keys. 'We can grab brunch at Brindisa. I'm starving.'

'Can't think why.' Simi winked as she pulled on her multi-coloured mirrored mosaic over-the-knee Tom Ford boots. 'We have to be back by three. I've got a delivery and it needs to go in the fridge.'

'What?'

'Dauphinoise potatoes, twice-cooked soufflés and choc-olate cheesecake.'

'You cheating little hussy.'

'It's better than poisoning our friends. And if you let on, you'll never have sex again.'

'We should get some flowers for Amanita.' Martin held the door open.

'Who's Amanita?'

'Ebenezer's wife.'

'Why does his wife need flowers? Don't tell me she's preg-nant again?' Simi regretted the words before she got to the end of the sentence.

'No, it's not good. She has breast cancer. He told me yes-terday. The poor bloke – he's so worried. She starts chemo next week.' He slapped Simi's bottom. 'Come on! You said we had to rush.'

Simi didn't meet his eyes. Martin had been back for five minutes. How could she not have known what was going on with Ebenezer? She pictured him sitting at his reception desk, smiling as he greeted her. Only last night she had pre-tended to be on the phone to avoid a chat.

One of her boots had slipped down her knee. She leaned over to pull it up. A few seconds ago they'd made her feel sassy. Now she felt selfish.

'Simi! You OK?'

'Yup. Let's stop at Chez Michele. They do amazing bouquets. I'll get them to deliver on Monday.'

∽

FORTY-NINE. FORTY-EIGHT. FORTY-SEVEN. Simi's eyes flicked between timer and oven. She had no idea what she was looking for. All she knew about soufflés was that they made an impact, which was why she'd chosen them. The leaflet said eight minutes and she was going to be precise.

She smoothed down her dress, a silk-chiffon DVF mini wrap with a palm print and a ruffled neck. The dress was as iconic as her evening was going to be. Classic, classy and effortless. Martin had refused to change out of his old jeans and vintage Arsenal top. And he refused to put on shoes (Simi had made him swap his holey socks at least). He poured wine – topped the glasses too full and too often, passed around spiced nuts and slapped Simi on the bottom whenever they passed each other. He was in his element.

Ronke was in jeans (as usual). Earrings were her idea of pulling out all the stops. But Boo looked different – almost stylish – in a black jumpsuit instead of her tired leather skirt. The shoes were wrong though, way too clunky. 'Love the jumpsuit, Boo,' said Simi. 'Where did you get it?'

'Iso chose it.' Boo did a twirl. 'She has a real eye for fashion. She thinks I should get a weave.'

Simi felt herself bristle. She worked in fashion. She had *two* real eyes.

Boo seemed chattier too. A bit like she'd had too much sugar. Or coke. But no, Goody-Boo-Shoes would never do drugs – not even in uni, when everyone experimented. Boo was high on Isobel. It was all, Isobel this (so athletic, we're doing 5k in thirty-two minutes now), Isobel that (incredibly creative, her hip-hop party idea is inspired), Isobel the other (she's healing at last – Chase did so much damage, she'd forgotten how to trust people). At one point during one of the eulogies, Didier had stretched his arms with a yawn and made an exaggerated eye-roll. Simi knew how he felt.

Simi hadn't realized how easy-going Kayode was. Or how funny. He looked relaxed and natural. He pulled back Ronke's chair when they sat for dinner and kept touching her – playing with her hair, stroking her arm, resting his hand on her knee. It was sweet. They even had inside jokes.

And then he told them the story of how they met.

'So nobody likes the dentist, right?' Kayode paused and looked around the table. 'But we all know we've got to go. So you book an appointment and pray they won't mention the drill. In I walk. And BOOM!' He threw his hands dramatically in the air, then took Ronke's hand. 'The most beautiful woman I have ever seen.'

Simi watched Ronke's cheeks redden. She looked so happy.

'Ah,' said everyone. Except Boo.

'Now you may not appreciate this, but even I struggle to impress a girl when I'm dribbling down my chin.' Kayode beamed a toothy smile. 'I look over at her assistant – he's winking and twitching. I figure either that I'm sending out the wrong signals or he's trying to tell me something.' Kayode put his arms around Ronke. 'It's all down to Rafa really. Thanks to him I worked up the courage to ask her out.' He kissed Ronke gently on the forehead.

'Ah,' said everyone. Even Boo.

Nineteen. Eighteen. Seventeen. This was bloody easy. The plates were warm and waiting with their little piles of micro herbs. 'A fiver for a sprig of cress – they must have seen you coming,' Martin had said. She'd ignored him. He'd blown the budget on six tomahawk steaks.

Beep. Beep. Beep.

Simi opened the oven and peeped in. They'd risen! Oh no, they were collapsing. She grabbed one, burned her fingers and yelped.

'They look amazing!' said Ronke, who had rushed over to help.

'That one's sinking. And they're tiny. They looked much bigger in the picture.'

'Don't worry, they're perfect.' Ronke grabbed a tea towel and placed a ramekin on each plate. 'Is there a sauce?'

'Sauce?' asked Simi, with a note of panic.

'Ignore me. They don't need sauce. You go first – it's your gig.' Simi took two plates. Ronke followed, balancing four like a pro.

The soufflés were OK. Minuscule but edible. They all cleared their plates. Which wasn't difficult.

Martin grinned at her. 'You'll have to give Ronke the recipe.'

Simi kicked him under the table. 'I assume you'll be OK cooking the steaks by yourself, seeing as I've done everything else?'

Martin kissed her, topped up the glasses and headed to the balcony with Didier and Kayode.

'Isn't this nice?' said Ronke, once they were out of earshot. 'The six of us together. And the boys get on so well.'

'Men,' said Simi. 'But yeah, I can't wait for Martin to come home for good. I'm better when he's here.'

'How come you didn't invite Isobel?' asked Boo. 'She was really upset.'

'Boo! You idiot.' Simi knew how petulant Isobel could get if she felt excluded. At school once she'd made Simi's life hell just for sitting next to someone else at lunch. She had thought of asking her but in the end decided not to – Iso could be a diva and Martin hated drama; they probably wouldn't hit it off.

'Sorry,' said Boo, 'you didn't say it was a secret. I just assumed she was coming.'

'She's never met Martin, and it's a couples thing,' said Simi. 'She takes over a bit and I wanted a relaxed evening.'

'I'm glad she's not here,' said Ronke. 'She's way too intense. She keeps calling me, wanting to meet up.'

'It's called being nice.' Boo tapped her nails on the glass dining table.

'I wish you hadn't told her.' Simi was becoming irritated with Boo, acting like Isobel was *her* friend, as if she was the first person in the world ever to have a gel manicure.

The balcony door opened and cold air rushed in. Simi hugged herself; her skimpy wrap dress offered no protection.

'Five minutes' rest and we're on,' said Martin. 'Who's for red?'

'Bugger! The potatoes!' Simi dashed to the kitchen, tailed closely by Ronke. 'Oh no! Oh no!' she wailed. 'I was meant to take them out twenty minutes ago.'

'We can do a salvage job,' said Ronke calmly.

'It's cremated. Ruined.' Simi poked at the dried-out crust. Ronke laughed. 'You'll do anything to avoid carbs.'

'It's not funny.' But Simi was glad Ronke was here. You could count on her to diffuse tension. The opposite of Isobel, who could be relied on to amplify it. She had a sudden vision of Isobel's pinched face as she said 'Bloody men' a few weeks ago, and realized she didn't actually want Martin to meet her.

'Have you got any bread?' asked Ronke, pulling Simi back to the present.

'There's an artisan baguette,' said Simi.

'Who needs potatoes when there's posh bread?' Ronke grabbed a bowl. 'Pass the vinegar and olive oil. I'll mix up a quick dressing.'

The steaks were perfect, the bread was bread, the salad was crunchy, Ronke's vinaigrette was yummy. And of course, she'd brought a tub of pepper sauce.

Simi scraped the burned bits (the top inch) off the potatoes and put what was left in the middle of the table.

'Yum, just how I like them.' Martin reached over and shovelled some on to his plate.

'You've invented potato brûlée,' said Didier, doing the same. 'You should patent it.'

They all laughed, even Simi. She didn't have to be perfect, not with this lot. Ronke was right: this felt good, like old times.

'Next to Kayode,' said Ronke, 'you get a Michelin star. The first time I cooked in his kitchen, the instruction manual was still in the oven.'

'Not fair.' Kayode smiled and touched Ronke's cheek. 'I'd just moved in.'

'Ah, so Kayode is like *ma chérie*.' Didier put his arm around Boo. 'Lukewarm baked beans in a microwaved potato is her idea of a good meal. If not for me, our little Sofia would starve.'

'That's rubbish.' Boo pushed his arm away. 'I might not like cooking, but I do plenty of it.'

Simi was not going to let a Boo–Didi domestic spoil her evening. 'What were you guys plotting on the balcony? You looked furtive.'

'Well, funny you should ask . . .' Martin grinned and raised his glass to Kayode. 'This lovely man has got three tickets for the Emirates tomorrow.'

'Ah, it's nothing,' said Kayode as the three men clinked glasses.

'No way,' said Simi.

'It's only a couple of hours,' said Martin. 'We have the whole day.'

'But it's not, is it? It's drinks first, drinks during and drinks after – to celebrate or drown your sorrows. By the time you get back you'll be pissed.'

'He'll behave.' Kayode gave a three-finger salute. 'Scout's honour. No pub, straight home.'

'Let them go,' said Ronke. 'It's good for them to have boy-time.'

'They're not boys. Oh, I give up. Go! But do not get blotto and make sure you win. I don't need a grumpy husband.' Simi would use the free afternoon to meet Isobel and face the music.

'I'll make it up to you,' whispered Martin. 'And I don't care if you can't cook. I fucking love you.'

∽

Isobel had turned down Simi's suggestion of lunch but after a lot of cajoling agreed to a quick coffee. She turned up late, looked sullen and sounded petulant. 'You look tired,' she said. 'And pale. Is that a spot on your chin?'

Simi didn't take the bait. 'Not enough sleep. I told you I'd keep him chained up.'

'You don't have to lie,' said Isobel. 'I know you had a party last night. You invited everyone except me. I guess I'm chopped liver.'

'It was supper, not a party. And it was Martin's idea, so don't be cross. I'm sorry. You know I love you. We all do. Boo was singing your praises all night, twirling around in her jumpsuit, saying what a supportive friend you are. And I'm here now.'

'Only 'cos he's at football. I'm not good enough to come to your party but fine to fill an empty afternoon. I get it.' Isobel scowled. It made her look like her dad.

'Look, Iso, I've said I'm sorry. I don't know what else I can do.' Simi forced a short laugh. 'We're not in primary school any more. You're my oldest friend. Come on.'

'OK, I forgive you.' Isobel's tone changed, became huskier. 'I'm in a foul mood. I got a call from my lawyer yesterday. My ex is coming to London. I've got a restraining order but apparently I can't stop him if it's for work, and he's doing a recce for some job. I know it's pathetic. We're divorced, I'm safe and I've got Vadim. But I can't bear it. I'm thinking of going to Abuja for the week to escape. Just hearing his name puts me on edge.'

'That sucks.' Simi rubbed Isobel's shoulder. She'd been a shit friend. She knew that Iso always masked her insecurity with aggression. 'Why do you still use Adams? You should use your maiden name.'

'That's worse. At least Adams is anonymous. As soon as people know who my father is, they become sycophantic or jealous.' Isobel gave a hollow laugh. 'That's if they don't run for the hills. I want to be liked for me. Promise you won't mention his name to Boo and Ronke.'

'OK,' said Simi. 'They won't care though.'

'But still, I'd rather you didn't. Now enough of me, how did it go with my headhunter?' Isobel patted Simi's hand. 'I told him to pull out all the stops.'

Simi was happy to move things along. 'He was fantastic, found me my dream job. They want to do a Skype interview next week. But they're looking for someone with media planning experience, online in particular. I don't have that.'

'So you lie.' Isobel leaned forward so her face was inches away from Simi's. 'How hard can it be? You can't let the perfect job slip away.'

Simi pushed her chair back and took a sip of her coffee. 'It's in Shanghai. So apart from not being qualified, it's in the wrong country.'

'You're not a tree. You can move. Shanghai's wonderful. I've been twice. I loved it.'

'My home's here. Martin's here – well, he isn't, but you know what I mean. Plus, I'm not likely to get pregnant if I'm in China.'

Isobel gripped Simi's wrist. 'Darling, you're on the pill. You're not likely to get pregnant full stop.'

10

RONKE

RONKE WASN'T GOOD AT saying no, so it was only a matter of time before she caved and agreed to meet Isobel. She picked The Lighthouse, Kayode's favourite watering hole (live sports on a giant screen). It was homely rather than hip, and would be quiet on a damp Tuesday evening.

When she arrived, Isobel was already there – a dialled-down version in jeans and T-shirt (no side boob), sipping sparkling water (not champagne). She still had the fake hair (red today), but it was in a neat bun (no swishing). Ronke reckoned Isobel's jeans, faded and distressed, with a gold label, probably cost more than her sofa.

'I'm so glad you finally said yes.' Isobel laid a soft hand on Ronke's arm, her now familiar greeting. 'I was starting to feel like a stalker. And you already have one of those.'

'I'm sorry.' Ronke wondered how Isobel managed to function with those nails. Did she never open a screw top, peel an onion or tap her PIN? 'Work's been full-on and we've been viewing flats most evenings. I'm sorry.' She willed herself to stop saying sorry.

'Relax!' laughed Isobel. 'I'm joking. I'm pleased you're here.

I really want to get to know you properly. One-on-one is so much nicer, don't you think?' She reached into her bag. 'Speaking of stalkers, I've got you something.' She handed Ronke a shiny pink can that looked like a teenager's body spritz.

Ronke took it hesitantly. 'What is it?'

'Pepper spray. I got it in the States. You can't buy it here. I hope you never need it, but if you do, aim for his eyes.' Isobel mimed squirting into Ronke's face.

Ronke flinched. 'Wow! Is it legal?'

'Not exactly. But we won't tell anyone.'

'Well, er, thank you.' Ronke was sure Isobel meant well, but there was no way she was going to start carrying around an illegal weapon. She buried it in her bag. 'I'm sure I won't need it. He's creepy, not dangerous.'

'They all start off that way. You need to be careful walking home after work. If you're ever worried, call me.' Isobel snapped her fingers. 'I'll send Vadim over. Now, what's this about flat-hunting? Did I hear you say *we*?'

'Yeah, Kayode and I are buying a place together. We've seen seven so far. The only suitable one went to bids – we missed by a mile.' Ronke sipped her ginger tea. 'Kayode wants to look north of the river but my work and friends are here. What we need is a bigger budget.'

'Moving in together? Sounds serious. Boo said you two were all loved-up at Simi's party.'

Ronke was under strict instructions from Simi to play down the dinner. 'It wasn't a party. But yeah, we're serious. And happy.' It was true. She'd never been happier.

'What does Kayode do?' Isobel shifted so she was closer to Ronke. 'What's his background? I want to know *everything*.'

'Well, um . . .' Ronke stalled, uncomfortable with this interrogation. 'He's a risk analyst, for a hedge fund. He studied Maths in Cape Town. He's . . .'

'I used to live in Cape Town. That's where I had my stalker.' Isobel paused, a deep frown on her face. 'So many men are evil. You've got to be so careful.'

'Kayode's very protective. He gave me a rape alarm and got one of his mates to fix a camera on my intercom. So now I'm a walking self-defence advert.'

'You light up when you talk about him. I'm jealous,' Isobel said with a wistful smile.

'Don't be. We've had our fair share of ups and downs. I know Simi and Boo have their doubts, but this time they're wrong. Kayode is the one.'

'He certainly charmed Boo at Simi's party.' Isobel strummed her fingers on the table. 'It sounds like you all had a wonderful time.'

'It wasn't a party,' Ronke said dutifully, trying to hide the fact that she was thrilled. Had her friends finally accepted Kayode? She really hoped so.

'Whatever. I can't wait to meet him in the flesh,' said Isobel.

∽

BEING SMUG TEMPTS FATE AND karma's a bitch. It was half past ten the next evening and Ronke was about to go to bed with a book when her phone pinged.

Hey baby . . . I'm on my way. We lost. I need cheering up.

She hadn't expected him – he was watching the game with

his mate Toks. But Ronke did the usual – out of her baggy tee, into her camisole, off with the scrunchie (lots of hair-tugging as she tried to turn bedlam hair into bed-hair), on with the lip balm.

Kayode was drunk. Not falling-over drunk, but drunk enough. Ranting on about what a shit day he'd had, how the ref was a cheat, how Arsène's tactics were all wrong. 'You couldn't fix me something . . . could you?' he added.

'Beans on toast?'

'I've been dreaming of your whore's spaghetti.'

And like an idiot she was flattered. 'Pasta *puttanesca* coming up. I'll put the kettle on – you look like you could do with a coffee . . .'

Before she'd finished, he'd opened the fridge, grabbed a beer, wandered through to the living room, turned on the TV and started flicking through the channels. 'You need to get Sky Sports,' he said, plonking his feet – still in shoes – on to her glass coffee table.

He wasn't here to be with the woman he loved. He was here for food. Because there's a limit to how many takeaways anyone (even Kayode) can eat. And you don't get sex with a kebab.

Ronke pushed the word 'doormat' out of her head and put a generous fistful of spaghetti into a pan of boiling water (salty as the sea, like Nigella said). In another pan, she warmed slivers of garlic in a glug of home-made chilli oil and melted in a few anchovies. She stirred in capers, fresh chopped chillies, sliced black olives and a jar of tuna (not a tin, the best albacore). Whore's pasta wasn't meant to have tuna in it, but Kayode was a real man and couldn't possibly survive a vegetarian meal.

Ronke couldn't cook for one, to be honest she struggled to cook for two, so she had a small (medium) bowl too. Which meant that her new intermittent fasting regime was blown. Still, she'd stuck to it for two whole days, longer than most of her diets.

Kayode grunted when she handed him the bowl.

She sat beside him on the sofa. 'Did I tell you Rafa and Luca are flat-hunting in—'

'Sshhh, I'm trying to watch this,' he said, mouth full of pasta.

After she'd cleared up, he pulled her on to the sofa. 'I can't stay. I'll have to go after. I don't have any clean shirts here.'

'After what?' Ronke tried to wriggle out of his arms.

'Oh, come on . . .'

'No, I don't want to.' Ronke pushed harder but he was too strong. 'I'm not some booty call.'

'Come on, babe.' He manhandled her so she was underneath him.

'Stop – let me go. You're hurting me! Get off.' Ronke struggled to free herself. 'What is wrong with you? Why are you being such an arsehole?'

Kayode staggered to his feet and fell against her little bookcase. The picture of her parents clattered to the floor.

'I don't need this shit.' Kayode picked up his jacket and slammed the door so hard the walls rattled.

Ronke cleared up with shaky hands. She picked up the frame to find the glass shattered. One of the shards pierced her finger and she dropped it to the floor – she didn't want to leave a bloody fingerprint.

She kicked her special cushion under the bed. He'd come for food and a fuck. And when he didn't get what he wanted, he'd fucked off. She might as well be a whore – at least she'd get paid. She lay awake fuming, too angry to sleep.

∾

ANY OTHER TIME, A MORNING at Fifi's with Boo for company would be the perfect way to start a day off. But Ronke was in a foul mood. She was tired (she'd finally cried herself to sleep at two). She didn't want to talk about what had happened last night. Certainly not to Boo.

And anyway, this whole weave idea was daft. Boo had lovely hair – glossy, smooth waves, no frizz. It was long too, way past her shoulders. Ronke's stopped growing once it hit her chin. Boo was the queen of the ponytail – topsy-turvy pony, messy pony, half pony, loose pony, side pony, high pony – anything to keep her hair out of her face.

Now, out of nowhere (well, out of Isobel's head), Boo wanted a weave. Not any old weave though – she was set on a full-on blaxploitation/Pam Grier/Foxxy Cleopatra Afro. Ronke wondered if Boo would shave off her eyebrows if Isobel suggested it.

Ronke remembered the moment Boo had announced this existential crisis weave at Simi's dinner party, ten days before. 'You'll hate it,' Ronke had warned. 'It will be all over your face. You've never even had plaits. You do know your hair gets cornrowed first?'

'I want a change,' Boo had said. 'Isobel says she feels like a different person every time she changes her hair.'

She must have a multiple personality disorder then, thought Ronke.

'So can your hairdresser do it?' asked Boo.

'Yeah, 'course,' said Ronke. 'Fifi can do anything. But it takes hours. At least three, maybe four. You'll have to go in the week; it's mayhem at the weekend.'

'You'll come with me, won't you? I'd be too nervous on my own; I wouldn't know what to ask for. I don't even know what hair to buy.'

Ronke loved going to Fifi's and she loved Boo, so of course she said yes. But now she wished she hadn't. She wanted to hole up with a tub of ice cream and *Location, Location, Location*. By the time she got out of the Underground at Balham, she'd had eight missed calls from Kayode and five texts.

I'm sorry. x

I'll never drink again. I'm ashamed of myself.

Ronke. I love you. I'm sorry. You've got to forgive me.

Please answer the phone. I'm worried. Let me know you're OK. Please?

Where are you? I've tried work, you're not there. Please tell me you're safe, I'm panicking. PLEASE REPLY.

Ronke called him back.

'Ronke! Are you OK? I kept thinking about that oddball who's been texting you. I was starting to panic. I don't know what to say. I'm a complete idiot. I can't believe I scared you. I'm so sorry.' Kayode's voice was shaky.

Ronke's mood lifted. He was grovelling. And anyway, he hadn't scared her. She'd been angry but never frightened.

She wouldn't tell him that though. 'I didn't get any sleep, and I'm still upset. I can't talk now. I'm meeting Boo.'

Fifi had lived in England since she was fourteen but had managed not to assimilate any English habits. She wore native clothes – bright hand-woven *Kente* fabric made into figure-hugging skirts and tops. Her hair was in intricate narrow embossed cornrows that zigzagged around her head and met in a high bun with plaits spiralling down her back. She had a strong Ghanaian accent with a proverb for every occasion, and a tendency to mix up pronouns – 'he' could refer to a woman or a man, it was potluck. She listened to West African pop, loved Nollywood movies and was religious – the born-again, speaking-in-tongues, hallelujah-Jesus-is-risen kind of religious. And Fifi loved to gossip. She didn't care who it was about, she wanted *all* the details.

Boo stopped Ronke at the entrance and pointed at the sign. *Banana Braids by Fifi.*

'What?' said Ronke.

'A bit racist?'

Ronke tipped her head. 'Huh?'

'Banana boat?' said Boo. 'You know. Banana republic? Monkeys?'

Ronke burst out laughing. 'Boo, you are so culturally illiterate. Sometimes I think you live under a rock. Banana braids are famous. Alicia Keys had them in her "Fallin" video. It's not racist. Well, it wasn't till you said it.'

Boo scrunched her face. 'It's a bit of a dive.'

'It's not Vidal Sassoon, but she's the best – I promise.' Ronke gestured for Boo to go first. Boo hung back. 'Come on, don't be such an *ajebutter*.'

'A what?' said Boo.

Fifi opened the door. '*Akwaaba*. Sister Ronke, you are welcome. Please enter.'

'Hey, Fifi.' Ronke pushed Boo through the open door.

'Hello, ma, you are welcome, ma. Please come and sit, ma.'

An hour later, Ronke was eating *kelewele* – soft plantains fried in palm oil with peppers, ginger and garlic, having her usual deep-conditioning hot-oil treatment. Her hair was covered in thick greasy moisturizer, piled up on her head and wrapped in a plastic cap. Rivulets of oil had escaped and dribbled down her face and neck. Ronke was supposed to stay under the steamer hood – the heat made the conditioner penetrate – but it got in the way of eating and talking.

Boo picked at a tub of jollof rice. She'd chosen it despite Ronke's hushed warning (she didn't want Fifi to hear) that Ghanaian jollof was not a patch on Nigerian jollof. Fifi had finished cornrowing Boo's hair – step one in the weave process.

'Did I tell you what happened to Aunty K last weekend?' Ronke asked. She knew she hadn't, but she wanted to start this story casually.

'No. What?' Boo turned to face Ronke.

'Keep your head straight, ma!' said Fifi. 'I am holding big needle, *ehn*.'

'Please don't call me ma,' said Boo for the fourth time.

'I'm sorry, ma,' said Fifi.

'It's going to be one big 'fro,' said Ronke. Boo's hair was now a spiral of cornrows snaking round her head. Fifi was stitching on hair extensions, wefts of frizzy brown and blonde hair.

'I look like a mollusc,' said Boo.

'The braids should be tighter, *ehn*,' said Fifi. 'This is not lasting a long time, ma.'

'It's tight enough.' Boo peered in the mirror. 'I look like I've had a facelift. I think it might be too long, I don't want to be Chaka Khan.'

'I'm cutting it after, ma.' Fifi muted the sound on the TV. 'Sister Ronke, you are telling us about your aunty.'

She pronounced it 'anti'. It made Ronke feel homesick. In Nigeria everyone older than you was an *anti* or an *uncoo*.

'It was terrible. She'd only been home for two weeks when it happened,' said Ronke. She ate the last piece of *kelewele* and wiped her hands on a napkin.

She'd heard the story three times now, first from Uncle Joseph, then Aunty K herself and finally her cousin, Obi. And she'd told it three times. To Rafa, Kayode and Kayode's sister, Yetty. It got more exaggerated with each retelling. She spun her chair round so she was more central, then decided standing would be more dramatic. This was proper Naija gist – it had to be told the right way. In a loud voice and with lavish gestures.

'It was a regular Sunday,' Ronke began. 'Aunty K had been to Lagos for the weekend. After church, she set off for home – an easy two-hour drive. Aunty K is always careful, she never uses the expressway at night, doesn't venture out after dark. She keeps the doors locked and windows wound up. And all her valuables – even her wedding ring – were stashed in her handbag, hidden in the footwell. She'd even put her dummy bag on the passenger seat.'

'What's a dummy bag?' asked Boo.

'A cheap bag to fool the robbers, standard practice in Lagos. Aunty K has a set of keys, a broken phone and some old makeup in hers. It's a decoy – if you get carjacked, the thieves snatch it and run. By the time they find out, fingers crossed, you're miles away.'

'Bloody hell,' said Boo.

'Lord, in your mercy, protect us.' Fifi touched her hand to her forehead, chest and shoulders.

Ronke paused, worried Fifi would stab herself with the big needle. Once Fifi was safe from puncture wounds, she resumed.

'Now, Aunty K isn't rich and her car isn't flashy. We're talk-ing dusty five-year-old Toyota Sienna. No leather seats, no air-con, no central locking. A standard *tokumbo*.'

'*Tokumbo*?' Boo stumbled over the word.

'A used car – you know, second-hand.' Ronke had got so carried away with her story, she'd forgotten how little Boo knew about life in Nigeria. 'It means from across the sea – an import.'

By this point, Fifi had stopped working on Boo's hair, the comb and needle abandoned. She held one hand up to her face, a stricken but eager expression on it. Even Boo looked spellbound, if a little odd with a quarter of an Afro. Ronke turned her voice up a notch.

'So, Aunty K's on the expressway, singing along to her church programme, thinking about supper. She was pretty sure she had some *edikaikong* soup in the freezer. Then out of nowhere, a car zooms up beside her and forces her off the road on to the hard shoulder. This is Nigeria, Boo, so the hard shoulder is not a safe haven. It's pot-holed and full of crap – old burst tyres, burned-out cars. You don't know what's lurking there. Or who.'

'Oh, my sweet Jesus.' Fifi crossed herself again.

'Bloody hell,' whispered Boo.

'Aunty K is trembling like a leaf, cursing the idiot who ran her off the road. The church music is still blaring out on the radio, she's taking deep breaths. CRASH!' Ronke clapped her hands together. Fifi and Boo jumped gratifyingly.

'The driver's side window explodes,' Ronke continued. 'A shower of tiny shards of glass rains down. Aunty K thinks it's a bomb. Rough hands yank her out of the car. Someone is shouting but she has no idea what he's saying. She's thrown down on to the hot filthy tarmac. Three men are leaning over her; they have machetes in their hands. Her wrapper is pulled open. She knows this is the end. She's going to be raped and murdered.'

'Pray God, save our aunty,' breathed Fifi.

'Bloody hell,' said Boo.

'Then God speaks to Aunty K. He tells her to sing. To sing for her life.' Ronke realized she'd gone a bit RuPaul on the last line – Rafa's influence. 'So, she closes her eyes, crosses her hands around her chest and bellows at the top of her voice.'

The God-speaking hadn't actually happened. Ronke had added that bit for Fifi's benefit. She considered lying on the floor, doing a full arms-crossed impression, but the salon was dirty. She sang, aiming for soprano, improvising as she didn't know the tune. 'Save me, Jesus, Save me, Jesus, From this godforsaken place.' Ronke paused to ramp up the tension.

'Then what?' said Boo.

'Sweet holy Jesus,' said Fifi.

'The next thing she hears is a sweet, soft voice asking if she's OK. Aunty K opens her eyes and there's a beautiful woman dressed in white – an angel – kneeling beside her and telling her she's safe. Turns out the thieves were scared of God and they scarpered. A passing car had seen it all and rushed to help. The driver of that car was the angel – a nurse in uniform. She picked Aunty K up, dusted her down, and gave her an escort all the way home to Ibadan.'

'*Onyame ye!* God is truly wonderful. He works in mysterious ways,' said Fifi.

'That's it. I am never going to Nigeria,' said Boo.

'Shit happens everywhere,' said Ronke.

'Sister Ronke, madam is correct in what he said. Nigerians are violent and money-mad,' said Fifi. 'Me too, I'm not going there. If they force me out, I will return to Ghana – at least I will be safe.'

'Fifi, they can't force you out,' said Ronke. 'You're British.'

'Do you not hearing the news, ma?' said Fifi. 'Hostile! Hostile environment. It's on LBC – you should listen, ma. They can be kicking us out anytime.'

'How's Aunty K coping?' asked Boo. 'She must have been terrified. I mean, that's how your dad died.'

'God rest her, Sister Ronke.'

'Him, Fifi. But yes, amen.' Ronke had thought the same thing but hadn't said anything to Aunty K. 'I'm just so relieved she's OK. She's coming back again next week, staying till just before Christmas. Uncle Joseph wants her to have a break. I'm going to take her to see the Oxford Street lights switched on. You can come!'

'No, ta,' said Boo.

'Grinch,' said Ronke. 'Anyway, you'll see her at Sofia's party. If that's OK.'

'Of course it is,' said Boo. 'You know I love her.'

Fifi turned up the TV, picked up the needle and went back to sewing wefts of hair on to Boo's head. Ronke popped back to the Ghanaian takeaway. She was still in her plastic cap, but they were used to people wandering in with curlers or half-woven heads. Telling the Aunty K story again reminded her life was short. There was no point pretending to Kayode she was still angry.

Got you some kelewele and fried chicken. Come round later, but not too late. I need an early night – didn't get much sleep.

He replied a nanosecond later.

I love you. I don't deserve you. And I am so sorry. See you at 6. Kx

Boo still had a quarter of a head to go when Ronke got back. 'Your turn,' she said. 'Come on, you must have some gossip.'

'Nothing happens to me,' said Boo. 'I haven't been anywhere since Simi's.'

'Well, how's work? What's the new boss like?'

'Seems all right,' said Boo. 'Actually I do know something you don't. You'll never guess what Martin told Didier.'

'What?'

'They're trying for a baby.'

'Simi?' Ronke was surprised but delighted. 'Are you serious?'

'Yup.'

'It makes sense, I guess. He's nearly forty. How exciting.'

'But why hasn't she told us?' Boo turned to face Ronke, then shouted 'Ow!' as Fifi yanked her head back.

'Sorry, ma. Remember, I hold big needle.'

'I don't know,' said Ronke. 'Simi bottles things up. I reckon it's a control thing. She won't talk about stuff till it's sorted. Remember how she was at uni? All that time we thought she was going to classes when she wasn't?'

'Pregnancy and fire cannot be kept secret, ma,' said Fifi.

'Huh?' said Boo.

'It's an African proverb,' said Ronke. 'But not right for Simi. She's great at keeping secrets. She'll probably tell us she's pregnant when she's in labour.'

'I thought about asking her but decided not to. She obviously doesn't want to talk about it,' said Boo.

'It's odd though.' Ronke tried to imagine Simi with a baby. She couldn't. 'I'm not sure she even likes children.'

'Everyone loves children, ma,' said Fifi. 'They are a blessing.'

'Hmm,' said Boo. 'You haven't met Sofia.'

'Stop it! Sofia's a joy,' said Ronke. 'Simi's still drinking. I'm going to stop when I start trying for a baby.'

'That's a bit judgemental,' said Boo.

Ronke bit her lip. 'You're right, don't tell her I said that.' She meant it though. She planned to stop drinking, avoid caffeine, take folic acid supplements – maybe even lose half a stone. She couldn't wait. House, then babies. It would be perfect if she and Simi were pregnant at the same time. Their kids would be best friends.

'*Obroni* are always drinking, ma,' said Fifi.

'She's not *obroni*,' said Ronke. 'She's half Nigerian.'

'Who's an *obroni*?' asked Boo.

'White people, ma,' said Fifi. 'Them think they have a God-given right to touch our hair. *Obronis* are stupid, *o*! One day they see you with teeny-weeny Afro – less than one centimetre. The next time they see you with long hair reach your buttocks. Your hair is growing so fast, they will say.'

'A bit racist,' said Boo.

'Takes one to know one,' said Ronke.

Five hours after they'd stepped through the door, Fifi proclaimed Boo done. 'I am finish, ma. It suits you *well-well*.'

'It feels weird.' Boo poked at her head.

'It will settle, ma. I will give you some oil, in case it scratches you.' Fifi did a jerky dance, touching her palms to her head repeatedly. 'Don't scar your head, *o*! It is better to be patting.'

'Yeah, like the Beyoncé song.' Ronke put one arm on her hips and patted her head with the other.

Boo had no idea what they were both on about. She peered at herself in the mirror and cautiously patted her head. 'I don't look like me.'

'I thought that's what you wanted,' said Ronke.

11

BOO

'MAMA! YOU LOOK LIKE a black woman!'

'*Tu es belle*.' Didier stooped to kiss her. 'But who are you? And what have you done with my Boo?' He circled her as if she was an exhibit. 'It's like cheating on my wife.'

Boo smiled and patted her head. Sofia had the same urge. Her little fingers poked and prodded. It was almost soothing.

'Eugh! There's a long fat slug underneath.' Sofia's voice was a mix of disgust and awe.

'It's going to take some getting used to,' said Didier.

There was no way Boo would get used to this. It was so itchy. And patting didn't help. This was worse than when Sofia had come home from nursery and proudly announced that Rudy had nits and all the mummies were to check their children's hair. 'What's wrong with the daddies doing the checking?' Boo had asked as she scratched her head.

Luckily Didier was happy to be the self-styled 'Lord of the Lice'. He combed Sofia's kinky curls on to a white piece of card. Sofia hated having her hair combed but this time she didn't complain. They were both gutted when the card stayed clean.

'Don't worry, *bébé*, I'm sure you'll get nits soon,' Didier said consolingly.

Sofia stuck out her bottom lip. 'I was going to keep them.'

'You're both deranged,' said Boo.

'Why are you scratching your head, Mama?' Sofia had asked at the time.

'She thinks she has nits,' said Didier.

'But, Papa, we checked.'

'They are not *on* her head, *bébé*.' Didier tapped his forehead. 'They're *in* her head.'

Didier and Sofia thought this was hysterical and cracked the same joke again and again. Boo had suffered from delusional parasitosis since. It came back whenever Sofia brought a nit letter home. Which was way too often.

But this weave was worse than imaginary lice. And it wasn't fucking delusional. Fifi said it was human hair, but it didn't feel like any hair Boo had ever touched. It was frizzy and dry, like the hair of a doll. Boo resisted the urge to pat it again.

They cooked supper together. Salmon, couscous, green beans.

'Yummy! I love green beans,' said Sofia. Yesterday she had thrown an enormous tantrum, claiming that green beans tasted like poo. *Is it possible I gave birth to a sociopath?* Boo wondered.

Didier did most of the work; Boo was too busy patting. She caught a glimpse of herself in the silver splashback of the cooker and did a double take. She looked familiar but different. A more exciting version of herself. Hot Boo? What would Neil think? Pat. Pat.

'Boo?' Didier nudged her.

'She's not listening, Papa,' said Sofia.

'Huh?' Boo said.

'Penny for them,' said Didier. 'They must be good thoughts – you were smiling.'

'Nothing. Sorry, just work. Boring stuff.'

'Supper's two minutes away. Sofia's laying the table.'

Later, Boo sat in the snug while Didier did bath and bed. The TV was on but she wasn't watching. She was thinking about her review lunch. Neil had cancelled twice, but yesterday he'd emailed to say that next Tuesday was definite and he'd cleared his diary for the afternoon. Was an Afro professional? She decided to get her nails done tomorrow; they were starting to grow out. She wasn't going to turn into a gel manicure junkie – this would be the last time. Shoes? She thought her black boots were OK, but Simi had said a higher heel and splash of colour would work better with the jumpsuit. Boo pulled out her laptop. She had a twenty per cent off voucher code for ASOS.

JUMPSUIT. NEW RED HEELS (NOT Simi high, but high enough for Boo). Red shiny nails. And massive Afro. The old dull Boo had been sloughed off. This was new cool Boo. No, new hot Boo. Confident and in control. She hadn't quite got used to her yet. Each time she caught a glimpse of her profile – reflected on the screen of her phone or in a window – she turned to see who the stranger was. Even her walk was different, her lope replaced with a pared-down version of Isobel's strut.

Her full-time colleagues, who had ignored her for months, smiled or stopped by her desk to chat. Three people offered to make her coffee.

'You look great, Boo – that haircut suits you,' said Elaine from the next cubicle. Boo was surprised she knew her name.

'It's not *my* hair!' Boo touched her head. How could she think it was real? 'It's a weave.'

'Oh! I thought maybe you'd permed it.' Elaine's hand moved over Boo's head. She pressed. Stroked. Pulled. Boo was shocked. A woman who'd never said more than 'hello' to her was actually groping her. 'Oooh, it's all springy,' said Elaine. 'Do you think it would work on me?'

'Probably not. It's a black thing.' Boo turned to her computer. For the first time in her life she felt black. She kind of liked it.

Her laptop pinged.

Back-to-back meetings all morning . . .

Boo's heart sank.

Can we meet at the restaurant? One pm. Hutong. Level 33, The Shard.

Boo's heart pounded.

∽

Boo had never been 'up the Shard', although Simi often suggested it. Ronke always pooh-poohed it. 'Twelve pounds for a glass of champagne? In a building that looks like a giant middle finger? What's wrong with All Bar One?' Boo had agreed with Ronke. Until now.

She stepped out of the lift, red heels clacking on the metal walkway. The restaurant looked like a Bond set – opulent and sexy, carved doors with intricate lattice work dividing the tables, turning them into private little rooms. Her new walk felt natural here. New Boo fit in.

A sharp-suited waiter escorted her to the table. A good one, next to the floor-to-ceiling windows – London laid out below them like a tableau. Neil stood, looked into her eyes and kissed her gently on each cheek. Her stomach fluttered, neurones firing along the brain–gut axis. Fight or flight? She sat.

'Wow! You look stunning. I love the hair. It's so you.' He smiled and his eyes sparkled.

Yes, Boo thought, *a me that's been suppressed for far too long*. Isobel had been right. Why the hell shouldn't there be an impulsive, strong and sexy Boo? An incredible Boo.

Neil handed the cocktail menu to their server without looking at it. 'We'll both have No Smoke Without Fire.' Once the waiter had left, Neil leaned forward and looked into her eyes. 'Their Peking duck is famous. The best in London, they say. And we must have the soft-shell crab and the lamb rack. What don't you eat?'

'I'm not fussy, I'll try anything.' Old Boo hated anything too hot or salty. She wasn't keen on lamb either.

He ordered for both of them. If Didier had tried that, she'd have called him sexist and controlling. New Boo was different in lots of ways.

The duck was carved at the table, the waiter brandishing the long knife like a Samurai. The crab was served in a lantern of bright red chillies, like an art installation. It was all too spicy for Boo (even new Boo). The rice was plain – a huge relief. Boo moved food around her plate with her chopsticks, barely eating any of it.

It was refreshing to debate genomics with an intellectual equal – someone who knew what he was talking about. A bit like being back in post-grad college, except that no one there had been this good-looking. Neil's shirt sleeves were rolled up to his elbows; the hair on his tanned arms was golden; he wore a silver and leather bracelet on his left wrist. He insisted she try the prawns, trapped one between his chopsticks and placed it between her lips. They were numbed by the chilli. She licked them. It felt dangerous.

He wanted to know if she was coming to the conference in York. She hadn't planned to. Mindless tedium was the norm at these awaydays, and it meant a night away from home. 'I'm not sure,' she said. 'I wasn't going to . . .'

'It would be great if you did.'

'Then I will.'

Outside it had begun to drizzle. Standing in his tan trench coat, umbrella aloft, he held open the door of her taxi. As Boo stepped into the back, he leaned to kiss her cheek. He missed and his lips touched hers for the briefest of moments. Her pulse quickened.

Boo wondered what she'd say if Didier bothered to ask about her review. 'Great. Couldn't have gone better,' she decided.

∽

WHEN BOO GOT IN AROUND five, the kitchen was in a state of chaos. Sofia and Didier sprawled on the floor surrounded by rubber snakes, neon erasers, plastic starfish, finger puppets, bags of Haribo – crap, crap and more crap.

'What are you doing?' Boo asked. 'Why are you home?'

'*Salut!* My meeting finished early,' said Didier, 'so I rescued Sofia and we went to Flapping Fish.'

'We're making bags for my party,' said Sofia. 'I was in charge of choosing. Papa said I could have anything I wanted.'

Boo rubbed her temples. 'Didier, we pay for after-school club.'

'I don't mind wasting ten pounds to spend time with my favourite girl.' He tickled Sofia.

Boo looked more closely at the toy assortment on the floor. 'Are those guns?' Her head started to throb.

'Tiny water pistols,' said Didier. '*Très petits*. Harmless.'

'I would have sorted this, you know,' said Boo. 'It was on my list.'

'Now we can do it together. Come and help.' Didier patted an empty inch of floor with a foam dinosaur.

'No, thanks. I'm going to change. You started it, you finish it.' She headed for the stairs. 'And you both know how I feel about plastic.'

By the time Boo got back downstairs, the mess was gone and Sofia was gobbling up broccoli.

'Broccoli was poison yesterday,' said Boo. 'You're playing me, Sofia.'

'Papa makes it tasty.' Sofia stuck her tongue out.

'Papa! *Un chef extraordinaire*,' said Didier.

'*Oui!*' squealed Sofia.

Boo glared at them both. They responded with synchronized Gallic shrugs.

'Boo, you need to look at the credit card bill.' Didier wiped the island. 'It's in the snug. There's some strange stuff. £180 at some Banana company . . .?'

'That was my hair.'

'You said eighty pounds.'

'No, I didn't.' She had. But only because it seemed like such a ridiculous amount to spend on a hairdo. 'Are you keeping track of what I spend?'

'Of course not. Sorry. What about Net-A-Porter? Over a thousand there?'

'Don't worry, I sent most of it back. I only kept the jump-suit. There'll be a big refund next month.' Boo tugged the sleeves of her hoodie over her hands and crossed her arms. 'Would you like me to check with you before I buy clothes? Should I keep the Waitrose receipts for you to inspect?' She heard her voice getting shriller.

'Hey, Boo, I said I'm sorry.' Didier lifted his hands in sur-render. 'I didn't mean . . .'

'I can't believe you're monitoring me like this.'

'I'm not. Why are you so angry, *chérie*?'

'Stop shouting!' Sofia stuck grubby fingers in her ears.

Didier took Sofia for her bath. Their squeaks and giggles made Boo's head hurt. One fucking jumpsuit. She kicked the kitchen door shut to block them out and messaged Isobel.

Hutong was amazing. Wish I was still there. Back home with tubby hubby and bratty child. See you tomorrow. Boo.

She refused to feel guilty. Didier had put on weight and Sofia could be a brat. It didn't mean she loved them any the less.

Half an hour later, Didier poked his head round the door. 'Glass of wine?'

'No,' Boo said icily.

He collapsed on the sofa and put his arm around her shoulders. 'You know I don't care what you buy. I check the bills – I always do. I didn't recognize the names, that's all.'

Boo stiffened and jerked away from him. 'I shouldn't have to ask for permission to buy a lipstick. It's not 1962. And this is Clapham, not Stepford.'

'It wasn't like that. Please, let's move on.'

Boo didn't want to move on. She kept her face hard and narrowed her eyes.

'So tell me,' Didier said, leaning into her, 'how did the big review go?'

'Fine,' Boo snapped. 'They want me to do more days. I think it's a good idea. I'll earn more, be able to spend my own money.'

'Boo, it's our money. You know that. But if that's what you want, let's see if we can make it work. Maybe I could work from home on Fridays? I'll talk to Robin.'

She knew he wouldn't. He'd use Sofia as blackmail. She could hear him in her head already. *I don't like it, Boo. Seven to seven is a long day for a child.* She sprang to her feet. 'I'm going to get an early night.'

'But it's only half past eight.'

'My head's banging.'

Boo fell asleep dreaming of a man with a golden tan. Not the sort you get from a sunbed. The healthy outdoorsy kind.

∽

'*BOZHE MOI!* YOU LOOK LIKE sisters today.' Vadim held the car door open. It was the first time Boo had heard him speak.

'Yeah, yeah. All black people look the same,' said Isobel.

'It's the hair,' said Boo. Isobel was in an Afro wig. She'd had it cut to match Boo's. And they were both in black leggings and black long-sleeved tops.

It was good to be able to talk about Neil. Boo didn't mention the kiss – well, it wasn't a kiss, more of a touch. But she did talk about the York awayday.

'A night away with your sexy boss.' Isobel nudged her in the ribs as they sat side by side in the back. 'Boo-time. You deserve some fun. You're a beautiful woman – enjoy the attention.'

Boo was relieved that Isobel got it. It was nice to be noticed. When Neil had said she looked stunning, she'd felt alive. And yes, Boo-time would be good. 'There's no harm in flirting, is there?' she said.

'A bit of fun can make your relationship stronger. It may help Didier appreciate what he's got. And anyway, what happens in York, stays in York.'

'I'd never cheat on Didier,' said Boo.

'So no new sexy lingerie, then?'

Boo decided it was time to change the subject. 'Did *you* know Simi was trying to get pregnant? Martin told Didier.'

'Is she?' Isobel raised her eyebrows. 'You don't say!'

'You already knew!' Boo exclaimed. 'Spill!'

And Isobel spilt. Big time.

An abortion. Poor Simi, thought Boo. Having to go through it on her own. Not even telling Martin. She looked at Isobel.

Why had Simi told *her*? 'How come she didn't tell me?' she said. 'Or Ronke?'

'Maybe she didn't want Ronke to know,' said Isobel.

'But why?'

'Come on, Boo! Open your eyes. Ronke's jealous of you – it's so obvious. She's desperate to get married and have a kid.' Isobel pointed a long nail at Boo. 'She wants *your* life. Simi didn't tell Ronke because she knew how judgemental she'd be. How bitter.'

Boo shook her head. She couldn't think of anyone less likely to be jealous. Or bitter. 'No, you're wrong,' she said finally. 'Ronke's not like that.'

'We'll see. You know her better than me. But I have a knack for spotting these things. Don't breathe a word about the abortion. I promised Simi.'

'I won't.' Boo reached for her ponytail and felt frizz instead. She knew it would be hard not to tell Ronke. Her Afro felt heavy; it was weighing her down.

12

SIMI

SIMI WAS RATTLED. THERE were children everywhere. Running, screaming, spinning, crying. Sticky fingers, muddy trainers, snotty noses. Surely that boy was old enough to use a tissue? A toddler wearing nothing but a nappy yanked at Simi's cream suede skirt and she recoiled. She caught Ronke's eye and mouthed, 'Help!'

Ronke laughed and picked up the stinky child. 'Looks like you need changing, little one. Do you think Aunty Simi wants to help?'

'Aunty Simi would rather poke her eyes out with a sharp stick.' Simi wrinkled her nose. She used the upstairs bathroom (she'd seen too many children go to the downstairs loo) and scrubbed her hands in scalding water. She hadn't touched the child, but better safe than sorry.

When Simi came back down, the kitchen was empty. Everyone was out in the garden. She joined them. It was cold but at least it wasn't raining.

Martin was playing football with a group of kids and dads. Sofia scored, or, to be precise, Martin collapsed like a sack of spuds and let the ball trickle over the line. He scooped Sofia into the air, sat her on his shoulders and did a victory lap of the garden, shouting, 'Gooooaaallll!' Spotting Simi, he called, 'Come and play.'

As if. Simi pointed at her white ankle boots.

'I told you not to wear white.' Martin turned back to the game. He charged round the garden barking instructions. 'Shoot! Shoot!' His new Stan Smith trainers (Simi had bought them) were ruined, his jetlag forgotten. It should have been her turn to visit New York this weekend but they'd swapped to be at Sofia's party.

Couldn't he be satisfied with being an uncle? Ronke wanted a dozen kids – he could borrow a couple from her now and again. Ideally when Simi was out.

She headed back to the kitchen. Boo was flitting about accomplishing nothing, wearing her martyr face – manic but ineffectual. She was always like this when she was hosting, getting stressed and complaining about how much work it was. It always surprised Simi how someone so intelligent could be so stupid.

Simi looked more closely at Boo. She was wearing her typical joggers and zip-up jacket, but something was different. Her outfit was more athleisure than slob. And it wasn't just the bonkers Afro or the new red heels. Boo had got sexy – if you ignored the neurotic head-touching. Simi ran her fingers through her poker-straight bob. She'd rocked an Afro when she was fourteen, before she'd discovered GHD straighteners.

In contrast to Boo, Ronke and Didier were the calm at the epicentre of chaos. They cuddled crying babies, soothed grazed knees, corralled kids into games and high-fived manic toddlers. Simi wasn't sure what the technical definition of toddler was – small person who couldn't string a sentence together, she decided. Ronke and Didier acted through instinct and in harmony. If a stranger walked in, they'd assume Ronke was Sofia's mother, Didier's wife.

Simi wandered over to Aunty K, who appeared to be acting out a one-man play to Didier's parents, over from France. It was the carjack story. Simi had now heard it twice. But it was more fun than watching children pick their noses. Besides, Simi had a soft spot for Aunty K. She'd always treated her and Boo as if they were her nieces too. She'd been there for Simi when she dropped out of medical school, the only 'grown-up' to visit her dreary Easton bedsit. 'Don't mind your daddy,' she'd said. 'He's in shock.'

Simi hated the word 'daddy'. Her stepsisters used it all the time and it pissed her off – so infantile. But from Aunty K it was OK.

'He will come round. He loves you. Give him time and trust God. You have to do what is right for you. I will always be proud of you, and so will he.'

That was the only time Simi stopped pretending she was fine during the depressing and distressing 'I'm a dropout' episode. She'd sobbed and Aunty K had cradled her like a baby. Although to be fair, next to Aunty K, Simi was baby-sized. She'd also given Simi a Nigerian leather pouffe. Simi wished she hadn't got rid of it.

Back in Bristol, when Boo first met Aunty K, she had struggled with the 'Aunty' thing. 'She's lovely but we're not related. I don't even call my real aunts Aunty. Why can't I call her Kehinde?'

Simi had tried to explain. 'It's a respect thing. In Nigeria, anyone older is an aunt or uncle.'

Now Boo insisted Sofia called them Aunty Simi and Uncle Martin. It was sweet.

The oldies moved on to griping about immigration, Didier's parents lamenting the damage that illegal migrants were doing to their community, how no one spoke their language any more, how people should stay where they were supposed to be. Aunty K joined in with gusto. 'They let anyone in nowadays,' she said, without a trace of irony.

Ronke and Didier ferried plates to the island. As usual, Ronke was in charge of the food. And as usual, she'd gone overboard: finger sandwiches, sausage rolls, plastic cups filled with popcorn, mini bagels paired up to look like headphones, bowls piled high with crisps, pretzels, vegetable sticks and fruit. Simi knew there'd also be a huge pot of jollof and chicken for the adults. And pasta salad and quiche for vegetarians and the less adventurous. Classic Ronke: a fat Lorraine Pascale.

'Can you believe they're whingeing about immigrants invading Europe?' said Simi. 'Is there a law that says you have to turn into a bigot when you get old? Are *we* going to be racist when we grow up?'

'Probably.' Ronke sprayed edible glitter on to a plate of sausage rolls. 'Boo's halfway there – but that makes sense: she's the oldest.'

The doorbell rang. 'I'll get it,' said Simi.

It was Isobel, straight off a *Yo! MTV Raps* set. It hadn't occurred to Simi to dress for the hip-hop theme and now she wished she had. Her pale suede skirt was a big mistake.

Isobel was wearing black Adidas joggers, the three white stripes lengthening her already long legs. They were low-slung and showed off the white logo strip on her pink Calvin Klein pants. A shiny pink crop top and an open Adidas jacket exposed her abs. Her hair was a big black Afro.

Boo rushed over and unzipped her jacket. Now it made sense. They'd planned it – coordinated outfits. Boo's crop top was lime green. Same clothes, same height, same skin tone, same fake hair. Boo a Poundland version of Isobel. Weird. Simi wished they'd told her. She could do rapper chick. She'd have done it better.

Vadim, in head-to-toe black, trailed behind Isobel, a huge cake in his beefy arms. Three tiers, red, white and blue, the French *tricolore*, topped with a fondant breakdancing Sofia, complete with corkscrew curls and cheeky pout.

'Oh, Isobel, it's perfect. Quick, let's take it in here. I don't want Sofia to see it,' said Boo. 'I was so worried you wouldn't make it.'

Boo had turned into Iso's lapdog. It was amusing but pathetic. Isobel saw more of Boo than Simi these days. They went running on the Common three mornings a week and now Simi heard more about Boo from Isobel than she did from Boo herself. Isobel's Boo was bored, frustrated and put upon by Didier the tyrant. Simi thought this was utter crap. Didier was a saint. He did almost all the cooking, most of the shopping, his fair share of tidying and he was brilliant with Sofia.

'Everyone in a circle!' yelled the entertainer. He started a slow-motion running-man demo. The kids, decked out in baseball hats, gold chains and faux microphones, jerked annoyingly. Eager parents (excluding Boo) and desperate-to-be-parents (Martin and Ronke) joined in. It wasn't Ronke's dance; she really should have worn a sports bra.

At least the kitchen was calm. Simi, Boo and Isobel sipped champagne, perched on stools around the kitchen island, far away from the action. Simi relaxed, watched the dancing, and listened to them chat. The music was good – old-school hip-hop from the nineties – and it was nice to see Martin have fun.

'Boarding school,' said Isobel. 'Better for the kids and definitely better for the parents. It's the smart solution.'

'Or not having them at all,' said Simi.

'You guys are awful,' said Boo. 'Sofia is the best thing I've ever done.'

'So how come you're in here with us and not out there with them?' Simi gestured at the garden.

'I deserve a five-minute rest,' said Boo. 'I've been non-stop all day.'

'Non-stop moaning,' said Simi.

'Give her a break,' said Isobel. 'She deserves some Boo-time.'

The doorbell rang again.

'I'll get it. I need to go to the loo.' Boo dashed off.

Moments later a smiling Kayode strode into the kitchen. He stopped suddenly and the smile vanished. Simi followed his eyes. He was staring at Isobel. Simi shivered involuntarily.

Isobel leapt off her stool. 'Oh my God. It's Kayode King.' He walked slowly towards them and she pulled him into a hug. 'Long time no see,' she said, her voice huskier than usual.

'You know each other?' asked Simi stupidly.

'Of course we do.' Isobel tugged at Kayode's sleeve. 'We used to be a couple. Didn't we?'

Kayode fiddled with a button on his canvas jacket. 'A very long time ago.'

'Thirteen years,' said Isobel. 'You still look good.'

'Where's Ronke?' asked Kayode. His left leg bounced and his eyes darted around the room.

If he wasn't so dark, Simi thought, he'd be bright red. 'In the garden,' she answered, gesturing with her chin.

'I'm going to join her.' Kayode backed out of the room.

They watched him go silently. Then Simi turned to Isobel. 'Well, that was awkward. He couldn't get away fast enough.'

'You think?' Isobel was smiling. 'So poor Ronke thinks *he's* Mr Right.'

'It's not funny, Iso. She's going to be pissed.' Simi knew Ronke would be more than pissed. She'd be gutted. 'You should have said you knew him.'

'Oh, come on, it was years ago,' said Isobel. 'And it's not my fault, I didn't know her Kayode was my Kayode. How could I?'

'He's not *your* Kayode. And I'm not stupid. He was in the picture.' Simi glared at Isobel, but she looked blank. 'You know . . . the one at Asari's wedding? On Facebook.'

'Was he? I didn't notice. I thought you didn't do Facebook?'

Before Simi could challenge Isobel further, Boo arrived with three bottles of beer. 'Where's Kayode?' she said.

'Garden.' Simi pointed. 'It turns out Isobel *knows* Kayode. She just forgot to tell us.'

'You're joking! Do all Nigerians know each other?'

'Not in the biblical sense, Boo.' Simi glowered at Isobel. 'You can explain.'

'I don't understand. Why didn't you say so before?' said Boo.

'I didn't know it was the same Kayode.' Isobel gave Simi a pleading look. 'No one said it was Kayode King.'

'How many Kayodes can there be?' asked Boo.

'It's a common name,' said Isobel.

Simi stared at Isobel. She sounded so sincere. And it was true: Kayode was the Yoruba equivalent of Kevin.

'I swear I didn't know.' Isobel put her hand on her heart. 'Come on, if I said I'd dated a Martin, you wouldn't assume it was Simi's Martin, would you?'

Simi forced a smile. She decided she needed some air. 'Pass the beers, Boo. I'll take them out.'

She joined Martin on the patio. Kayode's arm was around Ronke's waist. They looked good dancing together, fluid and natural.

The dance instructor was demonstrating a new move and Simi tried to follow. Martin was taking it very seriously. What he lacked in technique, he made up for in enthusiasm. Didier was awful, playing the fool.

Martin danced over to Simi. 'And they say all black people have rhythm,' he said.

'It's not fair,' said Simi. 'You've had lots of practice. I missed the instructions.'

'Let's try this instead.' He pulled her into the waltz position and turned her in circles. It was their wedding dance. Simi closed her eyes and let him lead her, even though the music was much too fast. 'Let's hope our baby hasn't got your two left feet,' he murmured into her ear.

Simi broke free. Couldn't they enjoy one solitary day without babies coming up? 'I'm going back in.'

Didier called out to her as she walked away, 'Tell Boo it's nearly cake time.'

Back in the kitchen, Isobel and Boo were whispering like teenagers, heads together, Afros touching. They fell silent as Simi approached.

'Didier needs you,' Simi said to Boo. 'Something about cake?'

'Always something. Never a moment's peace.' Boo nodded at Isobel and dashed off.

Once she and Isobel were alone, Simi asked, 'What were you two gossiping about?' She tried to keep her voice bright.

'The Kayode thing. Boo thinks Ronke will be upset. Please don't mention the Facebook picture. I swear I didn't recognize him. I really like her and I don't want this to become an issue.'

'She'll be fine. It was years ago.' Simi jutted her chin towards the garden where Kayode and Ronke were still dancing. 'I mean, look at them.' They watched Kayode pull Ronke into a bump and grind. As she turned to look at him, her face lit up. He kissed her. 'Anyone can see he loves her.' Simi hoped she was right.

'I'm not so sure. He pressed himself into me when I hugged him.' Isobel thrust her hips forward. 'He's the same dog he always was.'

'Don't be daft. He was desperate to escape.' Simi was sure Isobel was being silly; she'd always been an attention-seeker.

'I know what I felt.' Isobel waggled her head. 'Anyway, what's happening with your interview?'

'It's on Tuesday. But don't talk about it now.'

'You haven't told Martin, have you?'

'Not yet.'

Isobel moved her mouth to Simi's ear and dropped her voice to a whisper. 'Don't worry, *alobam*, I won't say a word.'

Simi could feel her 'not-lies' pushing her down. The birth control pills. The other pills. The interview for the job she wouldn't get. The Facebook picture. She picked up her glass and sighed. Martin was going back to New York on Tuesday. Let sleeping lies lie.

13

RONKE

RONKE DECIDED, AFTER A near fatal slip, that the shower was not a good place to practise her running man. Imagine being found naked two days later – she'd die of shame. Except that it wouldn't take two days: the water would cascade into the downstairs flat and Lisa had a spare key. Ronke would be mortified if Lisa saw her naked. Even if she was dead. It would be even worse it if was Kevin, Lisa's husband.

She was still buzzing from the weekend. Kayode had been wonderful at Sofia's party – he'd even helped to clear up. And he'd been great with the kids, comfortable and easy. Prospective parents ought to like children. Simi froze when one came within two feet of her. Even Sofia seemed to frighten her on Saturday. Was she really trying for a baby? Her outfit was ridiculous, even by Simi's standards. Cream suede at a child's birthday party? And she'd drunk way too much. Martin was practically holding her up at the end.

Kayode had made a real effort with Didier's parents. He'd listened to their long (and boring) Ryanair outrage story, then told one of his own that involved paying extra for a safety belt.

Ronke was pretty sure he'd made it up, but it had Didier's parents in stitches. Boo kept rolling her eyes when they spoke French, as if it was a crime to speak your own language.

In fact, Boo had been off all day. The matchy-matchy hip-hop outfit thing with Isobel was bizarre. Why bother going to all that effort to look the part if you weren't going to join in with the dancing, help with the food or offer your in-laws a cup of tea? And making fun of Didier was plain nasty. Didier might not be buff (like Kayode) but he was far from tubby.

But what Ronke couldn't stop thinking about was Kayode meeting Aunty K. After two no-shows, Ronke had worried she'd be prickly, which would make Kayode defensive. But no! He had charmed the pants off her.

'At last, *ehn*. The elusive Kayode makes his appearance. No excuses today, we thank God. I was starting to worry my little niece had fabricated you. Come, sit down. Let me examine you *well-well*.' Aunty K patted the small space next to her on the sofa. 'Little Ronke, I'm parched. Bring one small cup of tea. And take your time.'

Ronke yanked at her hair. 'Be nice. You promised.'

'It's fine, Ronke.' Kayode sat. 'You've got stuff to do. Let me and Aunty get to know each other.'

Ronke went back to tidying. She hoped Aunty K wasn't giving him a grilling: Who are your parents? What are your qualifications? Are you financially stable? Do you go to church? She looked over. Aunty K was definitely giving him the third degree. She hoped Kayode wouldn't get riled.

When she rejoined them, after as long as she could bear, Aunty K was ending her carjack story. Kayode said 'amen' when Aunty K did the prayer bit, her most recent addition to the tale, which now ended with a full service on the motorway. The angel (nurse), a gaggle of onlookers (who appeared from nowhere), holding hands and praising Jesus.

'God bless you, Kayode,' Aunty K finished up. 'Make sure you look after my little niece.'

'I will, Aunty K. I know how lucky I am. And God bless you too.' Kayode gave Aunty K a small bow and bounded off to join Martin and Didier.

In her head, Ronke punched the air. She knew Aunty K would love the bow.

'Very handsome. I approve,' said Aunty K. 'He comes from good stock. You should have told me his mother is a warden at Ikoyi Baptist Church.'

'So you like him?' Ronke beamed.

'Nice manners and a good job. God is great. You should settle down *now-now*.'

'He's perfect, isn't he? Just like Dad.'

'No man is perfect, *o*. Your father was a good man, but he had his faults, believe me.' Aunty K lowered her voice. 'Now, who is the girl always talking to Bukola? The one dressed like a carbon copy. Is she family?'

'No, that's Isobel Adams,' Ronke laughed. 'She's an old friend of Simi's. From Grange School.'

'What is her father's name?'

'I don't know,' said Ronke. 'There are a hundred and ninety million Nigerians – even you can't know them all. Does it matter?'

'I'm not sure,' said Aunty K.

That was another good thing about the weekend. Unlike everyone else, Kayode was completely unfazed by Isobel.

'Loud and manly,' he said disparagingly as he drove them home. 'I've met her before: didn't like her then, don't like her now. She's the worst kind of Nigerian – entitled, pretentious, vulgar.' Kayode reached over to touch her knee. 'Everything you're not. She's bad news. Stay away from her.'

Ronke sank back into her seat, clutching the container of leftover jollof and chicken. She wasn't sure if her warm glow was external or internal.

As if that wasn't enough, on Sunday they'd had lunch with Yetty and Abayomi. It was becoming a thing. Their thing.

Ronke turned off the shower. She'd used up all the hot water and was running late. At quarter past eight, she pulled her coat over her scrubs and bounced down the stairs. She bumped into Kevin, on his way out too. Ronke blushed as they said hello. What if she had slipped and died! He'd be in her bathroom investigating the leak. And she'd be naked.

Tina was ending a call when Ronke got to work; she seemed harassed. 'That was your favourite patient,' she said.

'I like all my patients.'

'Not Mr Owen. It's the third time he's called and it's not even nine.'

Ronke felt her mood sour. 'He's not a patient any more.'

'I know! I told him,' said Tina. 'Sorry, I shouldn't have mentioned it. Don't worry. I'll sort it.'

'*Buenos días*, Ronke. How was the big party?'

Ronke smiled broadly at her assistant, Mr Owen forgotten. 'It was amazing. I've got so much to tell you.' But they had back-to-back appointments all morning, and there was no time to catch up, no gaps for dance lessons. Ronke managed to fit in one loo break and three sips of warm, tepid, then cold coffee as she bashed out post-appointment notes.

'Last one.' Rafa opened the file on her screen. 'Then lunch.'

A new patient. Mr Watkins. Emergency chipped filling. His first visit so she'd have to do a full exam and X-rays. Please let it be a simple bond. She was starving.

When Mr Watkins entered, Ronke stood to say hello but she needn't have bothered. He headed straight for Rafa. 'Good morning. Or is it afternoon?' He held out his hand. 'So you're Ronke Tinubu. Such an unusual name – is it Catalan?'

Rafa returned the handshake, his ears bright red. 'I'm not the dentist, I'm the nurse.' He was embarrassed for Ronke, for himself and for the dickhead. It had happened before, of course. It happened to women all the time. But it happened to black (and brown) women more. Ronke could hear Simi in her ear: Do not *think* of apologizing.

'*I'm* Ronke, your dentist. And it's not Catalan, it's Nigerian. This is Rafa. He's from Galicia, which is six hundred miles west of Barcelona. Please, sit.' Ronke gestured to the chair and snapped on her gloves. 'Seeing as you're into onomastics, Ronke means "precious" in Yoruba. Luckily I'm not.'

She pulled the loops of her face mask over her ears and grinned. But her speech was wasted on Mr Wanker Watkins – he didn't even have the decency to look embarrassed.

Ronke winked at Rafa, who was still bright pink. 'Let's give Mr Watkins a pair of safety glasses. We wouldn't want to stab him in the eye with the periodontal probe. Would we?'

∽

LUNCH WAS A RUSHED AFFAIR — TEN minutes with a very average supermarket sandwich. As she chewed the last stale mouthful, her phone pinged.

Can't make the viewing. Toks has tickets for the match. Red Army! Love you. Kx

Ronke called. Straight to voicemail. She left a long (calm) message.

He didn't call back. He texted.

Chill. Rebook for tomorrow. Or go on your own — I trust you. Don't get psycho. Come on you Gunners!!

When their last patient left, Rafa had the sense not to hang around. '*Adiós*, Ronke. See you tomorrow.'

Ronke called the agent. He doubted it would be on the market tomorrow — they had six back-to-back viewings that evening. She tried not to get upset but why wasn't finding a home more important than football? It wasn't like he was doing her a favour. This was for *them*.

At home, she changed into her warm shapeless PJs and sank into the sofa to check her emails. An alert from Prime Location (why bother opening it?), one from her brother (a picture of his dog rolling in a muddy puddle, no message, a row of 'x's – typical) and one from her mum.

From: Mary Payne
To: Ronke Tinubu
Subject: Sunday?

Hello, darling
Did you have fun at the party? I bet your food was fantastic. Your Aunty Sheena is coming to visit on

Sunday. She'd love to see you. And I would too.
Please say you'll come. I'll make pineapple upside-
down cake if you say yes.

Love, Mum x

Aunty? What a joke, Ronke thought. If she's an aunt, I'm a size zero. Sheena was a bitch. Ronke made excuses for her grandparents: It was the 1970s, mixed marriages were unusual, they lived in the sticks and were old-fashioned. But it was hard to make excuses for Sheena. She lived in metropolitan, multicultural London; she'd grown up in the swinging sixties. What was her excuse? When Ronke was fourteen, the evil cow had suggested she straightened her hair – so she would look normal. Yup, she used the word 'normal'.

Ronke bashed at her keyboard.

From: Ronke Tinubu
To: Mary Payne
Subject: Re: Sunday?

Hello, Mum
YOUR FAMILY ARE RACIST BASTARDS
Sheena has never been an aunt to me. And if you
were honest, you'd admit she's been a shit sister to
you. She wanted nothing to do with any of us until
Dad died. And even then, she had the nerve to say
you shouldn't have married him. In front of me.

I'm not going to give Sheena a pat on the back for
finally realizing I don't have a bone through my nose.
Remember the time she asked if I knew how to use a

knife and fork? I cried for an hour. And you didn't tell her off. Or when she made horrid comments about my 'plump African arse'?

Sorry, Mum, but she's a stupid, mean, UKIP-voting old bag with yellow teeth. I hope she chokes on the pineapple upside-down cake.

All good here, about to order a takeaway, talk soon.

Love

R xx

P.S. The party was amazing – thanks for asking. Sofia had a ball. And my real aunty was there. Aunty K. Remember her? Your dead husband's twin sister? She loves me. Even though my hair isn't straight.

Ronke swallowed hard and jabbed at the delete icon. Of course she'd be on the train to Maidenhead on Sunday. She'd smile and be nice. Even take a gift for not-Aunty Sheena. A fancy soap or potted plant, not a jar of her home-made pepper sauce.

Ronke's phone rang. Kayode. She steeled herself and pressed decline, then opened her local Indian's online menu. Just one main course. And a naan. Maybe a couple of poppadums. No dahl. Ronke loved dahl. Fuck it, and a dahl. But she'd make her own rice.

14

BOO

'SHOUTING AT HER ISN'T going to help.' Didier picked up Sofia; she buried her head in his neck. '*Ne pleures pas, mon bébé*. It's all right. Mama didn't mean to be cross.'

'*She* should say sorry,' Sofia said between sniffs.

Didier looked at Boo. She ignored him and picked up a J-cloth. He held up his free hand enquiringly.

'OK. I'm sorry I shouted at you, Sofia,' said Boo. 'But I still need to know what you've done with your PE bag.'

'It's gone,' said Sofia.

Boo fought the temptation to scream. 'Yes, that much we've established. But where has it gone?'

'I gave it to Simon,' whispered Sofia.

'*Mais pourquoi, bébé?*' Didier stroked her hair.

'Because,' sniffed Sofia, 'my bag, the one that's gone, has a big pink S on it.'

Boo counted to ten. 'And?'

'Simon loves pink. And I don't. So we swapped.'

'What did you swap it for, sweetheart?' Didier dabbed at Sofia's eyes with kitchen roll.

'For Simon's bag, of course.'

'And where is Simon's bag?' asked Didier.

'It was from Tesco. And Mama says plastic is bad for the fishes. I put it in the bin because I didn't want Mama to be cross.' Sofia snaked her hands around Didier's neck and glared at Boo.

Boo sighed and tapped her watch.

Didier kissed Sofia's head and lowered her to the floor. 'Go upstairs and find a bag for today. *Vite! Vite!* We go in two minutes.' As Sofia scampered away, Didier put his arm around Boo's waist. 'It's only a bag, *chérie*. It's not worth screaming about.'

Boo tried not to flinch. 'Last week it was a pencil case. Who knows what will be next? She has to learn to value things. She can't keep giving stuff away.' She shrugged off his embrace. 'And you need to back me up, take my side. I'm always the bad cop.'

'OK, OK. But shouting isn't the way to teach her. You scared her.' Didier sounded exasperated.

'She was putting it on.' Boo knew she was being defensive. 'You're right. I'm sorry, I'm just stressed about the conference.' At least that was true – she was stressed. She'd been thinking about Neil since she woke up. 'You won't be late for pickup, will you?'

'I'm not the idiot, Boo.'

'I know. But you don't usually do Fridays. And it's *an* idiot. Not *the* idiot.'

'*Pour l'amour du ciel!*'

'Talking in French doesn't help,' said Boo.

Sofia bounded down the stairs with a raffia beach bag festooned with beads and tassels. Another ridiculous gift from Simi. 'That's not a school bag,' said Boo.

Sofia fixed her big round eyes on Didier. 'But Papa said . . .'

Boo relented. 'OK, but only for today. Now say goodbye to Mama.'

'Bye.'

'Don't I get a hug?'

Sofia delivered a stiff one-armed brush-off. Boo pulled her into a cuddle. 'Mama loves you and I'm sorry I was cross. Be a good girl for Papa and I'll see you tomorrow.'

'Don't worry about us.' Didier pecked her cheek. 'Go have fun.'

'It's work,' said Boo.

'It's a country house hotel. Try and enjoy it. Come on, Sofia – race you to the corner!'

'Don't run on the street,' Boo said to the closed door. She sighed. Her husband thought she was a bitch. Her daughter didn't want to touch her. She couldn't really blame them.

She picked up the case she'd spent ages packing. Her new M&S undies had gone in first. Isobel had suggested Agent Provocateur but it all screamed *I'm having illicit sex*. And even New Boo couldn't spend seventy-five quid on fifty grams of fuchsia polyamide. Jumpsuit, red shoes and new wrap dress. Isobel had called it a 'work to flirt' frock. Boo had put it on her own debit card this time. The last thing she needed was another inquisition.

～

THE NEXT DAY, BOO OPENED her front door and dumped her case by the stairs. Bobby Womack was crooning in the background. 'Please Forgive My Heart'. She closed her eyes and listened to Sofia giggling. The house smelled wonderful, but Boo felt nauseous. She shook her head. No. No. No. But it was still there. She unclenched her fists, forced a smile and stepped into the kitchen.

Sofia was in her little apron, the one Ronke had bought for her birthday. They had a matching set: Sofia's said *mini chef*, Ronke's said *head chef*. She was on her stool, whisking. Her tongue was stuck out, the way it always did when she was concentrating. Didier was singing out of tune as he peeled potatoes.

A pang of self-loathing ripped through Boo. A sharp and sudden spasm. Like a stitch from running too fast. No. No. No.

'Mama!' Sofia dropped the whisk. A spray of batter arched across the island. She hopped off the stool and ran into her arms.

Boo buried her face in Sofia's hair.

'Too tight, Mama!' Sofia wriggled free. 'I've been so good. I didn't give Simon my bag even though he said please. I almost did because he's going to the beach at Christmas. But I said no – because I want you to love me.'

Boo doubled over, disguised it as part of the hug, pulled Sofia back and breathed her in.

'Hey, you, what time is it?' Didier dried his hands on the tea towel draped on his shoulder and peered at his watch. 'You said one. We're not ready.'

'We're making a welcome home lunch,' said Sofia. 'I've done the mostest.'

'It smells wonderful.' Boo wanted to throw up. 'What are we having?'

'*Rôti de boeuf, pommes de terre rôties et des legumes,*' said Sofia.

'Sounds amazing,' said Boo. 'What does it mean?'

'Sunday lunch. Sofia is making *le pudding de Yorkshire*. And don't worry, we've got lashings of gravy for my Yorkshire lass.' Didier lifted her chin and kissed her. 'You don't have to lift a finger.'

'It's not Sunday,' said Boo.

'But it's your favourite. And Papa said our job is to make you happy.'

Boo swallowed hard. 'You always do.'

'Back to mixing, *bébé*. Try and keep some of it in the bowl.' Didier picked up a potato. 'Go and unpack. Relax. We've got this.'

Boo headed upstairs. She wouldn't be able to eat. She couldn't unclench her stomach. It felt like a stone. She kicked off her red shoes and crumpled on to the bed, face squashed into the pillow. She started counting. She would get up when she got to ten. Twenty. A hundred. A thousand. She forced herself up and unpacked, chucked clothes into the laundry basket. She balled up her new underwear and stuffed it in the empty bin. No. No. No. She pulled out the bin liner, tied a knot and put it in her handbag. She'd get rid of it later.

'I made you a brew.'

Boo jumped as Sofia pushed open the door. She looked so young, tiny little steps, mug held in both hands, forehead wrinkled.

'I only spilt a little.' Sofia put the mug on the dressing table. 'Not even two drops.'

'Thank you, darling. I'm being so spoilt.'

'Did you like the flowers? I chose them.'

Boo turned to look where Sofia was pointing. How could she not have noticed? Three giant sunflowers, too tall for the vase; it looked precarious. Boo curled and uncurled her hands.

'What's wrong, Mama?'

'Nothing, darling. They're beautiful. I love them. I love you.' Boo stroked Sofia's hair.

'You're strange,' said Sofia.

'I missed you,' said Boo. 'And now I'm home, I'm happy again.'

'I missed you a little. But we were busy so I forgot to miss you all the time. After school I took Papa to the park. I went on the slide and the swing. And I fell over. But . . .'

Boo pulled Sofia on to her lap. She clung to safety in the minutiae of Sofia's babbling. 'The flowers smiled at me. I wanted ten but Papa said money doesn't grow on trees and we have to save up for my new bag. Then we made pizza but we went out to play and the alarm went off and the kitchen was brown and smoky. But it was OK because Papa ate all the burned bits.' Sofia wriggled out of her arms. 'I've got to go. I'm in charge of the Yorkies.'

'OK. I'll be down in a little bit.' Boo couldn't meet her daughter's eyes.

After Sofia left she pushed the wrap dress deeper into the laundry basket, buried it under Didier's shirts. Didier must never know. It was the most stupid, reckless thing she'd done in her whole life. But also the most meaningless. She had started regretting it the second she stepped into his room. So why had she stayed? Why was she trying to blow her life up? How could she be so fucking stupid? So desperate for attention?

She stood under the shower, her third in twelve hours, and tried to retune her head – away from last night, back to Sofia's sunflowers, the swings and burned pizza. But last night replayed on a loop. What a stupid, self-satisfied fool she'd been in her slutty wrap dress and racy underwear. Her pathetic, puffed-up smile when he made a beeline for her, claimed the next seat and pressed his thigh into hers. She'd sipped her caipirinha, excited to be the last two saddos in a tired hotel bar. She had willed him to suggest a nightcap in his room, felt powerful when he did.

Boo rubbed her eyes to blot it out. The soap burned so she rubbed harder. Images from last night flooded her brain. No. No. No.

She'd anticipated it all. Bought the fucking underwear. Night after night, lying next to her husband, she had imagined what it would be like, dreaming of sex with another man. She'd spent ages getting ready for dinner, rubbed cream into her skin, walked into a mist of perfume.

The first prick of repulsion had come when he pushed his key card into the slot and the lights came on. His room was a clone of hers. Same forest wallpaper, orange headboard, grey flecked carpet. Overheated and stuffy, with windows you couldn't open. Oversized wall-mounted TV screening hotel info. Over-dressed bed – bolsters, shams, drapes and coverlets.

What are you fucking doing? She'd pushed the thought away. Sent boring Boo packing.

Boo made a plan. She would tell Neil it was a huge mistake, it couldn't happen again. Then she'd blank it out. Didier must never know. He wouldn't understand. He wouldn't forgive. He'd never cheat on her. He was loyal. Decent. Honourable. He was better than her.

15

SIMI

'I'm sorry,' said Simi, for the zillionth time.

Her superstar pitch had turned into a shitshow. The client had gone into administration and the agency was twenty grand out of pocket. Simi had spent the week trying to cancel things that were way too far down the line to cancel, in a futile attempt to limit losses. She'd been talked down to by a sweary, prima donna choreographer ('This is fucking ridiculous, I've spent days working on this. I thought you were a fucking professional. If my invoice isn't paid, I'll see you in court.'), shouted at by a bolshie grime artist with a limited grasp of the English language (thank God it was on the phone – she reckoned he was a spitter; he'd called her a *wasteman*, she Googled it, wished she hadn't), and Gavin was sulking because his ballet-dancing sister had missed out on fame ('She's sensitive, you know. And the rest of the company blame her. It's so awful, Simi. You have to do something.').

Worst of all, QB was being extra evil. She made out it was all Simi's fault. But how could Simi have known the company was under *severe liquidity constraints*? Her job was to win the pitch, not check their blasted financials.

'You need to get back in the saddle. You need to win something. And make it something big,' QB barked.

But the new business meeting hadn't gone well. Simi had wanted the Danish rainwear pitch. She was mad for Scandi chic, worshipped at the temple of Acne Studios and had been to Copenhagen. Twice. Her flat was the definition of *hygge* in a stripped-back, less cosy way. And she'd watched *The Killing*. All four seasons.

But no. Because according to QB, Simi's urban (black) roots made her a shoo-in for the Chitrita Phaishan launch. Chitrita was a Bombay designer and Phaishan her first diffusion (cheap crap) range for a Spanish high street chain.

'I don't know anything about Indian fashion,' said Simi.

'It's ethnic. Right up your street,' QB said breezily.

'I've never been to India. I don't even like curry.'

'Simi, we're on the verge of going bankrupt, thanks to *your* cancelled project. I've got corporate on my back and we – *you* – need to win this. If that means chomping down on fucking chicken tikka masala while prancing around in a sari, that's what you're going to do. Or do you want to tell people why they're being made redundant before Christmas? I didn't think so. Chop. Chop.' The bitch had actually clapped her hands in Simi's face.

So here she was, alone in the office at quarter past eight, Googling Indian fashion, trying to work out the difference between a *churidar* and a *salwar*, and hoping nothing else would go wrong. Letting yourself down was bad enough. Being responsible for your colleagues losing their jobs was unbearable.

Martin was the one person who could be relied upon to

put things in perspective. But not this time. He didn't get it. 'Cheer up,' he'd said, 'nobody died. Someone should have done a credit check before they let you loose with purchase orders. If QB gives you any crap, tell her to ram her job. Come and join me here – we can practise baby-making.'

Arghhhhh!

One goodish thing had happened this week. Her Skype interview with the local recruiter, a friendly Australian, had gone well. He hadn't mentioned media planning, so she hadn't had to bluff. She was through to the final stage, a face-to-face interview with the CEO and head of HR in Shanghai, a city 6,000 miles from home, for a job she hadn't mentioned to Martin. Going would be a waste of time.

When she told Isobel, Isobel did her 'clap bow' thing. 'I knew my man would come good. I'll call him tomorrow, put the pressure on. He needs to realize how important this is, especially now QB wants to force you out.'

Simi's eyelid twitched. She was being interviewed because of her skills and experience, not because of 'Iso's man'. Wasn't she? And one bad day – OK, bad week – at work didn't mean she was going to lose her job. Did it?

'You'll love Shanghai,' said Isobel. 'Why don't I come with you, show you around? We could go shopping in the old city and have supper at Ultraviolet; it's got three stars. I went there with Dad – sixteen courses, unbelievable. Let's invite Boo and Ronke. Yes! A girls' trip! My treat!'

'We're not girls. And it's an interview, not a minibreak.' Simi didn't have unlimited holiday and she had to be back to lead the Chitrita pitch anyway. She'd be in and out. Airport, taxi, interview, taxi, airport. Ronke had a job. Boo had a child.

Isobel forgot that not everyone lived in her rarefied bubble. Mere mortals had real lives, mortgages, jobs, alarm clocks.

Still, despite Isobel's faults she could be relied on for a good night out. And Simi needed to get pissed.

∽

WHEN SIMI CRAWLED OUT OF bed on Saturday, all she wanted to do was curl up on the sofa. She was miserable and hungover. But she'd agreed to meet Ronke. At bloody Buka.

Last night, when she was out with Isobel, things seemed to make sense. But when she got home, sleep evaded her. She lay awake, trying to figure out if Isobel was bigging her up or bullshitting her.

When she finally fell asleep, she relived a childhood memory, one she had thought she'd erased for good. She was back at Ikoyi Club. As a girl she had spent every weekend there – swimming, playing air hockey or table tennis, eating chips with pepper sauce, sipping Fanta from frosty bottles. When her father's business went pop, he stopped paying his dues and told her she couldn't go any more. But Simi kept going – all her friends were members, and no one ever asked the kids for ID.

She was sunbathing by the pool in her pink halterneck bikini, a three-month-out-of-date *Jackie* (hot off the press by 1990 Lagos standards) by her side, when the security guard, the one who sat in the kiosk by the gate, who'd smiled at her when she'd been dropped off, grabbed her arm and told her she had to leave. The nightmare was so vivid – the aquamarine pool water, the dark denim of the dress she pulled over her head. She heard the slap of her flip-flops as she followed him, felt the heat of her cheeks – red with embarrassment, not sun. Isobel had been there that day but they'd stopped talking by then. Simi couldn't meet her eyes. She tried and failed to keep her shoulders up as she was frogmarched out.

Simi woke drenched in the same shame and mortification she'd felt as an eleven-year-old. She toyed with the idea of cancelling Ronke, but she'd have to come up with an excuse and that would mean more lies. Instead she downed two aspirin and dragged herself to the shower. Maybe goat pepper soup would help? Or maybe she'd go crazy and order a carb fest – pounded yam or *asaro* with *dodo*. She'd lost three pounds this week; if she lost any more, her brand-new Fusalp stirrups wouldn't fit.

She took the Tube, hoping the walk across the river would shake off her fug. But the train was hot, and the rattling made her headache worse. A fat, greasy, gum-chewing man wedged himself into the seat opposite, legs splayed so wide he risked groin strain. He stared at his phone like a halfwit as he poked and prodded his bits. Simi locked eyes with the woman next to him and they synchronized eye-rolls. This was why she used Uber. The further north they went, the slower the Tube ran. Chew, chew. Poke, poke.

Simi hadn't walked to Buka from the station before. Tower Hill was shiny and clean, packed with funky tourists and cool locals. Hendon Central looked decrepit and dirty, full of miserable-looking mothers dragging blank-eyed, slack-jawed children.

Simi clacked down the stairs of the underpass. The crossover straps on her rainbow-striped, block-heeled platforms dug into her feet. There was a lingering hint of piss so she pulled up her scarf and used it as a breathing mask. She walked under the A41 as fast as her vertiginous shoes would allow, clattered up the stairs and inhaled fresh (well, less putrid) air into her lungs.

The Sainsbury's Local had lopsided dayglo banners in the window – *Bargain, BOGOF, Meal Deal*. The Turkish grocery had crates of weird stuff stacked outside it, vegetables Simi didn't recognize, loaves of bread without any packaging – it couldn't be hygienic. The girls in the Thai nail bar looked like zombies. Simi hoped they weren't modern slaves. At last she reached Buka. The filthy flag drooped in despair. She stepped in and sighed as the stale smell and clamour washed over her. She'd have to get her jacket dry-cleaned. And why did Nigerians always have to shout?

Ronke was already there (which was a first). Simi hoped she wasn't too upset about Kayode's history with Isobel; she didn't have the energy to console her. 'Hey, Ronks,' she said, forcing a smile on her face.

'You look tired,' said Ronke. 'And thin. Are you OK?'

'I'm fine. Work's a bit shit. And I was out last night. Anyway, some of us like being thin.' Simi knew it was bitchy but she didn't like the anxious look on Ronke's face.

'I'm crap at pretending, so I'm just going to say it.' Ronke poured Simi a glass of water. 'Martin told Didier you guys are trying for a baby.'

Simi was completely blindsided; it felt like she'd been punched. The corner of her left eye quivered and she didn't trust herself to speak. She closed her eyes to calm the involuntary spasm, and then turned, trying to catch the waiter's eye. 'I hate the tap water here, it's musty. I need a proper drink.' She crossed her arms and turned back to Ronke. 'He shouldn't have said anything. It's personal.'

'Simi, I'm your best friend.' Ronke leaned forward, a smile on her face. 'You can tell me anything. You know that.'

Simi sighed loudly. This was an ambush. And she didn't need it. Not today. 'OK, yes, we're trying for a baby. But he shouldn't have told anyone. I don't need the added pressure. I've been on the pill for ever – it could take years. Look, I promise I'll tell you when I'm pregnant.'

'But you didn't,' said Ronke.

'What are you talking about?' Simi uncrossed her arms and waved at the waiter. He ignored her.

'Simi, it's all right, I know,' said Ronke. 'Isobel told Boo about the abortion and Boo told me. You don't have to lie. This is me.'

'I can't believe this!' Simi could hear how shrill and angry her voice was. She glared at Ronke. 'You've been bitching about me behind my back?'

'Of course not,' said Ronke. 'I just want to help.'

'I don't need help. I'm fine. Everything's fine.' Simi was furious with herself. She should have known better. Isobel was good at collecting secrets, not so great at keeping them. 'Look, it's none of your business. Did you ask me to lunch to have a go at me?'

'No! I'm sorry,' said Ronke. 'I didn't mean to upset you. I'm sorry.' She fiddled with her hair.

Ronke's hair-tugging and serial apologizing only annoyed Simi more. 'Look, it's not a big deal – that's why I didn't tell you. I panicked. Martin was in New York, I was alone, I wasn't ready. I'm fine. I don't need looking after.'

'I'd have come with you,' said Ronke. 'You shouldn't have had to do it on your own.'

Simi heard the judgement in what Ronke didn't say. 'It wasn't what you think. I just took two tiny pills. No different to the morning-after pill – and you know all about those. Twice, wasn't it?'

'I was nineteen. And single. It was a bit different,' said Ronke. 'I'm not judging you. I just think you should tell Martin. He deserves to know. And he'll understand. You two will work it out.'

Simi couldn't believe how self-righteous Ronke was being. How dare she decide what Martin did or didn't deserve to know? 'I really don't need relationship advice from you.'

But Ronke wouldn't back off. 'OK. But you can't let him keep thinking you're trying when you're not. It's not fair. Deep down you know that.'

Maybe it was the hangover, the lack of sleep, the shitty week. Maybe it was guilt. Or perhaps it was bloody do-gooder Ronke making out Simi was being cruel to Martin. Simi banged two palms on the table, spilling her water and knocking the dusty fake flower arrangement to the floor. 'How bloody dare you tell me what to do? You of all people. When you've wasted your life on a string of losers who treat you like shit! You've never had a real relationship. You don't understand how they work. You have no idea of the sacrifices I've had to make. No two people have the same dream. My career matters. My freedom matters. You really think Kayode is the one? You're stupid! Deluded.' Simi didn't realize she'd been shouting till she stopped. The noisy men had fallen silent and were staring. Even the waiter looked attentive.

Ronke scrambled to pick up the flowers. 'Simi, stop it. Please. I'm sorry. I don't know what I've done wrong.' Her voice quavered.

'You're making out I'm a crap wife. I'm not. I love Martin.' Simi spat out the words. Tears were running down Ronke's face. They reminded Simi of her mother, the master of manipulative crying. Crocodile tears, designed to make her the victim, Simi the bully.

'Of course you do,' sniffed Ronke. 'And he loves you. It's all going to be fine.' She blew her nose and dried her eyes.

The loud men stared. And for the first time in Buka's history, there was a deafening silence.

'I'm sorry,' said Ronke.

'Stop apologizing. It's getting on my nerves,' Simi snapped. Ronke winced.

Simi took a deep breath. She wished she hadn't lost her cool; it was so unlike her. 'It's fine. I overreacted. Isobel shouldn't have told Boo. And Boo shouldn't have told you.' She tried a smile. 'I'm fine, Ronks. I know you care but there's honestly nothing to worry about. It just wasn't the right time. Living apart is hard – harder than I expected. Seriously, don't worry about me. I'm sorted. Now, let's order some food.'

'I don't think I could eat a thing,' said Ronke. 'I really didn't mean to upset you.'

'Look, I will get upset if you don't eat. Come on, I'm having *asaro*.' Simi forced another smile. The last thing she wanted was a bowl of sloppy carbs but she needed to make amends. Ronke hadn't done anything wrong. She was just being Ronke. It was Simi who'd fucked up. She should never have told Isobel.

'You always have pepper soup.' Ronke's voice was slightly less strained.

'I know, but you're right, I've lost a few pounds.' Simi touched Ronke's knee under the table. 'Let's share a starter. You choose.'

16

RONKE

RONKE FELT UNEASY AS she walked up Bolton Place in the biting wind. Isobel had asked her to come over. It hadn't really been an invitation – more of a summons. What could Isobel have to say that couldn't be said on the phone? Ronke hoped it wasn't about her disastrous lunch with Simi. They'd sort of made up but when it came to fibbing about feelings, Simi had form. It's what made the whole episode so out of character – Simi didn't do emotional.

Ronke still didn't know what she'd said to cause the explosion. Or why Simi had taken it out on her. She hadn't broken her confidence (that would be Isobel). She hadn't talked about her behind her back (that would be Isobel and Boo). She'd tried to do the right thing – be a good friend, give honest advice. Big mistake.

She suspected Simi had lashed out because it was easier than being honest with herself. Ronke tested her theory on Boo. Another mistake. Boo made it all about Boo: 'Oh no, now she'll think I'm a gossip.' (Well, you kind of are.) Then all about Isobel: 'She'll be mad with me.' (Well, maybe Isobel should have kept her big mouth shut.) And to end on a high,

Boo had belittled Ronke: 'Marriages are complicated. You don't understand and you shouldn't have interfered.'

But Ronke's misgivings about seeing Isobel were also tinged with curiosity. She was dying to see Isobel's house (described by Simi as sleazy). She turned on to the almond-shaped crescent and caught her first glimpse of the massive white three-storey townhouse. Stucco pillars – tick. High walls to deter snoopers – tick. Lion's head door knocker – tick.

Ronke ignored the lion and pressed the (plastic and surprisingly ordinary) doorbell. She heard a tinny, chimed version of the Nigerian national anthem, took it as a good sign and sang along. *Arise, O compatriots, Nigeria's call obey* . . .

Vadim answered the door. He led her through to the sitting room, bigger than Ronke's entire flat and dazzlingly ostentatious. Flock gold wallpaper, gold tapestries, an ornate sideboard covered in gold leaf, photographs (all of the same unsmiling man) in gold rococo frames. On the cream carpet (stencilled with swirly gold initials – DB), two overstuffed, metallic-gold Chesterfield sofas flanked a gold marble fireplace. Anything not gold was spangled with crystals. Sparkly chandeliers, twinkly table lamps and a vile drinks trolley cluttered with gem-encrusted bottles and glittery flutes.

Ronke smiled and bit her lower lip. It was revolting. So much worse than she'd dared hope.

'Welcome!' Isobel was in jogging bottoms and a hoodie, her arms outstretched. Ronke wasn't sure if she was displaying the room or offering a hug. 'I know, I know! It's a bit flashy, isn't it?' Isobel embraced Ronke. 'Dad makes Trump look subtle. You should see our place in Abuja – even the swimming pool is gold-plated.'

'*Na wa, o!*' Ronke laughed and walked up to one of the portraits. 'Is this him?'

'Yes. With my grandma, *nne nne* Bukola. She died when I was three; I never got to know her.'

'She was beautiful. Boo's a Bukola too but no one calls her that. Well, apart from Aunty K.' Ronke was drawn to a small sculpture of a head on a wooden plinth, the only thing in the room that wasn't gleaming. Distinctly African, a little smaller than life-size, it had an oval face, high cheekbones, a wide nose and facial scarring. The scars, around his mouth, were symmetrical and somehow made him more beautiful. Unmistakably royal, you'd have known he was a ruler even without his headdress, but the crown took away any doubt. Heavily beaded, it had a striking vertical plume – picked out in red paint.

'You like it?' asked Isobel.

'I love it. It's like the Ife head at the British Museum.' Ronke leaned closer to get a better look. She really wanted to touch it.

'It's heavier than you'd think.' Isobel picked it up and handed it to Ronke. 'Leaded brass.'

Ronke cradled the head. It looked alive. She felt it assessing her – face alert, lips parted as if about to speak. 'He's almost spiritual,' she whispered.

'Dad says it's one of the three missing heads, which would make it fourteenth century.'

'It should be in a museum,' said Ronke.

'Probably. If you tell anyone we have it, I'd have to kill you.'

Isobel placed the head back on its plinth and laughed. 'Only joking.'

Vadim reappeared and set a tray on the frosted table in front of Ronke. She smiled her thanks. He ignored her and retreated.

They both sat, Ronke rigidly, worried that the shiny leather would fart if she moved. Isobel squeezed in next to her, too close for comfort. They made small talk – work, the weather, Sofia's party. No mention of Simi. Ronke relaxed and decided she could risk reaching for her cup.

'I'm so relieved you're cool about me and Kayode.' Isobel's voice was low.

Ronke froze, her arm outstretched. 'What do you mean, *you* and Kayode?'

'Oh God!' Isobel turned, her face now directly in front of Ronke's. 'I can't believe he didn't tell you.'

Ronke was sure she could detect triumph in Isobel's smile. Her stomach flipped. 'Isobel, what *are* you talking about?'

Isobel spoke slowly. 'Kayode and I. We used to be a couple.' She put her hand on Ronke's rigid arm. 'I'm sorry, he really should have told you. This is so embarrassing.'

Ronke forced a smile, determined to hide her shock. Yes, he *really* should have. 'Oh, that,' she said. Her mouth was dry, her voice hoarse. She grabbed her cup with both hands and took a long sip. 'Yeah, he said he knew you. But we didn't go into details.' She could hear Kayode's voice in her ear: 'She's bad news. Stay away from her.' She took another long sip, playing for time. 'It's ancient history,' she said, her voice nearly steady.

'What a relief.' Isobel finally looked away. 'We had so much fun. I was only twenty-two and had just moved to Cape Town. It was fizzing. But if he's told you, you know all this already.'

Ronke did the maths. Thirteen years ago. 'Like I said, history.' She shifted on the slippery leather, eager to put some space between them.

'It was such a shock when I saw him at Sofia's party. I said to Simi, that's Kayode King! Please tell me he's not poor Ronke's Kayode. I could have died.'

So Simi and Boo knew and hadn't warned her. Ronke wanted to believe they were trying to protect her. But they must have known that hearing it from Isobel would be so much worse. 'Small world,' she said, desperate to leave.

'It makes sense though – he always had a thing for mixed-race girls.' Isobel smiled. 'But who knows! Maybe he's changed? Decided to settle down?'

'I'm sure we've all changed over the last decade,' said Ronke quietly.

'Well, I'm just glad you're cool about it. More tea?'

RONKE HAD CHEWED OVER THE Isobel and Kayode thing all week. She kept replaying their conversation in her head. Kept pushing Kayode to explain. Kept trying to believe that Simi and Boo were looking out for her, not laughing at her.

'Is it wrong to have a type?' she asked Rafa. She was sitting on the Spanish armchair in Rafa and Luca's new flat. The chair was yellow with two red cushions. Luca was on the Italian armchair, white with one green and one red cushion.

Rafa was on the floor at his feet. Ronke sipped her red wine, glad she was on Spain. White was a stupid colour for upholstery.

'Type of what?' said Rafa.

'You know . . . have a thing for Asian guys. Only fancy blue-eyed blondes? Or mixed-race girls?'

'For me it's about personality. They have to be kind. And funny. Being gorgeous is a bonus.' Luca patted Rafa's shoulder.

Ronke was chuffed for them, and a little envious. Rafa and Luca had been together nine months – three fewer than she and Kayode. But here they were, living together, buying stuff together. They'd struck gold with this flat. She wondered if Kayode would consider Mitcham. They'd get so much more for their money – a little house, not a flat. A proper garden. Off-street parking. And it was only half an hour from town. She must check what the schools were like.

Rafa and Luca even had a joint bank account. Ronke imagined a debit card printed with *Kayode King and Ronke Tinubu*. Or better still, *Kayode and Ronke King*. Deluded. That was the word Simi had used.

Their new flat was only partially furnished so supper was on the rug. Salami, cheese, olives, roasted peppers, almonds, artichokes in olive oil and a delicious rosemary focaccia. Ronke was glad she'd worn high-waisted jeans and a long loose top. If she ate any more, she'd have to undo a button. She took another slice of focaccia. It was so good. Mitcham even had a posh deli.

'But what if a guy *only* dates mixed-race girls,' asked Ronke. 'Is that weird?'

'Why? You *only* date Nigerian guys,' said Rafa. 'And you're not weird. Well, maybe a little.'

'That's not true. Kofi was Ghanaian. And Boyega was British.'

'Come on, you're cheating,' said Rafa. 'His parents were Nigerian.'

'It's something Isobel said. As well as politely letting me know she used to shag my boyfriend, cheers for that.' Ronke raised her glass peevishly. 'She made me feel Kayode was only with me because I'm mixed.'

'She sounds like a bitch. Nobody is just a colour. Or any other feature. You might always fancy men with hairy chests.' Rafa tickled Luca's chest. 'But if he turns out to be a bastard, you don't stay with him because of his hairy chest. Kayode fancied you the first time he saw you. I was there, remember? And he fell in love with you. Not your skin. You.'

'I just wish he'd told me. Or Boo. Or Simi. It was devastating hearing it from Isobel. I felt like an idiot.'

'What did he say?' asked Rafa, passing her the cheese plate.

'Not much.' Ronke shook her head. 'He didn't want to talk about it. Said it was just a fling. When I pushed, all he said was she's trouble. Oh, and that she looks like a man. Which she doesn't.'

Ronke didn't tell Rafa that they'd ended up rowing. She'd asked Kayode why he hadn't told her. OK, she hadn't asked, she'd yelled. She had every right to be upset.

'It's not a big deal,' he'd said. 'It was years ago; it meant nothing.'

This made Ronke even more angry. 'You know you should have told me,' she ranted.

'Will you drop it?' He got up from the sofa and started pacing her small sitting room.

'No! You must see how degrading it was to find out from her? I had to pretend I knew.'

'I assumed Simi or Boo would have told you. They're always quick to slag me off. I know they think I'm not good enough.' He paused his pacing and glowered at Ronke. 'And I warned you to stay away from Isobel.'

'And now I know why.' Ronke rubbed her eyes and then looked up at him. 'Do you still fancy her?'

'Oh, come on! This is stupid.' Kayode was shouting now. 'I can't stand her. She looks like a fucking bloke – all bones and muscles and veins.'

Ronke was pleased with this but still couldn't let it go. 'Are all your ex-girlfriends mixed race?'

'I told you, she wasn't my girlfriend. It was just sex. Not even good sex.'

Ronke tried to dig but Kayode had been evasive and defensive. The more she pushed, the more belligerent he got. Eventually she dropped it.

Ronke considered asking Yetty. But how could she steer the conversation to Kayode's exes without sounding like a total psycho? And so what if lots, or all, of his exes were mixed race? All her exes were black. If dating only mixed-race girls was bad, dating only black guys couldn't be good.

Ronke told herself to let it go. But she couldn't stop thinking about it. Why did she think Isobel had been mocking her? And why did Kayode hate Isobel so much?

∽

FOR WEEKS, ISOBEL HAD RAVED about Come-Chop, the new Nigerian fusion restaurant in Mayfair. Ronke was dreading it – the last person she wanted to see was Isobel. But she couldn't get out of lunch without looking churlish. And she didn't want friction with Simi and Boo – falling out with them was like falling out with herself.

Come-Chop's head chef had won a Michelin star at a fancy Nordic eatery and his business partner was a Nigerian mixologist. What could a Swede know about West African food? Had he even been to Nigeria? If he had, she hoped he'd used factor thirty – all the Swedes she knew were pale and blond. (Ronke didn't actually know any Swedes, apart from ABBA and Björn Borg.)

She spent more time than usual on her makeup – they'd all be glammed up. She didn't want to feel like a blimp so she battled into her Spanx. At least she wouldn't have to worry about them exploding: posh food meant minuscule portions. She put on her brand-new wrap dress, the one Simi had convinced her to buy. It was dark red with a single button and a black tie belt. Ronke used a tiny safety pin to fasten the under layer to her bra. She wasn't brave enough to flash her underwear the way Simi did.

She was running late but didn't hurry. It was cold and she buried her hands in her coat pockets. She ambled to Berkeley Square from Green Park station. She paused to gaze through the window of the Rolls Royce showroom, took a selfie with a baby blue Phantom and sent it to Aunty K. Paused at a coffee shop. *Today's special: Kopi Luwak. Eaten, digested and excreted from civet cats. £30 per cup.* She took another selfie. For Rafa this time – Aunty K would have an apoplectic fit.

She arrived half an hour late, handed over her woolly coat and took a deep breath. Nothing. She wrinkled her nose and tried again. Still nothing. No smell at all.

Isobel stood to greet her, cloyingly warm. 'Yay! You're here. I was starting to worry. I love your dress. No Mateus Rosé, I'm afraid, but they've got Lagos-inspired cocktails. I ordered you an *agbalumo* spritz. I hope that's OK? We were going to do the tasting menu: ten courses, all small. But if you'd prefer . . .?'

Ronke recognized nervousness when she saw it. Simi and Boo must have told Isobel she was hurt. 'Sorry! Sorry I'm late.' Ronke noticed Simi's withering look. 'Sorry. I'm apologizing too much, aren't I? The tasting menu sounds perfect. Thanks.'

The food looked incredible. Acres of white plate and an inch of delicious gorgeousness. A delicate slice of plantain adorned with a dehydrated raspberry. A two-inch disc of malted barley bread (like Soreen, which Ronke adored), topped with mushroom *kilishi*. A sliver of guineafowl breast with *epa sise* satay.

It wasn't Nigerian, but it did have distant echoes of home. The scotch bonnet powder was a masterstroke – Ronke was determined to try to copy it. The Club Chapman sorbet tasted like the Chapman at Apapa Club – she'd drunk gallons of it as a child. The crab jollof had the burned smoky flavour of party-jollof – Ronke wished it came in a massive bowl, not a thimble.

The drinks kept coming and Simi and Isobel got louder. Ronke could hear other diners tutting. 'Keep it down – people are staring,' she whispered. 'This is why we go to Buka, so we can be loud.'

'Fuck 'em,' said Isobel. 'This isn't regular Michelin, this is Naija Michelin. At these prices, we can make as much noise as we like.'

Even Boo was drinking a lot, which was out of character. She was wearing her old leather mini and turned ashen when Isobel made an incomprehensible joke about a wrap dress.

'You OK, chick?' Ronke bumped Boo's shoulder gently.

'Yeah. Just having a bad week. Would you mind babysitting Sofia one night? We need a date night.'

'Boo–Didi time!' Simi did her filthy laugh.

Of course Ronke didn't mind. 'I'd love to. She can come to mine for a sleepover.'

'And can you do one other thing? Help me take this weave out? I hate it. It's not me. And it itches like hell.' Boo scratched her head.

'No problem. I'm off Wednesday; I'll come to yours.' Ronke was surprised the stupid weave had lasted this long. And it would be good to have some one-on-one time with Boo, find out why she was sad.

Ten courses took a long time. The wine pairing meant ten different drinks – on top of the champagne and cocktails they'd started with. It wasn't long before they were all a bit merry.

As the last course, a mango and *ogbono* panna cotta the shape and size of a kidney bean, was cleared, Isobel clapped her hands three times. 'I know there's been a little tension lately and I think it's my fault. If I've upset any of you, I'm truly sorry. You've all been wonderful, so welcoming.' Isobel looked at each of them in turn. 'You know I've been through a rough time. Finding you has helped so much. I've got something for each of you – a little thank you for being here for me.'

'So much drama,' said Simi. 'This had better be good.'

Three waiters appeared, each holding a large box, which they placed one by one in front of Ronke, Simi and Boo. The boxes were so big they had to peek over them to see each other. Ronke's first thought was 'takeaway' – she hoped it was crab jollof.

Isobel pushed her chair back, its metal legs shrieking on the concrete floor. She paused dramatically and then commanded, 'Go on! Go on! Open up!'

Ronke lifted the lid of the balsa wood box to reveal a white cardboard box, crisscrossed with black velvet ribbon. Definitely not food, she thought, disappointed, untying the bow. She yanked out sheet after sheet of cream tissue, creating a mound on the floor beside her. Finally she got to the prize – nestling on a bed of shredded raffia. 'Oh my God,' she breathed, lifting it out of the box. 'It's the Ife head.'

Isobel beamed, like Lady Bountiful. 'You inspired me, Ronke,' she said. 'I wanted you, well, all three of you, to have something special – a sisterhood thing, to show how much you mean to me. Please say you like?'

They all had the same head. Boo was stroking hers, picking out the beads in the plumed headdress with her fingertips. 'Oh, Isobel, thank you,' she said. 'I'll treasure it for ever.'

Simi turned hers in her hands as if appraising its weight. 'It's heavier than it looks. You could do some real damage with this.'

'It's beautiful.' Ronke was still transfixed, staring at the face. 'Is it from the shop at the British Museum? We can't accept this, it's too much.' She'd seen the resin replicas there, had been tempted till she saw the price tag. £1,600.

'No, no – these are unique. Exact copies of my dad's original. I had them made specially, out of leaded brass. You should get them insured – they're worth a small fortune.'

Ronke glanced from Boo to Simi. They looked quite unfazed, clearly didn't agree it was absurd and over the top. 'It's too much,' she said again.

'Nonsense,' said Isobel. 'It's not enough. You'll never know what finding you has meant to me. Now I can do more than survive.' She paused and smiled, nodding at each of them in turn. Ronke was last to come under her gaze. 'You've given me a purpose. I can thrive.'

'Well, mine's going to live on my bedside table. It'll be like sleeping with royalty,' said Simi.

'Yes, me too,' echoed Boo.

'You already sleep with a king.' Isobel placed her hand on Ronke's arm. 'Now you can sleep with two. I'm so glad you don't hate me.'

Ronke smiled weakly. She couldn't refuse the gift but she couldn't keep it – it would rile Kayode. She'd give it to Aunty K for Christmas.

Simi followed Ronke to the loo. 'I owe you an apology. I was out of order the other day. I said some awful things.'

Relief rushed through Ronke and she pulled Simi into a tight hug. 'No, it was my fault. I shouldn't have poked my nose in.'

'Come to mine after,' said Simi. 'We can curl up on the sofa and watch a crap movie. I've missed you.'

'I can't. I'm meeting Kayode.'

'Come on, I'll get us a takeaway.' Simi smiled warmly. 'From Buka. We didn't get to enjoy it last time and this meal didn't touch the sides.'

Ronke laughed. 'That's bribery!'

'Pounded yam. *Egusi* stew. *Puff-puff*.'

Ronke decided to blow Kayode out. He wouldn't mind, he was always changing plans on her. 'You had me at pounded yam.'

'Don't say anything to Isobel,' said Simi. 'She'll insist on joining in and I want it to be just the two of us.'

Ronke felt ridiculously pleased.

17

BOO

Boo WISHED THE IFE head would stop staring at her. She was changing out of the work clothes she'd put on an hour ago and into her running gear. She was supposed to be at work but she couldn't face Neil. She couldn't face this creepy head either. She threw her blouse over it to stop its eyes following her around the room.

Didier thought she was still going in. On Mondays and Tuesdays for the past two weeks, she'd got dressed in her work clothes, kissed them goodbye, then hidden in a coffee shop until the coast was clear. She made up reasons for getting home early – a meeting in town, a headache, a fire drill.

When she phoned the office, she made up different reasons. Last week she'd invented chicken pox for Sofia. Yesterday, she made the poor mite even worse with a cooked-up streptococcal infection. She couldn't keep it up for ever but she reckoned she could drag it out another week.

She'd been avoiding Isobel too. She didn't want to talk about Neil, didn't want questions about York. But Isobel was persistent, had badgered her all weekend. So here she was, getting ready for a run on a sleety Monday morning.

Boo pushed herself hard. Good exercise hormones – endorphins, serotonin and oxytocin – rushed through her. They made her feel strong. Much better than bad lust hormones – testosterone and estrogen. She made it back to their start at the outdoor gym long before Isobel, where she patted her Afro as she stretched – the sweat made it itchier, if that was possible. She couldn't wait to get rid of it. Boo couldn't believe people kept a weave in for months.

Isobel insisted on a post-run coffee, steering them to a table tucked away in the corner. 'So, did Didier like my special gift?' she asked after their drinks arrived.

'Yes,' lied Boo. In fact, Didier had wondered why someone she'd only known for five minutes would give her such an extravagant present.

'Ronke was thrilled with hers, wasn't she? She seemed on good form at Come-Chop,' said Isobel.

'Yeah, I'm seeing her tomorrow.' Boo patted her head. 'She's taking this weave off.'

'It's funny – I thought she'd be more upset about me and Kayode,' said Isobel. 'She made out he told her about us, but I know she was lying.'

Boo shook her head firmly. 'Ronke never lies. Maybe we're all wrong about Kayode. Didier is convinced he's in love with her. He's got a soft spot for Ronke himself.'

'Be careful it doesn't turn into a hard spot,' Isobel snickered.

'Stop! It's not like that. She's like a sister to him.'

'Well, don't say I didn't warn you. It's obvious Ronke wants your life. And Kayode is definitely not in love with her. If he was, he wouldn't have come on to me at Sofia's party,' Isobel giggled.

'No!' Boo stared at her. Was Isobel pleased that Kayode still fancied her? Or was this her idea of a joke? 'He wouldn't,' she said finally.

'Ask Simi – she was there. I don't know why you're surprised: you said it yourself, she always picks arseholes. But . . .' Isobel paused and pointed a perfectly manicured nail at Boo. 'Not a word to Ronke. Don't go blabbing like you did about Simi's abortion.'

Boo sat on her unmanicured hands. The gel polish had ruined her nails; they were thin and flaky. She felt drained and on edge. She didn't need any more secrets. She had enough to deal with.

'It's all right.' Isobel gave her a condescending pat on the hand. 'I forgive you. Now come on, I want to know all about York.'

'There's nothing to tell. You know how these things are.' Boo chewed on a split nail.

'Didn't you hear what I said? I have a nose for these things. You're here, not at work. That's how I know you had sex with your boss.' Isobel laughed throatily. 'You've got guilt written all over you.'

'Don't be ridiculous.' Boo's mouth was dry. She tried to blink but her eyelids wouldn't move.

'It's obvious! You were running away from something just now – you flew up that hill. I could hardly keep up.'

'I'm getting fitter,' said Boo. 'That's all.'

Isobel put her hand over Boo's. 'Don't look so upset. It's me. Go on, you'll feel better when you get it off your chest. You can trust me.'

'Oh, Isobel, it was awful.' And Boo found herself pouring

out the whole horrid story. 'He kept saying I was exotic.' Boo shuddered.

'What a prick!' spat Isobel. 'Parrots are exotic. Carpets are exotic. Not people. It's a fucking insult. I've met men like him, wanting to chalk screwing a black girl off their list. What would he have said if you were Asian? Your eyes are like almonds? Does your vagina go sideways?'

Boo was stunned. Isobel was indifferent to her sleeping with Neil but outraged that he called her exotic? She sipped her cold coffee. It tasted acrid. 'I can't face him. I've been pretending Sofia is ill. Oh, Isobel, I don't know what to do. If Didier finds out, I'll die. You can't tell anyone. No one. Not Simi. Not Ronke. No one.'

'Of course we won't tell anyone. Your secret's safe with me. In this case, honesty is the worst policy.'

'Yes. As far as I'm concerned it didn't happen,' said Boo. 'I never want to see him again. I'm going to resign.'

'Why?' said Isobel. 'Stop being so theatrical. Just tell him it's over.'

Boo knew Isobel was right. She needed to go back to work, tell Neil where she stood. 'I feel like such an idiot. We've been flirting for months. I led him on.' Boo squeezed her eyes shut.

Isobel poked Boo's shoulder. Hard. 'Open your eyes! You're a grown woman. Take control, tell him how you feel: *Last week I wanted to shag you; this week I don't. End of. And don't use the word exotic again. You wanker.*'

'Maybe I won't put it quite like that,' said Boo, rubbing her shoulder.

∽

Boo stood waiting for the kettle to boil, inspecting the stainless-steel pasta server in her hand. The stiff prongs were perfect for getting under the frizz, stabbing through the corn-rows and massaging her itchy scalp. She put it back to her head.

'What are you doing?' shouted Ronke. 'You're going to hurt yourself.'

'I can't bear it any more. I hate it.'

'It's OK,' said Ronke. 'That's why I'm here. Go get a comb and a pair of scissors – little ones. I'll sort the teas.'

Five minutes later Boo sat silently with a towel around her shoulders, listening to Ronke natter away. Her sing-song voice and the snip-snip of the scissors were hypnotic.

'You have such beautiful hair,' said Ronke. 'The whole point of a weave is to get hair like yours, not to cover it up. I don't know what you were thinking.'

'Hmm.' Boo didn't know either. She was glad Ronke was behind her, sure the shame in her face would be apparent.

'I can't wait for Sunday. I'm making lunch for Yetty and Abayomi – you know, Kayode's sister and her husband. I'm doing roast chicken with all the trimmings, including jollof rice . . .'

Boo tuned out the specifics and tried to make sense of the logic. Ronke was turning a Sunday lunch she had to cook into something exciting and joyful.

'We're viewing another flat tonight. It's in Mitcham, not far from Rafa's place,' said Ronke. 'Kayode wasn't sure at first; he was a bit snobby about Mitcham. But Rafa took us for a drink at his local. Turns out the landlord's an Arsenal fan. And this flat has a garden and a shed. He's as excited as me.'

Boo wondered how Ronke could make her little life sound so happy. Here she was talking about an outpost of Croydon as if it was the Holy Land. Was it because she expected nothing? Did Boo expect too much?

Ronke shook Boo gently. 'Are you asleep?'

'No, I'm listening. It's nice hearing you talk.' Boo decided not to slag off Mitcham or mention Isobel and Kayode. 'I'm so glad you and Simi have made up.'

'Me too,' said Ronke. 'I felt awful. And you were right, it's not my business. She and Martin are strong – like you and Didier. They'll work it out.'

'Hmm.' Boo pinched the bridge of her nose. She had to move the conversation away from couples. Christmas. Ronke was obsessed with it. 'What's your work doing for Christmas?'

'A *Drag Race* party.' Ronke paused, snipping for a moment. 'You know, the RuPaul TV show.'

Boo didn't have a clue, which was fine.

'We're doing lip-sync battles. I'm going as Michelle Visage – I've got the boobs for it. Rafa's going to be Ru. I'm trying to convince Kayode to come in drag. He's got amazing legs! But shoes might be a problem – his feet are massive, size fourteen. What's your company doing?'

Boo didn't want to go there. She'd got the email last week. Xmas on the Beach. A hotel in Studland – dinner, dancing, overnight stay and a 'walk off the hangover' stroll in the dunes the next morning. Partners optional. 'I'm not going,' she said. 'I'm not like you – I'm not bothered about Christmas.'

'Don't be a grinch. You have to go.' Ronke put down the scissors. 'Almost there. Let's unplait you. Oh dear, your scalp looks sore.'

Boo grimaced as her hair emerged from its twisted bonds. She couldn't wait to wash it. She was going to use a whole tub of deep conditioner. 'Did you know Simi got headhunted?'

'No,' said Ronke. 'We talked for hours on Saturday. She didn't mention it.'

'Isobel told me.'

'That girl is a proper *amebo*,' said Ronke with a deep frown.

'A what?'

'A gossip,' said Ronke. 'Someone who can't keep their mouth shut.'

Fuck. Fuck. Fuck. Boo shut her eyes. *Oh God*, she thought, *what have I done?*

18

SIMI

SIMI BURIED HER FACE in Martin's rugby shirt. Synthetic blueberry and jasmine from the fabric conditioner but no trace of him. She was alone. Apart from the Ife head on her bedside. It looked as miserable as she felt.

She'd told Martin Shanghai was a work trip. She had re-invented Chitrita Phaishan as a Chinese brand. QB wanted her to see their flagship store and meet the team. And budgets were tight so it was in and out.

Martin had been sympathetic. 'This is slave labour – you'll be shattered. It had better be business class.'

'I bloody hope so,' Simi lied again. The flights were steerage.

And today, she had knitted in another untruth. 'Yeah, it went well. Didn't get to see the city, but met the team and got some ideas for the pitch. It's all good.'

What a waste of a lie. Shanghai had been an unmitigated disaster.

She had cleared customs at Pudong and tried her best to disguise her exhaustion with foundation. It didn't work. Her face somehow managed to be both thin and puffy. Too many late nights, hangovers, skipped meals.

A sullen driver took her to the Trade Zone. She was expecting bustle – she'd Googled – population twenty-four million. But she hadn't expected to see every single one of them. And she hadn't expected them all to look the same. Simi knew she was being ignorant. No, she was being plain racist.

Martin had said something similar on his first trip to Lagos. They'd been gridlocked at Ojuelegba in the morning rush hour. The junction teemed with people. Workers squashed into overloaded danfo buses, hawkers shoving newspapers into people's faces, children in dusty uniforms playing *ten-ten* and a gang of area boys demanding donations. Cocooned in their air-conditioned car, Simi was glued to her phone, oblivious. Martin prodded her, eyes wide.

'There are so many people. And they all look the same.'

Simi had read him the race relations act. Told him the other-race effect was a poor defence for small-minded, little-Englander bigotry. Now she understood.

The interview with the CEO was toe-curlingly embarrassing for both of them. He quizzed her on media planning, fired questions at her in a language Simi didn't speak – ROI, reach, frequency OTS, direct buy vs pragmatic buy, engagement, platform preferences, flighting, pulsing. They both knew she was out of her depth. He was kind but kept glancing at his watch. Simi hated being pitied; she wanted it to be over as much as he did.

Two hours later, she was back at the airport. She'd failed. It was becoming a habit. She would lose her job and probably never get another. It was a five-hour wait for her flight so she found herself calling Isobel. 'I shouldn't have come. It was awful.'

'Typical,' said Isobel. 'They hate black people. You should see them in Nigeria. There's a Chinese restaurant in Lagos and it's segregated. I'm not joking. There's a separate area for Nigerians. You don't even get the same food. And this is in our own country, where they are the fucking visitors. You couldn't make it up.'

Simi tried to make this narrative fit. The HR woman had been a bit dodgy, asking where she was from and acting surprised when Simi said she was British. But she couldn't kid herself. It hadn't gone wrong because of her skin colour, it had been a disaster because she'd been crap. And now Isobel, who had been pushing Shanghai like a dealer, had suddenly changed tune. Simi knew she was doing it to make her feel better, but it wasn't working.

'What time do you land? I'll send Vadim,' said Isobel. 'I know how to cheer you up.'

'I can't. I need my bed.'

'Chin up, *alobam*. They don't deserve you. And who wants to live in bloody Shanghai?'

Simi folded the rugby shirt and put it away. She needed to stop overthinking. She was meeting Ronke, Boo and Iso later. The gym would kill two hours. Then a bit of retail therapy – she needed a new ski jacket; her old one was two seasons out of date.

She was heading out with her gym bag when her phone beeped with a message from her stepmother.

Bawo ni Simisola? Call me urgently. God bless you. Mama Tosan.

Simi's already bad mood darkened. What did she want? And why couldn't *she* call? WhatsApp calls were free in *both* directions. She considered ignoring it. But what if something was wrong? She sighed and dialled. 'Hello, Mama T. You OK? Dad all right?'

'Hello, Simisola, it is good to hear your voice. You never call us. We are all fine, *o*. I am so happy. We are coming to visit you. Me and Daddy.'

Simi's headache went from dull to sharp. 'Right. Er . . . when?'

'Next week, *o*! Friday. I cannot wait to see you. Hold on for Daddy.'

'Hello, *Dad*.' Simi flung the bag on the bed. The word *daddy* had set her teeth on edge. 'How are you? Um, the thing is, next week isn't great. I've got a big pitch at work, then I'm off to Vermont. So it's like manic.'

'Since when do I need your permission to travel? *Ehn*? Simisola! You should be wishing me journey mercies. *Ah-ah*! You *dis* girl. I didn't kill my father so you will not kill me.'

Simi lowered her head. She wasn't a girl. She was a thirty-five-year-old woman, running on empty. She had no reserves left to play good daughter. 'Um . . .'

'It's a flying visit. Only ten days. I must see my son and my grandchildren. You will arrange a taxi to meet us, *abi*? I will email my requirements.' And the line went dead.

Simi threw her phone at the Ife head, watching her morosely. Her father screwed with her confidence at the best of times. She loved him, but if they hadn't happened to be related, she'd have nothing to do with him. And to be fair, he'd have nothing to do with her.

After the divorce, Dad had discovered religion. He met Aunty Moji in church and two years later Simi had two stepsisters, Tosan and Temisan. Aunty Moji became Mama Tosan, or Mama T.

They were born-again Christians, the kind who took no responsibility for things going wrong and credited God and/or Jesus for everything good. Prime example: God gave Simi the power to help them financially.

They were messy. In Surulere they had a live-in house girl who cleared up after them, but the house was still a tip.

They were nosy. She had caught her stepmother rifling through her wardrobe and Dad thought he had the right to read her bank statements.

But worst of all was Dad's incredible ability to talk about himself. He didn't give a shit about her life but was determined she should know all about his. The price of petrol, erratic electricity supply, problems with the generator, dwindling pension, lazy house girl, greedy pastor, terrible weather, annoying mosquitoes, pot-holed roads . . . Nothing was too small to whine about.

Simi toyed with putting them up in a hotel – an apartment hotel – where Mama T could cook her stews (you couldn't expect her to eat English food in England), but it would just be another stick to beat her with. She sighed and picked her phone up from the floor. The screen was cracked. *Gah!* She checked the head – no damage. She sat back on the bed and looked at her father's list of 'advance requests'.

- Four jars of honey (*Simi knew full well you could buy honey in Lagos. You could buy anything at Shoprite in V.I.*)

- One large Harrods Christmas Pudding (*Not to eat. To display proudly so visitors could see how sophisticated he was.*)
- Ink Cartridges x 4 – cannot remember the brand of the printer, it's the one you bought for us, make sure you check
- 6 bottles of Vitamin C – I don't like those yeye dissolvable ones you got last time. I want the correct ones from Holland & Barrett. (*If he was so particular, why didn't he get them himself: he'd have ten whole days, enough time to buy – and pay for – his own crap.*)

The list ended with some obscure generator parts – an alternator, spark plugs and a voltage regulator. But the last item was a new low.

- Viagra. 12 tablets.

Fuck right off, Simi thought. *I am not buying Viagra for Dad. Or Daddy.*

∽

Funky Nation at Ronnie Scott's had been Ronke's idea, but the VIP booth was all Isobel. Simi hadn't been out in Soho for years – too touristy, too smelly – but this was good. The crowd was the right age (not old, not teenage); the dance floor was rammed but their booth was roomy; they could sing along to the music (stuff she recognized) but still hear themselves talk.

Simi told them about her father's upcoming visit. She didn't do pity parties so she made it light and funny, not letting on how distressed she was. Boo moaned about her outlaws and how she was dreading Christmas. She'd got rid of the dreadful Afro and was back in her leather mini. Ronke didn't join in the folks-trashing session because her parents were wonderful.

'Ladies! I've got exciting news. A date for your diaries.' Isobel beat out a drum roll on the table. Her nails were black with tiny golden dots.

Simi rolled her eyes. But Isobel wasn't looking at her. She was focused on Ronke.

'An *owambe* for my niece's sweet sixteen,' Isobel continued. 'You're all invited.'

'An owam-what?' asked Boo.

'A proper Naija party!' Ronke gushed. 'Food, dancing, music.'

'You'll love it, Ronks,' said Isobel. 'She's such a princess, it's going to be so OTT. The brat wanted Versailles but she's had to settle for Sky Garden.'

Simi bristled. Why was Isobel sucking up to Ronke? 'It hasn't opened yet,' she said snidely. 'I looked into it for a launch.'

'Money opens doors, darling,' said Isobel. 'And you'll love this, Ronke – there's *aso ebi*.'

'Now you're making words up,' said Boo.

'Oh my God! I haven't worn *aso ebi* for years. Not since Aunty K's sixtieth.' Ronke turned to Boo. 'It's like a uniform. So, say it's a wedding, the bride's family are all in one fabric and the groom's in another. Cloth is *aso*, family is *ebi*. Family cloth. Get it? You make it into whatever you want – so everyone looks different but the same. We'll have to find a tailor. That's going to be tricky.'

'Don't worry, Ronks, Patience will sort you all out. She's been my tailor for ever,' said Isobel. 'She's super-quick. And I'm paying. My treat!'

'Not for me,' said Boo. 'I'll wear my jumpsuit.'

Isobel flicked her hand in the air. 'You can wear whatever you want. But Patience can do a little dress for Sofia. And something for Didier.'

'He's French,' said Boo.

'He'll love it,' said Ronke. 'Me and Sofia can have matching dresses!'

Simi looked at her friends. Ronke bouncing with excitement. Boo anxious. Isobel lapping up the attention. 'Will your dad be there?' she asked.

'Don't know yet. Maybe, if he's in town.' Isobel touched Simi's knee. 'But don't worry, he'll have forgotten all about his little spat with your dad.'

Simi hadn't been worried, just curious. She resolved to win the *aso ebi* off. Her mind whirred.

'Let's hit the dance floor, Simi,' said Isobel.

Simi was still irritated with her. 'Not to Shalamar.'

Isobel stood and held her arm out. 'Come on, Boo.' It wasn't a question.

Boo obeyed. Simi rolled her eyes at Ronke, who rolled hers back. They both knew Boo hated dancing.

'How long are they staying?' asked Ronke.

Ronke was the one person Simi could be honest with about Dad. She knew how much he got to her. 'Ten long days. I'm dreading it. He makes me feel like a guest in my own home.'

'It's just his way. You know he loves you. And you can escape to mine whenever you want. I can stay at Kayode's, give you a bit of space. I'll even make a big pot of stew. In fact, I'll do two. You can put one in the freezer – save you worrying about cooking.'

Simi had no intention of cooking. Or worrying about cooking. 'Are you sure?'

''Course. But you should tell him how you feel instead of bottling it up.'

'It wouldn't change anything. He doesn't care. I'm the dropout, the family failure.'

'More fool him. Anyway, you've got Martin, me and Boo. We love you.'

Simi put her arm around Ronke. 'You're right, as always.'

Maybe God did exist and was listening, because at that exact moment the unmistakable sound of Bernard Edwards' bass blared out the opening chords to Sister Sledge and 'We Are Family'.

Ronke looked at Simi and smiled. 'Come on. They're playing our song.'

19

RONKE

RONKE KICKED OFF HER shoes and lowered the dental chair so she was horizontal.

Rafa, perched on her stool, swivelled to face her. 'So what seems to be the problem, Ms Tinubu?'

Ronke closed her eyes, trying to work out where to start. She'd waited a week before mentioning Isobel's party to Kayode. She knew he didn't like Isobel (which was a good thing) but she hadn't anticipated how violently he'd react.

They'd been lazing in bed reading the Sunday papers when she brought it up. They were relaxed and happy; she was sure it was the right moment. He had flipped. Leapt out of bed, stomped about the room, accused her of never listening, said he wouldn't go to the party under any circumstances and insisted *she* couldn't go either. Ronke tried to explain that he was being childish, and that Isobel was Simi's oldest friend, but he wouldn't listen.

'Come on, Ronke,' said Rafa. 'It can't be that bad.'

Ronke opened her eyes. 'He won't come to the party.' She sighed dramatically. 'And I really wanted Isobel to see us together.'

'Who cares what she thinks?' asked Rafa.

'I do,' said Ronke. 'I go to his rugby games even when it's pouring with rain. Why can't he grit his teeth and do this for me?'

'Why doesn't he want to go?' Rafa spun himself round in a circle. 'It's not like him to miss a party.'

'He can't stand Isobel. And he says it'll be a vulgar display of stolen wealth. And there's nothing worse than hanging out with a bunch of spoilt brats dripping in designer clobber.' Ronke kicked her feet against the chair. 'He's right. But I don't care – I want to go and I want him to come with me.'

'It sounds right up my street.' Rafa leapt off the stool. 'Take me!'

They spent the rest of their break scrolling through *ankara* outfits on Pinterest. Ronke was going traditional – tight around the boobs and bottom, mermaid skirt, peplum.

'Look at this! Ozwald Boateng. From last year's spring/ summer collection.' Rafa passed Ronke his phone. 'Do you think the tailor will be able to make it?'

'Ozwald who? You sound like Simi.' Ronke peered at his phone: two good-looking black guys on a catwalk, both wearing tightly fitted suits made out of *ankara*. She wished Kayode wasn't being so difficult – he'd look amazing in a suit like that. 'Cool.' She handed the phone back. 'According to Isobel, her seamstress can do anything. We'll find out soon enough. Bring your favourite suit in – she can use it for size.' She prodded her tummy. 'Isobel's coming round to take measurements on Thursday. Do you think I can lose a stone in three days?'

∽

RONKE WAS LATE AS USUAL. She hoped Kayode wouldn't be waiting. But with Rafa's suit draped over her left arm (in a cerise garment carrier) and a bulging bag for life in her right hand (a six-pack of lager and the makings of supper – chicken, Boursin, prosciutto, new potatoes, green beans), she couldn't text.

Someone was sitting on the low wall opposite her flat, a bunch of flowers on his lap. He looked out of place, but that was daft – anyone could sit there, Ronke had done it herself, waiting for her neighbour, Lisa, to come home when she'd forgotten her keys.

As Ronke pushed at her wrought-iron gate with her knee, she sensed the man move. Next thing he was beside her, hand extended, yellow roses inches from her nose. Ronke's instinctive smile vanished as she realized who it was. Her hands shook and she clutched her bags more tightly. 'Mr Owen. Why are you here? What do you want?'

'I had to see you.' He stepped forward and thrust the flowers at her again. The sharp acetate wrapping scratched her face. 'I got you these.'

Ronke stepped back, her heart thumping. 'I can't accept them. You need to leave.' She tried to push through the iron gate but it was latched.

He leaned closer. 'But I bought them for you,' he said, his voice agitated.

'How do you know where I live?' Ronke frantically fumbled the gate open and lurched through. She tried to swing it shut but he caught it with his free hand.

'I've been following you. I'm looking after you.'

'You need to go. Now. My fiancé will be here any second.'

Ronke backed towards her front door, but she didn't open it, scared he'd push in with her. She felt a wave of panic.

He came closer. 'I love you, Ronke.'

'Mr Owen, you're confused.' Ronke's voice wobbled; even she could hear the fear in it. She looked around desperately, but the street was empty. She tried again more firmly. 'I want you to leave now. Please go away.'

'I'm coming inside. Give me your bag – it looks heavy.' He reached for her shopping.

Ronke pulled her arm back. He held on.

The bag split. Potatoes rolled into the street, the six-pack of lager landed on her toes. The pain brought tears to Ronke's eyes.

'Now look what you've done!' Mr Owen shouted, smashing the flowers to the ground.

The next bit was a blur. Suddenly Kayode was between them, a foot taller and a lot wider than Mr Owen. Ronke heard herself giggle. A high-pitched nervous titter.

'Who are you?' Mr Owen backed away from the front door, almost tripping over a potato.

'I'm her boyfriend, you fucking weirdo. Touch her again and I'll break both your arms.' Kayode gave him a push, his palm flat against Mr Owen's chest. Mr Owen stumbled and fell backwards. His glasses flew off and he lifted his hands to his face as if to ward off incoming blows.

Ronke giggled again – she couldn't help it. The small white man sat on the pavement, the big black man looming over him. It was the perfect moment for the police to arrive.

There was a screech of brakes and two uniformed officers piled out of a patrol car. Time seemed to slow.

The male officer barked at Kayode. 'Step back, sir. Calm down. Hands where I can see them. I don't want to have to cuff you.'

The female officer crouched beside Mr Owen, comforting him, fetching his glasses and helping him place them back on his nose. She sat him back on the wall. 'Are you OK, sir? Are you hurt? Did he hit you?'

Ronke stood rigid, unable to speak. She clutched Rafa's suit like a shield, her breathing fast and ragged.

And then time sped up. Lisa flew out of their shared front door, waving her arms dramatically, her long blonde hair trailing behind her.

'I was the one who called you,' she tried to explain. 'This man's been loitering here for hours, staring up at Ronke's flat and muttering to himself. I knew he was up to no good.'

Kayode was backed up against the police car. 'Name and address, sir?' The male officer's voice was level and calm. 'And what's your business around here today?'

'Fucking typical racist bollocks. This is bullshit!' Kayode's voice was loud and angry. He took a step towards the policeman.

'Steady, sir.' The officer placed a hand on Kayode's chest and eased him back against the car. 'No need to swear.'

'Listen to me, you moron.' Lisa had a potato in one hand and a packet of green beans in the other. 'The white guy is the one you should be talking to. The black guy is her boyfriend.'

Ronke took a deep breath and forced her mouth to work. 'Yes, he's my boyfriend,' she said to the policeman. Her voice was squeaky. 'Calm down, Kayode,' she added.

Kayode objected to this. 'I am fucking calm,' he said, in a tone that was anything but.

By this time, a small crowd of onlookers had gathered. It took half an hour for Ronke to make a statement. The police wanted her to file a stalker's report and she agreed to visit the station the next day. They released Mr Owen with a warning. Everyone watched as he stumbled off with his battered flowers.

Kayode was still angry. He ranted to the police about institutional racism, threatened to make a complaint.

Lisa egged him on. 'Classic unconscious bias,' she said. 'I did a course at work. Don't ask questions, just take one look and decide white man good, black man bad. It's disgusting. I'll be your witness, Kayode.'

'Let's drop it,' Ronke said quietly. 'Please.'

'No, she's right,' said Kayode. 'If Lisa weren't here, I'd be in a cell. They'd probably have planted some fucking drugs on me too.' He hugged Lisa, his new best friend.

Ronke followed a fuming Kayode up the stairs, potatoes stuffed in her pockets.

'Why didn't you use the rape alarm?' Kayode threw the chicken breasts on to the worktop. 'And why were you giggling?'

'I don't know. Nerves, I guess. Sorry.' Ronke couldn't think straight. She needed a hug not an inquisition. 'You shouldn't have hit him – you could have got in trouble.'

'For fuck's sake, I was protecting you. He could have been carrying a knife. And I didn't hit him.' Kayode opened the fridge. 'I can't believe you're making it my fault.'

'I'm not. But getting mad didn't help.'

'You don't get it. You have no idea what it's like to be a

black man in the wrong place at the wrong time. A, you're a woman; B, you're light-skinned. It's completely different.'

'Kayode, please stop shouting – this isn't *Mississippi Burning*. I've said I'm sorry. Let's make supper.' She moved to hug him but he turned away.

'Are you saying the police aren't racist?' Kayode grabbed a beer and slammed the fridge door.

'I'm not saying anything. Look, I'm still shaking.' Ronke put her arms around him. 'Please give me a hug.' This time he didn't push her away, but his arms were stiff.

Supper was awful. The chicken undercooked, then burned. The evening was tense. Kayode angry, then sullen. Ronke tearful, then miserable. He walked her to work the next morning. They held hands, but she knew he was still pissed off.

'We need to go to the police station and make your stalker's report,' he said. 'Today.'

'I know. I will.'

'I'm going with you. What time will you finish?'

'I'm meeting Isobel after work. I'll go at lunchtime, I promise.'

Kayode stopped walking, dropped her hand and glared at her. 'What the fuck are you meeting her for?'

Ronke rubbed her eyes. She had planned to tell him she was going, just not like this. 'She's bringing the fabric for the *owambe*,' she whispered.

'You agreed not to go.'

'No. You said you wouldn't go. Rafa's coming with me.'

'I give up. Do what you want.' He turned and left. No goodbye kiss.

THAT EVENING RONKE WALKED HOME the long way, her head on a constant swivel, the rape alarm Kayode had given her clutched in her right hand. Her street was deserted but she rushed up the stairs and fastened the door chain anyway. Minutes later, at seven on the dot, her buzzer went. She peeked out of the window. Yup, large car, blacked-out windows, massive bald chap holding the door open. Isobel.

Isobel breezed in, looking casual in a girl-next-door way, if you happened to live next door to a beautiful rich girl.

'Wine?' asked Ronke. 'Have a seat – just chuck the cushions on the floor.'

'Do you have any herbal tea?' Isobel's 'herbal' had a silent 'h'. She ignored the sofa and wandered around Ronke's small living room, taking it all in.

'Hell yeah!' Ronke stepped into her kitchen. Isobel followed. 'Take your pick. Matcha, ginger, mint, apple, green?'

'Matcha, please. I love your flat. Can I look round?' Isobel was already opening the bedroom door. Ronke was glad she'd remembered to take the Ife head out from the back of the wardrobe.

'Go for it – won't take you long.'

Isobel put her head round the kitchen door. 'The head looks quite happy in your bedroom.'

Ronke yanked at her hair. 'I call him *Ooni*.'

They spread the fabric out – a riot of purples and greens in bold sculptural shapes. The round metallic embellishments glistened in the light. This wasn't ordinary *ankara*. It was Vlisco – the Louis Vuitton of Dutch wax, twice the price of most brands and twice as nice. Kayode was being unreasonable – why should she miss out on a good party?

She pulled up her Pinterest page and showed Isobel her outfit shortlist.

'Patience doesn't use patterns, she cuts by eye,' said Isobel. 'She needs a week, so you have to see her this weekend.'

Ronke almost moaned in relief. She'd been dreading Isobel asking for her measurements. She reckoned her upper thigh was bigger than Isobel's waist.

'I've put her in a flat in Kennington. It's a dive – best if she comes to you.'

'You've put her . . .? What do you mean?'

'She lives in Lagos. I flew her over. Easier than trying to find a good tailor here.'

'*Na wa, o!*' said Ronke.

Isobel zoomed in on a narrow skirt with a fluted peplum and a fitted off-the-shoulder bodice. 'This is the one for you. It'll show off your wonderful curves.'

Ronke was surprised. 'Snap! That's my favourite too. The top's a bit revealing though.'

'Nonsense. If I had your boobs, they'd always be on show. Go for it. Kayode won't be able to keep his eyes off you.'

Ronke yanked at her hair again. 'What are you wearing?'

'You'll have to wait and see,' said Isobel. 'Can you give Patience some ideas for Sofia? Boo doesn't have a clue. If I didn't know better, I'd say there was no way she was half Nigerian.'

'Yeah, no problem. I'm seeing them tomorrow. Maybe Patience could meet us there? Measure us all together – save her rushing around?'

'Whatever works for you. She's getting paid so she'll do what she's told. I'll drop the fabric off at Boo's on my way home.' Isobel wandered over to Ronke's small bookcase and picked up the framed photo of her parents. 'Don't you hate him for leaving you?'

'What?' Ronke felt a sudden urge to snatch the frame out of Isobel's hands. She'd fixed it with superglue, but it was fragile. 'He didn't leave me. He was killed.'

Isobel stared at the photo for an inordinately long time, before handing it over. 'I know what it feels like,' she said. 'My mother left me too. My *mamochka*. She committed suicide when I was twelve.'

'I'm so sorry. I didn't know.' Ronke returned the frame to the shelf. Kayode's warning rang in her ears. She ignored it and gave Isobel a half hug.

'I don't talk about it. I try not to think about it.' Isobel's low voice cracked. 'She broke Dad's heart and when they split up, I blamed her. The last time I saw her I was so mean. When she died, I hated myself. I was away in boarding school, in New York, which didn't help. I went a bit crazy. Swallowed some pills. Lots of pills.' Isobel's voice dropped to a whisper. She seemed smaller, fragile. 'It was a cry for help; I was torn up inside.'

'You poor thing.' Ronke couldn't imagine how she'd have coped without her mum, brother and Aunty K. She went in for the full hug.

'Three years of psychotherapy didn't help.' Isobel hugged her back so tight it hurt. 'Sorry, this is the first time I've talked about it in years. Even Simi doesn't know the pain I went through. But I knew you'd understand.'

Ronke pulled out of Isobel's grasp. 'You never really get over it.'

'I know,' said Isobel. 'But I learned to hide my feelings. It was the only way to get away from the fucking shrink.'

Ronke wondered if Isobel's brashness was just a coping mechanism. Ronke hadn't had to hide her emotions; she didn't have to pretend to be brave. 'It's crap, isn't it?' she said.

'Dad doesn't say it, but I know I remind him of her. I'm his *tsarina* now.' Isobel's voice became brighter. 'Enough of this. Let's talk about happier things. Tell me, where did you meet Kayode?'

Ronke hesitated. She didn't want to talk to Isobel about Kayode, but maybe it would make her see what a tight couple they were. And she loved their *how we met* story. Kayode had walked into the surgery for a check-up. Black suit, white shirt, wonky tie. He'd towered over her as he shook her hand. Her knees had wobbled. She'd mimed at Rafa, 'He's gorgeous.' Rafa had mouthed back 'He's gay.' She'd relaxed then because Rafa's gaydar was never wrong. 'I looked into his mouth and fell in love. With his teeth. They're perfect, like my dad's. White, straight and big. Not too big though, just right for his frame. He's tall – six foot four in socks. He plays rugby, so he's pretty beefy.'

'Yes, he is big.' Isobel's laugh was like a tinkly bell. A very annoying tinkly bell.

Ronke pictured them together and felt nauseous. Her heart wasn't in the story any more.

20

BOO

Sofia wouldn't shut up. 'Poor Aunty Ronke, she lives all by herself so I'm a special treat. I bet she'll want to keep me for ever.'

'I doubt it.' Boo scrambled on the floor gathering toy soldiers. 'There are some good things about living by yourself.'

'Like what?' asked Sofia.

'Peace and quiet. Time for yourself. Freedom.' Boo dumped the soldiers into an overflowing toy box. 'No toys – now that's a distinct advantage.'

'No toys?' Sofia grabbed a handful of soldiers and chucked them into her Trunki. 'Poor Aunty Ronke. Maybe I'll let her keep one.'

It had seemed like a good idea on Saturday. Pack Sofia off for a sleepover, date night with tubby hubby (she needed to stop using that moniker, even in her head). But now she was dreading it. Sofia was a convenient buffer and go-to excuse. Don't want to talk to your husband? Make sure Sofia is always in the room. Want to avoid your boss? Fake an illness for your child. Not sure how to get rid of an unwanted visitor? Pretend it's Sofia's bath time.

Which was precisely what she'd done when Isobel stopped by yesterday, unannounced, to drop off a huge bag of cloth. Didier was upstairs doing bedtime with Sofia and Boo was desperate to get rid of Isobel before he came back down. He'd met her once, at Sofia's birthday party, but only for a brief hello. If he came down now, he'd put olives in a bowl, dig out the nice glasses, open a bottle of red and invite her for supper. Boo didn't want them in the same room, couldn't stomach the idea of them chatting. She'd sent Isobel away firmly and a bit rudely, promising to message her.

The doorbell rang and Boo answered it to find a red-faced Ronke clutching a pink suit carrier. 'You look like you've done a marathon,' Boo said.

'I have! I jogged all the way from the junction,' Ronke panted. 'I wanted to get here before Patience.'

'Who's Patience?'

'The tailor. She's coming to measure us. Isobel said she'd drop the fabric off yesterday. Don't say she forgot?'

'No, it's here,' said Boo. 'I was doing bath time; we didn't get to chat.'

Sofia bounded into the room from the garden, hands covered in mud. 'Look, Aunty Ronke! I found a slug.' She threw her arms around Ronke.

'Now look what you've done.' Boo pointed at the brown handprints on Ronke's red jeans. Sofia's face crumpled.

Ronke gave Boo a look and knelt and cuddled Sofia. 'Don't worry, roomie, mud washes off. Guess what? I've got us face packs for later.'

Boo clenched her teeth. Ronke's disapproving look was almost as irritating as Didier's disappointed look.

Ronke spread the cloth over the island, smoothed out the folds and swooned. 'Isn't it wonderful?'

'A hundred happy colours,' said Sofia.

'It's certainly bright,' said Boo. It was hideous. Lurid.

'It's not too late to change your mind – there's enough for everyone,' said Ronke.

'You're all right,' said Boo. 'I'll pass.'

Didier came in from the garden. 'Wow! *C'est magnifique!*'

'That means good,' said Sofia. Boo was pleased she wasn't the only person Sofia talked down to.

Ronke hoicked Sofia on to the island. 'You are so clever.'

Didier kissed Ronke twice on each cheek and stroked the cloth lightly. 'Ah, it's stiff, crispy.'

'It's wax. They embed the fabric in it. It gets soft when you wash it, but I love it like this; my peplum is going to be so sticky-outy. Look, Sofia . . .' Ronke scrolled through images on her phone. 'I bet your dad would look great in *buba* and *sokoto*?'

Sofia giggled.

'What do you think, Boo?' asked Ronke.

'I think we're in England and should stick to English,' Boo bristled. All this eulogizing over a bit of cotton – you'd think it was cashmere.

Ronke ignored her and spouted more gibberish – *Vlisco. Dashiki. Agbada. Fila. Gele.* Didier and Sofia cooed, nodding as if they understood. The doorbell rang; none of them looked up. 'Don't worry, I'll get it,' said Boo loudly.

Patience turned out to be short and round with a wide smile and a wider arse, skin the colour of milky tea and lips of bubble-gum pink. She wore a huge kimono-style jacket-dress made of African fabric but in more subdued tones of brown and grey, and with a less bonkers pattern.

'You're fat!' said Sofia.

'And you are rude,' said Boo. 'I'm sorry – she's at that age.'

Patience cackled and slapped her hip. 'Don't you worry, Miss Boo, she is right.' She turned to Sofia. 'I come from Calabar, where they measure beauty by the pound.'

Sofia stared, dumbstruck.

Boo was as amazed as her daughter, but managed to keep it off her face. 'Can I get you a tea? Or coffee?'

'Iced water, please, Miss Boo,' said Patience.

'I'll have one too,' said Ronke. 'I'm dehydrated after my run.'

'And me, Mama.'

'I'll do a jug.' Boo hoped Didier had filled the ice tray. Why couldn't they drink tea like normal people?

'Did you have to come far?' asked Boo as she handed Patience a glass.

'Miss Isobel has located me in a fine house. It's not far. Five stops to here on the black line from animal and something. Easy journey.'

'What?' Boo decided the woman was mad. She looked at Ronke for confirmation.

'Northern line from Elephant and Castle,' said Ronke, before turning to Patience. 'You should try Obalende Suya Spot – it's right outside the station.'

Patience pulled a tape measure from her bag and joined the huddle. There was more ooh-ing and aah-ing, more unintelligible gobbledegook, and now, thanks to Patience, added cackling. Boo knew she *could* join in – she was half Nigerian, for fuck's sake – but it all sounded so foreign. For once she was envious of Ronke. Her own waste-of-space father had stolen her heritage – she'd been left with half an identity. No wonder she felt like an intruder in her own life.

Didier draped the fabric around his shoulder and struck a pose. How dare he be more comfortable than her? Resentment flared and came out as spite. 'You'll look like a prat in an African outfit. It's not a costume, you know. It's culture. Your appropriating it is almost as bad as blackface.'

Didier laughed, her venom wasted on him.

'Boo!' Ronke said. 'Don't be horrid. That's like saying Kayode isn't allowed to wear a suit. My mum wore native all the time in Lagos. Take no notice, Didier. Rafa's going for it and he's so excited.'

'Rafa? Why's he going?' asked Boo.

'He's my date,' said Ronke. 'Kayode can't make it; he's doing something else.'

Doing someone else, thought Boo. 'Typical,' she said out loud. And then felt bad when Ronke's face reddened. It wasn't her fault her boyfriend was a cheat. Boo closed her eyes and tried to shake the word 'cheat' out of her head.

'Let's measure this little one first.' Patience pulled out a pad and pencil. 'You won't need much cloth – you're a skinny little thing.'

Sofia stood on tiptoe to make herself taller as she always did – the height chart on the back of the door was forever two inches out.

'How did Isobel find you?' asked Boo.

'*Ehn*, I've known Miss Isobel since she was little girl, longest time. When she call me say come sew cloth in London, I know say *God don butta my bread*! Her mama was my best customer in the old days. Beautiful woman. Very shapely, *ehn*. You know white people no get bottom, but Mrs B, she get am, *o*!'

'Papa is white, and he has a bottom,' said Sofia.

'White people's bottoms are like pancake. You are lucky your mama has Naija blood. Or you might have pancake bottom too. Where are your people from, Miss Boo?'

'My people are from Yorkshire,' snapped Boo.

'My bottom is round!' Sofia stuck out her bum.

Didier stuck his bottom out too. 'Mine's bigger than Mama's. Maybe I've got some Nigerian in me.'

'*Ikebe* super,' laughed Ronke as she patted her own backside.

Patience cackled. Boo squeezed her bottom in. She was standing a foot away from the group and it felt like an abyss. *My* home, *my* family and still I don't fit in. *You don't want to*, said the voice in her head.

Ronke passed Boo her phone. 'How about something like this for Didier?'

Boo looked down. A man wearing a tunic with slim trousers. She laughed. 'It looks like a dress. Didier would never wear that.'

Didier peered over her shoulder. 'I like it. Is there enough fabric?'

'Yes, *o*! Plenty, plenty. Miss Isobel's costume only requires one yard.' Patience kissed her teeth. 'I swear, that girl is allergic to cloth.'

Once they were measured, Sofia dragged Ronke to the garden to meet her slug. Didier followed. Boo hoped Patience would leave. 'More water?' she asked half-heartedly.

'Yes, please, Miss Boo.' Patience handed Boo her glass.

Boo filled it from the tap. 'So have you known Isobel long?' she said to break the silence. As soon as the words were out of her mouth, she realized they'd already covered this.

'Oh yes, since she was a small girl. Her mama was my best customer. She is still my favourite.'

'She's still in Nigeria?' asked Boo, surprised.

'No. She fled in 'ninety-one when everything scattered. She no go return. She was good to me – gave me money to set up my shop. And she remembers me at Christmas, sends me Western Union from Moscow without fail. God bless her.' Patience eyed Boo from crown to toe. 'Now what of you? Let me make you one nice dress. You don't want to look like a trespasser.'

'Thanks, but I've got something to wear.'

'*Na your choice be dat.* I go make you handbag and head-wrap. The *aso ebi* be like entry ticket – it shows you belong.'

The last thing Boo wanted was a bloody headwrap. 'That will be lovely,' she said. If only belonging was that easy.

∽

THE HOUSE FELT WRONG WITHOUT Sofia. Boo was used to being home alone or home with Sofia or home with Didier and Sofia. What did couples without children do? What had she and Didier done in the years before Sofia? What did Simi and Martin do? They went out. A lot. But they must stay at home sometimes. They couldn't be having sex all the time. Could they?

Didier rubbed her shoulders. 'How about I run you a bath?'

She could drag a bath out for half an hour. Forty-five minutes even. But she didn't want to sound too keen. 'Hmmm . . . maybe. Why are you being so nice?'

'I'm always nice. And I want you to be happy. Lately you've been so uptight.'

'I'm not uptight.'

'Sorry. Stressed? Angry? I don't know. Help me out here, Boo.' Didier lifted her chin and gazed into her eyes. 'One minute you want to work full-time, the next you don't want to work at all. I can't say the right thing. You're not you any more. So talk to me.'

Boo pushed his hand away.

'What's wrong, Boo? Are you unhappy? Depressed?'

'Trapped,' Boo whispered.

'Pardon?' said Didier sharply.

'Nothing.' She rubbed her temples.

'You said trapped.'

'If you heard me, why did you say pardon?'

'What's trapping you? Is it me? Sofia?'

'Of course not. I don't like being called uptight.' Boo stood up. 'Look, forget it. I'm going to have a bath.'

'Fine. Take your time,' said Didier coldly.

She ran the bath, stepped in, stepped out, wrapped a towel around her and went back downstairs.

'I'm sorry,' she said. 'I don't know why I'm being such a cow. I can't even blame my hormones. Maybe it's a midlife crisis?'

'You're thirty-five.'

'An early midlife crisis?'

'Well, you have another reason to hate me. I forgot to

book dinner and everywhere's fully booked.' Didier looked defeated.

'I don't hate you.' Boo moved over to his lap, climbed on and kissed him. 'I love you.' Her towel slipped and he bent his head and kissed her breast. She felt herself respond. It didn't feel seedy. She didn't feel exotic. An image of Neil flashed into her head and her stomach lurched.

'Stop! I've left the bath running.' She jumped up, clutching the towel around her.

'We could share it.' Didier leapt to his feet.

'I'm not in the mood.'

'We haven't had sex in weeks. What's wrong, Boo?'

'There's nothing wrong. I'm allowed to not feel like it.'

Minutes later, she heard the front door slam. She closed her eyes and sank under the water. But it didn't help – the guilt went with her.

When Didier got back, dripping with rain and laden down with groceries, he was contrite. As if he had been at fault. 'I'm sorry, *ma chérie*,' he said. 'Let's start again. You've always loved my *vongole*.'

'No, *I'm* sorry, Didier.' Boo rubbed his wet hair with a clean towel. 'I know I've not been nice lately. I'm going to snap out of it. I do love you.'

Boo sat at the island while Didier scrubbed clams. She told him about Ronke's stalker turning up and Kayode hitting him. Ronke had said pushed, but Boo reckoned she was playing it down.

'Thank goodness he was there.' Didier filled a pan with water and added a fistful of salt.

Boo bit back the *too much salt* comment. 'He nearly got arrested for assault.'

'Then the police are stupid. He was protecting the woman he loves. I would do the same if anyone touched you or Sofia.'

For the first time in for ever, Boo felt comfortable. She considered telling him about Simi – how she hadn't told Martin she'd got pregnant. It was illogical (and cruel), but part of her wanted Simi to seem like a bad wife. As if it would make her seem like a good one. But Martin was Didier's best friend. And Simi was hers. She couldn't betray her.

After supper, Boo sat contemplating her life as Didier washed up. Her phone pinged. Picture messages from Ronke. 'Come,' she said, taking Didier's hand and leading him to the sofa. They flicked through the images together. Sofia and Ronke with slices of cucumber over their eyes, in party dresses. Sofia wearing a pair of Ronke's shoes, in the kitchen. Sofia making Jenga out of fish fingers, on the bed, surrounded by toy soldiers and cushions. Didier laughed. Boo kissed his neck. The phone fell to the floor. They made love in the kitchen, like they used to before Sofia. He felt right. He smelled right. It was comfortable. It was wonderful.

21

SIMI

SIMI REPEATED HER MANTRA: *Three more sleeps till I get my flat back. Ten more sleeps and I'll be with Martin in Vermont. I can get through this.*

Mama Tosan seemed to have upped her game this time around. Simi's pristine flat had turned into a dump. Each evening there was more crap to trip over. Why in God's name had they bought two sheepskin rugs when they lived in one of the hottest countries in the world? And a massive wicker picnic hamper, complete with chintzy blue and white crockery.

'Mama T, you live in Surulere, not Hampstead,' Simi had said, trying to keep the irritation out of her voice.

'*Ehn*, we can have picnic in the Harmattan, when it's cold,' her stepmother replied. 'I saw it on the TV, *Downton Abbey* programme, so elegant.'

Cold? You were lucky if it dropped below seventy-five in Lagos. And there was zero chance of them sitting outside, being eaten alive by mosquitoes. 'Lovely,' Simi said.

With Dad and Mama T in her flat, Simi's office should have been her refuge. But it wasn't. The Chitrita Phaishan pitch had not gone well. They hadn't had an official 'no', but Simi could feel it in her bones – it was going to be another failure. A repeat of Shanghai.

'Sorry, not the right fit,' the headhunter had said. Simi had expected it but the rejection still hurt. She hadn't mentioned any of it to Isobel, whose constant flattery and praise made Simi feel worse, if that was possible.

Simi was always on edge when Dad was around, and without Martin it was worse. Today she'd had a panic attack at work, the second since Dad arrived. Her hands shook, her knees quaked, her heart thumped. She managed to hold it together until she got to the loo, locked herself in, took big gulpy breaths. She knew the drill: own your accomplishments, separate feelings from facts, love yourself, break the silence. But she had no accomplishments. She felt like a failure because she was a failure. And as for breaking the silence – she'd tackle that once she was with Martin in Vermont.

When she got home that evening, Simi crossed her fingers as she turned the key. Dad and Mama T were meant to be spending the night at Olu's, babysitting the wonderful (terrible) twins. Thank God. That was another thing: the constant thanking of God was infectious. Simi had done it at work today; Gavin had given her a worried look.

The flat was dark and quiet, and she stepped cautiously in. She turned on the lights in the sitting room. It was tidier. Not up to Essie's usual standard, but she couldn't blame her – it was difficult to clean around so much stuff. The coffee table was piled with rubbish. Two Bibles (his and hers); a three-inch-thick wad of filthy naira notes, bound together with an elastic band (less than a fiver in proper money); four pens with chewed lids, three notebooks, two Argos catalogues (they had a real problem with sharing); a tub of multivitamins; a blood pressure monitor (Dad was a hypochondriac who checked his blood pressure twice a day) and two pairs of reading glasses.

On top of all the junk was a note from Essie.

Greetings, Simi. I tried my best, but I ran out of time. I had to run an errand for your daddy. Please can you settle next time – I have left the receipt. Kind regards, Essie.

What the hell? She had told him Essie's job was to clean, not cook, make tea, wash clothes, run bloody errands or offer short-term loans. This was so embarrassing. Treating her house like a hotel was bad enough. Treating Essie like a house girl was bang out of order.

Simi went to the kitchen with her sushi supper. Three pots were soaking beside the sink, another note from Essie sat next to them.

Simi, the pots need to soak for some hours. The bottom was burned. I didn't want to scrape them. I know they are expensive.

Black specs floated on top of brown, dingy, spumy water. It made Simi feel sick. She donned rubber gloves and scrubbed. She wasn't sure her beautiful, barely used, teal Le Creuset would ever recover.

It would be worth it if they were even a tiny bit grateful.

But they weren't. Dad had been sulking since he'd arrived. Nothing was good enough. She should have been at the airport to meet them, taken time off work to ferry them around, stocked the cupboards with proper food. Simi explained that work was busy, pointed out that he'd given her no notice. He scowled and compared her (unfavourably) to Olu: 'Praise God, Olu shows respect for his father. He booked his annual leave as soon as I informed him of my visit.'

No praising God for Simi, who had paid for the cab from the airport, whose flat they were squatting in, who had spent last weekend at their beck and call – even though she was wiped out with jetlag.

'You should take Wednesday off and follow us to Madame Tussauds. Spend some time with the twins. Olu never sees you. He said you are a stranger to your niece and nephew, Simisola! It is not good, *o*.'

'I've got meetings on Wednesday,' Simi explained. 'I could do Friday?'

But no, Friday was no good. Olu needed them to babysit so he could take his tired, stressed wife out for dinner.

Fitting around Simi wasn't important. She wasn't important. And nothing she did would ever be good enough. This wasn't new. She'd known it all her life. So why did it still piss her off?

She headed to her bedroom, shutting the spare room door, but not before she saw the mess inside. Two huge open suitcases on the floor – billowing clothes and shoes. What was wrong with using the wardrobe?

She stripped off and put on her workout clothes. Gym. Shower. Sushi. Meditate. Sleep.

Three more sleeps till I get my flat back. Ten more sleeps and I'll be with Martin.

∾

SIMI HAD JUST COME BACK from her run when Dad and Mama T, terrible twins in tow, barged into her room. They didn't even have the decency to back out when they saw she was half-naked.

'*Ah-ah!* Still lazing about at this hour? *Abeg*, get up,' said her dad. 'The children are hungry.'

Simi backed into the en suite. 'What are *they* doing here?'

'Olu had chores. When it's your turn, you will understand. And you should stop wasting time, *sha*: you are no longer a spring chicken – approaching forty.'

'Where did you get this effigy, *ehn*?' Mama T picked up the Ife head. 'It fine pass, *o*! Where is my own?'

Simi shut the bathroom door and screamed silently.

After a quick shower, Simi took the brats to McDonald's. She let them order whatever they wanted, which turned out to be nuggets drowned in gunky sauce, McFlurry ice creams *and* full-fat Cokes. If Olu was bothered about what they ate, he should have fed them.

Simi checked her watch. Two. Ronke was due at six with the dresses from Patience; they were getting ready for the party here. She picked up her phone.

Ronks I need you. I'm babysitting the twins. You need to rescue me. It's for their own safety. Please come soon. Like RIGHT NOW. Sx

When they got back in, Dad was snoring on her sofa and

Mama T was in the kitchen chopping onions – smashing Martin's Japanese Global cleaver on to the white Carrara marble worktop. Simi managed to swallow back a yell. She grabbed the green Joseph Joseph chopping board out of its nest and slammed it down. 'Please use this. I don't want scratches on my marble.' Chopping boards existed in Nigeria, but sometimes Mama T acted like she'd never left the bush.

Mama T ignored the board. 'You are back at long last. Where are the tin tomatoes?'

'Did you buy any?'

'All normal people keep tin tomatoes.'

'I don't. I don't cook.'

'A woman must be able to cook or she won't keep her husband. *Ehn,* you must go to the shop. Let me write a list. And take the children; I don't have time for them now.'

'But I've just got back,' said Simi.

'Daddy is hungry,' said Mama T. 'Do you want him to starve?'

When Simi returned for the second time, the flat smelled acrid (Mama T believed in burning food to get rid of the germs) and Dad was awake. But there were sunlit uplands – Ronke had texted, saying she was on her way.

Simi dumped the kids in front of the TV and collapsed into the armchair opposite her dad. 'Did you have fun at Olu's? Were the kids good?'

'They are wild. No discipline. They need to come to Nigeria and learn manners.' He picked up his notebook and put on his official face. 'Simisola, I need to talk to you. Olu is planning to do an MBA to bolster his career prospects. He's an academic so he won't have any problems. And we will all rejoice when he can put MBA after his name, in addition to LLB Hons.'

'First I've heard of it,' Simi said cautiously. She would rejoice if Olu held down a job and stopped sponging off her.

'He wanted to discuss it with me first. Of course I am delighted – he has my full blessing.'

'Good for him.' Simi stood. 'I'm going to make a coffee. Do you want one?'

'I don't drink coffee at this time. But wait now, I am talking to you.' He waved her back to her seat. 'Olu needs our support. He doesn't want to take advantage so he will do it part-time. That way he can continue to work.'

'Big of him.' Simi knew where this was going.

'The exchange rate is so bad. Nearly three hundred naira to the pound. Can you imagine? I remember in 1986 it was twenty naira for one pound. You don't know how we are struggling.'

'Yeah, it's tough for everyone.' Maybe he wouldn't ask, Simi thought. Maybe just this one time he wouldn't ask.

'Families must support each other. And Martin is doing well so you have no worries. It is an investment. Once Olu lands on his feet, he will pay you back. With interest.'

'I already pay the twins' nursery fees, Dad. £800 a month,' said Simi. 'I can't afford any more.'

'The MBA is £12,000. I will sell some shares and find £2,000. I want you and Martin to add £10,000. God will return it in triplicate.' He pulled out his notebook, picked up one of the pens with chewed lids and flipped through the pages till he found the right one.

Simi felt her insides shrivel. She'd grown up watching him tick things off his mundane to-do list. 'Dad, I can't. We don't have that kind of money sitting around.'

'Talk to Martin. He's a man. He will understand better. Tell him to contact me.' He waved her off dismissively.

'I need a coffee,' Simi said, stomping away.

'It is not good to be drinking coffee after midday,' he called after her.

She FaceTimed Martin from the bathroom, tap on full to drown out her voice.

Martin just laughed. 'Shake the magic money tree.'

'It's not funny. All I am is a cash dispenser. I'd love to take a year out to do a creative writing course – I wonder if he'll stump up for that.'

'Creative writing? You never said.'

'Well, no. I'd chop off my right leg before I went back to school. But how can he ask for ten grand?'

'Don't stress. Olu will have some other hair-brained scheme by next week. We'll work something out.'

The doorbell rang. 'I've got to go. Ronke's here.'

'Cheer up. Go have some fun.'

Simi ran to answer it. 'Ronks! Save me, before I kill someone.'

'Hello, chicken,' said Ronke. 'I've brought *chin-chin*.'

Simi hugged her but Ronke was laden with bags and had no free hands to hug her back. 'Should a dentist be pushing rock-hard, deep-fried pastry?'

'It's good for business,' said Ronke. 'My mortgage relies on broken teeth.'

Simi marvelled as Ronke morphed into a Nigerian; she

sounded as if she had never left Lagos. Simi had worked hard to master her English accent and didn't drop it for anyone ever. She knew it pissed off her dad – he told her to stop *blowing grammar*, said she was trying to be highfalutin. Simi raised her eyebrows sky-high as Ronke dropped a curtsy to Dad.

'Hello, *uncoo*, you are welcome, *o. Bawo ni, anti?* I hope your journey wasn't too stressful. I made vegetable stew with goat meat. I know it's *uncoo*'s favourite.' Ronke dug into her massive bag, pulled out two tubs and handed them to Mama T. 'And my pepper sauce for you, *anti*. Welcome, *o*! It's so good to see you.'

'God bless you, sweetheart. We have been starving here,' said Mama T. 'Simi's kitchen is not designed for cooking. I'm used to gas, not this *yeye* induction rubbish. You are looking fine as always. Come and give me a hug.'

They discussed ailments, petrol shortages, traffic and armed robbers. The chat was sprinkled with Yoruba and pidgin.

Ronke magicked lollipops out of nowhere and cuddled the feral twins as if they were precious. They seemed to become less annoying. How did she do it?

Dad asked about Ronke's work. He called her 'my dear'. He even smiled (for the first time since he'd arrived). He wanted to know all about her practice and the courses she'd been on. He listened attentively, told her how well she was doing, how clever she was, how proud he was. Well, of course he did – Ronke was a dentist, not a dropout. Dad had always liked Ronke. He took no notice of any of Simi's other friends but had welcomed Ronke like a long-lost daughter from day one.

Olu arrived at six to pick up the kids. It took half an hour to get rid of them – jackets, scarves, hats, gloves on, then off so they could go to the loo, then on again.

Simi snuck a bottle of wine and two glasses into her bedroom (Dad disapproved of alcohol except when he was drinking it) and sprawled on her bed. 'Ronks, it's been hell. They haven't stopped nagging since they got here. They'd swap me for you in a heartbeat.'

'Don't be daft,' Ronke said softly. 'They're not that bad.'

Simi sat up and opened the wine. 'Did I tell you I caught Mama T snooping around my bathroom? She said she was looking for lipstick, but I know she was lying. She was looking to see if I'm still on the pill. I'm not stupid; I hide all my stuff before they get here. Laptop in the cleaning drawer – no chance of her looking there – contraceptives in my Louboutin shoebox – she has clodhopper size eights, so she leaves my shoes well alone.'

'Clever,' said Ronke. 'I can't imagine Martin trying on your shoes either.'

'Don't start. I'm going to tell him in Vermont,' said Simi, refilling her glass. 'Now, where are these outfits?'

Simi had shown Patience photos of Lupita Nyong'o at the Golden Globes in her red Ralph Lauren cape dress and Patience had made her a floor-length off-the-shoulder cape. The *ankara* was perfect – rigid enough to give form and structure. Underneath, Simi wore a sleeveless, thigh-skimming, black body-con dress. She felt like a superhero – the cape had achieved what meditating and running hadn't.

'You look incredible,' said Ronke.

'So do you.' It was true. Ronke had a good figure; it went

in and out in all the right places. The peplum emphasized her curves, turned her into Jessica Rabbit. 'Kayode won't be able to keep his hands off you.'

'He's not coming. Rafa's my plus one,' said Ronke, after a pause.

'Why not?' Simi wasn't surprised but she wondered what excuse he'd come up with.

'It's not really his thing. He doesn't like big parties,' said Ronke.

Simi decided to let it go. If Isobel was right about Kayode flirting with her at Sofia's party, it was just as well he wasn't coming. 'Right, let's go. First challenge is to get out of here without Mama T telling me I look like a slut.'

As expected, Mama T loved Ronke's outfit. 'Elegant, traditional and fashionable – the perfect combo.' And as expected, she hated Simi's. '*Ah-ah!* It's indecent. It's as if you are going out in your undergarments.'

'Don't worry, I'm wearing boy pants,' said Simi. 'No chance of flashing.'

Mama T reached for Ronke's peplum and rubbed the cloth between her fingers, valuing it, estimating its worth in naira. Her brow wrinkled. Simi knew she was converting it into pounds.

'This is not *small-small ankara*, this is the real stuff,' said Mama T. 'Who is throwing this party, *ehn*? They have *plenty-plenty* money.'

'My friend Isobel. Dad knows her.' Simi raised her voice. 'Dad, you remember Isobel, from Ikoyi?'

'Isobel who?' said Dad.

'Isobel Babangari. You know – Mr Babangari's daughter.'

Dad lurched to his feet. 'Simisola! You want to finish me, *abi*? I told you not to be associating with her.' His voice was louder than his usual loud level. '*See me see trouble*. You *dis* girl, you want to kill me, *ehn*? Why are you going there? They are dangerous. Too much *wahala*. Simisola, you need to be more circumspect. Ronke – talk to your friend, she doesn't hear me.'

'It's just a party, *uncoo*.' Ronke patted his arm. 'Don't worry. We're big girls now.'

'We're women. More than old enough to look after ourselves.' Simi was shocked at her dad's reaction. She touched her cheek; it was hot. How could he still be holding a grudge? What was wrong with him? 'Come on, Ronke, let's go.'

'Wait!' He was practically yelling now. 'Simisola, I'm not joking. You are vexing me too much. Ronke, tell your friend!'

'It's OK, *uncoo*,' Ronke said sweetly. 'Don't stress yourself.'

'You need to be careful. Ronke, you especially. Never cross a Babangari – the whole family is rotten.' Dad shook his head and sat back down. He looked old and beaten. 'They can finish you. That's one thing I learned the hard way. Mind yourself, *abeg*.'

Simi's shock hardened into anger. He was treating her like a five-year-old. And Ronke behaving like one wasn't helping. 'We're off,' she said, pulling Ronke out with her.

She was ranting before they got to the lift. 'I'm thirty-five. I haven't had a penny off him for fifteen years and now he wants to dictate who I'm friends with? And you didn't help, going all girly on me.'

'Sorry, I wanted to calm him down. He's got a real bee in

his bonnet about Isobel,' said Ronke. 'Kayode's the same. He can't stand her.'

Simi was tempted to put Ronke straight. She stopped herself but couldn't resist a little dig. 'He liked her enough to go out with her.' She glared at Ronke, but Ronke stayed silent. 'Dad's just bitter,' Simi continued. 'When Isobel's father sacked him, Dad's business went downhill. He needs someone to blame, because it couldn't possibly be his fault. It's bad enough blaming Mr Babangari, but what's it got to do with Isobel? She was eleven! How can it have anything to do with her?'

'I don't know,' said Ronke. 'But your dad obviously thinks she's bad news.'

Simi rolled her eyes. She didn't care if Ronke saw her or not.

22

RONKE

RONKE HAD BEEN TO lots of Nigerian parties, in Lagos and in London, but she could tell this was on another level by the queue of cars on Fenchurch Street – stretch limos, Hummers and blinged-up four-by-fours with blacked-out windows. Their taxi was next in line, behind a pink-chrome-wrapped Bentley with bulging wheel arches; it looked like a gargantuan vibrator.

They'd spent the entire journey in an uncomfortable silence. Simi sat as far away from Ronke as she could and stared out of her window the whole journey, her head at an obviously uncomfortable angle. Ronke had been too scared to speak, worried she'd make Simi even more angry. If that was possible.

'I'm glad we didn't take the Tube,' Ronke said finally.

Simi didn't reply but at least she straightened her head. They both watched as two giggling teenagers clambered out of the pink monstrosity, twinkling as if they'd been dipped in a bath of sequins.

They found Rafa in the foyer. Skinny black jeans (they might be jeggings), slim-fit *ankara* jacket, black silk shirt, *ankara* tie, shiny black loafers, no socks. Rafa never wore socks. 'Why didn't you wear the trousers?' asked Ronke.

'They were too tight. I couldn't breathe.'

'Tighter than those?' Simi pointed at Rafa's crotch.

'Much tighter, darling,' said Rafa. 'Borderline indecent.'

One lift was reserved for *aso ebi* wearers. Ronke gave the long queue of 'not so important' guests a sheepish smile. They glared back.

The roof garden was breathtaking – three steel-framed terraces under a huge glass-domed roof, with acres of lush vegetation. Somehow the cavernous space managed to feel intimate. Floor-to-ceiling windows displayed a lit-up London but there was so much going on inside that the incredible view paled into insignificance. A forest of tropical plants – palm trees and crane flowers in a riot of greens, purples, reds and yellows – should have got all the attention, but the people were even more colourful. Women in gravity-defying *geles*, men with sweeping *agbadas*, teenagers in body glitter and not much else. Ronke stopped to stare at the six-tiered birthday cake, almost as big as herself. Each tier was different – one swirled with fondant roses, one studded with crystals, another gilded in gold leaf. She had to crane her head to see the bejewelled *Sweet Sixteen* cake topper.

'Come on.' Simi nudged her and pointed to a mezzanine where a few people were wearing the same fabric as them. 'That's where we belong.'

Ronke was happy to comply, pleased that Simi had stopped sulking.

The entrance was blocked by a large woman swathed in gold lace and weighed down with jewellery, teetering on skyscraper heels at least two sizes too small. The bouncer looked tiny next to her. 'Family VIPs only,' he said, unbothered by the size difference. 'I'm afraid you can't come in. Please step aside.'

'Do you *even* know who I am?' Her voice was loud, her accent strong. 'Even' came out as *heeven*. 'Am' was *ham*.

Simi smiled for the first time since they'd left her bedroom. 'Come on. This is much better than checking a list of names.'

Ronke mouthed a 'sorry' at the poor woman as they were ushered past. She felt bad but couldn't help being amused. It wasn't a proper Nigerian party if someone didn't play the *Do you know who I am?* card.

There were only a dozen or so people in the cordoned-off area and Boo was easy to spot. She looked like a waitress in her black jumpsuit.

Ronke pecked her on the cheek. 'How come they let you in?'

'Patience made me this.' Boo held up a baguette-style clutch bag made of the *ankara*.

'It's gorgeous.' Ronke wished she'd asked for a bag.

'At least I'm not decked out like a tribeswoman,' said Boo. 'Have you seen Didier? He looks ridiculous. But I must admit, Sofia's dress is pretty.'

'Where are they?'

'Downstairs. Exploring.'

'Have you seen Isobel?' asked Simi.

'She's around somewhere.' Boo turned her head.

'Is her father here?' asked Simi.

'I don't know.' Boo shrugged.

Simi reached for a glass of champagne, downed it in one and picked up another. 'Cristal,' she announced. 'Downstairs it was prosecco. Equality is a foreign concept in Nigeria.'

Ronke couldn't wait to join the action – it was too refined for her up here. 'Let's go find Sofia,' she suggested.

'You go,' said Simi. 'Boo and I are quite happy being segregated.'

Ronke looked at Rafa and gestured at the crowd below. 'You'll come with me?'

'Try and stop me.' Rafa held out his arm.

Ronke took it. 'Food first, then dancing.'

'You're the boss. Do you think I can take pictures? Luca won't believe me otherwise.'

They stopped to stare at a raised white cube on which three men dressed in white *agbadas* were drumming on *batás*, Nigeria's famous talking drums. The sound was haunting, like a group of people humming a secret coded message in perfect harmony. The men swayed as they squeezed the drums under their arms, their hands moving crazy fast. Eyes closed, heads tilted in some sort of rapture.

'It sounds Cuban,' said Rafa.

'Nigerian slaves took the sound to Cuba,' said Ronke. 'It was ours first.'

They watched for a while, until Ronke's stomach reminded her she was hungry. There was a group of food stalls at one end of the garden and she was determined to try them all. 'Let's do a quick recce, then we'll know what to pig out on.'

They started with the quietest: three trestle tables covered with green-white-green tablecloths. Ronke opened the stainless-steel chafer dishes one by one – jollof rice, fried chicken, *dodo*, cling-wrapped balls of pounded yam, *egusi* stew, seafood okra and peppered snails. She couldn't understand why it was deserted. The next stall – a Nando's pop-up – was mobbed. 'Heathens,' said Ronke.

'Teenagers,' replied Rafa.

There was a Japanese stand lined with tatami mats, where geisha waitresses presented trays of raw fish and a teppan-yaki chef flipped shrimps and tossed rice bowls. 'Simi loves sushi,' Ronke said. 'I'll take her a plate.'

But Rafa pulled her along. 'Simi's got legs. She can get her own.'

'There's no way she's leaving the VIP zone,' said Ronke. 'She's in her element. It's not that she's a snob . . .'

'Just superficial.' Rafa winked.

'Stop it,' said Ronke. 'She likes luxury. It's not a crime.'

They found Didier and Sofia at the burger truck.

'I'm like mini-you.' Sofia did a twirl. 'Have you seen the candy cart? Papa says I have to eat real food first.'

'Rafa, take a selfie of us.' Ronke passed him her phone.

'It's not a selfie if he takes it,' said Sofia.

'Don't be rude, clever clogs,' said Didier. 'Have you tried the mushroom *suya*? It's delicious.'

They roamed from stall to stall. Ronke sampled most things but kept returning to the empty Naija one. 'This is so good – the snails are fantastic. Crunchy, not chewy. Why won't any of you try one?' She skewered another peppered snail. Rafa looked squeamish.

Didier tried but failed to keep Sofia away from the candy cart. The pink and white awning, pick 'n' mix display and floss machine were too big a draw.

'Aunty Ronke, are you sure it's all free?'

'Yes, poppet,' said Ronke. 'But you don't have to eat it all.'

'You've had three bowls of jollof and four bits of chicken and a gazillion snails.'

'Nothing gets past you.' Didier scooped Sofia into the air.

Rafa had abandoned them for the dance floor and a bunch of new teenage friends.

'He's popular,' said Didier.

'They think he's loaded,' said Ronke. 'It's the *aso ebi* – anyone wearing it must be close to the family. And anyone close to this family must be filthy rich.' They left him with his new entourage and went back to Simi and Boo.

'Are all Nigerians millionaires?' asked Didier. 'Maybe we should hire a private detective to find your father. With any luck, you're related to one of this lot.'

'I doubt it.' Boo sipped her champagne. 'He was a con man.'

'You never know,' said Didier.

'Drop it,' snapped Boo.

Ronke changed the subject. 'I used to believe London was a leveller. Now I'm not so sure.'

'What do you mean?' asked Didier.

'In Lagos, the rich are isolated. They live in enclaves; the only normal people they see are staff. But here, we rub together – we all take the Tube, work in the same buildings, pay the same taxes. It's one of the things I love about London – we're all equal; it doesn't matter who you are. But this party is like being back in Nigeria. Haves up here, have nots – well, have a bit less – down there. The have nots are outside. That's why Kayode wouldn't come. He has a point – look around you: way too much *shakara*.'

'Oh, is that the reason he gave?' said Simi. 'Well, I like it up here with the haves.'

'I guess I'm not used to it,' Ronke said. 'I live on a different planet.'

'Me too,' said Didier.

Ronke smiled at him, then swallowed as a familiar cloying scent hit the back of her throat.

'Who's on a different planet?' Isobel whispered into Ronke's ear. 'And where's the lovely Kayode?'

Even in this riot of excess, Isobel was otherworldly. She was wearing *ankara* hot pants and a bandeau top. Her skin was covered in tiny gold flecks and she shone. Ronke exposed less flesh when she was sunbathing.

'Missing in action,' Simi answered for Ronke.

The bartender snapped to attention and opened a fresh bottle of Cristal. The one he'd opened five minutes earlier obviously wasn't good enough for Isobel.

Simi drained her glass and held it out for a refill. 'Is your dad here?' she asked Isobel.

'No. Still in Abuja – couldn't get away. Cheers!' Isobel took a delicate sip, then pointed at a frumpy pouting teenager. 'Face like a smacked arse.'

Ronke felt sorry for her, alone at her own birthday party. 'What's upset her?'

'Don't tell me – the cake's not big enough?' Simi's filthy laugh rang out.

'Worse,' said Isobel. 'She wanted a spraying gun and I said no.'

'What's a spraying gun?' asked Boo.

'It looks like a gun but it's not. You stuff it with banknotes, press a button and, *voila!* – money shoots into the air,' said Ronke. 'Landing like confetti over your awestruck guests who scrabble around, pocketing the loot. I've never seen one. Aunty K told me about it.'

'Why did you say no, Iso?' Simi splashed champagne on her cape. 'Spoilsport.'

'She wanted sterling. Can you believe it! Five-pound notes. My offer of fifty-naira bills wasn't good enough.'

Ronke looked at the dance floor. Sofia was teaching Rafa and Didier the *skelewu*, one hand akimbo, the other held up, swivelling her torso.

'Now, Ronks, come with me.' Isobel took her arm. 'I'm glad Kayode isn't here. There's someone who's dying to meet you. He's good-looking, single and loaded. Best of all, he's reliable.'

Ronke looked to Simi and Boo for support. Nothing. She shook herself free from Isobel. 'No, thanks. I have a boyfriend.'

'He's not here though. No harm in keeping your options open.' Simi's speech was slurred.

'I'm going to join Rafa.' Ronke stomped down to the dance floor. She loved dancing but now her heart wasn't in it.

'What's wrong?' asked Rafa, reading her face.

'Nothing. I'm being silly.'

'You sure?' asked Didier.

'I'm fine. Just tired. I might call it a night.'

'We should be going too,' said Didier. 'Sofia's had too much sugar and it's way past her bedtime.'

Sofia yawned. 'I need the toilet.'

'I'll take her,' said Ronke, holding out a hand. 'You go on up. I'll meet you there.'

As Ronke trudged slowly up the thick carpeted staircase, Sofia bouncing beside her, she heard Simi's drunken cackle. She stopped abruptly as the words registered in her brain.

'It's typical Ronke – she's wasting her life. He'll never settle down.'

'He was a dog when we were together and he's still a dog now,' Isobel chipped in.

'She always picks dickheads,' said Boo. 'By the time she figures it out, she'll be forty. And we know she wants kids.'

'Come on!' Sofia yanked at Ronke's arm. 'Why have you stopped?'

Ronke let go of Sofia and grabbed the velvet rope for support.

Didier saw Ronke and his face fell. 'Boo,' he said, 'enough.'

'It's true though.' Boo didn't bother to look at him. 'It's almost as if she likes being treated like shit.'

Ronke's heart tanked. She took a step back and stumbled into Rafa, who had just come up the stairs.

'*Qué pasa?*' he said.

'Boo, stop!' shouted Didier.

They all looked up and stared at her. Ronke blinked back tears. Her best friends were three feet away, but it felt like three miles. 'Can we go, Rafa?'

'Ronks, I'm sorry.' Simi lurched and grabbed her wrist.

'This is all my fault.' Isobel stepped forward and rested her palm on Ronke's other hand. 'I was telling them about the guy who wants to meet you – he has a thing for curvy girls . . .'

Ronke shook them both off with a powerful jerk. 'Leave me alone.'

Rafa grabbed her bag. 'Come on. We're out of here.'

Ronke still didn't trust herself to speak. She clattered down the steps and hurried to the lift, eyes down, trying to conceal the copious tears now sliding down her cheeks. Rafa followed close behind, talking into his phone.

'Won't be long. He's on his way,' said Rafa, patting her back as they stood shivering on the street.

Ronke was sobbing uncontrollably into Rafa's jacket when a car horn tooted. She'd expected a cab, had worried she might not have enough cash, but it was Kayode's battered Golf.

'I called him.' Rafa opened the door and pushed her in. 'Look after her, Kayode. Her friends are bitches.'

Kayode leaned over to kiss her wet face. Then he switched from Talk Sport to Heart FM and they drove home in silence, his hand on her knee between gear changes.

When they got to his, he gave her one of his T-shirts and made her a mug of green tea. 'You OK?'

Ronke nodded. 'Simi and Boo kept asking why you weren't there.' Ronke didn't want to tell him what they'd actually said. She didn't want him to hate her best friends.

'Is that all? Did you tell them I hate all that tacky fake shit? Women with creepy yak hair extensions, men carrying man-bags, stuck-up kids acting like entitled snobs, the do-you-know-who-I-am crap.'

Ronke remembered the *do-you*-even-*know-who-I-am* lady and almost smiled. She folded herself into Kayode's arms. 'I shouldn't have got so upset. It was something Isobel said. She wanted to introduce me to some bloke. She made it sound like we weren't serious.'

'I told you, she's trouble.' Kayode released her from his arms. 'You wouldn't listen.' His voice louder.

'I know.' Ronke took his hands in hers. 'I wish I hadn't gone.'

'Did Simi and Boo tell her where to get off? Did they have my back?'

'Please don't get mad.' Ronke's shoulders slumped; her tears were back.

Kayode kissed her gently. 'I guess that's a no. They don't trust me because I'm black. They've both got white husbands and I'm not good enough because I'm Nigerian. They're bigots, the pair of them. And as for Isobel, you know how I feel. She's trouble. I don't want you to have anything to do with her.' He wrapped his arms around her. 'Me and you. We're what matters.'

'You sound like Simi's dad,' said Ronke. 'He told me to stay away from her as well.'

'You should listen to him. He's right. Now, come on.' He pulled her up. 'Let's go to bed. I love you,' he whispered. They made love and when she woke up, they were spooning.

∽

THE NEXT MORNING, RONKE GOT Kayode to take her to the supermarket for essential supplies. Calling his kitchen spartan would be overstating just how ill-equipped it was. Ronke's was crammed with (essential and well-used) stuff. And not just food. She had a dozen wooden spoons – big ones, little ones, flat ones, slotted ones – each vital for a specific role: scraping, stirring or tasting. Kayode had two, and one of those still wore a price sticker.

His fridge had contained a pack of spreadable not-butter (eugh), a bottle of white wine (for her), a six-pack of Tiger

Beer (for him) and a carton of past-its-sell-by milk. That was it. Now it was properly stocked.

While he was at rugby practice, she listened to *The Archers* and cooked, enjoying being alone in his flat. She added a dash of Maggi sauce to the ready-made chicken gravy to zhuzh it up. He only had three saucepans, so she kept lunch simple: two roast chickens – it was as easy as doing one and he could have the other one in the week. She lifted the chickens out of the oven and rested the tray on a thick wedge of newspapers – Kayode didn't own a trivet.

She was admiring their beautiful, swollen, burnished breasts when he came in and hugged her. He smelled of sweat and grass. Almost as good as the chicken.

'Wow! I think I'm going to have to marry you.'

Ronke's heart thumped.

He reached out to snaffle a piece of chicken skin but pulled his fingers back and licked them. 'Hot!'

Ronke grinned and tented the chickens in foil. 'Go take a shower, you filthy pig.'

Her phone pinged. Another grovelling message from Simi. She ignored it and turned her attention to the potatoes – crunchy and golden. The veg was prepped; she'd warm it through with a knob (slab) of butter. Real butter, not weird spreadable crap. She opened the wine and enjoyed the moment. Ronke King. Wife. Mother. Amazing cook. Handsome, rugby-playing, sexy husband. Two perfect children (one boy, one girl); twins would be ideal.

Kayode came back in, damp from the shower. He pulled her into his arms and kissed her ear. 'Come to Lagos with me for Christmas,' he said. 'I want you to meet my mum.'

Ronke had imagined their first proper Christmas together. Scrambled eggs and smoked salmon in bed as they opened presents. They'd go to Mum's for lunch, come back and cuddle on the sofa to an Xmas special, eat catfish *banga* soup (an Aunty K tradition – turkey for lunch, *banga* for supper). She'd dreamed of a white Christmas – walking hand in hand with her fiancé, roasting chestnuts on an open fire (well, not that bit – she didn't have a fire and she hated chestnuts). But this was so much better. Christmas in Lagos. Meeting his mum. 'Yes.' Ronke felt weepy. Happy weepy. 'Yes!'

23

BOO

Bumps & Babies. Such a stupid, undignified name for an NCT group. Boo had hated the name when she had a bump. She despised it now she was bump-free.

Five years later the meetings were annual (not weekly) and children were banned. There were four BBs left. Cassie had dropped out when they ganged up on her for being an anti-vaxxer. Lynne had moved to Singapore. Alas, she kept in touch, sending pictures of Tulip and Tree living the expat dream, supervised by their uniformed nanny.

The first few minutes were stilted but soon the battle was in full swing: Whose husband was more useless? Child most annoying? Mother-in-law most horrific?

Jenny, who used to be the wild one, was pregnant again. With twins. She sat stroking her bump, swathed in a black jersey dress, blathering on about how hard it was to find a people carrier big enough and how Peanut and Piglet would complete their family (all with a straight face).

Boo couldn't have another child. There'd been complications after Sofia's birth which had led to secondary infertility.

She'd got over it. But she didn't need a 'friend' banging on about how fucking fertile she was.

Mel, who ran her own advertising agency, was pregnant again too. But sullen. She'd discovered her husband was having another affair. He'd had one the first time she was pregnant. The silly cow had forgiven him because it wasn't his fault. Women (sluts) kept throwing themselves at him. He had needs. And she was so tired all the time. Boo tried to remember if Mel had always been this stupid.

Gracie was fretting. She kept checking her phone. Her mum was on holiday, so her husband was babysitting (looking after his own child). It was the first time he'd been home alone with his five-year-old son.

Boo felt disconnected. None of them were happy (apart from Jenny – and happiness was easy if you'd had a lobotomy), but they were all happier than her. Even Mel – married to a cheating bastard – seemed more content.

She'd hoped that seeing the BBs would steady her, make her feel normal – wife, mother, part-time exec – but it had done the opposite. She wanted to scream, shock them with her secret: *You think you've got problems, well, check me out! I was bored, so I let my boss fuck me. He sends me dirty messages; I keep re-reading them. On Monday I was going to tell him it was over. But he said I looked nice and I was flattered so I flirted back. Maybe it's because my husband cares about my best friend's feelings more than mine.*

Boo grabbed her phone, stared at the blank screen and leapt to her feet. 'I'm sorry. Sofia's throwing up and she's got a temperature. Didier's worried it might be chicken pox. I'd better go. I'll message you tomorrow.' She had to stop making Sofia sick. And why did she always default to chicken pox?

Out on the street, Boo gulped in cold, fresh air. She didn't want to go home. Guilt was eating her up. It was unbearable. After date night, she thought she had a handle on it. A plan. She would put it in a box and go back to her old life.

On Monday, she'd gone to work with a mission. Rehearsed her speech on the Tube: *Look, Neil, I made a mistake, an error in judgement, and I regret it. It needs to stop. I can't do overnight trips, so you'll have to find someone else to front the podcast idea. I'm sorry if I gave you mixed signals.*

She didn't get to use it. Neil was out. When he slid into her cubicle at twelve, brushed his knee against hers and told her she looked beautiful, she smiled.

Boo had never had casual – meaningless – sex before. She'd been proud of being a prude, felt superior to Ronke with her string of useless boyfriends and Simi who dressed like a porn star. She'd had her first kiss at eighteen, a fumble with a fellow fresher from Yorkshire at the students' union bar, no tongues. She dated the next guy she kissed for two years. There were two more snogs before her second proper boyfriend, and they were together for nine months. Didier was the third man she'd slept with. Simi had set them up on a blind date and they were engaged nine months later.

She despised herself for having sex with Neil. Hated herself for not having the backbone to tell him to fuck off. She was turning into a monster. She could see it but seemed incapable of stopping it. Being nasty to Didier made her feel better – she couldn't help it, the desire to wipe the calm, contented look off his face was too strong. She was even snapping at Sofia. It was narcissistic (*if I'm not happy, no one else should be*) and it was ineffective – it didn't make the guilt smaller, it made it overwhelming.

It was too cold to wander around Clapham in the dark. Boo gritted her teeth and headed home. She hoped Didier would be asleep.

∾

THE NEXT MORNING, THERE WERE three WhatsApps from the BBs.

Is Sofia OK?

Can I do anything to help?

Pip's had the pox, so if Sofia wants a playdate call me!

The messages made Boo feel worse. These were nice people who cared about her. They had their own crap to deal with. Why had she needed to escape them? And what kind of mother invented a disease for her child (so many times)? She tapped a group reply.

Didier panicked. She's fine this morning. Typical man! Take care. Boo x

The door slammed and Sofia rushed into the kitchen with a bag of pastries. 'I'm having *pain au chocolat* for breakfast. Papa said I can because I'm French.' She opened the bag. Boo reached for a plain croissant and Sofia swatted her hand away. 'You're not French so you shouldn't have any.' Then she relented and held the bag out. 'But we'll let you, 'cos we're nice.'

'Thanks,' Boo said, taking the croissant.

'I'm extra special because I have three cultures. Aunty

Ronke said so. You have two, which isn't as good. Poor Papa – he's only French. It's sad.'

'He'll survive,' said Boo.

'It's a day-to-day struggle,' Didier said. He bit into pastry, showering crumbs all over his top. 'Boo, are you coming to swim school?'

Boo couldn't face happy families this morning. 'Does it need both of us . . .?'

Didier shrugged. 'Family time?'

'I was going to call Ronke, meet her for lunch . . .' She knew the Ronke card would let her off.

'Good idea,' said Didier. 'You need to apologize.'

'And me! I want to see Aunty Ronke,' said Sofia.

'*Non*,' said Didier. 'We'll go to soft play.'

Perfect Didier. Sofia loved soft play. Boo couldn't stomach it – the smell (a combo of urine and vomit); the kids (pierced ears and Hello Kitty leggings); and worst of all, the adults (shouty and tattooed). Boo wasn't a snob like Simi but she did have standards.

Boo arranged to meet Ronke at Happy Joseph, an Aussie-themed café on the Common. She knew Ronke would be fine; she wasn't the type to hold a grudge. Ronke had over-reacted, but then Ronke cried at the drop of a hat. Boo hadn't said anything that terrible. She'd called Kayode a dick – and he was. Isobel agreed and she had insider knowledge. The fact was, Boo was being a good friend, trying to stop Ronke wasting yet another year of her life. And anyway, it was unimportant compared to what Boo was going through. Ronke was kind, practical and positive – she'd help Boo work this out.

'I've done something stupid,' Boo started, before Ronke had taken her coat off. She felt like she was outside her body looking in – her story a mix of fact and fiction. Boo a victim, Neil a monster, Didier a catalyst, Sofia a burden.

'It was just the once,' she finished up a few minutes later. She decided to gloss over the second time – one night counted as once. 'I'm not sure why I did it. It's like I was drugged or something. It just happened. It was a huge mistake. But it wasn't my fault. Didier has made me feel like a passenger in my own life. I know he loves me, but he makes me feel invisible.'

'Hang on, slow down,' said Ronke. 'You slept with your boss? You cheated on Didier? Seriously? How could you?'

'I don't know. He made me feel important. Look, Ronke, I didn't ask for any of this. All I've done wrong is say yes to people. I've done it all my life, I'm a people-pleaser. And somehow, I've got lost along the way.'

'You need to own this,' said Ronke. 'You can't make it someone else's fault. And you're not a people-pleaser – you've never cared what anyone thinks. What's happened to you, Boo? It's as if you don't care about anyone else. Not me. Not Didier. Not even Sofia. Remember when Akin cheated on me – you saw how much it hurt. You were there.'

Boo had expected sympathy, kindness, reassurance. She couldn't believe Ronke was being so self-obsessed. 'This isn't about you. Are you still cross about the party? I've said I'm sorry. Surely you can see this is more important?'

'But you haven't said sorry, Boo.' Ronke's voice was sharp. 'I stupidly imagined that's why you wanted to meet up.'

Ronke's superior tone grated on Boo's nerves. She was almost tempted to tell her that Kayode was still flirting with Isobel. 'You weren't meant to hear.'

'That just makes it worse. But you're right – this is more important. You have everything, Boo: a wonderful husband, a beautiful daughter. Don't throw it away.'

Boo's tea had gone cold. She drank it anyway. She tried again – she had to make Ronke see things from her side. 'I won't. I love Didier – you know that. But I need him to put me first sometimes, not side with Sofia all the time.'

'I wish you hadn't told me,' said Ronke. 'You've made me complicit.'

Boo tugged at her ponytail. 'I really thought you'd understand. You think my life is a fairy tale. Well, it's not. You had an idyllic childhood in Lagos. You've always fit in. I want to be noticed. Is that so wrong?' Boo studied her reflection in the window.

'Boo, I lost my dad when I was eleven. There was nothing idyllic about it.' There was a crack in Ronke's voice.

'At least you knew who he was,' Boo snapped.

'What's that got to do with anything? You're looking for excuses, trying to justify what you've done. You can't. Boo, I've known you for ever. I love you. I know you're a good person. But you're making bad choices.' Ronke stood and wound her scarf around her neck. 'You've got it all. What more do you want?'

'You don't get it,' said Boo. 'At least Isobel understands.'

'You told Isobel? Why am I not surprised?' Ronke grabbed her coat off the back of the chair. 'You know what I think? I think you should hand in your notice. Today. Stop working there and start working on your marriage. And stop listening to bloody Isobel.'

'You hate her because she's beautiful and she used to date Kayode.' Boo watched Ronke's chin tremble. 'Sorry, I shouldn't have said that.'

Ronke pulled on her coat. She didn't look at Boo.

'Ronke, wait!' shouted Boo. 'You won't tell anyone, will you? You can't tell Didier.'

'I won't tell anyone,' said Ronke.

Boo put her hand on Ronke's bag to keep her there. 'And you'll still take Sofia to *Frozen*?'

'Of course I will. She hasn't done anything wrong.'

Boo watched her leave. She knew she shouldn't have made that awful comment about Isobel and Kayode. She wouldn't have if Ronke hadn't been so judgemental. How dare she suggest that Boo was like Akin? This was completely different. Maybe Isobel was right. Maybe Ronke was jealous.

24

SIMI

THE PROBLEM WAS, SIMI couldn't remember what she'd said at Sky Garden. But she knew it must have been awful because Ronke was ignoring her calls. And Ronke never did that.

Didier had told Boo he was ashamed of her. And Didier never told Boo off. Boo didn't want to talk about Ronke, but then Boo didn't want to talk about anything. Isobel on the other hand wouldn't shut up. As far as she was concerned, Ronke was being neurotic.

So after a week of silence, Simi decided to go large. She turned up at Ronke's bearing gifts. A takeaway from Buka (pounded yam, *egusi* stew, croaker fish special), a fistful of Ronke-friendly DVDs (*Pitch Perfect, Coyote Ugly, Magic Mike*), a bottle of Mateus Rosé, a tin of Teapigs peach lemonade tea and a Hemsley and Hemsley spiralizer. Simi had Googled 'best gifts for foodies' for inspiration.

It wasn't about the gifts though. Simi said sorry and meant it – even if she wasn't quite sure what she was sorry for. For once, she stuck to the truth. 'I'm so sorry I upset you, Ronks. It's the last thing I'd ever want to do.'

'Do you really think I'm wasting my life?' asked Ronke.

'No!' exclaimed Simi. 'I was talking rubbish. It was Dad's fault, banging on about Mr Babangari. It stressed me out and I drank too much. But it's no excuse. I'm truly sorry. Please forgive me.'

The takeaway and the tea had gone down brilliantly. Ronke was less convinced by the spiralizer; she didn't get the courgetti over spaghetti thing. Simi ate the fish special and drank the wine. Ronke demolished the pounded yam with three mugs of disgusting fruit tea.

They chatted for hours, Channing Tatum and his posse gyrating silently in the background. They talked about Kayode (who, according to Ronke, had pretty much proposed and was taking her to Lagos for Christmas – which meant Isobel had been wrong); about Boo (who, they both agreed, was turning into Iso's poodle); about Simi's dad (who had kept ranting about the Babangaris but had, thank God, gone home). And, of course, about Martin. Ronke still thought Simi should tell Martin *everything*, but Simi knew better. He didn't need to know she'd got pregnant. In fact, he mustn't know. But she'd be honest about everything else. How she'd gone back on the pill (he needn't know she'd only been off it for four weeks) and wanted to wait until he was back home to try again. She'd admit to second thoughts – put them down to being home alone. She wouldn't tell him about the interview. What was the point?

Ronke was right about one thing though – Martin loved her and she loved him. Baby or no baby, they would be fine. She'd come clean with Martin in Vermont. Tell him the truth. Well, most of it.

SIMI HAD DREAMED ABOUT THEIR holiday in Vermont for weeks. Her and Martin, skiing in slow motion, a bit like a *Ski Sunday* replay. She heard the iconic clubby soundtrack in her head, fizzy and bright with its sweeping strings and bombastic percussion, as she flew down the slopes in her new Moncler ski jacket, white powder blowing in her wake. Simi didn't let the fact that she was crap at skiing get in the way of her fantasy.

After days of counting sleeps, it was time to see Martin. But the flight out was delayed and she missed her transfer. Finally, six hours late, tired and dehydrated, she arrived at the resort. It lived up to the hype – snow-capped roof, double-height glass window, wooden deck, hot tub. Inside, there were fluffy reindeer hides everywhere, the open fire was lit and a bottle of champagne sat chilling on ice.

The only thing missing was Martin. He'd left a cheery note.

You must be shattered. Chill out at the spa. No point in wasting snow. I'll be back by six. Love you xx

The spa felt too much like hard work, so Simi took a shower and crawled into bed naked. She was still asleep when he crept in beside her four hours later. It was the best way to wake up. Three hours later they resurfaced and crunched through the snow, hand in hand. The resort sparkled with fairy lights. *It's going to be fine*, Simi said to herself, squeezing his hand tightly.

The restaurant was fancy American – Martin's heaven, Simi's hell. Steak *or* lobster or steak *and* lobster. Huge portions with whipped white butter and mountains of French fries. Her chef's salad drowning in gluey, gloopy ranch dress-ing that tasted like sour mayonnaise.

She was all set to tell him. She would have told him. But he beat her to it.

'They want me to stay in Manhattan. Three years, maybe five. It's all we've ever wanted. We'll be set up. And you love New York. Think of all the shopping! The little one will have triple nationality – British, American and Nigerian – not bad, eh?'

He'd worked it all out. She could spend the first few months looking for an apartment – or house – he thought Brooklyn made sense. She could have hobbies – do a course or start a little business – although why bother, she'd be preg-nant in no time. He misread her look.

'Hey, it's only been six months. Like you said, it's not going to happen if we're not in the same country. Did I tell you we get full-spec private health insurance? I insisted on it. If we need IVF, we'll have IVF.'

Simi pushed her salad around her plate, emptied her glass and told Martin to order another bottle. She couldn't tell him. Not now.

'Take it easy, Simi.' Martin stabbed a piece of rare steak. 'We're skiing tomorrow – you want a clear head.'

Simi thought of her father, tutting every time she had a glass of wine. Her anger began to bubble. 'You sound like Dad,' she said, downing the glass.

'Oh, I emailed him,' said Martin. 'Told him we'd help with Olu's MBA but we couldn't stretch to the full ten grand. He has a real problem with your friend Isobel – he's more worried about her than the money. He wants me to warn you off her.'

The warning infuriated her and she clung to the anger like a life raft. 'Let me see if I've got this straight. You've accepted a position without talking to me. Assumed I'll jack in my job and morph into a twee homemaker. And you and Dad are working out how many kids I'm going to push out, how to spend our money and who I can be friends with?' Simi waved the waiter over. 'Same again,' she said, pointing at the wine cooler.

'Simi! Come on. It's not like that. What are you mad about? We both want a baby and you asked me to talk to your dad. I never tell you what to do. I wouldn't dare.'

He was right. The problem wasn't Martin telling her what to do. It was her not telling Martin what she wanted. How could she be mad about him helping her brother? But it was too late to back off, so she doubled down instead. 'I can't believe you're making decisions that affect me without talking to me. My job matters. My life in London matters. We're supposed to be a team. You're not supposed to accept a role in Manhattan without talking to me.'

'We are a team.' Martin waited while the waiter opened the bottle and filled their glasses. 'I haven't said yes and I'm talking to you now. If it doesn't work for both of us, I'll tell them no.'

Simi decided to try a smidgeon of honesty. 'I love London. It's home – all my friends are there. New York is great but I don't know if I want to live there. I don't want to be a stay-at-home mum.' *I'm not sure I want to be any kind of mum*, she left unsaid.

'Hey! I've never wanted you to be a housewife. You'd be crap at it anyway.' Martin held her hand across the table. 'You could work anywhere – you're brilliant. Look, I think it'll be great and the gang can come and stay any time. But if it's a no from you, then it's a no from me. Us against the world, remember?'

Simi sipped her wine in silence. She couldn't work out why she'd got so angry. She was sick of being semi-single, drinking too much, being anxious. She never panicked when Martin was with her. 'When do you need to decide?'

'Not me. Us. It's our decision. Your decision really. I'll tell them I need a couple of weeks.'

'Maybe it could work,' she said. This could be just what they needed. A fresh start. A reset. Loft apartment, shopping at Barneys, cupcakes (not that she'd eat them) from Magnolia Bakery, furniture from ABC Carpet & Home.

'No pressure.' Martin filled her glass. 'Do a pros and cons thing. I'll come home the weekend after next. We can talk it through then.'

For the rest of the trip they were inseparable. They breakfasted in bed, drank champagne in the hot tub and ate dinner in their lodge, in front of the fire. They only ventured out to ski, and even then Martin insisted on staying with Simi on the nursery slopes. She knew it was torture for him, tried to persuade him to go on the black runs where he belonged, but he wouldn't. So they hung around with the six-year-olds, all of whom were better at skiing than Simi.

Martin told her she looked amazing in her new jacket. She glowed, warm and snug under the hood. But the white powder wasn't flying in her wake, it was billowing around her as she hit the snow. And it wasn't in slow motion. It was fast. And furious. And painful. The soundtrack different too. No strings or percussion. Just Martin's laughter as he picked her up after she fell for the thousandth time. It was wonderful.

∽

SIMI MADE HER MIND UP on the flight back. New York would be perfect. She'd get a new job – that would put babies on the back burner for a year. Or two.

She rang Martin as soon as she landed, but he insisted she think it through. She didn't need to. She was sure. She was ready for this new life. She'd start now with a mini detox.

On her first night back in London, Isobel insisted on meeting. Simi acquiesced. It was easier than arguing. Iso tried to talk her into having a drink, called her a lightweight. Simi stuck to her guns and sparkling water.

She filled her in on Martin's job offer. Isobel did what she always did when Simi's plans didn't include her. She'd been the same when she was seven. She sulked (you're abandoning me, after all I've done for you). She stropped (you'll hate New York, it's crowded and dirty, too hot and too cold). And she got bitchy (Martin seems very controlling, you won't be able to work without a green card, you'll be stuck at home).

Isobel's hostility had the opposite effect to what she intended. Simi added getting away from Isobel to the list of New York pluses.

And, for the first time in her life, Simi felt *almost* positive about a child. Not right now. But in a couple of years. A baby in New York would be much better than a baby in London. Manhattan mums weren't expected to do it all. Having staff (a full-time, live-in nanny) was a sign of success, not of bad parenting. Martin was right – they could do it their way. Their kid would enjoy weekend breaks as much as they did. Go to boarding school, like Simi had wanted to. She decided her imaginary child would be a girl. She'd give her everything she herself had missed out on and protect her from the crap of warring parents that she'd been saddled with.

Simi wanted to share her excitement with friends who would be happy she was happy – even if it meant she was moving away. She realized how much she missed the old threesome – the way things used to be. They had celebrated all their milestones together – first jobs, promotions, break-ups, engagements, weddings – they should share this too. She tried to arrange lunch with Ronke and Boo but they both made silly excuses. So she visited them separately.

Ronke was thrilled – her face lit up. She twirled Simi round the living room, whooping.

Simi had to confess she hadn't talked to Martin and for once Ronke didn't scold. 'Hey, you know best. But you should tell him you're not sure about kids. You can work it out together.' Simi dismissed this; she was sure about kids. Sure now wasn't the right time. Sure one day would be.

Boo was grumpy and self-absorbed (it seemed to be her new norm). 'Lucky you,' she'd said. 'I wish I could change my life.'

But nothing could kill Simi's mood. Life was back on track; she was golden again. Martin and her, against the world. Winning.

And this weekend she wouldn't be sitting around at home, trying to fill the hours. It was annual competitive godmothering time. Ronke's Christmas gift was taking Sofia to some awful show. A thousand screaming children in a cinema. Simi couldn't imagine anything worse. Her gift was much more civilized – afternoon tea at The Julius. She invited Isobel as a sop for neglecting her. Iso could sit between Boo and Ronke – stop them behaving like children.

25

RONKE

I'M IN HELL, THOUGHT Ronke.

She was trapped. Squashed into an uncomfortable seat, hemmed in on all sides. There was a sharp pain in her side as Sofia prodded her with the snowflake wand. Again. Her head was throbbing, and the tight plastic tiara wasn't helping.

Ronke had never seen the attraction of the cinema. There was no pause button, no tea, the food was crap and you couldn't snuggle into a soft throw. But today was supposed to be different – a wonderful Disney-inspired extravaganza of joy, balloons, sweet harmonies and magic. Sofia would be a gorgeous little poppet, wide-eyed with wonder, enjoying one of the best days of her little life. All thanks to Aunty Ronke, who would be crowned godmother of the year. Five years running. Take that, Simi!

Ronke had spared no expense. VIP tickets to the *Frozen* sing-along at the Royal Albert Hall, upgraded to include The Fairy Brunch and Interactive Prop Bag. What a bloody con. Twenty pounds for a tacky plastic bag containing three foam snowballs, a light-up carrot nose and the lethal snowflake wand Sofia was putting to good use.

Ronke had shunned the cheap Princess Elsa outfits on Amazon (way too flammable for precious Sofia) and forked out for the eye-wateringly expensive Disney Store original. She'd tried to get one for herself. How sweet they'd look in matching outfits – brown royalty. Now she was grateful they didn't make them in size fourteen. Looking like a Michelin-sized princess in itchy acrylic would have been the icing on this frozen fiasco.

Sofia had been the opposite of a gorgeous little poppet. Godbrat from Hades would be more accurate. She hadn't stopped whining since Ronke picked her up three very long hours ago. She preferred *Beauty & the Beast* to *Frozen*, she wanted to be Olaf not Elsa, the Tube was too hot, the sandwiches too brown, the Elsa blue jelly too jelly-like, their seats too far back.

The lights went up and yanked Ronke back to reality. She looked around. A couple of hundred Princess Elsas, two dozen less glittery Princess Annas and a smattering of Olafs. All off their heads on the processed sugar-fest brunch. The annoying sing-along host demonstrated another daft dance move and the overexcited children mimicked her, demonstrating a total lack of coordination, caterwauling at the tops of their tuneless voices.

What was I thinking? Ronke tried to remember how this competitive godmothering malarkey started. And how come Simi's treats involved alcohol, swanky eateries and not much Sofia? *Not that I'm being judgy,* she told herself.

She snuck a look at her phone. *Shit, another hour to go. Breathe . . . This is supposed to be fun.*

A text from Simi:

Setting off now. See you at four. Sx

They were meeting at The Julius for The Mad Hatter's Tea Party – Simi's Christmas treat for Sofia. Surprise! Surprise! It involved cocktails. And Isobel and Boo.

For the first time in her life, Ronke wasn't looking forward to spending time with Boo. She'd been deliberately late in picking up Sofia to avoid any chance of a chat. She'd thought about inventing an excuse to get out of this pretentious tea, but she and Simi were good again and Ronke didn't want to piss her off. But why did Isobel have to be there? Ronke blamed her for everything – for dating Kayode, for Boo's sleeping with her boss, for Simi's lying to Martin. She knew she was being unfair. The Isobel–Kayode thing was an unfortunate coincidence and her friends were both grown-ups. But fact was, pre-Isobel, their friendships had been rock solid. Now there were cracks.

Sofia grabbed hold of her with warm sticky fingers. 'I love you, Aunty Ronke. This is the best!'

Tears welled in Ronke's eyes. She pulled Sofia close, kissed her head and laughed as the itchy blonde wig tickled her nose. 'And I love you right back.'

The auditorium exploded into 'Let It Go'. Ronke and Sofia sang along at the top of their lungs, waving their arms in unison – almost exactly as the host was demonstrating.

Ronke's mood lifted and her headache faded. This had been such a good idea. And she still had her favourite song, 'Fixer Upper', to look forward to. It reminded her of Kayode.

∽

SOFIA WAS STILL ON A *Frozen* cloud when they got to The Julius. It didn't matter how amazing this tea was, Sofia was going to talk about *Frozen* for weeks. Ronke had won. She hoped the portions weren't stingy; the Elsa blue jelly hadn't touched the sides.

She heard them before she saw them: Isobel's transatlantic twang and annoying laugh, Simi's trademark cackle.

Sofia skipped across the room. 'Mama! Mama! We danced and we sang, and I've got a wand!' She poked Boo in the chest.

'Ow! Where are your manners?' Boo scolded. 'Say hello to your aunties.'

'Hello, Aunty Simi. Hello, Aunty Isobel,' Sofia said dutifully. 'How does your hair go long and short, Aunty Isobel? My friend Gemma has a doll whose hair grows when you press her belly button.'

Simi beamed at Ronke and patted the chair next to her. 'Ronks! Come sit.'

'She's a bit overexcited.' Ronke sank into the chair, glad she wasn't next to Boo, sad she was next to Isobel.

'Look, Sofia, I bet you've never seen anything as good as this!' Simi pointed at the two waiters approaching, each carrying a massive cake-stand, tiers separated by giant tea-cups decorated with clubs, spades, hearts and diamonds.

For the first time since they'd walked in, Sofia was silent. She swayed on her feet, wonderstruck. Ronke was gob-smacked too. Meringues disguised as red and white mushrooms, test-tubes of frothy milkshakes with *DRINK ME* signs, miniature scones that glittered with silver icing sugar, home-made Jammie Dodgers with heart-shaped holes filled with strawberry jam, mini diamond-shaped tomato quiches, round sandwiches with Marmite clock hands.

'Would you care for a tea infusion, madam?' A third waiter appeared next to her, dressed in a riot of colours and a huge top hat festooned with flowers.

'Oooh yes – mint, please,' said Ronke.

'And another round of cocktails,' barked Isobel.

'And a bottle of sparkling water,' added Simi.

'Next year, Sofia,' chirped Isobel, in a put-on childish voice, 'I'll take you to Lapland to see Santa. We'll all go. My treat!'

Sofia stared at Isobel adoringly. Ronke slumped in her chair. Maybe Simi was right, she thought. Maybe you can buy happiness.

But the food didn't taste as good as it looked. *All style, no substance*, thought Ronke smugly. Sofia ignored the savoury bits and gorged herself on sugary crap – three meringues in three seconds. Boo was oblivious. The three of them had met for brunch and it would appear that Isobel and Boo had been drinking non-stop.

'Have a sandwich, Sofia – they're so yummy,' Ronke lied.

'Eugh! Meringues are yummy,' said Sofia, mouth full.

'How's Kayode?' asked Isobel. She dragged out each syllable, an ugly twist to her mouth.

Ronke smiled. She was ready for this, had hoped it would come up. 'We're off to Nigeria for Christmas. He wants me to meet his mum.'

'Wow! Well, I hope he's flying you first class,' said Isobel. 'Nigerian flights are awful. Especially at Christmas with all those proles going home. I'd rather not go at all than fly steerage.' She flicked a hand under her nose twice, as if trying to get rid of a bad smell.

'Premium Economy. For me it's a treat. I guess I'm a prole.' Ronke looked at Boo for support. When Simi had suggested they upgrade on their trip to Rome last year, Boo had called her a poser with more money than sense.

'Let's hope he turns up this time,' said Boo.

Isobel did her tinkly laugh and touched Boo's arm. 'Oh yes! He left her standing at St Pancras like a lemon. If he'd done that to me, I'd have killed him.'

Boo tinkled with her.

Simi nudged Ronke's knee: *ignore them*. Ronke felt her nails bite into her palms. She wasn't surprised at Isobel but what had happened to Boo?

'Martin's coming home on Friday,' said Simi. 'We're going to say yes to his job.'

'Friday? I'll make him a cake. He was disappointed I didn't do Sofia's this year – said her birthday cake was sickly.' Ronke was pleased with this put-down. 'Don't worry, I won't inter- rupt you love birds, I'll drop it off with Ebenezer.'

'He'll love that. But he'll want to see you. I'm sure I can unchain him for half an hour.' Simi did her dirty laugh.

They all joined in. Except Isobel.

'What's wrong?' asked Boo.

Isobel looked around furtively then scooted forward in her seat. 'I wasn't going to say anything; I don't want to ruin the mood. But all this talk of happy couples makes it so much worse. It's Chase.'

'What's he done?' asked Simi.

'Nothing yet,' said Isobel. 'He's got a shoot in London. The bastard is going to be here for six fucking weeks and I can't do anything to stop him.'

'Little pitchers have big ears.' Ronke raised her eyebrows and tilted her head at Sofia.

'Show a bit of compassion, Ronke,' said Boo. 'And where on earth do you get these parochial sayings?'

An hour later, Isobel was still ranting about Chase, Simi and Boo were still consoling her and Ronke was trying to convince an overtired Sofia that lying on the floor was not a good look. The waiter stepped over Sofia to deliver more drinks. Cocktails for Boo and Isobel, tea for Ronke, an espresso for Simi.

'You should take her home, Boo.' Ronke pointed at Sofia, in case Boo was too drunk to know who she was talking about.

'I don't want to go home,' Boo pouted.

'Vadim will take her,' said Isobel. 'Let's make a night of it. I feel like dancing.'

'I need my bed,' said Simi. 'This is the first drink I've had all week. I'm out of practice.'

'What's happened to Simi?' asked Isobel. 'She used to be fun.'

'I'd love a night out,' said Boo. 'I've been so stressed.'

'You deserve Boo-time,' said Isobel. 'Tubby hubby will understand.'

Ronke was amazed. Stressed! Boo-time? Tubby hubby? What was wrong with them? Was Boo having some sort of breakdown? And she wouldn't send her child home with a steroid-pumped Russian. Would she?

'Vadim won't mind?' asked Boo.

'He does what he's told.' Isobel reached for her phone. 'You can be my *alobam*. Simi's sacked; she's become a bore. You're coming too, Ronke. I insist.'

It appeared that Boo *would* send her daughter home with some random bloke. Ronke lifted Sofia off the floor. 'Sorry, I'm meeting Kayode.' She wasn't. 'I'll take Sofia home.'

∽

'THANK YOU FOR BRINGING HER back.' Didier joined Ronke in the kitchen. 'She's tucked up in her princess dress. I didn't have the heart to wake her.'

'Will she sleep through?' asked Ronke.

'Till six with any luck. Please stay for a quick drink?' Didier pulled out a stool for her. 'Are you hungry? I can make you an omelette?'

Ronke was about to say no, but there was something melancholic in the way he asked. And she was starving. She smiled her assent.

'*Maman* recommended this red.' Didier opened the bottle in showy French waiter style, sniffed the cork and poured a splash into a huge glass. 'Spicy and rich. I think you'll like it.'

Ronke swirled it pretentiously, stuck her nose in, took a sip and smacked her lips. 'It's all right – not Mateus Rosé, but it'll do. I'm kidding – it's delicious!'

He grabbed a bowl and three eggs. 'So, who is she out with? Wait, let me guess – Isobel, *la magnifique*?'

'Yup. Her new bestie. Can I be honest? I don't like her. I've tried to be empathetic. I know what it's like to lose a parent when you're young – it changes you. And losing your mother must be even worse . . .'

'*Non*,' said Didier. 'Her mum lives in Moscow.'

'She's dead. She died when Isobel was twelve.' Ronke yawned.

'Boo told me her mum was in Moscow. Maybe I'm wrong. I glaze over when she talks about Isobel.'

While he cooked, Ronke talked about her Christmas plans. Unlike Boo, he was pleased for her. She ran through her must-do list – eat original *ofada* rice in Sagamu, catch a speedboat to Tarkwa Bay, visit the slave museum at Badagry. 'I'm a bit worried about meeting his mum. It's a big deal, you know.'

Didier ran the spatula around the pan and folded the omelette into thirds. 'Anyone can see you're good for him. He loves you. She will too.'

'I hope so.' Ronke took a mouthful. It was delicious – light, fluffy, almost perfectly seasoned (just missing a heavy pinch of cayenne). 'Thanks – it's so good!'

'You're welcome.' Didier sipped his wine then blurted out, 'I'm worried about Boo. I don't know where her head is. Has she said anything to you?'

'No! Nothing.' Ronke kept her eyes on her plate, shovelling egg on to her fork.

'I don't know if we're enough for her. I thought we were happy. But she's not.' Didier sounded close to tears.

'Look, it's a blip. You guys will work it out. Take her away for a weekend break. I'll have Sofia.'

'I think it's more than that. Ronke, tell me.' Didier's eyes were pleading. 'Is she having an affair?'

Reckless, stupid Boo. Ronke looked straight into Didier's eyes. 'No! Of course not. She loves you.'

Didier's face brightened. 'Don't tell her I asked you. Please. I'm being paranoid. I trust her.'

'My lips are sealed.' Ronke studied her feet.

They moved to the snug, Ronke with a green tea, Didier with his wine. They talked and talked. She closed her eyes to let them rest. For a minute.

26

BOO

Boo TRIED TO FORCE the key into the lock. The pavement shifted. She leaned on the door to steady herself and toppled when it flew open.

'What time do you call this?' Didier gave her the look.

'I didn't realize I had a curfew.' Boo wished the floor would stop undulating.

'Don't shout – you'll wake Sofia.'

Boo decided her shoes were the reason she was wobbling. She kicked them off and followed Didier into the snug. Ronke was asleep on the sofa, a Welsh blanket tucked around her. How fucking cosy. 'What is *she* doing here?' Isobel was right – you couldn't trust a friend when she wanted your life.

'*She* brought our daughter home,' Didier whispered coldly.

'That was hours ago. Why is she *still* here?'

Ronke stirred and rubbed her eyes. 'What time is it?'

'It's late. I'll give you a lift home,' said Didier.

'What's wrong with an Uber?' Boo snatched the blanket and wrapped it round herself.

'I want to see she gets home safe. I'll be ten minutes. Go to bed.' Didier walked out of the room.

'What have you been talking about?' said Boo.

'You mostly. He's worried,' said Ronke.

'What did you tell him?'

'Nothing.' Ronke held a finger to her lips.

'You need to stop being jealous of me. And of Isobel.'

'Go to bed, Boo,' said Ronke. 'You're talking crap.'

Boo decided sleep was a good idea. She stumbled up the stairs, twisted her ankle and yelped. 'Sorry,' she whispered dramatically. But it was too late. Sofia's door opened and she peeked out, still in her stupid Elsa dress. Didier had obviously been too busy entertaining Ronke to put her to bed properly.

'Is it morning, Mama?'

'No, darling. It's sleep time. Back to bed.' Boo hiccupped. Ronke and Didier stood at the bottom of the stairs, looking up, judging her. Sofia didn't look too impressed either. Fuck the lot of them. Having fun wasn't a crime. She collapsed on top of the bedcovers. If Sofia could go to bed with her clothes on, so could Boo.

She woke at seven. Her head felt like it had been pierced with an ice pick. Sofia was sitting cross-legged on the bed. 'What are you doing?' Boo asked.

'I'm talking to the head.' Sofia tried to lift the Ife head, but it was too heavy and tumbled to the floor. Its malevolent eyes stared up at Boo.

'It's not a toy, don't touch it,' Boo said sharply. When Sofia's eyes welled up, she added more gently, 'I mean, it's heavy – you could hurt yourself.' And, of course, Didier chose that moment to walk in.

'Papa!' wailed Sofia.

'Let's get breakfast, *mon bébé*. Mama needs more sleep.'

Didier left her a bottle of water and paracetamol. 'Take two, it might help.'

Boo checked the head – no damage –'popped the pills, took off her clothes and got back into bed. She was still asleep when Didier came back with a tray two hours later. 'I feel sick,' she said.

'I'm not surprised – you were smashed.' Didier kissed her forehead. 'Stay in bed. I'll take Sofia to soccer school.'

She sipped the tea. Dark and strong. Perfect. 'Thanks.'

'You're welcome.'

She nibbled a corner of the toast – light on butter, heavy on Marmite – exactly how she liked it.

Didier put her phone on the bed. 'It keeps buzzing. Your friend Isobel. What is it with her? You talk to her more than me. Ronke thinks she's—'

'So Saint Ronke has been bad-mouthing her,' said Boo with a sudden flare of anger. 'I should have guessed. You know what, I don't care. Isobel is my friend. I can't do this now.' Boo pulled the covers over her head. When she peeked out, he was gone.

∽

AT TWELVE, BOO FORCED HERSELF out of bed and read Isobel's messages.

Alobam! What a good night! I'm hitting the gym, join me? We could do lunch after.

Wakey! Wakey!

I've given up. Guess tubby hubby has you on lockdown. See you Wednesday. Ix

Boo liked being Isobel's *alobam*. She wished she could be as commitment-free as her. Green-eyed Ronke didn't know how lucky she was – it was easy to believe you'd make the perfect wife and mother when you didn't have a husband or a kid.

She checked her emails – a raft of rubbish. Net A Porter, Sweaty Betty, ASOS, Jenny from the BBs checking on Sofia (how many times did Boo have to tell her Sofia didn't have chicken pox?). One from Neil.

> **From:** Neil@ModernScience.com
> **To:** Boo@ModernScience.com
> **Subject:** Lunch?
>
> Hey you,
> We keep missing each other. I'm in the office
> Monday – let's do lunch. Wear the sexy dress again –
> you know the one I mean. We can make it a long one.

She felt disgusted. And excited. Guilty. And empowered. She'd kept all his messages, re-read them most days. They went from flirty to filthy. Her replies were all about work. She wasn't encouraging him. But she wasn't telling him to stop. Maybe she had schizophreniform disorder? Or maybe she was just fucking stupid. She heard the door.

'I scored a goal, Mama!' Sofia ran into the kitchen, the plastic studs on her football boots clattering on the wooden floor.

'Good girl, well done. But not so loud.' She watched Sofia deflate.

'How's the head?' asked Didier.

'It was fine. It's pretty solid.'

'I meant your head,' said Didier.

'Oh, much better,' Boo lied.

'Lunch?' asked Didier. 'I could do pasta. Or we could go to Pizza Express?'

'Pizza Express!' shrieked Sofia, pogoing around the kitchen, her football boots making an awful squeaky sound.

'Pasta.' There was no way Boo could cope with a room full of rowdy kids being ignored by their stressed-out parents. One child was enough. Today, one child was too much.

While Didier cooked, Boo played Sushi Go with Sofia, letting her win round after round. It wasn't difficult; she couldn't focus.

She popped to the loo and when she came back, Didier was using her laptop. Boo couldn't remember logging out. Which meant her emails were open. Which meant . . . Fuck. Fuck. Fuck. She felt a pulse beat in her neck as she yanked the laptop away from him, her hands clammy. 'Excuse me, that's my work computer.' She risked a glance. *Sky Sports*.

'What's the problem?' he said.

'Nothing,' she said. 'I'm tired. Sorry, I'm being a cow.'

'Moo,' said Sofia.

Boo knew she shouldn't have overreacted. Even laid-back Didier could get suspicious. She looked at his emails all the time. She even opened his sent folder to make sure he wasn't slagging her off to his mum. He never was. He was too fucking perfect. She should delete Neil's messages. She would delete them. She just wanted to read them one last time.

She managed to get through the afternoon. She did bath and bed (Didier didn't offer).

'Are you working from home tomorrow?' Didier asked when she was done.

'Does it matter?' Boo hadn't decided if she was going in or not. She couldn't risk seeing Neil. She definitely couldn't risk lunch.

'Just checking who's taking Sofia to school.'

'It's Monday. Your day,' Boo snapped.

'OK. Sorry I asked.'

Boo closed her eyes. 'No, I'm sorry.'

'For what, Boo? For not being able to look at me? For sending your daughter home with Ronke? For being miserable? Or is it trapped?' Didier put his head in his hands. 'Talk to me, Boo. *Je comprends pas.*'

His sanctimonious tone riled Boo. 'I'm sick of this. I don't need to apologize for wanting a night off. I'm thirty-five, not sixty. Stop making me feel guilty all the time.'

'I've never minded you going out.' Didier sounded crushed.

'What were you and Ronke talking about last night? Were you slagging me off?'

'Of course not. This is crazy talk.'

'Whatever. I'm going to bed.' Boo stormed upstairs. She knew she was behaving badly, but what was she supposed to do when she was under attack?

27

SIMI

Simi rubbed her arm. Smooth and soft after the top-to-toe body polish. Her nails were shiny, her hair straight and glossy (thanks to the keratin blowout). Pedicure, then eyebrow threading. No rush – Martin's flight didn't land until six.

She couldn't wait for their New York adventure to start. Her list of pluses was extensive – amazing shopping, the best sushi in the world, Broadway shows, the brownstone she was determined to live in (they'd need two spare bedrooms). The one minus – she'd miss her friends (hence the spare rooms). Although after the disastrous tea, she wasn't sure she wanted them in the same place at the same time. Iso had sniped. Boo had simpered. Ronke had sulked. It was saying something when the five-year-old was the most mature person in the room.

Simi's life was back on track. On Monday she'd had a meeting with QB. She'd expected the worst and was determined to keep her game face on. She was off to Manhattan. No one would ever find out she'd been sacked.

When Simi arrived, QB was on the phone, barking instructions at some hapless victim (probably her husband). She'd pointed at Simi (accusatory), then at the chair opposite (patronizing), and held up two fingers in a gesture that could have meant 'two seconds'. Simi had been sure it said 'fuck you'.

When she finally hung up, QB smirked at Simi. 'Right. You have no idea what this is about, do you?'

'I can guess. You're letting me go. I'm on a six-month rolling contract. You'll have to pay me off.'

'Are you high?' asked QB.

'I've got the paperwork.' Simi wouldn't let QB wriggle out of their contract. 'It was agreed at my last review.'

QB snorted. 'Don't be so bloody stupid. You're not getting fired. You're a star – my biggest star! This is good news, Simi. Extraordinary news.'

Their boutique agency had been bought by a global communications group. QB was to head up the merged London office and she wanted Simi to run the Manhattan start-up. Her own team, an expense account, generous relocation package and lots of travel (turning left as standard). 'Your husband's out there, isn't he? When does his contract end?'

'He's had an offer to stay – long term.'

'Sounds like serendipity.' QB raised her glass.

Simi dipped her feet into the mini-jacuzzi of warm scented water and indulged in her favourite Manhattan fantasy. She was a brown Carrie Bradshaw (with a bigger shoe closet), Martin a better-looking (not so sleazy) Mr Big. It was time to let go of the stupid impostor syndrome. She wriggled her toes. She could add baby-soft feet to her list of accomplishments. She had it all – happy marriage, dazzling career, straight hair.

Her phone interrupted the daydream.

'I'm in a cab – got an earlier flight,' said Martin. 'Where are you?'

'Carnaby Street, making myself beautiful.'

'You're always beautiful. No rush – I'll see you at home. I need a long hot shower to make myself less stinky.'

∽

EBENEZER PRESSED THE LIFT BUTTON. '*Salaam alaikum*, Mrs Simi. I know why you are smiling! Mr Martin is already here.'

Simi burst into the flat and scanned the living room. No Martin. A cake tin on the coffee table: six cupcakes with 'I heart New York' toppers. Ronke was a sweetheart. She was surprised he hadn't eaten one. Or three.

'Hi honey, I'm home,' she called in a sing-song voice. No answer. He must be in the shower.

She found Martin on their bed. His eyes were red. He wasn't smiling. Simi's eye twitched. What could have happened? He was fine an hour ago.

'I found these.' Martin opened his palm to expose her contraceptive pills. 'And this.' He tapped a piece of paper against the Ife head.

Simi knew what it was. The consent form she'd signed for those two pills, stapled to the aftercare leaflet with 'Medical Abortion' in big bold type. She'd put it in the shoebox with her contraceptive pills. She felt a sudden sharp pain in her chest.

'How did you find it?' she said. Her hands shook as she rubbed her breastbone.

'Does it matter?' Martin flung the contraceptives at her. They bounced off her shoulder and fell on to the rug.

'I can explain.' She stared at the floor, the pills a barrier between them.

'Great. I can't wait to hear this.' He sat back and placed a pillow behind his head. 'Fire away. I'm all ears.'

She couldn't. She wanted to tell him the truth. But she wasn't sure what the truth was. 'It's not what it looks like.'

'Good. Because it looks like you're a fucking liar and I'm a fucking idiot.'

'No,' said Simi. 'I did come off the pill but ... I got pregnant.'

'That was the idea,' said Martin. 'But you're not pregnant now. Are you?'

'I panicked. You weren't here.'

'You seriously want to make this *my* fault?'

'It's not *anyone's* fault. I was going to tell you.'

'Bullshit. You had an abortion. You made a decision about our child without me.'

'Don't be so dramatic. It's my body. And it wasn't a child – it was a few cells.' Simi clutched her stomach, saw his eyes follow her hands and dropped her arms. 'It wasn't an ab . . . ab . . .' She couldn't say the word. 'It was a tablet. Two tablets. Like the morning-after pill.'

With one sudden movement, Martin swept the Ife head off the bedside table. He waved the leaflet at her. 'I can fucking read. All this time I've been thinking we were trying. Thinking we were a team.'

Simi took a step back; she felt faint. 'Martin, you're over-reacting. We can work this out. I had a wobble but I'm OK now. I've got a job in New York. A brilliant job. We can have a baby. We will have a baby. I'll be ready soon. In a year . . .'

'Shut up!' Martin stooped to pick up the head. 'Why didn't you tell me?'

'I was going to.' Simi's eye twitched again.

Martin raised his arm and lunged at her. 'Enough of your fucking lies!'

'Stop! What are you doing?' Simi screamed. 'Let go of that horrible thing.'

He staggered away, held his arm out and dropped the head.

Simi sank to the floor. 'You've chipped the wood,' she said. 'It's ruined.'

'Like us,' he said, stepping around her.

Simi didn't have the words to make him stay. She heard the door slam. How had he found out? It wouldn't cross Martin's mind to open one of her shoeboxes. Something had made him. *Someone* had made him. But Ronke was the only one who knew her secret hiding place. Simi rocked the head from side to side, like a baby. *Oh, Ronke. What have you done?*

∽

FOUR DAYS LATER SIMI STILL hadn't spoken to Martin – the longest gap since they'd met fourteen years earlier. She'd left voice messages, sent text messages and emails. Tried him at home and at work. Tried in the middle of (his) night, hoping he'd pick up on impulse. She left begging messages, angry messages, calm messages. Nothing.

She couldn't tell anyone. So she didn't. She channelled

her inner Dad, slapped on her flawless facade and kept the pain hidden. She'd taken to wearing sunglasses. Sunken eyes were bad enough, but the persistent twitch was doing her head in.

Ronke called and texted. Simi ignored her. If Ronke had told Martin (and she must have), Simi couldn't face her. And if she hadn't (stupid thought – she must have), it would mean admitting that her marriage was on the rocks. She was the one who picked Ronke up when her relationships fell apart – it didn't work the other way round. Simi had to accept the unbearable truth: their friendship was over. She just had to hope her marriage wasn't.

At work, Simi stuck to the script. She was golden, Martin was great, nothing to see here apart from wall-to-wall success. She must have inherited this senseless mix of pride and shame from Dad.

Her father's face flashed into her head. Back in Lagos when they were forced to downsize, his biggest worry had been what people would say. He couldn't afford to service his Mercedes, but no way would he sell it, so it sat on their drive rusting away like a big white elephant. All that mattered was being seen as the *big oga* with the big car.

Like father like daughter, thought Simi. *I might feel like shit, but in my Burberry Prorsum sheepskin jacket, at least I look fantastic.* Now she just needed to fake it with Isobel for as long as it took to have a drink. She'd avoided her for as long as she could, but Isobel had pushed and pushed. So here she was at Gotham. Showtime.

'Hey, Isobel!' Simi rubbed her twitching eye and gave Isobel a hug.

In her sleeveless halterneck dress, Isobel's arms looked pumped, her biceps protruding. But it wasn't just physical. She was more theatrical than usual. 'Sorry I was such a bitch about you moving. It was selfish.' Isobel reached for Simi's hands across the table. 'I'd just found you and I couldn't bear to lose you again. But I've had words with myself and I'm truly happy for you, honest.'

'Oh, it's fine.' Simi tried to pull her hand back, but Isobel's grip tightened.

'I'm stressed out, you see. Chase will be here next week and the thought of being in the same city as him has made me paranoid. I'm not sleeping. I'm not eating. But it's no excuse for being a bad friend. So let me make up to you. I have this brilliant real estate guy in Manhattan. If you give me Martin's details, I'll put them in touch.'

'No! No. His office has someone. But thanks.' Simi was glad they were in a dark alcove – her spasming eye was out of control.

'OK, but if you change your mind, let me know. And I've got you a moving gift.' Isobel waved an envelope in the air. 'Well, it's for you *and* Martin. Tickets to the *Hamilton* premiere! They're like gold dust; I had to pull lots of strings.'

'You shouldn't have.' Simi squirmed.

'Rubbish. You deserve it. You've got to tell Martin. Call him now!'

'He'll be at work. I'll tell him tonight.' Simi downed her drink and changed the subject. 'Have you seen Boo?'

'Yes, I ran with her today.' Isobel cocked her head. 'Did you know she's been sleeping with her boss?'

Simi was shell-shocked. Shagging your boss was such a cliché. Goody-Boo-Shoes having an affair. It was hard to believe. According to Isobel, it was all Didier's fault – poor bloke. Even little Sofia got to shoulder some blame. At least Simi wasn't blaming her fuck-up on anyone except herself. Well – apart from Ronke. She wished she could text Martin. *Look what Boo's done – now that's what you call bad.*

'Are you listening?' said Isobel.

'Yes. I'm dumbfounded,' said Simi. 'I don't get why she told *you*? No offence, but I'm her best friend. Well, and Ronke.'

'She told Ronke. Big mistake. Ronke pretty much called her a slut. Boo was in pieces. I had to console her.' Isobel's eyes seemed to gleam as she spoke.

So that's why Boo and Ronke had fallen out. It was like being back in primary school – back-stabbing, rumours, he-said, she-said.

'I just hope she keeps it to herself. Ronke can be spiteful,' said Isobel. 'Remember when you told her about the abortion? Unhappy people are vindictive.'

'It wasn't an . . . Iso, what do you mean?' Simi was taken aback. She studied Isobel's face. 'Ronke's not unhappy.'

'She should be. Kayode keeps pestering me. It's kind of desperate.'

'What does he want?' said Simi distractedly, her mind still on Boo.

'The kind of things a man with a girlfriend shouldn't want from his ex.' Isobel nodded suggestively.

Simi was silent while she tried to process this new revelation. Was this why Ronke wanted to ruin her marriage? Out of vindictiveness? I'm unhappy – you should be unhappy too? No. She couldn't make that fit. Ronke wasn't like that. 'Shit,' she said. 'I have to tell her.'

'No,' Isobel said firmly. 'It should come from me. I don't want her blaming you. Or Boo.'

Simi's eye twitched. How on earth had their lives got so complicated?

28

RONKE

RONKE DIDN'T MIND WORKING Saturday mornings – half day, full pay and Wednesday off. Plus, Saturday patients were more relaxed. The one downside was that Rafa point-blank refused to work weekends. So she had Eliza, who was good at her job but zero fun. If the conversation veered from *Coronation Street* or *Loose Women*, Eliza shut down. She wasn't remotely interested in burning issues like how to impress Kayode's mum in Lagos or how to fit nine restaurants into a one-week holiday.

Ronke's streamlined list of restaurants included three *mama puts* – the best in Lagos, according to Aunty K. Ronke loved everything about these hole-in-the-wall *bukas*, built from tarpaulin and rusty corrugated iron. The food (cooked in blackened pots over firewood pits) was ridiculously cheap and unbelievably delicious. The scowling cooks guarded their recipes like state secrets. Customers travelled for miles on *okadas* or in luxury limos. Bankers sat on mismatched plastic chairs next to impoverished students, inhaled the same car fumes and listened to the same soundtrack of blaring horns, squawking chickens and shouting. Ronke couldn't wait.

Eliza walked in with their last patient. 'Your friend is downstairs – I told her you'd be twenty minutes.'

'Who?' Ronke asked. She wasn't expecting anyone.

'Don't know. She said she was your best friend.'

'What does she look like?'

'Long brown hair in a pony. Pretty.'

Boo. Please let her have come to her senses. She wouldn't have come if it wasn't to apologize. Would she? Being pissed off with Boo had made Ronke miserable. She was more than ready to forgive her, even though her siding with Isobel at Simi's tea had really hurt.

The patient was a regular – an easy six-monthly check-up – no cavities, no X-rays, no stress. Ronke was done in fifteen minutes. 'You get off, Eliza. I'll load the autoclave. Send Boo up – she knows the way.'

Ronke heard the footsteps, peeled off her gloves and turned round. 'Oh, it's you.' She dropped her arms. 'What are *you* doing here?'

'Hi, Ronks.' Isobel's smile didn't reach her eyes. She was shrouded in an over-the-top floor-length white faux fox-fur coat. At least Ronke hoped it was faux. 'I would have called but my phone's dead. I don't know what's wrong with it. Actually, can I borrow yours? I need to let Vadim know I'll be a while.'

'Er . . . yeah, sure.' Ronke unlocked her phone and handed it over. 'I'll let Tina go, she's meant to finish at twelve.'

'Take your time.' Isobel looked around the room imperiously as she pulled off her white leather gloves, one finger at a time.

Ronke stomped down the stairs. Why was Isobel here?

What did she want? And how could she get rid of her? She had plans for the afternoon, a critical mission – Kayode's family had a pool; she had to find a flattering swimsuit.

When Ronke came back in, Isobel was sitting cross-legged on the patient's armchair. She was wearing a long white wrap dress – the sort of thing you'd wear to get married on a beach. The dress had fallen open at her upper thigh, the fabric pooling on either side of her toned brown legs. Her black bovver boots were incongruous with the dress. She looked thoroughly out of place in Ronke's little surgery.

Ronke wiped her palms on her trousers nervously. Kayode had called Isobel manly – Ronke could see it now. The dress was soft and silky but Isobel looked strong and muscular. The veins in her neck stood out like cords. Ronke was her complete opposite – short and dumpy, in faded black cotton scrubs.

'I have to tell you something. Promise you won't shoot the messenger.' Isobel tilted her head. Ronke took in her patronizing half-smile.

'I promise.' Ronke sank on to her little stool.

'The thing is . . . Well, there's no easy way to say this, so I'll be blunt. It's Kayode. He's been hounding me. He keeps calling, saying he wants me back. I haven't given him any encouragement – the opposite in fact. I've told him to stop, to leave me alone, but he's getting more and more intense. Maybe it's best if you hear for yourself.' Isobel tapped at her phone.

'You said it wasn't working.' Ronke's voice was croaky.

'Silly me. I'd turned it off by mistake. I'm crap with technology. Now hush.' Isobel held out her phone.

Kayode's rich baritone filled Ronke's treatment room. 'Hey, Izzie. It's me. Look, enough is enough. I'm going to tell Ronke about us. It's not fair on her. I can't lie any more. Call me. Don't ignore this. You know how I feel. I've got to see you. Please. I'm going crazy.'

Ronke's vision blurred; she felt spaced out.

'He's sending texts too. Loads of them.' Isobel thrust her phone into Ronke's face.

Ronke pulled her head back, her eyes swimming with tears. She blinked.

Izzie, I'm going mad. Stop ignoring me. We need to meet.

It had to be a joke. But it was his face in the little circle, his name beneath it: *Kayode King*.

Ronke couldn't bear to read more; she pushed the phone away.

Isobel reclined, a bitter little smile on her face. When she next spoke, her voice was wistful. 'It started at Sofia's party. I couldn't believe *he* was *your* Kayode. There was something I didn't tell you. Maybe I should have. It was the way he hugged me – it wasn't platonic. He pressed himself against me, if you know what I mean.'

Ronke knew what Isobel meant. It was how Kayode had hugged her after their first date. It had made her knees tremble. 'Yeah,' was all she could bring herself to say.

Isobel leaned forward. 'The last thing I want to do is hurt you but when you said you were going to meet his mum, well, I knew I had to tell you. I don't want you to be humiliated like I was. She's an awful woman, prejudiced and spiteful.'

'You met her?' Ronke's whisper was flat.

'Of course. And his sister, Yetty. I met the whole family.

Didn't he say? We were practically engaged. Until his mum put a stop to it. As far as she's concerned, mixed-race girls are loose, not marriage material. That's what she said to me. Can you believe it? Deep down, Kayode's a mummy's boy – it's why we split up.' Isobel put her hand on Ronke's arm. 'He won't marry you, Ronke. Girls like us are for messing around with. Not for keeps.'

Ronke imagined reaching for the ceiling-mounted dental light, swinging it hard into Isobel's spiteful face. The vision was so realistic, she heard the bone crack. She jerked her arm away.

'I'm so sorry, darling. I know this must be hard.' Isobel wiped a non-existent tear off her face with a manicured nail. 'But men are so weak. Kayode reminds me of Chase – he was a mummy's boy too. I told Simi and Boo how Kayode had made a pass at me, but they laughed it off.'

Ronke closed her eyes. Was this why Simi had been ignoring her? She looked at Isobel. 'You're saying that Boo and Simi know about this?'

'Oh yes. They've known for ages. I showed them the messages,' said Isobel. 'I begged them to tell you; I knew you'd rather hear it from them. But they said you needed to find out the hard way.'

So, this was how betrayal felt – like being punched in the stomach. Ronke stood and stared at her ugly plastic shoes. 'I need to be on my own.'

'Are you sure? Do you need a hug?' Isobel stood and held out her arms.

'Yes. Yes. No. Just go.' Ronke stepped back, bumping into the stool.

As Isobel left, she gave a small wave from the door. Ronke sank back down. She felt dead inside.

She texted Kayode.

I need to see you. Now. Are you at home?

He replied in seconds.

What's up? Leaving at two. Home game.

Ronke swallowed hard and tapped.

Stay there. I'm on my way.

∽

HER BELOVED KAYODE. HIS BULK filled the doorway. Black jeans, Arsenal hoodie, a wide smile on his face. Ronke shook her head; she felt a dull ache in her chest. He reached out to hug her; she pulled away.

'What's wrong? Has that arsehole come near you again?'

'Isobel told me,' Ronke said.

'Told you what?'

'Everything.' Ronke looked into his eyes. She'd been clinging to a shred of hope. A minuscule part of her still believed it would be a lie. But his face said it all.

'Whatever she's told you, it's crap.' Kayode stepped aside and ushered her in but Ronke stayed put. 'OK, OK. I should have been honest. But I don't talk about it. It was all so degrading. She's a total psycho.'

Suddenly weary, Ronke slumped against the door frame. 'Kayode, stop. No more lies. She's told me everything.'

'Ronke, listen . . . It's not . . .' Kayode lowered his eyes.

'I don't know why I even came. She's welcome to you.' Ronke turned and walked towards the lift.

Kayode darted in front of her to block her path. 'Listen to me. I'm going to tell you the truth. All of it. You've got to believe me. Come inside.'

'No. You can talk here.'

'It wasn't serious, not even exclusive. But when I tried to end it, she got obsessive, wouldn't take no for an answer. She kept coming to my flat and we'd end up in bed. I was young and stupid. I'm not proud of it.'

Ronke felt defeated. She spoke slowly. 'Kayode, you introduced her to your family.'

'No! I went to Lagos for a holiday. She turned up at our house, told Mum she was my fiancée. Caused a scene. Crying, screaming, threatening to kill herself. It took hours to get rid of her. We were on the verge of calling the police. Ask Yetty if you don't believe me. She was there.'

Ronke shook her head. 'Oh, come on, this is ridiculous. If this was true, you'd have told me. Why would you hide it?'

'I was ashamed, OK? When I got back to Cape Town my name was mud. She'd spread nasty rumours – said I'd beaten her up, stolen her jewellery, owed her money. Then my office got an anonymous complaint saying I was on the take.' Kayode rubbed his head. 'I lost my job. I lost everything. I had to leave South Africa. It took me a year to get my life back.'

Ronke's face was aflame with rage. 'Do you think I'm a complete idiot? I heard your message. You begged her to meet you.'

'She's twisted it. Yes, I did want to see her. But not like that. She's obsessed with me. I wanted to tell her to back off – to leave me alone, leave us alone.'

'You know what . . . I give up. I'm sick of all the lies. I don't care any more.'

'Ronke, I'm telling the truth. Look, I'm not perfect. I'm no saint. I'm not your dad.' He looked down at her pleadingly. 'But I swear to God, that bitch is out to get me.'

Ronke felt her face crumple. 'I don't give a shit about her. This is about you and me. It's about you not being able to tell me the truth.' Hot angry tears ran down her cheeks. She turned to leave.

Kayode pulled on her arm, trying to stop her. 'Ronke, listen – I love you.'

For the first time in Ronke's life, she hit someone. A hard slap, palm open, on his lying, cheating face. It shocked them both.

Ronke didn't give him a chance to react. She ignored the lift and ran down the stairs, chest heaving. He didn't follow. She yanked her phone out. 'Rafa, can I come over?'

29

BOO

Boo squeezed her eyes shut and listened to her heart bang against her ribcage. Thump. Thump. Thump.

An hour ago, she'd got back from soccer school. Sofia had skipped ahead, looking like a hoodlum in her 'We Kick Balls' sweatshirt, a stupid name for a stupid team. Boo hated Saturday football, standing around in the mud, but her mood slumped further when they turned the corner. Home and its tedious monotony, Didier and his infuriating chirpiness, Sofia and her constant neediness.

She watched her little girl bang on the door with both hands, almost smiled when she jumped into Didier's arms. He scooped her up, kissed her head, turned and walked into the house. He didn't look at Boo. She trundled after them. 'Don't mind me.' No answer.

Her laptop was on the island. Open. Her chest tightened. Her heart pounded. Didier wouldn't. He just wouldn't.

Sofia clung to Didier like a limpet. 'We practised dribbling. And I was the best at keepy uppy.'

Didier didn't shave at weekends. There was a time – forever ago – when Boo found it sexy and rugged. Today he looked haggard. Boo's arms tingled; she looked down and they were dotted with goosebumps.

'I wanted to be the striker, but we had to take turns and it was never my turn,' said Sofia. 'I bet I'd have scored, like . . . ten.'

Boo looked at her laptop screen. Blank. She glanced up; his eyes were on her. Was she projecting, or was torment staring back? She pressed the space bar. Woke the string of messages between her and Isobel. *Tubby hubby* leapt out as if highlighted in fluorescent ink. She tapped the red circle to close the window. The one behind was worse. Her work email, open on Neil's last message. *Stop being a tease. If your plan is to drive me mad with desire, it's working.*

Her hands shook as she closed the laptop. It didn't mean he knew. Didier wasn't suspicious – he trusted her.

Didier crouched down so he was Sofia's height. 'Are you hungry, *mon bébé*?'

'*Oui, Papa, un petit peu.*' Sofia held two fingers an inch apart.

'*Bon! Alors, on va à McDonald's.*'

'Yay!' Sofia spun around.

Boo bit back her 'fast food is evil' lecture. 'I'll come.'

'*Non.* You're sick and tired of your mundane existence. You stay.'

Thump. Thump. Thump. She'd said that to Isobel. Used those exact words.

'Get your coat and scooter, Sofia. Do you need the loo?' Didier locked eyes with Boo.

'Mama can come too,' said Sofia.

'*Non*, Sofia, Mama needs Boo-time. Tubby hubby will

manage. You can tell me all about the game.' Didier grabbed his wallet.

Boo-time. Tubby hubby. It was light-hearted banter. Not so funny when he said it. Boo trembled. He'd read her messages to Isobel. He'd read Neil's emails. She paced round the island. At some point she opened her laptop and pressed the delete button over and over. But she could still see them in her head; she knew them by rote. *Twice in one night – if you hadn't left, I'd have managed a hat trick. What are you wearing under that dress? Thinking about you makes me hard.* She clamped her eyes shut. Why hadn't she deleted them? Because she was a fucking moron who got a kick out of reading them, that's why.

Last week, she'd told Neil it was over. She'd flattered herself he'd be upset. Was sure he'd try to convince her to meet him one more time. But no:

'Hey, it's fine. We had a little fun. The thrill's always in the will-we-won't-we, don't you think?' He grinned. 'Don't look so worried – no one got hurt, consenting adults and all that. We're good.' And just like that, Neil went from pornographic sex pest to professional colleague.

Boo opened her trash folder and read the emails again, looking for ways of making them innocent. Or at least less damning.

As she held the shift and delete buttons, it struck her – Didier wasn't curious; it wasn't in his nature. He wouldn't poke around her laptop. Not off his own bat. Ronke's judgemental face loomed in her vision.

She called Ronke. Straight to voicemail. She toyed with the idea of calling Simi. But where to start? Simi didn't know about Neil. Isobel. She'd know what to do.

'*Alobam!* Let's meet for lunch,' said Isobel. 'Can you escape? We could—'

Boo cut her off. 'Didier knows.'

'Knows what?'

'About me and Neil.'

'Oh dear. Is tubby hubby terribly upset? What did he say?'

'Nothing. He's not talking to me. I don't know what to do.' Suddenly shattered, Boo slumped over the island.

'How did he find out?'

'He saw the emails,' said Boo. 'He's read our messages too.'

'Something must have made him look,' said Isobel. 'Or someone. My money's on Ronke.'

'Why, though? She's my best friend.' Boo saw Ronke wrapped in her Welsh blanket, sucking up to Didier. She heard her censorious attack: *You need to own this*.

'No, she's not. I am. Jealousy makes people ugly, makes them do awful things. Look, don't worry, Didier will get over it. Don't act guilty. In fact, do the opposite. Go on the attack. His ego has taken a bashing – you wait, I bet he joins a gym next week,' Isobel tinkled.

Boo squeezed her eyes shut. Her life was imploding and Isobel was laughing. 'I've got to go.'

'OK. But if he asks for a divorce, call me. I know a brilliant lawyer. And if he touches you, come here. You and Sofia can stay with me.'

'Don't be ridiculous. Didier would never hurt me.'

'Well, be careful. Some men go mad when they find out their wives are cheating. Sure you don't fancy lunch? We could go to Hutong. You liked it there. We could ask Ronke and Simi to come too. We're all single now.'

Thump. Thump. Thump. Isobel was mad. Boo tried Ronke again. Straight to voicemail.

∽

BOO SPENT THE AFTERNOON ANALYSING potential outcomes, none of them good. She wanted a confrontation, was ready for Didier's anger, but when he and Sofia finally got home, he ignored her. Didn't say a word. Didn't even look at her.

'Are you OK, Mama?' Sofia asked.

'A little bit under the weather, darling.'

'Do you need a plaster?'

'No, but a hug would be nice.' Boo buried her face in Sofia's hair. It smelled of grass.

Didier insisted on doing bath and bed. So Boo went to the snug and sat in the dark. She tested words in her head – but couldn't find any to make this go away. She settled on the truth: *I don't know why I did it. I really messed up. I'm sorry. I love you.*

She heard the door close. 'We need to talk,' said Didier.

Now the moment she'd been waiting for had arrived, Boo wasn't ready. 'I'll go and kiss her goodnight,' she said.

'*Non.* She's asleep. We need to talk about your hot boss.'

Boo let the words, her words, stab her. She deserved it.

'Why?' Didier stood with his back to her, staring out into the garden.

'It's not what it looks like,' said Boo. 'I made a mistake. It meant nothing. I regretted it straight away. I'm sorry.'

Didier turned and looked at her. 'Do you love him?'

Boo was outraged. 'Of course not. I love you. Only you.'

'*Je comprends pas*. You slept with this *fils de pute* and then you came back here to play happy families.' Didier held a palm out to silence her protest. 'All the time you are laughing at me with your new *meilleure amie*.'

'No. It's been eating me up. That's why I've been so unhappy. I'm glad you know. Now we can work this out. We can move on.' Boo stepped towards him, arms open wide.

Didier pushed her arms away. 'I can't look at you. I need air. I'm going out. I'll sleep on the sofa.'

'You can't go. We need to sort this out.' Boo's voice was coming out wrong, high-pitched and reedy. 'Think of Sofia.'

Didier poked her in the chest with his finger. 'I always think of Sofia. You and Sofia. That's all I ever think about. For me, it has always been enough.'

'It's enough for me too,' Boo whispered. 'You can't run away – we need to talk.'

'Talk?' He jabbed her in the chest again. 'What should we talk about? My wife with another man?'

'Us,' said Boo. 'We need to talk about us.'

'You've said it all. Boring tubby hubby.' Didier's voice was a crass mimic. 'Not like hot boss,' he said, one hard jab in the chest with each word.

Boo stepped back, shocked. Didier was never cruel. 'Stop it, Didier! You're hurting me.'

'*Moi?*' This time Didier slapped himself on the chest. 'You accuse *me* of hurting *you*? *Tu es folle*.' He spat the words out, then shook his head and walked out.

Boo stood rooted to the spot, the slam of the door echoing in her head. Her eyes were drawn to the mobile he'd left behind. She scrolled through his messages with shaky hands.

She didn't want Isobel to be right. But the most recent message was from Ronke.

She's cheating on you. Look at her emails. Sorry, you don't deserve this.

Boo stumbled, suddenly light-headed. She sank to the floor and cried. Silently.

30

SIMI

SIMI STILL HADN'T HEARD from Martin. Ten days. Two hundred and thirty-three hours. She must have called him sixty times, sent a hundred texts, forty emails. She'd contemplated flying to New York. She could surprise him at his office, or lie in wait at his apartment – he'd have to talk to her then. One minute she was sure it was the right move, he'd take one look at her, realize how sorry she was and forgive her. The next she knew it would make things worse – he would say something he couldn't take back. She had to let him come to terms with it in his own time. They were a team. Us against the world.

Simi was still in bed when Boo called. It was Sunday, and there was nothing and no one to get up for. Another sleepless night, lying in the gloom, convinced the Ife head was staring at her, appraising her, finding her lacking. At dawn, she turned it to face the wall.

Boo was incoherent, tripping over her words, repeating herself, making no sense. Simi tried to get her to focus. 'Boo. Stop. I already know about you and your boss. Now calm down and tell me slowly. What on earth has happened?'

'So she told you too. I don't believe this,' sobbed Boo. 'What is wrong with her? Why didn't you say you knew?'

'She asked me not to. I was surprised you'd told her.'

'I tell her everything. I always have – you know that. I trusted her. And now she's told Didier. How could she do this to me?'

'Isobel told Didier?' Simi was beginning to think Boo was unhinged.

'Not Isobel. Ronke.'

'Are you sure?' Simi was now wide awake.

'I saw her text.' Boo's voice was panicky. 'She told him to read my emails and messages. Isobel warned me – I didn't listen. And now Isobel says Didier will want a divorce.'

'Boo, I'm coming over. Sit tight. We'll work this out.' Simi was dressed and in an Uber twenty minutes later – a record, only possible because she went scrunchie and hat. A new sequinned Saint Laurent beanie, perfect for a Manhattan winter.

Simi's left eye twitched and she pressed her palm into the socket. Boo's panic made Simi's own problems seem even bigger. What if Martin didn't forgive her? What if he wanted a divorce? She hadn't even considered this. Now she couldn't get it out of her mind.

Was Martin talking to Didier? Were they comparing notes on their lying, cheating wives? Surely screwing your boss was a million times worse than not telling your husband you were still on the pill. Not that she thought Didier should divorce Boo – of course not. But what Boo had done was much, much worse. On a scale of fucked-upness, Boo was a seven, Simi a two. Three at most. Simi found herself wishing that she and Martin had a child. He wouldn't be able to ignore her for ten days if there was a little person to care about. The irony of this wasn't wasted on her.

Boo opened her front door, her body posture the opposite of inviting. 'We can't talk here,' she said. 'Wait, I'll get my bag.'

It was Sunday brunch time for couples (lunch for families) and all the eateries around the Common were rammed. They ended up in a Wetherspoon's. Simi chose the quietest table, told the waitress they weren't hungry and asked for a bottle of house white. This wasn't the time or place to be a wine snob.

The teenager twiddled her nose ring and snapped on chewing gum. 'You're in the restaurant section.'

Simi sighed. 'I'm happy to pay for two meals but we don't want them.' Boo flopped over the grubby table, head in hands. She was going to start rocking back and forth any minute.

'Not how it works.' The waitress slapped two greasy menus on the table. 'If you wanna sit here, you gotta order food. And I gotta serve it.'

'Chicken Caesar.' Simi shoved the menus back. 'Two bloody Caesars. And the wine. Hurry with the wine.'

'Watch your tone. We've got zero tolerance for staff abuse here.'

'I'm sorry. I'm having a bad day.'

Once the waitress had trudged off, Boo started babbling. 'He won't talk to me. He can't look at me. And poor Sofia, she knows something's wrong. She's so quiet and you know Sofia, she's never quiet. Simi, I can't bear this . . .'

Simi was tempted to give Boo a slap – bring her to her senses. She glanced at the waitress. A slap was a bad idea. Simi was sailing too close to the 'aggressive black woman' stereotype already.

'Boo, breathe . . . Go on, deep breaths. Good. Now have a drink – a long drink. Start at the beginning. Tell me everything.'

It took ages to get the full story out of Boo and it still didn't make sense. Didier had read all the (senseless, moronic) emails Boo hadn't deleted. And not just emails from her boss (bad enough) but the (nasty, thoughtless) messages Boo had sent to Isobel. Simi revised her scale – Boo was nine and a half, she was still a two.

'Why didn't you delete them?' Simi asked. But she knew. *Why hadn't she thrown away the leaflet?* She tried to comfort her. 'Didier loves you. You and Sofia are his world. He's hurt. You need to make him realize how sorry you are. He's worth fighting for, Boo. Your family is worth fighting for.' Simi meant every word. Martin was worth fighting for too.

'You don't understand,' said Boo, tears sliding down her face. 'Imagine if this was you and Martin.'

'I would never cheat on Martin.' Simi regretted the words before they'd even left her mouth. 'I'm sorry, that came out wrong.'

'What if he found out about your abortion?' said Boo. 'What if someone told him? How would you feel? How would *he* feel?'

Simi went rigid. She wasn't ready to talk about it. She took a sip of the cheap, over-oaked, urine-coloured wine. She'd never be ready to talk about it. What the hell . . . 'He knows.

He found my pills.' Simi told Boo everything. It didn't make her feel better. It didn't halve the problem. It just made it more real.

'It must have been Ronke.' Boo banged her fists on the table. 'Who else could it be? She must have told him about your shoebox. How could she do this to us?'

Simi was confused. 'How do *you* know about the shoebox?'

'You were laughing about it at Sky Garden – you said it was the only place safe from your stepmother. You called her Bigfoot. Don't you remember?'

'No,' said Simi. 'I'd drunk too much.'

'It was just before Ronke caught us talking about her and Kayode.' Boo tapped her fingers on the table; her eyes were wide. 'Is that why? Some kind of warped revenge?'

'I don't know,' said Simi. 'But I'm going to find out.'

∽

It was a twenty-minute walk to Ronke's flat. Simi made it in fifteen. Her feet, toes crushed into three-inch kitten heels, screamed in protest.

Ronke was in joggers and a baggy jumper. Her springy curls pulled off her face in a tight bun. It didn't suit her. She looked shapeless, tired, drab. Her face was shiny, her chin spotty.

For the second time today, Simi wasn't invited in. 'What do you want?' asked Ronke.

'Martin knows.' Simi studied her face for signs of guilt.

'Good. Secrets aren't healthy.' Ronke moved to close her door.

Simi put her sore foot in the way. 'My marriage is on the rocks. Is this what you wanted?'

'You know what?' said Ronke. 'I don't care.'

'And what about Boo? Or don't you care about her either? She's convinced Didier is going to divorce her. Is that what you want too?'

Ronke sighed. 'I'm not surprised. I hope they work it out. For Sofia's sake.'

'Why are you being so mean?' Simi wanted to shake her. Or punch her.

'Simi, for once this isn't all about you. Please go away. I've got my own problems. You knew Kayode was texting Isobel. You and Boo both knew. You've been treating me like shit for weeks, laughing behind my back, humiliating me in public. We've split up. I hope you're satisfied. You were right.' Tears were running down Ronke's face.

'You can turn off the waterworks,' said Simi. 'It's pathetic. Are you telling me you fucked up my marriage because your boyfriend is a dick? Seriously?'

'Don't you dare. You fucked it up all by yourself,' said Ronke. 'And you can tell Isobel she's welcome to Kayode.'

'Is that it? All this, because you're jealous of Isobel?'

'I'm not jealous of her, I'm sick of her. There's been nothing but *wahala* since she arrived. Your dad was right about her. Now go. Just go.' Ronke slammed the door.

∽

THE LAST THING SIMI NEEDED was small talk with Ebenezer. But he was in the foyer and escape was impossible.

'*Salaam alaikum*, Mrs Simi. How is Mr Martin? When is he coming next?'

'Fine. Soon.' Simi glanced at the stairwell, but her feet were killing her. Six flights would finish them off. She headed for the lift, hoping Ebenezer wouldn't follow. He did.

'I have good news – my wife has finished her chemical treatment. Yesterday I cooked *thiéboudienne* and she ate well for the first time since it started. We added some of Sister Ronke's pepper sauce – she is such a kind lady. When she brought the cakes for Mr Martin, she gave me two jars and some ginger tea for my Amanita. She recommended it for the nausea; it was very effective. Please thank her for me.'

Simi's ears roared and she felt a surge of hatred for Ronke. Cupcakes. Pepper sauce. Ginger tea. Spite. She gritted her teeth and willed Ebenezer to shut up. She pressed the lift button.

'It was so busy that day,' Ebenezer prattled on. 'First Sister Ronke – we had a nice discussion; she is excited about her trip to Lagos. Then after my lunch break, that other friend came. She is not so nice.'

'Who? Which other friend?' Simi stopped jabbing the lift button and turned to face him.

'The flash one.'

'You mean Isobel?'

'The one with the big car and the bodyguard. She gave me an envelope and instructed me to give it to Mr Martin in person and only him. She was very rude – shouting as if I am stupid. I am not. I am used to handling important deliveries.'

'Did you give it to him?'

'Of course. I have not misplaced one parcel in over twelve years. I gave him the cake from Sister Ronke and also the envelope.'

'And you're sure it was the same day?' Something fizzed in Simi's brain. 'Ebenezer . . . are you sure?'

'Yes. Of course. I keep a record in my desk. Let me show you?'

It was ten minutes before Simi could get away. Ebenezer took her through his logbook (spidery writing, inordinate detail). He talked about his children, all six of them, and the holiday in Senegal they were planning once Amanita got the all-clear. The whole time he was talking, Simi's mind was racing. When he stopped for breath, she made her excuses and ran. She took the stairs, feet be damned – this had to be done now.

Boo called before Simi got to the sixth floor, desperate to know what Ronke had said. Simi tried to get her off the phone, but she wouldn't stop ranting. 'I never want to see her again,' said Boo. 'Now I know what Isobel meant. It makes sense.'

'What?'

'She said we're all single.'

Simi paused for a long time.

'You still there?' asked Boo.

'I'll call you later.' Simi rushed into her flat, threw the phone on the sofa, freed her feet from their kitten-heel traps and picked up her laptop.

Dear Dad,

I know we never really talk but this is important.

Strange things are happening. I need to know what you meant when you said I shouldn't associate with

Isobel. I know you fell out with her father. Was it just
about work? Is there something you haven't told me?

And I should have said this years ago . . . I'm sorry I
let you down by dropping out of medical school. I
know you think it was a terrible mistake. But it was the
right thing for me, and you have to let it go. I'm tired of
being ashamed – it's weighing me down. You have to
forgive me, so I can forgive myself.

Love
Simisola

Simi pressed send. She felt a bit heady.

∽

SIMI STAYED UP UNTIL THREE A.M. No reply. Nothing. She knew
she could, should, stop torturing herself. All she had to do was
pick up the phone. But her father had a knack for reducing her
to a recalcitrant teenager – monosyllabic and defensive.

The next morning, she was full of regrets, wishing she
could unsend the email. By the time he finally called at midday, she'd given up. She took a deep breath. 'Dad.'

'Simisola, *ololufe mi*. I just saw your message – I don't
check my emails. You should have used WhatsApp. That's
the best way to reach me. You know we don't always have
electricity – I can't be charging the computer every time.'

'Sorry, Dad, it doesn't matter.' Typical. He'd turned a plea
for help into a critique of her communication skills.

'No. You must listen to me. Your email made me sad, Simisola, and humbled. I would not change one single hair on your

head. I am so proud of you. I am always telling Tosan and Temisan they should follow in your footsteps. You have always been so self-sufficient, so independent, so generous. It is me who let you down. I am a fool – an old fool – and that's the worst kind. I should have supported you when you left Bristol, but I was too arrogant. Every day I regret the way I handled it. Simisola, I am so sorry. It is you who must forgive me.'

Dad sounded emotional. He didn't do emotional. Simi had never heard him say 'sorry'. Ever. She felt her cheeks – they were wet. She didn't do crying. 'I'm sorry, Dad. I should have talked to you. I should have been honest.'

'No, this is my fault,' said Dad.

They spent a few minutes trying to outdo each other in claiming blame and apologizing. Finally Simi said, 'Dad, I need to know about Isobel. What did you mean when you said they weren't good people?'

'It's not something I wish to discuss with you.'

'Please, Dad. This is important.'

There was a long silence. And then he cleared his throat. 'It concerns your friend, Ronke. Her father's death was not an accident. He was having an affair with Irina and when Dele found out, he had him killed. He bragged about it to me. Boasting, banging his chest. I told him I could not work for a murderer and he laughed at me. But I wasn't brave enough to go to the police. I am a coward.'

'Oh, Dad.' Simi felt a rush of pity for her father. All those years he'd been hiding his shame, putting on a front. They were so alike. 'And that's why you lost your business?'

'*Ehn*. When you met Ronke in university, I was overjoyed. *Ah-ah!* I fasted for three days. It was a sign that God had forgiven me. He sent my beloved child to protect Ronke. To compensate for my failure.'

'But why didn't you tell me?'

'I was ashamed. I didn't do anything and still I lost every-thing. But you won't make the same mistakes I made. You are smart.'

'Hmmm,' said Simi.

'Those Babangaris are rotten to the core. You be careful, Simisola.'

Simi raked a hand through her hair. So Isobel's father really was a beast. Could Isobel have inherited his passion for revenge? 'OK, Dad.'

'Simisola, I am not even joking, *o*! Listen to me: I am your father. I am still the head of this family. She is a bad apple. From a bad tree. Don't see her again!'

'I promise, Dad. I have to go. I love you.' Simi had no intention of seeing Isobel again. But she had to see Ronke. She owed her that much. She couldn't do it on her own though. She needed Boo.

31

RONKE

RONKE PULLED UP HER fat jeans (thank goodness she'd kept them) and shrugged on a baggy sweater (long enough to cover her tummy). They'd have to take her as they found her, miserable and sorry for herself. She'd tried to get out of it, knew she'd be shitty company, but Rafa had insisted. 'You're not spending Saturday night on your own and that's final,' he'd said. 'Besides, we need you. We've got a new paella pan and no idea how to use it. You'll be doing us a favour.'

While Rafa was a glutton for punishment, Ronke was just a glutton. 'Eating your feelings' was a real thing. And crappy, shitty feelings craved crappy, shitty food. Ronke had done heart-break binges before – she knew how it worked: wallow in memories, listen to love songs, stuff your face with ice cream and chocolate. But she'd never done it on her own. She'd always had Boo and Simi beside her.

Boo would prescribe fresh air, frogmarch her on enforced walks, smuggle salads into her fridge and tell her she never liked him anyway.

Simi could be relied on to find an upside (lucky escape – your kids would have had bowlegs), make her laugh, convince her she deserved better and bully her into going dancing – which always made her feel good.

Being betrayed by Kayode was horrendous. Being stabbed in the back by her two best friends was almost worse.

Ronke caught her reflection and flinched. You are what you eat, as Boo would have said. Which made Ronke a take-away pizza (the kind that left an oil slick in the box), a polystyrene carton of egg-fried rice from the dodgy end of Queenstown Road (salty, synthetic and sickly), or a fried chicken thigh from a dive called Cluck Me Up (which had somehow managed to be both soggy and dry).

Ronke knew she was being melodramatic, but she couldn't help it. She could cope with work – in fact the routine was helpful. When she snapped on her gloves, pulled the straps of her mask behind her ears and put on her loupes, she could forget about Kayode. But outside work there was nothing. She'd go home, collapse on the sofa (in her scrubs, why bother changing) and cry. She kept the TV on, sound off. She didn't look at the flickering images, she just wanted to know they were there.

She had tried her damnedest to make Kayode 'the one'. Ignored the fact that she did all the heavy lifting in their rela-tionship, airbrushed his flaws, oversold his positives, forgave him when she shouldn't and defended him to her friends. It had almost worked – she'd convinced herself he was perfect.

Ending it had been the right decision, but she still felt bereft. She was never going to find a man as good as her father. He didn't exist.

She started blubbing as soon as she got to Rafa's. It was the kindness that did it. Seeing Luca at the window, looking out for her. Rafa opening the door before she got to the bell. They cared. They thought she was worth investing in. It disarmed her.

And as tears sometimes do, these helped. Soon Rafa was crying too. Luca passed them tissues and dabbed his own eyes. When Ronke pulled herself together, she felt lighter. 'I'm hungry,' she said. 'We need to stop blubbing and start cooking.'

They let her take over the kitchen. It was obvious they'd planned it and their thoughtfulness made her eyes fill again. 'Onions,' she said. 'It's the onions. Happens every time.' Ronke realized she'd missed cooking. She thought of all the awful things she'd eaten, disappointed in herself. If you were going to put on a stone in two weeks, at least let it be with food you love. *Ewa agoyin*, coconut rice, steak and kidney pie, scones with jam and clotted cream.

Ronke scooped the fried chorizo out of the paella pan. She chucked in the diced onions, stirred them till they were coated with delicious orange oil. 'Kayode turned up again last night,' she said.

'Did you let him in?' asked Rafa.

'No. Well, not really. Lisa must have buzzed him in. He banged on my door for five minutes – I watched him on the CCTV. He looked demented, veins popping on his forehead. I had to open it – I didn't want another encounter with the police.'

'Poor Kayode,' said Rafa.

'Don't you dare!' Ronke laughed for the first time in ages. She added three handfuls of bomba rice to the onions, stirred and added a fourth. You always needed one for the pot. 'That's when I realized it was truly over.'

'Why? What happened?'

'Nothing. I didn't look in the mirror. I didn't try and make myself pretty. And I looked like shit – in my scrubs with dried-up noodles down my front, shiny face, red eyes, crazy hair. But I didn't care.'

'What did he say?'

'The same old stuff. I love you, blah, blah, blah. Isobel is lying, she's obsessed with me, blah, blah, blah. I can't let you go, blah, blah, blah.' Ronke shelled the prawns – twisted their heads off, peeled back their shells. She twisted one prawn more aggressively than necessary and it split in two. 'I told him I didn't love him. And he left.'

'Brutal,' said Luca.

'Poor Kayode,' said Rafa.

Ronke added a ladle of stock to the rice, then placed the prawns and strips of red pepper on top. She tore off a strip of foil, tucked it over the pan and turned the heat down. 'Ten minutes. I'll make a salad dressing. Did I tell you Simi came round?'

'To apologize?' asked Rafa.

'No! To shout at me.' Ronke was still in a state of disbelief about Simi. 'She accused me of wrecking her marriage. I told her she did that all by herself. Then she said I was jealous of Isobel. I was so angry, I kicked her out.'

'What a bitch,' said Luca.

Ronke stayed over. Rafa tucked her up in their spare room with a hot water bottle. She dreamed of Dad. He told her she didn't need a man – she was enough.

∽

RONKE HAD SWITCHED OFF HER mobile at Rafa's and hadn't turned it back on – she'd heard enough of Kayode's lies. She got home to find her answerphone blinking madly.

Three messages from Kayode: 'Please pick up.' (*Nope. Even if I was in.*) 'I don't know what else to do.' (*Piss off.*) 'We need to talk, I don't want to go to Lagos without you.' (*You should have thought of that before.*) Delete. Delete. Delete.

A confused message from Didier. She listened to it twice and it still didn't make sense. He was off to France with Sofia and wanted to say thank you before he left. For what? Sofia's Christmas present was still sitting on Ronke's coffee table; she hadn't wrapped it yet. And why were they going to France now? They always went on Christmas Eve. Why was *he* calling instead of Boo? Delete.

A message from Aunty K checking Ronke was still on for Sunday lunch and asking her to bring baking soda, which meant she was making okra soup. Ronke was dreading telling her she wouldn't be coming to Lagos for Christmas after all. *Sorry, Aunty K – I'm single. Again. I picked the wrong bloke. Again. I failed the relationship test. Again.* Still, okra soup would help numb the pain. Delete.

A message from Isobel. Upbeat and chirpy. 'Hey, Ronks! Where are you? I've called your mobile five times! Why aren't you home? I thought you might want to go out, take your mind off things. Kayode is still hounding me, by the way. Boo and Simi have gone AWOL and I need someone to have fun with. Say you'll be my *alobam*. Please call me. Any time. Bye. Oh, it's Iso.' Ronke felt sick. The woman was off her rocker. Certifiable. Delete.

The last message was from Simi. 'Ronks, I know you're

angry with me and you have every right. But we need to talk. There's something you have to know about Isobel. I've been talking to Boo. We love you, Ronks. Please call.' What was wrong with them? Kayode, Boo, Simi – all obsessed with bloody Isobel. *Leave me alone*. Delete.

∽

RONKE BLURTED OUT THE WHOLE story to Aunty K within minutes of arriving. 'Turns out I was wrong. Kayode didn't love me.' Tears were running down her cheeks; she dabbed at them with a tissue. 'I don't think I'll ever meet someone as good as Dad.' She couldn't keep the whine out of her voice.

Aunty K enveloped her in a bear hug. 'Little Ronke! Are you crying? Stop it *now-now*. Don't be wasting tears on that *oloshi*. He's a fool. *Ehn*, let him vamoose. Useless *yeye* boy. It's even good, better to find out now. Come and help me chop the okra.'

Aunty K was a feeder. She believed that a good meal cured all ills, even heartbreak, and she was always on Ronke's side. But she was very particular about how okra should be cut. No way could you use a food processor or a box grater. It had to be done by hand, one finger at a time. And you had to have a mix of sizes – a few thin slices, some little chunks, but most of it had to be diced so finely it was practically a purée.

As Ronke chopped, Aunty K ranted. '*Ehn*, let him go with that other woman. She can even keep him. What is her name, *sef*?'

'Isobel,' said Ronke. 'You met her at Sofia's party. Boo's carbon copy, remember? Isobel Babangari.'

'Adams,' said Aunty K. 'You said Adams.'

Her tone was off. Ronke stopped chopping. Aunty K looked older. Her face was still smooth (a thick layer of Mac Studio Fix hid her wrinkles) and her hair (a wig) was glossy black and helmet-like as usual. But her eyes were different. Fearful. Old people's eyes. She was going to be sixty-five next year – but life expectancy in Nigeria was fifty-four. Ronke recalled the blood pressure tablets and felt a wave of panic. 'Are you OK, Aunty K?'

'Ronke, leave the okra. There is something I must tell you. I should have told you a long time ago.' Aunty K's voice cracked. 'I loved my brother but he was a weak man. That Russian *ashewo*, she bewitched him. She must have used Soviet *juju*. Meeting her was the biggest mistake of my brother's life. It got him killed.'

'What do you mean?' asked Ronke. 'Dad died in a carjacking.'

'*Ehn.*' Aunty K sucked her teeth. 'They made it look like a random attack, but it was murder. Everyone knew Mr Babangari had orchestrated it. As your father used to say, God rest him, in Nigeria, you can get away with murder as long as you are rich enough. Mr Babangari was above the law. The police told me if I had any sense, I would shut up before I suffered the same fate. In those days the police were corrupt.' Aunty K hissed again. 'They are no better now.'

'I don't understand.' Ronke listened as Aunty K ripped the last good thing in her life to shreds. Her perfect dad was a lie. The man she had idolized all her life was a cheat. He was sleeping with another man's wife. He had planned to abandon Mum, Ayo and her. He'd broken Mum's heart before he died.

Tears rolled down Ronke's cheeks as she thought of her mum. All the times she'd accused her of being cold and callous. 'Did Ayo know?' she asked.

'Yes. Yes. He and your mama had too much to deal with,' said Aunty K.

'Why didn't anyone tell me?'

'Little Ronke, you loved him so much. We didn't want to hurt you.' Aunty K put her arms around her. 'I blame myself. I knew what my brother was doing. Poor Mary. She suffered so much. I do not blame her for not associating with me.'

Ronke wriggled out of the embrace. *No*, she thought. *But I did. And you let me.* For the first time in her life, Aunty K couldn't comfort her.

32

BOO

It was amazing how new routines, like your husband sleeping on the sofa and avoiding all eye contact, could become bearable. Normal even.

Didier was civil to Boo in front of Sofia. The highlight of yesterday's dialogue: 'Pass the mustard.' When Sofia went to bed, he retired to the snug – his new bedroom. If she joined him, he turned up the TV.

They lived like single parents. Two single parents who happened to share a house and a child. They ate together, but she knew Didier was only doing that for Sofia's sake. He made sure he was awake before her, shoved his nest (pillow, sheet, blanket) into the wardrobe and took his clothes into the shower. Didier, who used to drive her mad walking around in boxers, had turned into a prude. He was never naked any more. *Tubby hubby with his pasty flabby belly.* Boo hated herself for making her husband hate himself.

The only topic that interested him was Neil. He had so many questions, was morbidly obsessed – wanted details. Sordid details. Boo knew that telling him would make him feel worse, make it harder to move on, so she clammed up. He'd swear, in French. They'd go back to silence.

Boo had a new calendar – BR and AR – before and after Ronke destroyed her marriage. She couldn't stop thinking about her. Ronke who'd been her maid of honour (she'd sobbed at the vows). Who'd been there when Sofia was born (much more useful than Didier – he'd thrown up). Ronke, who'd been her best friend for as long as she could remember, had turned into a back-stabbing traitor. She made the mistake of telling Didier how she felt. 'I blame Ronke. She shouldn't have told you. She betrayed me. I don't think I can forgive her.'

'Betrayal!' he shouted back. 'Are you seriously preaching about betrayal and forgiveness? Ronke is a good person. This is not her fault.'

On Day Three AR, Boo resigned by email. In a short cold message, she told Neil she'd be working her notice from home. He didn't argue. The next day she got confirmation from HR and three months' pay in lieu of notice. Smart Neil.

When a courier delivered a jiffy bag stuffed with her bits (framed photo of Didier and Sofia, *J'aime Maman* mug, box of tampons), it felt like closure. It had been so easy. Why hadn't she done it weeks ago? *Like Ronke told you to*, said an unhelpful voice in her head.

That evening, Boo rushed through Sofia's bedtime so she could tell Didier. She snatched the remote control before he could drown her out. 'I've resigned. I'll never see him again. It's over. It's time to go back to normal.'

Silence. She expected him to be pleased. Or at least relieved. 'Didier . . . say something. Please.'

'Normal? Back to being trapped here with me, the tubby hubby?' He grabbed his coat and stormed out.

He came home at two, collected his nest and went to the snug. Boo was awake, waiting, but he didn't look at her.

There was another change in their 'separate but together' life. Cleaning. Boo heard Didier scrubbing the loo each time he used it. She knew why. *I'm not sure who's less toilet-trained – husband or daughter. LOL.* It wasn't funny. It was tragic.

On Day Five AR, Sofia stumbled into their bedroom at some ungodly hour and found Boo alone. '*Où est Papa?*' she howled. '*Où est Papa?*'

Didier appeared, bleary-eyed, in a long-sleeved sweatshirt and old joggers. 'I'm here, *mon bébé.*' He didn't even sleep naked any more. Boo felt the weight of the damage she'd caused; it crushed her.

'Where were you, Papa? Why weren't you here?' Sofia snivelled. 'Why don't you love Mama any more?'

Didier climbed into bed, with Sofia in the middle as a human barrier. He looked at Boo, their first eye contact in days. 'I couldn't sleep, *mon bébé*. Of course Papa loves Mama. And we both love you.'

After that they were back in the same bed. Not touching. Not talking. But it was progress. Until he dropped the bombshell.

On Saturday morning, Didier gave Sofia his iPad, shut her in the snug and made his announcement. 'We're going to France on Monday. I've booked the flights. I don't care if there's a fine for taking her out of school four days early. I need a break. I'm not asking.'

'That's a great idea.' Boo was thrilled. At last, a thaw. 'Yes! Yes! It's exactly what we all need.'

Didier raised his arms, palms out. 'Not you. Me and Sofia. It's you I need to get away from. I need space. And the tension isn't good for Sofia.'

Boo's stomach contracted; it felt like the air was being sucked out of her. 'But what will you tell your parents? What will we say to Sofia?'

'I'm sure you can come up with a lie,' said Didier.

Boo winced and Didier became almost kind. He told her he loved her but was buckling under the strain. He wanted to go home.

'But this is your home,' she said. 'It's our home.'

'I know,' he said. 'I'm struggling, Boo. Please don't make this difficult.'

'I feel so horrible about what I've done,' she said.

'I'm glad,' he replied.

'Didier . . .' Boo sank on to the sofa.

'It means you care. And I want you to care.'

'I don't want you to go. I love you. I'll do anything to make things right.'

'Then let me and Sofia go to France. It's not for ever. Just two weeks.'

So Boo pretended she understood. What else could she do? They invented a story – Mama had to work on a big project, so Sofia got to go on a special adventure with Papa. She was excited about spending *Noël en France avec Mamie et Papy*. Boo tried not to take it personally, but failed – she felt unloved and unwanted. She listened to them chatter (in

French) about the fun they would have without her. Most of it she couldn't understand, which somehow made it worse.

Worst of all, Didier seemed happier since the announcement. He was nicer to her, made eye contact, smiled (once or twice) and resumed bringing her a mug of tea in the morning. The thought of leaving her had cheered him up.

∽

BOO SOMEHOW MANAGED TO HOLD things together until they left. She had to. For Sofia's sake. But once they'd gone, her thoughts bounced around the empty house. She felt lost. Cut adrift.

She tried to work out why she'd done it. What had she thought was missing? What had she resented so much? Was it cleaning? Had she fucked her life up because she hated vacuuming? Was it because her husband and daughter sometimes chatted in French? Because she only worked two days a week? Had it not occurred to her to get a cleaner, take French lessons, change jobs?

All that time wasted, thinking she didn't belong. Now Boo ached for the two people she belonged to. She wanted to be imprisoned by Didier and Sofia. She wanted her old life back. Didier used to call her his down-to-earth Yorkshire lass. But was she? Or was she all take and no give? Just like her absent father.

Boo tried to see Simi. She suggested coffee, dinner, drinks, chill at mine or at yours – but Simi had retreated into her shell. Boo knew she regretted telling her about Martin. Simi couldn't bear it when people weren't dazzled by how wonderful her life was; she despised sympathy.

The one person who kept calling was the one person Boo didn't want to see. Isobel. In the unlikely event that Didier asked what she'd done today, she could hardly say, 'Oh, I met Isobel. But don't worry, I didn't slag you off.'

Boo knew she couldn't put her off for ever. She hoped Isobel would understand, was pretty sure she wouldn't. She plucked up the courage, put on her big-girl pants as Sofia would have said, and arranged to meet her at the White Lion.

When she arrived, Isobel eyed the room in contempt. 'What made you pick this dump? It smells of damp dog. And why have you been avoiding me after all I've done for you? What's wrong with all of you? Nobody wants to come and play.'

'We've all got stuff going on. Going wrong would be more accurate.' Saying it out loud made it hit home – all three of them imploding at the same time. It had never happened before. Ronke's love life was always a rollercoaster but Simi and Martin never wobbled (or if they did, no one knew), and she and Didier were the most boring couple in the world. Or they used to be.

Isobel rolled her eyes. 'Tubs still sulking?'

'Don't call him that.' Boo was regretting this already. 'He's gone to France with Sofia. It's awful. I'm not sleeping. I miss them so much.'

'You let him kidnap your daughter!' Isobel was apoplectic. 'You're so stupid. He's going to want custody. I told you to lawyer up.'

'I don't need a lawyer. We're not getting divorced. What's wrong with you?'

'There's nothing wrong with me,' said Isobel. 'You're the stupid one.'

'Isobel, you're talking about my family. We're going to work this out.'

Isobel wasn't interested. She launched into an inquisition on Simi. Was she still going to New York? Had she said anything about Martin?

'I don't know. I haven't seen her,' Boo lied.

'Last time I saw her she made out everything was fine, but I know she was faking,' said Isobel. 'She's hiding something. And now she's avoiding me.'

'She's probably busy at work,' said Boo.

Isobel changed tack, moved on to Ronke. 'She must be devastated. Maybe she'll lose some weight – God knows she needs to. Do you think she'll take Kayode back?'

'I haven't spoken to her,' Boo said truthfully.

'I don't blame you after what she did. Well, at least with Tubs away, you can play. Tonight! I'll pick you up. Eight?'

Boo put her hands on her knees to stop them from trembling. 'Isobel, the thing is . . . it's why I called.' She hesitated again, clenched her teeth and went for it. 'I can't meet you any more. I need to put Didier's feelings first.'

Isobel's nostrils flared. 'What are you trying to say? Are you unfriending me? How fucking dare you!'

Boo looked away. 'I'm sorry. Please try and understand. You'll always remind Didier of those awful messages.' She snuck a glance at Isobel; her eyes were stony. 'I've got to get my marriage back on track. You must be able to see that.'

'You ungrateful little bitch!' Isobel exploded. 'I treated you like a sister. I took you under my wing, wasted my time and money trying to raise you out of your miserable little life with your fat wimp of a husband and your ugly brat of a child. I should have known better. You're nothing. Just another coconut bastard. I wish you unluck for the rest of your pathetic life.' She stood up, the veins in her temple pulsing, then leaned over and shouted into Boo's face. 'How dare you choose him over me? You don't get to leave me. I decide! And I'm dumping you.'

And then she flounced off, leaving a quaking Boo to pay the bill.

∽

Boo was still in shock hours later. No one had ever spoken to her like that. She'd actually felt scared. Had Isobel always despised her? Boo remembered something she'd read in a journal about people who could switch empathy on and off. Was Isobel a psychopath?

When the bell rang, Boo peered through the peephole to check it was Simi. She started ranting as soon as she opened the door. 'You won't believe the things Isobel said. She called me a bitch, said Sofia was ugly. She wished me unluck! Is that a Nigerian curse? She was screaming. Everyone was looking. I was mortified.' Boo expected Simi to be astonished but she wasn't. Simi had news of her own.

Simi was stuffing Oreos down her face. Crunch, crunch, swallow. She'd already demolished three mini bags of Haribo – more sugar than Boo had seen her eat in all the time she'd known her.

'It's my fault,' Simi kept repeating. 'It's all my fault. She's a manipulative bitch. She wanted us to be single so we'd need her, so she'd be the centre of our world.'

Boo's view of Nigerian men, gleaned from her absent father, Ronke's ex-boyfriends and Aunty K's stories, had always been dim. They lied, they cheated, they shirked their responsibilities, they disappeared. But what Simi told her was batshit crazy.

As Simi demolished cookies, Boo processed the facts: Ronke's father and Isobel's mother had an affair. When Isobel's father found out, he had Ronke's father murdered. And because he was loaded, he bribed the police and got away with it. 'Bloody hell. Poor Ronke. Does she know?'

'No,' Simi answered between mouthfuls. 'I've left loads of messages but she's not calling me back. And there's more.'

'What?'

'I know it was Isobel who told Martin I was still on the pill. And I'm sure she sent Didier that text. I don't know how, but I know it was her.' Simi crunched the last Oreo.

'It was from Ronke,' said Boo. 'I saw it with my own eyes.'

'It was from her phone. But did she send it? Think about it. Did Ronke even know about the emails?'

Boo's knees started bouncing again. 'Isobel saw the emails. She wanted to read them and I let her. Ronke didn't know, of course she didn't. I've been so stupid.'

'Isobel's brilliant at getting people to talk, pretending she cares. It's all an act. She messed with our heads,' said Simi. 'And it's all my fault. I let her in.'

Boo wanted it to be Simi's fault. Without her, she wouldn't have met Isobel. She wanted it to be Isobel's fault. Without Isobel, she wouldn't have had a jumpsuit, a wrap dress, sexy underwear, a fucking Afro. She wouldn't have slept with Neil. She wanted it to be anyone's fault except hers. 'She made me hate my life. But why? Why did she do it?'

'I don't know,' said Simi. 'It's like my dad said: Never trust a Babangari. He said she's a bad apple. He was right.'

Boo heard her blood whooshing in her ears. 'What did you say?'

'Dad. He says the whole family is rotten to the core.'

'No!' Boo leapt up and wobbled. She had to hold on to the island. 'Not that. What's Isobel's dad's name?'

'Babangari.'

'That's a common name. Right? Like Kayode? Or Martin?' Boo asked desperately.

'What are you on about?' Simi scrunched up the empty biscuit packet. 'Is there anything else in Sofia's stash?'

'Simi! I need to know.' Boo grabbed Simi by the shoulders. 'Babangari. It's the Nigerian equivalent of Smith. Or Jones. There are loads of them. Yes?'

'No,' said Simi. 'Calm down. It's an unusual name. Iso used to brag how she was the only young Babangari. Not true any more, of course – her father sired a whole stable of bastards.'

Boo felt the room spin. 'What's her father's first name?'

'Dele. Dele Babangari. You sure you don't have any chocolate?'

Boo couldn't speak. She couldn't breathe. Isobel had known for months. She'd quizzed her about her father. All this time, she knew they were half-sisters. 'I need to pack. Come on – you can help.'

'Where are you going?' asked Simi.

Boo headed up the stairs. She was going to get her life back. She wasn't related to Isobel. She wasn't a Babangari. She was Didier's Yorkshire lass. 'I'm going to France. I need to be with my family.'

'Good,' said Simi. 'But we have to see Ronke first. We've treated her like shit. I can't do it on my own. We both owe her.'

Boo grabbed a bag and chucked clothes in randomly. She slid the jumpsuit off its hanger; it was going in the bin. 'I'm sorry, I can't. I've got to go now. You'll be fine.' Boo couldn't think about anyone else. Ronke and Simi were Nigerians – they'd grown up with this kind of madness. Her eyes settled on the Ife head. 'Simi, can you put this disgusting statue in the outside bin? Please? I can't bear to touch it.'

'Are you OK, Boo?' asked Simi.

'No, I'm not,' said Boo. 'I need my husband and my child. Tell Ronke I'm sorry. Tell her I love her.'

33

SIMI

Simi bundled Boo into an airport-bound Uber and set off for Ronke's alone. She wasn't sure she'd be let in, had no idea of what she'd say if she was. She dragged her feet, trying to work out where to start, but there was no template for the conversation they were about to have.

It turned out that Simi had worried for nothing. Aunty K had got there first. Ronke was eerily tranquil. She seemed to have short-circuited the five stages of grief (or were there seven?) and gone straight to acceptance. And in classic Ronke style was more worried about everyone else. Her mum ('I've been awful to her'), Aunty K ('She meant well, she tried to protect me'), Boo ('I'm so glad she's gone to France; I'll call her tonight') and Simi ('You should be in New York; you have to sort things out with Martin').

Ronke even managed to find sympathy for Isobel. 'What chance did she have with a father like that? She must be terribly unhappy. I hope she gets help – God knows she needs it.'

Simi tried to convince Ronke to talk to Kayode, give him a chance to explain. But Ronke wouldn't budge. 'He lied to me. He didn't trust me with the truth,' she said. 'Anyway, he's off to Nigeria next week – maybe when he gets back.' Simi didn't push it. She was hardly in a position to give relationship advice.

They went over it again and again, trying to make sense of it all. Ronke was astounded to learn that Isobel's mother was alive and well, and living in Moscow. 'I don't get how anyone could lie about their mum being dead. She had me fooled – there were real tears in her eyes.'

'She's a monster,' said Simi.

'It's over. We never need to see her again.'

Simi rubbed her eyes. 'All this *wahala* is my fault.'

'Enough.' Ronke put her arms around Simi. 'Nobody died.'

SIMI COULDN'T SIT STILL. THE room was like a low-rent hotel lounge. The fabric on the hideous sofa was scratchy, the coffee lukewarm and acrid. The door sign said, 'Comfort Room'. What did that even mean? Simi didn't feel remotely comforted.

When her phone had rung at 5.45 a.m., she'd lunged for it, her first thought Martin: he's listened to my message, he's ready to talk.

It was an unknown number.

The caller had announced herself as PC something or other. 'Are you a friend of Isobel Babangari-Adams?'

'Um . . . yes?' Simi wanted to say no.

'She's at Belgravia police station. She's asked for you. Can you come over?'

'Now?'

'The sooner the better.'

'What's happened?'

'Isobel will tell you herself. Please get here as soon as you can.'

So Simi called an Uber. What else could she do? She swiped her face with a flannel, threw on jeans, jumper, boots, hat and paced the lobby, waiting for it to arrive.

Simi had ignored Isobel's calls and told Ebenezer not to let her up. She didn't want an explanation (denials and excuses) or a confrontation (justification and insults). And now, as she squirmed on the scratchy sofa in the uncomfortable Comfort Room, she wished for the umpteenth time that Isobel had never found her. Wished the photograph at Asari's wedding hadn't been taken. Wished the police had called someone else. Anyone else.

The door finally opened and Isobel walked in, followed by a uniformed policewoman. Isobel was wearing a blue tunic and trousers; it looked like prison garb. Her feet were bare, her head bowed, her hands behind her back. For a second Simi thought she was handcuffed, but then Isobel looked up, burst into tears and rushed towards her, arms outstretched.

Simi was horrified. Isobel's face was puffy. There was a deep cut on her lip, her left cheek looked raw and her eyes were ringed with smudged makeup. Her always immaculate manicure was wrecked, and there were raw welts on her wrists. Her hair was a state, with a clump ripped out, exposing the cornrows.

Simi suppressed her revulsion and went to her. 'What happened? Who did this to you?' No one deserved this. Not even

Isobel. As Simi put her arm gently around her shoulders, Isobel keened like an injured animal.

The officer helped manoeuvre Isobel into one of the nasty chairs. 'Isobel, sit here for a few minutes while I talk to your friend.' She gestured for Simi to follow her. 'I'm WPC Simkins,' she said once the door was closed. 'I've been looking after Isobel. She's seen a doctor and been given painkillers. She can't go home for a few hours, not till the SOCOs are done. Can she stay with you?'

Simi hesitated, hearing Dad's warning in her head. 'Um, yes. I guess.'

'Good. Can I call you Simi?'

'Yes. Whatever. Was it her ex?'

'Yes, it was. I'm sure Isobel will tell you everything. She's been through a traumatic ordeal and has been helping us for the last five hours. She's been so strong. Right now, she needs a friend.'

'Of course,' said Simi. Isobel, always strong and in control, was crumpled and broken. Simi couldn't abandon her in this state, it would be inhumane.

'I've got an officer on standby to take you home. I need to confirm a few details; it won't take long.'

Back in the room, Simi wriggled out of her coat and draped it around Isobel's shoulders. Simi sat on the arm of her chair and rubbed her back. 'You're going to be fine, Iso. I've got you.'

WHEN THEY GOT TO SIMI'S, the policeman escorted them to her front door. He reminded her of Vadim, although half his age and width. *Where was Vadim? Wasn't it his job to protect Isobel from Chase?*

Once they were inside, Isobel spoke for the first time. 'I need a shower.'

'Of course, come on. In here.' Simi led her to the spare room, opened the en suite and turned the shower on. 'There's plenty of hot. I'll go and find you something to wear.' She rifled through her wardrobe and realized she didn't want Isobel in her clothes. She pushed away the thought and pulled out a vest, socks and knickers, then yanked out a pair of old joggers and a sweatshirt from Martin's drawers. She grabbed a few toiletries and went back to the spare room. 'I'll leave some stuff here. Take your time.' There was no answer but at least she couldn't hear crying.

Simi wanted to tell Ronke but didn't want Isobel to over-hear. It was nearly eight – Ronke would be on her way to work. She bashed out a text.

Ronks. Something terrible has happened. I've just picked Iso up from the police station. Chase has beaten her to a pulp. She's in a proper state. I don't want her here but what else could I do? Sx

Ronke's reply was instant.

Oh my God! Poor thing. Of course you have to look after her. I've got back to backs all morning, I'll call you at lunch. Rxxx

Simi filled the kettle and pulled out two mugs. Changed her mind and grabbed the brandy. When Isobel emerged, she looked tiny – drowned by Martin's clothes. Her wet hair clung to her neck like rats' tails. Pared down and dressed in faded cotton, she looked a little like Boo.

'Here, let me.' Simi lowered Isobel on to the sofa and

towelled her hair softly. She draped a throw around her shoulders and handed her a brandy. 'Drink this. You need it. God knows I do.'

'Oh, Simi, it was so awful,' whispered Isobel. 'He wouldn't stop hurting me. I was sure I was going to die. I didn't mean to kill him. I just wanted him to stop.'

Simi's hand wobbled and brandy dribbled on to her white sofa. She ignored it. 'Isobel, what happened?'

'It wasn't my fault. He said he had to talk to me. To put things right. He sounded so desperate.' Isobel sipped the brandy. 'Vadim had the night off and you know I don't go out on my own. So I told him to come over. It didn't cross my mind he could do this. I wanted to do the right thing. I've been so lonely. None of you talk to me any more.'

Simi raised her eyebrows but Isobel took no notice. Now she'd started talking, she couldn't stop. She could tell he'd been drinking, offered him a coffee but he insisted on a beer. Then he pounced, tried to kiss her. Grabbed at her. She pushed him away, asked him to leave. But he went crazy. Called her a whore. Said he knew what she wanted. Then he slapped her. So hard her teeth rattled. She was terrified. He dragged her across the room. By her hair. 'Look at it!' Isobel pawed at her head. 'He was deranged, Simi. And so strong. You know how big he is.'

Simi didn't have a clue how big Chase was. 'Oh my God,' she said, covering her mouth in horror.

'I screamed at him to stop. Begged him. He laughed at me. Then he grabbed my head and smashed it into the wall. Everything went black. When I came to, he was on top of me.' Isobel sniffed.

Simi patted her back, like you would a small dog. Her damp hair pressed into Simi's face. Simi wanted to pull away but didn't. 'It's not your fault.'

But Isobel hadn't finished. There was more, and it was worse. He started to strangle her. Somehow she had managed to grab the Ife head and swung it. She was scared she wouldn't be strong enough. But she was. She swung it again. And again. Until he stopped. 'There was so much blood,' she said, with an ugly twist to her mouth.

Simi didn't want to hear the rest, but Isobel kept talking. She called the police. They seemed to take for ever. She had to tell them every sickening detail. They made her stand on a sheet and undress in front of a nurse. They'd bagged her clothes like she was the criminal. And they kept asking the same questions. They swabbed her – her lips, her cheeks, her vagina, her arse. It was like being violated all over again. They cut a bit of her hair, scraped under her nails. And they took pictures. She thought it would never end.

Isobel put her hand on Simi's arm. 'Thank you for coming to get me. I didn't know who else to call. I'd never smelled fear before – I didn't know it had a smell. But it does, Simi. And it's disgusting. He reeked of it. I can still smell it. And the blood. Oh, Simi, so much blood.'

Simi recoiled. Something in Isobel's tone was off. Was she bragging? Simi shuffled on the sofa, putting space between them. 'It's over now.'

'Yes, it's over. He's dead.' Isobel poured more brandy into their glasses. 'I know I shouldn't have let him in, but he said he wanted to talk about Ronke.'

Simi gasped. '*Ronke?* What's Ronke got to do with it? Chase has never met Ronke.'

'Chase?' said Isobel. 'Chase is in LA. He wouldn't dare come near me. I can't believe you thought it was Chase. It was Kayode. Kayode King.'

Simi felt herself hyperventilating; she needed air. This didn't make any sense. Why would Kayode attack Isobel? She walked to the balcony. 'Isobel, what have you done?'

Isobel followed her, holding out her wrists, presenting the red welts like a gift. 'Look! He attacked me. *I'm* the victim.'

Simi opened the balcony door with trembling hands. The cold air blasted her face. 'You can't be sure he's dead. Was there an ambulance?'

'Oh, he's dead. I made sure of that,' said Isobel.

Simi tried to make sense of what she was being told. Isobel had killed Kayode. She was practically boasting about it. 'Oh my God, I need to go to Ronke.'

Isobel stepped out on to the narrow balcony, her face inches away from Simi's. 'I'm the one who needs you. I'm your *alobam*. Not her.'

Simi took a step backwards. The aluminium rail dug into her back.

'You look scared,' said Isobel softly, her breath hot against Simi's cold face.

Simi glanced down at Jacob the dray horse, eighty feet below. She imagined herself plummeting past the six balconies, landing broken at Jacob's hooves. She couldn't afford a panic attack. Not now. 'I want you to leave.'

Isobel's eyes were hard. 'Look at your pathetic little face – the same stupid expression as when I got you kicked out of Ikoyi Club. It was so funny watching you scrambling around for your cheap flip-flops, trying to pretend you couldn't hear us laughing. You're a joke.'

Simi felt dizzy with shock. 'You murdered Kayode. You killed him because he chose Ronke.'

'Choices have consequences. Surely you learned that from your stupid father?' There was white spittle in the corner of Isobel's mouth. Her nostrils flared. She took a step forward.

Simi screamed, barged past her and stumbled into the safety of the living room. 'Get out of my flat!'

'You smell of fear too. It's disgusting.' Isobel picked up her purse. 'Now, are you going to tell *poor* Ronke or will you leave that pleasure to me?' Her awful laugh hung in the air long after she slammed the door.

Simi snatched her phone and pressed the buttons frantically. She had to get to Ronke before Isobel did.

34

RONKE

Ronke dropped her phone. As she fumbled to catch it, her shoulder bumped the dental tray. She watched an anaesthetic cartridge glide to the floor, heard the crack as it shattered. The clear liquid seeped over the cream tiles, enough to numb a premolar. She'd heard what Simi said but her brain couldn't process it.

'What's wrong?' Rafa grabbed a wad of napkins, dropped to his haunches and mopped up the mess.

His black scrub trousers hitched up and exposed his bare ankles. *He really should wear socks*, Ronke thought. *He'll catch a cold.* 'Kayode is dead,' she said, her voice flat.

'*Qué quieres decir?*' Rafa leapt up.

'Isobel killed him. That's what Simi said.' Ronke's phone rang again. She didn't move.

Rafa took it out of her hand. 'Hello . . . yes, Simi, she's here . . .' Seconds later he turned to Ronke, his eyes glassy. '*Oh, Dios mío.*'

'So it's true?' Ronke felt foggy; her fingers and toes started to throb.

'I . . .' Rafa stuttered. 'She's on her way here.'

'Mrs Fanshawe is downstairs,' said Ronke robotically. 'I need to fit her temporary onlay.'

'I'll cancel her. I'll cancel everyone. You stay here. Simi won't be long.'

'I don't want Simi.' Ronke staggered to her feet. 'I have to go.'

'Where? I'll come with you.'

'No. I need to be on my own.'

'Call me. Promise you'll call me?' said Rafa. 'Wait, you need your coat. It's freezing.'

Once Ronke got outside, she realized there was nowhere to go. She started walking, one foot in front of the other, no idea where they were taking her. She found herself reciting the Lord's Prayer. *Our father, who art in heaven*. Did God help hypocrites? *Please, God, let him be alive*.

She tried to push away the memory of the last time she'd seen Kayode. He had told her he loved her. Begged her to trust him. The words she had said to him bounced around her head: *I don't love you any more*. Ronke closed her eyes and begged a god she wasn't sure she believed in. *Please. I will do anything. Forgive us our trespasses*.

It made no sense. Why on earth would Isobel kill him? *Deliver us from evil*.

Ronke found herself on a bench in Battersea Park, the Buddhist Peace Pagoda in front of her. She'd sat here with Kayode three weeks ago, planning their Lagos trip. He was supposed to fly tonight. She would have joined him on Christmas Eve. He couldn't be dead.

She fumbled for her phone. 'Yetty, it's me – Ronke.'

Yetty's voice was hoarse from crying. She said what Ronke had been praying not to hear. Kayode was dead.

'I can't understand why he went to her house,' said Yetty.

Ronke curled over herself on the park bench, weeping silently. She should have listened to Simi. She should have gone to him as soon as she found out what a liar Isobel was. But she hadn't.

Yetty told her how Kayode hated Isobel. Worse, he was frightened of her. And now the police were saying he had attacked her. Talking about him as if he were an animal, calling it self-defence. Saying he had a history of violence.

By the end, Yetty's voice was a broken whisper. 'What am I going to tell Mum? She thinks he's coming home tomorrow. Abayomi is working out how to repatriate his body. My brother is a body.'

Ronke gasped for air. Her chest felt tight. She slumped lower on the bench.

'I don't care what the police say,' said Yetty. 'She's lying. She murdered him in cold blood.'

'I know.' Ronke was sure. The only thing she didn't know was why. She rubbed her hands. Her fingers were so cold she couldn't bend them.

Something nagged at her, a fragment of a memory. She tried to grasp it. What had Simi's father said? *Never cross a Babangari.* No, not that. But something about fathers.

The damp cold had seeped into her bones but she didn't move. The memory crystallized. Isobel in her flat, holding the picture. *Don't you hate him for leaving you?* she'd said. Isobel had known who her father was. She'd known all along.

Ronke grabbed her phone. A dozen missed calls from Simi, three from Rafa, two from Isobel. She forced her frozen fingers to work. *Pick up. Please. Pick up.*

'Ronke.' Simi sounded frantic. 'I've been worried sick. I've been to your work. I'm outside your flat now. Where are you?'

'Listen,' said Ronke. 'How did Isobel find you?'

'On Facebook. A picture at Asari's wedding.'

'Was I in it? Was I tagged?'

'Yes. Now please tell me where you are,' pleaded Simi.

Raw righteous rage took hold of Ronke. It froze out the pain, the self-pity, the despair. Isobel had planned this from the start. Was it her sick idea of revenge? For the sins of their fathers? Ronke, who had avoided confrontation all her life, knew what she had to do. She stood up straight; it was as if her blood had turned to ice. 'I'm going to see Isobel,' she said.

'You can't!' Simi's voice was hysterical. 'It's not safe.'

Ronke cut her off and started walking towards Chelsea. It was snowing now but she didn't feel it. She'd spent twenty-five years not knowing why she'd lost her father. That was not going to happen again with the only other man she'd ever truly loved.

⁓

A STRIP OF YELLOW TAPE was tied to one of the ornamental bay trees flanking Isobel's front door. The other end had been ripped free and was fluttering in the swirling snow.

Ronke held her finger down on the plastic bell. She could hear her teeth chattering – clack, clack, clack. Loud enough to drown out the tinny National Anthem. But in spite of the cold, she felt steady.

Vadim led her through to the living room, gestured at the shiny gold sofa, and left.

Ronke remained standing. She was too tightly wound to sit. Her phone rang. She turned it off without looking at the screen.

A dozen photos of an unsmiling murderer stared at her from behind gold rococo frame prisons. Seconds later, another murderer stood before her. Isobel. Holding a bottle of champagne and two glasses. She was smiling.

'Oh, it's you! Sorry I'm not looking my best. My ex – our ex – got a bit overexcited.' Isobel waggled the bottle. 'Drink?'

Ronke didn't answer. She swallowed hard to stop the roaring sensation in her ears.

'Just me, then.' Isobel raised her glass. 'Cheers!'

Ronke's eyes were drawn to the empty plinth. She bit her lip hard and refocused.

Isobel followed Ronke's gaze. 'Ah, the head. Yes, it came in handy. The police have it. I'll send it to you – a little keepsake. I'm afraid it's a bit bloody.' She laughed.

'I know you murdered him.' Ronke was glad to hear her voice was steady.

'Yes!' Isobel beamed. 'But I admit I had a little help.' She tilted her head and stroked her bruised face. 'Vadim did this. He's really earned his Christmas bonus.'

Ronke felt her knees start to buckle. She put one hand on the wall to anchor herself. 'I need to know why.'

'Darling, I did it for you.' Isobel pointed at Ronke with a broken nail. 'The stupid fool begged me to tell you the truth. He kept saying you were the best thing in his life. He was desperate to get you back. Well, obviously I couldn't let that happen. You don't get to be happy. You're as stupid as your father, thinking you can take what belongs to me.'

'You *killed* Kayode because my father and your mother had an affair twenty-five years ago? You're insane.' Ronke spoke slowly, her voice loud and clear. 'I lost Dad. Haven't I suffered enough?'

'No, not nearly enough. Would you like to know why your father died? Me! I made it happen.' Isobel tilted her glass. 'You sure you won't join me?'

Ronke shivered. A million microscopic insects were marching under her skin.

'Fine – I don't mind drinking alone.' Isobel refilled her glass. 'I heard them, you see. She brought him to our house, took him to the bedroom she shared with *my* dad. What kind of a mother would do that? I was in her closet; I used to like it in there. I heard them talking about how they'd run away together. She was going to leave me. Leave me for some nobody – a pauper dentist. I couldn't let that happen. I told Dad what I'd heard. I knew he'd put a stop to it. We're very similar.'

Ronke thought she might throw up. 'Is that why you got back in touch with Simi? To get close to me?'

'It was fate. I recognized Kayode straight away. I couldn't imagine what he was doing with such an ugly frizzy blob. Then I saw the name: Ronke Tinubu. How many Tinubus could there be? And there was Simi – stupid, pathetic Simi. It was meant to be.'

'You planned this all along, didn't you?'

'Duh! You don't think I hung around with three halfwits for the fun of it, do you? It's been torture.'

'And Boo? What did she ever do to you?'

A vein throbbed in Isobel's forehead. 'Ah! Boo was a bonus.

I confess I didn't know she was my half-sister. When she told me her dad was Dele Babangari, I nearly fell off my chair. You can tell her from me, she's not a real Babangari. Just another of his worthless bastards.'

Ronke gasped. Poor Boo. Related to monsters. No wonder she'd run away.

'Now, is there anything else?' Isobel emptied her glass. 'I need to finish packing. I'm off to Abuja to spend Christmas with Dad. I've finished what I came here for.'

'This isn't Nigeria.' Ronke's voice finally cracked. She had her truth, but it didn't change anything. She felt her legs starting to give way. 'You won't get away with this.'

'I already have,' laughed Isobel.

Ronke staggered to the door and managed to get it open. The snow had settled in white ankle-deep drifts. Ronke stumbled to the pavement, icy damp seeping through her Crocs. She knew she wouldn't make it home. She swayed and reached out but there was nothing to hold on to. Just before she fell, she saw Simi, phone pressed to her ear, snow in her hair and fear in her eyes.

Ronke closed her eyes and let herself go. She collapsed into Simi's arms, sobbing. Her body shook, her chest heaved. Simi, two inches shorter and two stone lighter, held her up. 'You're OK. I've got you. I've got you.'

Epilogue

NINE MONTHS LATER

Ronke was running late, as usual. She was nervous. The three of them hadn't been in the same room since, well, since Isobel. They weren't the same people.

Ronke had seen Boo a few times, but never on her own – always with Sofia, sometimes with Didier. Boo was doing well, had a new job in academic research at UCL, and was loving it. She and Didier were in couple's therapy and it seemed to be working: they looked happy. Sofia was in love with Tosca, their Miniature Schnauzer. But not as besotted as Boo, who posted a new Tosca picture on their WhatsApp group every other day.

Simi had moved to New York in January, and if the messages were to be believed, the golden couple had taken it by storm. Their loft apartment in Tribeca didn't look like a dump. Ronke had Googled rental prices – they were definitely doing fine. No talk of babies – good for them. No pressure.

She was pleased her girls were good. And she was doing

OK too. She'd attended a grief support group – Rafa had enrolled her and gone to the first session with her. It had helped. But she still thought about Kayode every day.

She was closer to Mum and Ayo than she'd ever been. Mum had even gone with her to see Aunty K last week – her decision, Ronke hadn't pushed. Dad wasn't mentioned. Baby steps.

No one had heard from Isobel. The police said the case was still open, but with no evidence what could they do? Isobel was right – she had got away with it.

Ronke stopped at the cashpoint and withdrew a hundred pounds. She sauntered past the Sainsbury's Local, the Turkish grocery and the Thai nail bar, then paused outside Buka. The flag! They'd changed it. It looked wonderful – a triband of green, bright white and green. Maybe it was a sign. Fresh starts.

Ronke studied her reflection in the shiny mirrored door and yanked at an errant curl. She'd told the girls about Tony. They'd met at a dental conference in March. He was ten years older, a widower, with two (lovely) young kids, a boy and a girl. He was nothing like Dad. Not her usual type at all. He was dependable. He gave her flowers to see her face light up, not to say sorry.

What was she going to say when Simi inevitably asked, 'So what's new?' She decided she would tell them Tony had asked her to move in. They should be happy for her. He loved her more than she loved him – they both knew what that was like.

She wouldn't tell them Tony was for short for Tamunotonye. Or that he was teaching her to make *onunu* this evening – ripe plantain pounded with yam and palm oil, a speciality from Rivers State, where he grew up. They'd meet him soon enough.

Ronke pushed open the door and stepped into downtown Lagos. Simi and Boo looked up from their usual table. Simi with her wonderful smile and Boo's arms spread wide for a hug. It felt like coming home.

Bonus Scene

ISOBEL

The Babangari Residence, Abuja – before all the wahala

The three maids sat sweating under the palm tree, their starched white uniforms blending into grubby plastic chairs. Talking on duty could earn you a slap so they communicated with their eyes. But right now, six wary eyes were trained on Isobel. Madam got angry if she was kept waiting. And when Madam was vexed, she could be unpredictable. Yesterday, she'd thrown her phone at Aduka – her crime, serving red wine in a white wine glass. The screaming had been worse than the small cut. 'How dare you put your filthy blood on my phone! Go and get disinfectant, I don't want to catch your revolting germs.'

Isobel stood and stretched. The maids tensed, bottoms lifting, as she prowled to the edge of the gold pool. They relaxed back into their seats, exhaling in unison, as she dived into the gleaming depths.

Aduka ran her finger over the plaster on her cheek. '*Dat weave don spoil finish.*' Her voice was a whisper; she wouldn't be surprised if Isobel's special powers included underwater hearing. Uzo and Echioma sucked their teeth in reply.

Isobel's head emerged from the waterline, her long blonde hair trailing behind her like a mane. She turned, kicked her feet against the glittering tiles and swam to the other side, strong arms slicing through the water, slim ankles flicking rhythmically.

Twelve lengths later, Isobel grabbed the shimmering gold pool ladder, and the three maids sprang to their feet. Aduka grabbed a fluffy white towel from a towering pile, all monogrammed in shiny gold thread with the initials DB. Uzo rushed to the poolside bar to fetch a bottle of cold sparkling water and a crystal glass, placing them carefully on a gleaming gold tray. Echioma rearranged the sunlounger – smoothing the towel, plumping the pillow, wiping the iPad screen, polishing Isobel's diamanté-encrusted sunglasses.

The maids wished they had sunglasses. The sun was directly above them (and it was scorching) but they weren't squinting because of its rays. They were blinded by the gold. Mr Babangari liked gold.

The pool was lined with gold mosaic tiles, which made the water look like warm urine, but no one dared tell him. It was enveloped in an acre of Italian Calacatta marble tiles, streaked with thick gold veins. Each tile cost more than the three maids' combined annual salary. The sunloungers were bronze – glossy filigree metal topped with plush ivory cushions, each emblazoned with the obligatory gold DB monogram.

Isobel dabbed her face and hair and threw the towel at Aduka. 'Turn on the AC.'

'Yes, *mah*.' Aduka turned the large white portable air conditioning unit to high and made sure the vents were angled towards Isobel.

Later, the maids would laugh at the idea of using air conditioning outside in the midday sun.

'*Money don scatter her brain,*' Uzo would say.

'*Why him no buy golden AC, sef?*' Echioma would reply.

Aduka would laugh, a bitter laugh.

Isobel lay on her front, her gold-clad bottom facing the sky, and swiped through her iPad. Aduka risked a quick glance: Facebook.

The maids returned to their plastic chairs. The tree didn't offer much shade, but there was less gold and less glare at the servants' end (even Mr Babangari didn't feel the pump room warranted gold leaf).

A minute later, the big *oga* himself stomped down the marble steps and through the gold columns. The maids were at his side in seconds.

'Good morning, *sah*!' they chorused.

Echioma rushed off to drag his bronze throne closer to Isobel's lounger, the metal legs screeching on the marble tiles. Uzo joined her and together they managed to lift it off the ground and stagger six feet.

'Ice water, *sah*?' Aduka's eyes were downcast; eye contact was not advisable.

He waved them away, his rings glinting in the sun, and sat, arranging his white *agbada* around him.

'Tsarina,' Mr Babangari said, 'I'm travelling to Lagos. Till Sunday. Keep me company, *ehye*?'

Isobel gave a loud sigh and turned over. 'No, Daddy, I'll stay here.'

'Why are you sad like this? Forget the stupid Adams boy. The divorce didn't cost a penny and he dropped the assault charge. He was too feeble for you. You need a strong man. Like me.'

'I couldn't care less about Chase, he's a pussy.' Isobel tapped at her screen. 'I'm bored.'

'*Ehn?* So come to Lagos. A change is as good as a rest.' Mr Babangari clicked his fingers.

Aduka skidded across the tiles, almost tripping in her haste.

'Bring me Star beer. Cold one, *o.*'

'Yes, *sah!*'

'Tsarina, what will you drink? Cristal?'

Isobel ignored him, eyes glued to her iPad.

Aduka snuck another glance. Still Facebook. It looked like a photo from a society wedding. Three yellow women. Two *oyinbo* men. One very fine black man.

'Tsarina!' Mr Babangari touched Isobel's arm. '*Gini?* Have you seen a ghost?'

'No, not a ghost, Daddy.' She didn't take her eyes off her screen, but a smile spread over her face. 'Just a blast from the past. You're right, I do need a change. London. I'm going to London. It's time to catch up with an old *alobam.* And make some new friends. Is the house empty?'

'Yes, yes! Of course. It's good timing, *sef.* You must transport the Benin bronze for me. I have a potential buyer.'

'No problem.' Isobel swung her legs off the lounger. Uzo was already beside her, holding out a silk robe. 'I'm going inside to book my flight.'

'*Ah-ah!* You cannot be taking the head through customs. Too risky. Use the jet. You can drop me in Lagos and go from there.'

'Perfect.' Isobel slipped on her robe and stepped into her heeled slippers. She clacked away, and then stopped and spun around. 'Oh, Daddy, can I borrow Vadim? I might have a few errands for him.'

RONKE'S JOLLOF RICE

Serves 4

1 large onion, finely sliced into rounds

½ scotch bonnet chilli, deseeded and finely diced (Ronke leaves the seeds in, she's hardcore)

2 tbsp groundnut oil

Seasoning for jollof: 1 tsp curry powder, 1 tbsp thyme, 1 tsp white pepper, 1 tsp garlic powder, ½ tsp nutmeg, 1 bay leaf

2 x Maggi cubes (or 1 x beef/chicken stock cube)

1 tbsp tomato purée

1 tsp dried crushed crayfish (optional)

250g long-grain rice (Ronke uses Uncle Ben's)

150ml tomato passata

400ml chicken stock

- Warm the groundnut oil in a medium saucepan.
- Add the onions and chilli and fry gently on a low heat until soft. Stir every few minutes. Don't rush – this takes a good half-hour.
- When the onions are soft, turn heat to medium and add the jollof seasoning (see ingredients), Maggi cubes, purée and crayfish. Cook for 2 minutes, stirring.
- Add the rice (dry – don't rinse) and cook for 2 minutes, stirring twice.
- Add the chicken stock and passata. Stir.
- Check for seasoning – it may need a pinch of salt (but check: Maggi is salty).
- Bring to the boil. Then turn heat to low, cover and leave for 20 minutes. Don't be tempted to stir.
- Check after 20 minutes – if it's dry add a splash of water. You want the rice to be soft but not mushy and the water to have disappeared.

- Then check every 5 minutes. It takes about 40 minutes on low for the water to be absorbed and the rice to lose its bite.
- Serve with chicken stew and *moin-moin*. Ronke always has extra sides: *dodo* (fried plantain) and a crisp green salad.

RONKE'S CHICKEN STEW

Serves 4

1 medium onion, finely diced

1 red bell pepper, deseeded and finely diced

½ scotch bonnet chilli, finely diced (deseed unless you're Ronke)

2 tbsp groundnut oil

1 tsp white pepper

1 tsp garlic powder

1 Maggi cube

1 tbsp tomato purée

100ml tomato passata

200ml chicken stock

4 chicken thighs or drumsticks

Seasoning: 1 tsp curry powder, ½ tsp salt, 1 tsp thyme, 1 tsp white pepper, ½ tsp cayenne pepper, 1 crushed Maggi cube

2 tbsp olive oil

- Preheat oven to 200°C/Gas 6.
- Warm the oil in a medium saucepan and fry the onions, pepper and chilli over a low heat until they are soft. (Stir every 5 minutes. Don't rush – this takes a good half-hour.)
- Meanwhile, prep the chicken – put in a large bowl and add the chicken seasoning (see ingredients) and olive oil. Mix well. Put the chicken pieces in a roasting tin lined with foil.
- Roast the chicken for 40 minutes, turning every 10 minutes until cooked through, ending skin side up so it gets crispy.
- Back to the stew. When the onions are soft, turn the heat up to medium and add the white pepper, garlic powder, Maggi and purée. Stir. Add chicken stock and passata.
- Bring to the boil, turn to the lowest heat, cover and leave for 30 minutes. Stir every 10 minutes.

- Add the cooked chicken, stir, turn off the heat.
- Great with white rice, perfect with jollof and *moin-moin*.

AUNTY K'S MOIN-MOIN

Makes 6

190g Nigerian brown beans

½ scotch bonnet chilli, deseeded

1 onion, roughly chopped

1 red bell pepper, deseeded and roughly chopped

2 Maggi cubes

500ml chicken stock

1 tsp white pepper

¼ tsp nutmeg

1 tbsp dried crushed crayfish (optional)

3 tbsp groundnut oil

6 x 250ml ramekins

- Soak the beans in a pan of cold water for an hour.
- Rub the beans between your hands to loosen the skins, then rinse, drain and repeat. Keep going until shorn of their skins, naked and white. Drain.
- Blend (liquidize) the beans with the scotch bonnet, onion, pepper, crumbled Maggi cubes, stock, pepper, nutmeg and crayfish. This takes a while – start slow and work up to high speed. You want a mixture that's velvet smooth.
- Pour into a bowl.
- Add the oil and whisk. It may need a splash or two of water – you're looking for a smooth pouring batter a bit heavier than Yorkshire pudding mix.
- Pour into well-oiled ramekins.
- Steam for 75 minutes. A skewer should come out clean.
- Leave to cool for at least 10 minutes before turning out.
- Serve warm with jollof, stew and, if you're Ronke, *dodo* (fried plantain) and a crisp green salad.

Acknowledgements

Thank you to my Nigerian and British families for the wonderful gift of two cultures. With a very special mention for my sister, Victoria Oyegunle, who believes (wrongly) that I can do anything. Everyone needs an *alobam*; she is mine.

I owe an enormous debt of gratitude to the following people and organizations:

My incredible agent, Liv Maidment, and the entire team at my wonderful agency: Madeleine Milburn, Hannah Ladds, Liane-Louise Smith, Hayley Steed, Giles Milburn, Rachel Yeo, Sophie Péllisier, Georgina Simmonds, Georgia McVeigh and Valentina Paulmichl.

Catherine Cho, for her smartness and flair, and for holding my hand during two very crazy weeks.

Laura Marshall, for help and advice when I needed it most.

My book-to-screen agent Josie Freedman (I still miss our Zooms), the wonderful Liz Kilgarriff and her team at Firebird Pictures. Don't forget my rider – we are rocking *aso ebi* at the wrap party!

My brilliant editors, Jane Lawson and Kate Nintzel, for championing *Wahala* and making it immeasurably better.

You brought such wisdom and insight to the process; editing with both of you was a joy.

#TeamWahalaBook at Doubleday/Penguin Random House UK, especially Hayley (superstar) Barnes, Julia Teece, Laura Ricchetti, Laura Garrod, Emily Harvey, Charlotte Trumble, Kate Samano and Alison (legend) Barrow. Marianne Issa El-Khoury – you are a genius – my cover is banging.

#TeamWahalaBook at Custom House/HarperCollins US, especially Bianca Flores, Liate Stehlik, Molly Gendell, Jennifer Hart, DJ DeSmyter and Ronnie Kutys.

Shout-out to Daniel Morgan and his posse at Grindstone Literary. Winning your competition gave me the confidence to query – thank you.

Mike Cooper (my favourite photographer, ever) – thank you for getting rid of my chins ;-)

Writers are the most supportive group of people I've ever met. I'm grateful to my friends from the CBC and Penguin writing courses. A big thank-you to Barbara Henderson – the best creative-writing tutor, I learned so much from you.

So much love to My Special Ks – Kayte Genders and Karen Swann. I cannot wait to read both your books – heads-up: I will read the acknowledgements first ;-)

My MM fellow 2022 debuts: I couldn't be in better company. Nita Prose (unbelievably generous with help and advice), Lizzie Pook (we're going to DM every day, forever, right?) and (the ridiculously gorgeous) Charmaine Wilkerson.

Scarlett Down, for being the first person to read my opening chapters. (Yes, she asked for more!)

All my ~~girls~~ women, we need to make up for all those

missed lunches: Maxine Lowdon, Lucy Sreeves, Kemi Soyege-De-Koster, Nikki Popoola, Angela Richards, Rosemary Adebola and Rachel Down. Now, stop asking which one is you – it's fiction!

Two of my favourite ~~boys~~ old men: Andrew Stracey (my first and only boss) and Tom (Gussie) O'Donnell. Thanks for the most important life lesson: JFDI, then go for a long lunch.

To the greatest dogs in the world: Tosca, Petra, Fela and Lola. All the best ideas came on our walks.

Finally, I'm ending where it all began. Peter – look what we made. T-Unit for ever. xxx